MR. UNEXPECTED

THE BONDED BROTHERS SERIES

J R GALE

J R GALE PUBLISHING LLC

Editing: Ellie- My Brothers Editor

Proofing: My Brothers Editor

Cover: Sarah Paige- The Book Cover Boutique Cover

Photographer: Michelle Lancaster

ISBN: 979-8-9885905-5-2

"Love is like a butterfly, a rare and gentle thing." — Dolly Parton

AUTHOR'S NOTE

Please check the author's website to find the content warning for Mr. Unexpected.

MR. UNEXPECTED

BONDED

PROLOGUE

Harrison

Somber energy radiates through the room as we face the unbearable task of saying goodbye to our sister, which will no doubt be the worst day of our lives.

"Guys come closer. It's time to discuss Claudina," Camila's voice croaks out in a whisper, another stark reminder that she's deteriorating right before our eyes.

She has weeks, maybe days, left—she's dying of cancer, and there is nothing we can do to stop it.

Casting my eyes down to a peacefully sleeping Claudina in my arms, I untwine my other hand from Camila and reach around, gently pulling her toward us, hoping to give her the strength she needs to get through this.

Leo walks to her other side and kisses her forehead softly before taking a seat. Nate is next to me, rubbing her leg in comfort.

"Sebastian, come here, please," Camila whispers, reaching her hand out for our brother.

He pushes off the far wall and hesitantly walks toward her bed. His face twists with anguish.

He's trying to be strong for our sister, though he's failing miserably.

We've all seen the slow decline of his mental health, and I'm petrified about what will happen once she's gone.

Sadness knots my insides thinking about a life without Camila. She is the one who has given *us life* since we were young kids, always with a smile on her face and a fierce attitude to get through the day.

Why her?

Why is this sweet soul being taken from us so early in life? To suffer and leave her young daughter and family. It's not fucking fair; she had a whole goddamn life to live.

I clench my jaw to stop any reaction my face may give away, not wanting Camila to be upset or worry about my feelings.

I'm acting calm on the outside, but on the inside, it feels like I'm fucking dying alongside her.

Glancing down at Claud again, who's stirring quietly in my arms, I'm reminded that I need to man up and grow a pair. There's still a part of Camila that will live alongside us, and we need to stay strong for this precious angel.

Camila starts to speak, her voice low and slow. "I know the four of you consider yourselves brothers."

"We *are* brothers," Leo corrects her.

Nate and I are brothers, while Leo, Seb, and Camila are all siblings. The Morales family raised Nate and me; we are not family by blood but family by choice.

"And you're our sister. Don't forget it," Nate adds.

She musters up a small smile and mouths *I love you*, to him.

"Grief can be an ugly thing. I don't want any resentment toward one another, and I want to make sure you're still okay with the arrangement regarding Claudina."

Leo speaks up first. "I back you one hundred and ten percent. Both Nate and I agree that neither of us is ready to be a father. Not that I wouldn't step up if I needed to, but I promise to be the greatest uncle of all time. Better than this grumpy jerk over here," Leo answers, pointing to Seb, trying to lighten the mood.

Sarcasm has been his coping mechanism throughout this entire process.

I hold Seb's eyes, silently asking him to speak up now if he has any reservations about Camila's decision to make me Claud's legal guardian.

Camila has struggled with this since discovering she was pregnant: who will be the father?

After she went into remission, she decided to live life to its fullest —traveling the world, partying with her friends, meeting men—everything she missed in her early twenties. But letting loose with a man she didn't know had us welcoming Claudina into the world nine months later. It's been the highlight of our lives and a small distraction when Camila's ovarian cancer came back full force while she was pregnant.

We all knew the outcome when she chose Claudina's life over chemo in her first trimester. Even with the aggressive treatment she received later, there was nothing we could do other than support her wishes.

She would not sacrifice her daughter's life for a slight chance of saving hers.

So, when it came down to putting a name on the birth certificate, she asked if it could be me. She didn't want to leave it blank, and considering we have been lifelong friends and are not technically related, it made sense.

I reassured Sebastian that in no way, shape, or form did this mean I would automatically become her guardian when Camila died. We would all discuss it together and decide. However, as time passed and his emotions began to get the better of him, we all agreed I would be the best fit.

Sebastian's tormented eyes hold mine for a beat longer before he nods. "I agree. Harrison is Claudina's father, and we are her uncles. No more discussion is needed. It's done."

Claudina's father.

It's the greatest title I'll ever hold.

My fingers run tenderly along the apple of my daughter's rosy cheek and then her dark hair, just like her mother's. I turn toward

Camila. "Being this precious baby's father is the greatest privilege one can receive. I will cherish, respect, and love her for all of my days."

Tears glisten on her pale skin. "I know. She is the luckiest girl in the whole world to have you by her side. I know I always was." She sobs, and I wipe her tears away, then my own that have broken free. "I love you. Thank you for stepping up without one ounce of hesitation." She turns to everyone. "I love you all so, so much."

There's not a dry eye in the room. How could there be?

Camila points to the water. "I have one more thing to say, but I need water." Her voice is croaky, signaling her exhaustion.

"Okay, and then you rest," I tell her.

She nods, then gestures at Claud, wanting to hold her once more before she falls asleep. I place the baby in her arms and position mine around them to give her support. Camila isn't strong enough to hold her alone anymore.

"There is one thing I never told you about Claudina, and it's the meaning behind her name. Claudina is after the Claudina Agrias Butterfly. It is uniquely beautiful, adorned with bright, stunning colors, standing out among the rest, which I already know my Claud will, too. But most importantly, butterflies have a special meaning for the after-life. In many cultures, they represent the human soul, and in others, hope." She coughs, asking for more water, then takes a minute to gather the strength to keep talking. "So when you see a butterfly, know I am there with you. I can feel that my soul is not ready to leave any of you, and I promise always to stay connected." Her body shakes from the constant stream of tears, and I can't take it any longer.

"Enough. This is too much. You need rest."

She ignores me. "And do you know that saying when you're excited or nervous, you've got butterflies in your stomach? Think of me, okay? I'll be there for all the important things. When you land a big job at work. When you meet the girl of your dreams, and your stomach drops with constant fluttering. I'm there with you, experiencing it all."

Nate hands me and Leo tissues before passing the box to Seb.

This is all fucking wrong. She can't leave us.

Camila closes her eyes, and I think she's had enough until she whispers, "Promise me something."

"Anything," Sebastian speaks up as we all nod in agreement.

"When I'm gone, you may feel broken and alone. But please try to remember you still have a whole life to live. With my passing, Claudina will bring the four of you even closer together. She will be the reason for you to feel alive again. She will bond you forever. So promise me you'll live for Claudina, to give her the life she deserves, the one you gave me."

"We promise," we say without any hesitation.

Being bonded for life to my brothers is a privilege. I love these three men more than anything,

Plus, I would do anything to make Camila happy, and now Claudina.

My daughter.

1

Juliette

BREATHE IN.

Breathe out.

I repeat the mantra as I stare at the single piece of paper weighing down my hands *and my life.*

One paper officially changing the course of my future, the one I've had planned out since I was a young girl. And even though I've suspected this for a while now, I still can't get over my immense shock.

After months of hoping the outcome would be different, I finally let the tears I've been holding back fall, blurring my vision, but not enough that I can't see the dreaded words.

After much deliberation and discussion with your team of doctors, it is not without sadness and regret that we have come to the unfortunate decision to terminate your position as principal dancer at the New York City Ballet.

My door flies open, and my mom barrels in a rush, breaking me out of my mental stupor.

"Juliette," she cries in her soft French accent. "Tell me I'm reading this wrong. This can't be true." She thrusts a manila envelope in my face, then quickly pulls it back when she takes in my tear-streaked face. "What's wrong, my love." Her voice quickly changes, full of worry.

"It's nothing. Let me see what you have." I reach for the envelope, pushing my letter behind my back, only I'm too slow. My mom steps back out of reach, eyeing me with concern.

I know she won't let this go, so I huff and hand her the letter.

"Oh, Juliette," she croons with empathy. "I'm so sorry. So it's official?"

I nod. "They want me to come in today to hand in my building pass and wrap everything up."

She sits next to me on my bed and wraps me in a tight hug, engulfing me with the scent of my father.

Shortly after he died last year, she started wearing his cologne to feel close to him, and as morbid as that is, soon after, I, too, took comfort in the smell.

Like now, it feels as if he's here with us, joining in on our family hug.

Maybe he is.

"I know it feels like your life is ending, but something bigger and better will come along."

"Don't." My tone is sharp. I instantly regret letting my emotions get the better of me. I never want to upset my kindhearted mother, but I don't want to be coddled. "I'm sorry, Mom." I kiss her cheek, "I'm not ready for reassurances. I'd rather you tell me how it is. That my life is over at the early age of twenty-four."

She chuckles softly. "Don't be so dramatic. I won't lie and tell you it's going to be easy. You trained your whole life for this, and it's been taken away in the blink of an eye. I also meant it when I said it would all be okay. You're your father's daughter. Sweet but strong, and if anyone can work through this, it's you." She pulls back to look me in the eyes. "I know you don't believe this now, but there is more to life than ballet. You're young and have your whole life ahead of you. No matter what you do, you *will* succeed."

I subconsciously rub my injured leg as I think over her words, wondering if I'll actually work through it because I often worry that without ballet, I don't have much to offer and struggle knowing what to work toward now that my dreams have been ripped away.

Ballet has been my life since the age of three. Nothing else interested me, and it was clear early on that I had a natural talent.

My parents were proud but never pushed me to go further. In fact, they often wanted me to stop training, worried that it was too much for a child to stress over something that should be fun.

But I was addicted. I loved the thrill of succeeding, and though I often wanted to quit after grueling, intense classes, that high never went away for me.

Ultimately, I always wanted to be better, to do better.

The day I was asked to join the New York City Ballet was like winning an Olympic gold in my eyes—I had finally made it.

I worked diligently, day and night, and it paid off. I hit my next goal, becoming a soloist ballerina soon after, and within a year, I made it to principal dancer—the highest level, where I was the lead ballerina in performances like *The Nutcracker* and one of the most difficult to perform—*Swan Lake*.

Though nothing meant more to me than when I was chosen to dance *The Sleeping Beauty* for our fall season.

All of my hard work came crashing down on opening night when a taxi swerved and hit me. After just one performance, my dream of performing my favorite Disney movie, the one I repeatedly watched with my dad, came to a dramatic end.

And six months later, so did my career.

My phone buzzes beside me, breaking me out of my depressing thoughts. I lift my head from my mom's shoulder to see my best friend blowing up my phone.

"Becks?"

"Yeah, she wants me to meet her for dinner and drinks at some swanky place tonight, but I'm not in the mood."

"You should go. You need to get out more."

"We'll see, maybe." I shrug. "Hey, what's in the envelope that you wanted to show me when you barged into my room without knocking?" I raise an accusing brow.

I had finally moved out of my parents' apartment, only to quickly move back in when my dad died. There was no way I could leave my mom alone and devastated.

And if I'm being honest with myself, I didn't want to be alone either. My dad was my best friend. I think about him every day. Having my mom close is a blessing.

"It's nothing. I'm going to head back down to the bakery." She tries to get up, but I block her with my arms.

"Mom."

She sighs loudly. "If I had known about your letter, I wouldn't have brought mine up, but I guess we should just get all the bad news out of the way."

She hands me the large envelope embossed with the logo of our building management company.

I open it quickly and read it over.

Oh no.

"This can't be true," I murmur, re-reading the words repeatedly. God, if I thought my day started terribly, this puts the icing on the cake.

Not only is our building being purchased, but the financial firm is buying out the whole block, and there is no way we'll be able to afford the new rent.

I look up into my mom's tear-filled eyes, "What do we do, Juliette?" she whispers. "I can't lose the bakery. It would be like losing your father all over again."

I take her shaky hands in mine. "They can't just kick us out, right?"

"No, they can't, but our lease is up at the end of the year. Unless we can get the money for the new rent, we will be forced to move out."

Fuck. This is not good.

"We have some time. Maybe we can get a loan. I'm not sure, but let's not stress over it today. I'll figure something out, I promise."

Her big brown eyes, the ones that we share, stare back at me with defeat. She knows just as well as I do that this will be challenging, but I'll do everything and anything in my power to save Le Petit Boulanger, *The Little Baker*.

A surprise from my father. My mom's pride and joy.

When I catch a glimpse of the clock, it's a reminder I need to leave soon and put the final nail in my dancing career coffin.

This could possibly be one of the worst days ever.

Painful yet painless, all at the same time.

After handing in my card key, I signed discharge papers, said my goodbyes, and that was it.

In a matter of minutes, my career as a professional ballerina was over. Blood, sweat, and tears went into twenty-one years of training for what?

What a mess.

My new life starts today. I have to believe that because if I let myself wallow like I did earlier today, I'll head down a dark hole I have no interest in being in.

Before I leave, I walk the long, memorable hallway to make a quick stop one last time to watch my favorite little girls and boys.

The program inspired me as a young child and solidified my love for the art of dance. I remember catching glimpses of the older ballerinas and knew that was what I wanted to be when I grew up.

"Four, five, turn six, seven, eight. Yes! Well done, good job. Next group." I hear Adriana call to her students as I make my way over to the glass windows. She spots me instantly and gives me a sly wave so the kids don't see.

I watch them learn the basics, and no matter how many times I visit them, their innocent, determined faces and toothless smiles always warm my heart.

"I knew I would find you here," a familiar voice calls out behind me, breaking me out of the first happy bubble I've been in in some time. "You weren't going to say hello or goodbye?"

"Why would I?" I snap without turning around.

"Babe—"

"Don't. My name is Juliette. Better yet, don't utter my name again. You lost that privilege." I stand up straighter, grab Adriana's attention, and quickly wave goodbye before storming out, needing to get far away from my dickhead ex.

Always calm, level-headed, and someone who rarely raises their voice, that's how people would describe me, but the second you cross me, we're done.

"Juliette, just wait! I'm sorry, okay?"

I whip around and narrow my eyes. "For what? What are you sorry for?" I ask, glancing over his tall frame, taking in his shaggy blonde hair and dark eyes. It does nothing for me, and I suddenly have no idea what I ever saw in him.

"F-For everything," he stutters.

"Name one thing!" I yell, and I can see by his facial expression I've shocked him, but he's caught me on a day of weakness, and I can't stand to even look at his stupid face. "You can't, can you? Can't pick even one thing from the list?"

"You have to understand—"

I shake my head venomously. "No. I don't have to understand why my boyfriend only visited me once in the hospital when I was there for two weeks or why he stopped calling and checking in while I was in rehab. You disappeared, and then one day, I received a text saying it's better if we go our separate ways. A text, Hunter." I throw my hand up, annoyed. "Or are you sorry I saw pictures of you and *her* together on my birthday?" He stays silent, though I have to give it to him, he does look remorseful, but I don't give a shit. "Now that I'm not the best, I'm not good enough for you, am I right? You had to move on to my replacement? Well, guess what? Have a good time with second best," I spit. "She'll never be me."

Before he can answer, I leave him in shock and run down the busy street, weaving myself through the crowd toward Columbus Avenue, far away from that arrogant jerk.

All he cared about was status. I see that now. Hunter is a good dancer, great even, but he is nothing without his partner, so he latched on to me since we grew up together. When I got injured, I was no longer there, so he moved on to my replacement.

I was so blinded, so goddamn blinded. *Ugh!*

"Whoa, Jules. Slow down," a voice rings out as I slam into a familiar body.

"Isaac, oh my god," I pant. "I'm so sorry. I'm having a horrible day, and my head's not on straight. Are you okay?"

Isaac is a top hairdresser located on the Upper West Side. We usually run into each other a few times a week, although never literally, like today.

"I'm fine. Though I'd be better if you'd finally let me give you that makeover you've been promising me for years." He winks, and I smile at his forwardness.

He's been begging me to chop off my long, dull brown hair. With always having it slicked back in a bun, I didn't want to deal with shorter hair; it just meant more bobby pins and hairspray.

But now...

I turn and look into the shop window to see my reflection, and it's as if I'm seeing a whole new person.

I'm not Juliette Caldwell, ballerina, anymore.

The million-dollar question is, who is she?

One thing I know is I'm not someone who likes to sit around and feel sorry for myself, and I've done enough of that over the last six months. I have too much on my plate to pity my situation.

I'm lucky to be alive.

You know what...

"Okay," I say and shoot him a wide smile.

"Okay? Okay, what?"

"Let's do a makeover."

God, I'm so late.

Swerving through the busy streets of downtown, I yell a bunch of sorrys as I bump into people left and right. Even on a Wednesday at ten o'clock at night, New York, as always, is bustling, ready for anything.

The vibrance and liveliness pumping through this city are unmatched. You'll never experience it anywhere else, and while I appreciate the buzz, typically I like to experience it from my bedroom so I can get an early wake-up to enjoy a morning in the park.

But I'll trek downtown for a late dinner with my best friend, who works twelve or more hours a day and has always been there for me.

Finally arriving after what feels like hours, I push open the large, sleek black doors and rush toward the hostess for help, since—of course—my phone died, and I couldn't ask Becks where she was sitting.

While she directs me to her table, I take in the scene and smile, fascinated by fashionable people and their loud voices talking over the pumping music. It might not be my scene every week, but when I get out, the energy my city delivers is addicting.

"Holy hotness," Becks calls, whistling loudly across the trendy Tribeca restaurant.

My cheeks burn at the scene she's making, so I hurry over to the table. She stands as I approach, grabbing me by the shoulders to spin me around. "You like?" I waggle my brows.

"Fucking love."

There was no trim today.

Isaac not only cut ten inches off, giving me a blunt, cool girl lob that sits on my collarbone, he also added low lights to give my dark locks a subtle glow.

I feel rejuvenated.

We sit, and Becks reaches up and pulls her wig off her head, causing the uptight woman next to us to gasp loudly.

"Couldn't you have done that before you got to the restaurant?" I hiss.

She shrugs. "It was fucking hot under there."

I roll my eyes, "Then stop wearing them. Or better yet, keep your hair dark and wear fun wigs when you want some color."

She aggressively points at me, but her eyes sparkle with delight.

"Shut that pretty mouth of yours right now. I will never dye my hair back to black. I won't let those corporate assholes win."

"The ones that sign your checks, therefore paying for this extravagant dinner tonight?" I raise a judging brow.

Becks is an analyst at one of the largest financial firms in the country, hence the long work hours, and with that comes her abiding by their archaic rules and dress codes.

It's a boys' club—thousands of dollars are spent on perfectly tailored suits, with the reluctant casual Friday.

Unfortunately, for Becks, my crazy, outgoing, free spirit of a friend, that means hiding her blue-dyed hair under *corporate-approved* wigs.

We're interrupted by the waiter bringing over two drinks, and if I had to bet, they're two spicy margaritas.

"Thanks for pre-ordering," I say as we clink our glasses; her dark-green eyes never leave mine, even while sipping her drink. "What?"

A smile tugs at her lips. "I go on a work trip for a week and come home to a whole new Jules. You look amazing, like fucking banging."

"Thanks. I feel it for the first time in forever."

Her face drops, and she takes my hands across the table. "How are you, honestly?"

What's there to say? "I'm taking it day by day. The bakery has been busier than ever, and helping Mom has taken so much of my time that I'm not sure I've fully processed everything."

"Standing baking all day hasn't been painful for your leg?" she asks, concerned.

"It's tolerable. I occasionally get shooting pain from the nerve damage, but it usually doesn't last long. I'm sure wearing these heels won't help, but the doctor gave me the okay."

"Well, don't push it. If you need help, I have a ton of vacation days I can use. I still remember how to make a mean éclair."

Becks is the sister I've never had, and although I won't let her, I know that she would drop everything to help Mom and me at Le Petit Boulanger. We've known each other our whole lives, and even though we've gone on incredibly different paths, we will always be as thick as thieves.

I rub my thumb over her hand, silently thanking her for caring, before pulling back and taking another sip of my drink.

"You know, the cabbie who hit me came by the bakery the other day while I was working with Mom to apologize."

"Really?" Her eyes bulge. "You don't blame him, do you?"

"Of course not. He was swerving to avoid an idiot who crossed without looking. He was devastated. I think when the *New York Times* did an article about my doomed career, it set him spinning. He looked more upset than I did when I got the news."

She rolls her eyes, annoyed, "Fucking vultures. They were so insensitive in that article."

No shit.

"Ready to order, ladies?" the waiter interrupts, and of course, neither of us has opened our menu, focused on catching up, but Becks comes here often, so I'll trust her to order something scrumptious.

"This is on you, babe. You know what I like." I grin as I see her perk up with excitement.

Ms. Foodie loves to order for the table, and for years, I was limited by a strict healthy diet. It's only recently I've been indulging more, and it's never made her happier.

Behind Becks, near the bar, movement catches my eye.

Four insanely handsome men say goodbye to one another in a familiar way, hugging and patting each other's backs. Two kiss goodbye.

And when I say men, I mean *men.*

By the looks of it, they're older than me and Becks and hold the presence of sophistication.

One of the taller ones stays back and sits at the bar, flagging down the waiter, who swiftly takes his order and soon after, puts down a glass of water and a scotch neat.

I'd guess he's over six feet because he looks tall even while sitting there.

I try to look away, but my eyes drift back toward him. He lifts the drink to his lush lips, and my eyes trail down his lightly tanned neck to watch his Adam's apple bob up and down as he gulps down the liquid.

When did swallowing become sexy?

Ever so slightly, his tongue peeks out, licking the bit dribbling out, causing my stomach to flutter. Why this stranger elicits such a response is beyond me.

There's just something about him that I can't put my finger on.

Perhaps it's because he's the most beautiful man I've ever laid eyes on, or maybe it's because it has been a while.

The loud music pumping through the restaurant begins to drift away as I fall into a trance, staring at every inch of him.

He sits tall with broad, muscular shoulders that bulge through his light blue dress shirt, while his legs are spread wide, giving his already formidable appearance an extra dose of dominance.

As if he can hear my thoughts, he deliberately turns his head, pushing a rogue piece of honey-blonde swept hair away from his face, mesmerizing me with his square jaw and piercing blue eyes that, even through the dark of the restaurant, blaze through the crowd.

Our eyes lock, and neither of us looks away, lingering longer than normal. He rolls his lips and takes a deep breath, flaring his nostrils as my heart pounds against my chest.

"Earth to Jules?"

My eyes widen and snap back to Becks. "Sorry." I pick up and gulp down the rest of my drink, trying to regulate my breathing.

Holy fucking hell. What is wrong with me?

Even now, I'm trying to keep my gaze on Becks, not the Adonis across the way. He's like a magnet I can't pull away from. Commanding all my attention.

"You didn't hear anything I ordered, did you?"

"Not a single one," I admit, nervously running my hands through my hair and coming up short when it slips out the end of my newly shortened style.

Ah, that's going to take some getting used to.

Becks narrows her eyes and slowly turns around, wondering who or what had my attention. "Don't," I snap. "Don't make a scene, please."

It will be blatantly obvious if she turns all the way around. I already feel embarrassed enough that he caught me staring.

She crosses her arms and widens her eyes. "Now, why would you think I would make a scene, Juliette Caldwell?"

I look down and push my straw around the ice in my empty drink. "A very handsome man might have momentarily paralyzed me. He might have also caught me staring," I whisper without looking up.

"Oh, I already know that. I called your name three times before you realized, and I could see you had hearts in your eyes."

"I did not," I spit. What the hell is she talking about?

"Well, don't gate keep. If I can't look yet, you might as well give me the goods on him."

I lean back, subconsciously raising my eyes toward the bar, and catch him still looking.

Shit.

"Jesus. Act cool."

"Easy for you to say, you don't know the power this man has over my eyeballs." I laugh. "Oh, someone else just walked up. You can look —fast, though."

She turns inconspicuously but quickly sits forward, face ashen. "No."

"What do you mean *no*? No, what? You barely got a look at him."

She shakes her head rapidly. "Oh, I've gotten a good look. For the last two years at Abbott."

"Oh my god, you work with him? What a small world." Abbott is the asset management company Becks works at.

She laughs sardonically, not looking one bit amused. "Oh, I don't work *with* him. I work *for* him. He is my boss's, boss's, boss: Harrison Davenport, CEO of Abbott. And you're forgetting about that jerk right now. You're not going there."

Harrison.

"I wasn't going there," I mutter. "I was only looking."

"Well, don't even look," she says with finality, which shocks me because she constantly pushes me to talk to new people and get out of my comfort zone.

She never understood what I saw in Hunter. Looking back, I'm not sure what it was either, other than familiarity. So, I'm surprised she's not dragging me over there by my hair, introducing me.

A waitress this time shows up with a margarita, and I couldn't be more thankful to switch the conversation.

"Carrie, this is my best friend, Juliette. Jules, Carrie is the best waitress in all of New York, and a new friend of mine."

I shake her outstretched hand.

"Hi, so nice to meet you." She smiles warmly and returns the sentiments before returning to the bar.

Lucky bitch, serving *Harrison*.

Becks sighs and leans back. "I feel bad for her. Her ex-husband is a piece of work. They're in the middle of getting a divorce, and he shut off all her cards, both credit and debit, completely fucking her over."

"What?" I ask, stunned. "How can he even do that?"

"Everything was in his name; he manipulated her toward the end of their relationship, and this isn't even the worst of it."

"How can it get worse than leaving your wife high and dry, with no money, *especially* in New York, where everything is five times the price it should be?"

She takes a large gulp of her drink and slams it down. "They have three kids under the age of four that he gives no shits about. So now she is feeding them, paying for childcare, and trying to pay rent with her waitress job. It's impossible. Not to mention, she's been working double shifts here, then three hours later, getting the kids up for school. She has no family in New York."

Tears tickle my eyes; I feel for Carrie but also for Becks. I know this is hitting home for her.

Her dad left her and her mom with nothing when she was younger. Her mom struggled for a long time. Though her story turned out for the best, it left its scars.

She wipes a rare tear, which means this woman affects her more than she lets on. Unlike me, Becks does not cry.

An hour has passed, and we're waiting on dessert when I look up toward the bar where Harrison sits with the man who walked up earlier. And sure enough, just like the million other times I've looked up during our meal, half his attention is on his friend, the other on me.

We're getting brazen, sending small smiles back and forth. It's playful and flirtatious, and I haven't felt this alive in a while.

"Stop it right now, Juliette. Move those eyes away from the bar this instant."

"Stop patrolling me. I don't know why you're getting your panties in a bunch over this. I've only looked at the guy."

She presses her glass to her lips, contemplating her words. "He's just not for you. Okay?"

I huff, annoyed. "What could be so bad about this *stranger*, anyway?"

She holds up her hand and counts down. "One, he's way too old for you. He must be at least ten or fifteen years older than you."

"You love older men," I interrupt.

"Yes, me. You'd get walked all over by a man like him."

"Can you stop talking about me like I'm some naive child? You're starting to piss me off."

"Two..." She raises her voice, ignoring me. "He's an asshole. He's a fucking hard-ass. People avoid him at all costs in the office."

I shrug, "Must be tough being CEO of that big of a company, especially if it's as successful as you say."

"Three—"

"Okay, enough with the countdown, he's an older asshole. I get it. Good thing I exchanged looks with him, not bodily fluids or wedding rings," I snap and stand abruptly, causing a shooting pain in my leg.

"What's wrong?" Beck's panicked voice raises.

I take a deep breath and wait a second to let the pain pass. "My leg twinged, but it's gone already. I'm going to the ladies' room. I'll be right back."

There are still three girls ahead of me in the queue, so I do the only thing I've been thinking about for the last hour.

Google Harrison Davenport.

Harrison Montgomery Davenport is an American billionaire businessman. He is the current Chairman and CEO of Abbott, one of the world's leading investment firms with over $10 trillion in assets under management. Age 38, Davenport, the eldest son of former CEO of Abbott, Anderson Davenport, and his wife, Caroline Montgomery Davenport, studied at The University of Pennsylvania, graduating Summa Cum Laude.

His net worth was assessed at $10 billion, one of New York's youngest billionaires, alongside his architect brother, Nathaniel Abbott Davenport.

Last year, Davenport was named one of Forbes's 50 Most Influential People of the Year.

Ah, so he *is* older by fourteen years. Oh hell, that's a lot.

And he's freaking rich. I can't even afford tonight's dinner. He could afford to buy the whole city.

I read on.

Davenport is aloof even to his peers and is fiercely private about his personal life. Though rarely seen without a beautiful woman on his arm while attending outings, he has had no known relationships in the past five years.

He is the father to his young daughter.

What? He's a father?

It doesn't seem like the mother is in the picture if he has a different date for every event. But a dad, that even sounds old.

"Hello? Are you using the bathroom or not?" a girl snaps from behind me.

I turn, annoyed. "You could have just told me it's my turn. No need to be nasty."

She huffs as I turn back, and as I reach the door, the men's room opens—and out steps Harrison.

Holy shit, he's even more beautiful close-up.

My steps falter when he raises a brow, smirking, and I bite my lip to hide one myself.

Those blue eyes freely roam my body, sending goose bumps along my skin. "Hi," he murmurs deeply.

I blush and smile. "Hello," I rasp, not recognizing my own voice.

Hmm, is the new Jules flirty? I think I love that for her, even if it's the margaritas giving her courage. Or maybe it's *Harrison* that's bringing out a bolder side of me.

He reaches his hand out. "Harrison."

I place mine, which looks small and delicate, in his large, strong hand. "Juliette." I try to shake his hand. Instead, he squeezes mine gently and brings it to his lips.

Dear God, breathe, Jules!

His full lips on my skin send a warming shiver through my body that I can't explain. My brain is completely fried.

With his lips lingering over my skin, he asks if I have a last name, and before I can answer, I'm interrupted.

"Can you fucking go into the bathroom already?" the girl barks.

"Sorry." I cringe when I see more people have joined the line.

I glance up at Harrison one last time, letting my eyes rake over what I call perfection, burning the image into my memories, then turn and close the bathroom door, hearing a faint *"wait"* as I walk away.

The decision I make in that split second to walk into the bathroom is the right one. What business do I have flirting with someone like Harrison?

Older, mature, rich, and a father.

None. None at all.

It doesn't matter that I've never been physically more attracted to someone or how. In all the years I dated Hunter, he never made my heart beat a mile a minute.

It doesn't matter. *Right?*

When I return to my table, unable to stop, I glance at the bar, and he's gone. His drink is cleaned up, and his suit jacket is missing. My stomach drops in disappointment.

Well, I guess that's that.

"Oh. My. God. Oh my god. Oh my god!" Carrie cries, flapping her arms around, then throws something at Becks.

Becks's eyes widen. "Where the hell did you get this?"

"Christopher, the bartender, asked me for a life update. I got a little emotional, and I think one of my customers was listening the whole time. When he left, he looked me straight in the eye and said, 'Even though you might not feel it, you will get through it. Do it for your kids.'"

"What customer?" I ask.

"Did you see that hottie sitting at the bar earlier?" She points to Harrison's seat.

I sure did.

Glancing over to what Beck's is holding—it's a fifteen hundred dollar tip. I stare at Becks, and she rolls her eyes, "Fine. Maybe he's not as bad as I thought."

He's perfect. Too bad I'll never see him again.

2

Juliette

"THE BAGUETTES ARE FINISHED out here. How much longer for the new batch?" Alice peeks her head around the corner.

I glance at Mom, who's in charge of all things bread today, while I finish the mille feuille and macarons. She holds up one finger.

"One minute," I call back to Alice, who is operating the front of the shop.

The weather has changed for the better, spring is here, so spirits are high, and all the parents and nannies of the Upper East Side are bringing their kids in for after-school treats and pre-weekend pastries.

It's a madhouse, to say the least.

"Okay, they're done, my love," Mom calls over the romantic melodies of Tchaikovsky's Symphony No. 5 playing softly through the speakers. I may not spend my days training anymore, but familiarity with his compositions' sensuously rhythmic flow still calms my nerves on stressful workdays.

I carry my finished pastries out to the main case, placing them perfectly in a row while Alice chats up a customer, helping them choose between two options.

"I would go with the strawberry," I offer, glancing over the counter. A wide smile stretches my face when I see it's two of my favorite customers. "Pear Tarte Tatin is my favorite, but considering it's strawberry season, and they were freshly picked this weekend, I would go with that."

"Sounds perfect. Two to go, please. We'll be back next week to chat, but this one will be late for dance if we don't get out of here quickly." Willa pats the little girl she nannies for on the head, who excitedly waves at me, and then they're both rushing out the door.

After saying hi to one more regular customer, I run back to get the baguettes from Mom.

While kissing her cheek, I glance down at her swollen hands. "You okay?" I ask, worried that her severe arthritis is causing her too much pain.

It's the main reason I took over here, though she still helps most days. I think it would completely kill her spirit if she couldn't, but more often than not, she's overseeing the customers rather than creating beautiful pastries in the back like she's done for the last twenty years.

So far, today has been a good day for her.

I've seen a light in her eyes that's been missing recently, though I'm concerned with the extreme humidity that comes along with the impending summer months, her pain will soon be unbearable.

"I'm okay, Juliette. No need to worry," she says as if I have a choice. I'll always worry.

An hour later, Alice comes back to let me know Becks is here, and when I glance up at the clock, I see it's much later than I realized.

"We're done for the day, my love. Go see Becks, and I'll be up soon to say hi."

I kiss her again, then head toward Alice. "I'll come up front. Thank you, Alice."

Quickly, I wash my hands, throw my chef's coat in the dirty pile, and head out to see Becks, wondering why the hell she's all the way uptown during a workday.

"What in the ever-living hell happened to you?" I ask, wide-eyed and shocked as an extremely sweaty Becks stands in the middle of the shop, one hand on her hip, the other holding her wig.

"Do you have any cold water in the back?" she pants. "I already checked the fridge, and you're out."

"Um, sure," I answer, still confused.

Lovely Alice comes running with a cup of ice water. "I'd hug you, Alice, but I doubt you want any of me touching you."

"That would be correct." She laughs, then heads to the back to help Mom with the last of the cleaning.

Alice is the sweetest person I've ever met and has worked for my mom for over ten years. I've never once seen her get angry or raise her voice. And trust me, that's a challenging task when some of these entitled Park Avenue Princesses come in.

Becks strides over to one of the tables, and I follow suit, grabbing an extra chair to put my leg up. My poor body is sore today. On top of working all day, I had an intense physical therapy appointment this morning, and it's finally catching up with me.

"Care to explain why you're in workout clothes and look like you've jumped in the pool during work hours?"

"Stupid bitches."

I bark out a laugh. "What?"

"All these skinny bitches want to do work meetings at Barry's Bootcamp or SoulCycle." She rolls her eyes and uses air quotes, "'It's good for the working relationship,' says my idiot boss."

Continuing to laugh. "You hate working out," I say.

"No fucking shit. In a fucking wig to boot." She chugs more water.

"Rebecca Rosenberg, watch your mouth," my mom calls from the back.

Becks's eyes widen. "What does she have, bionic hearing?"

"No, it's your voice. It's raised about two hundred decibels."

"Sorry, Inès! Love you."

"Love you more, sweetheart!"

"You good?" She points to my leg, which I'm massaging with deep pressure.

"Long day." I lean back, close my eyes for a second, and try not to fall asleep. I could blame my lack of energy on the early hours bakery owners keep, but in all honesty, I haven't slept a wink since last week. I can't get my encounter with Harrison out of my head, and I hate to admit it's affecting me.

Every night, I play back the scene outside the bathroom, wondering if I should have at least given him my last name. Who knows, maybe he would have looked me up because something in my gut is telling me he felt the energy between us, too.

Should I have let that nasty girl who stood in line behind me go in front to give us more time to talk?

Maybe I was wrong about our differences; I should have spoken up. Or maybe it's all in my head, and he didn't feel one ounce of attraction.

Either way, I can't go back in time, nor can I tell my racing thoughts to stop, so I'm stuck in this hamster wheel of emotions.

"Hey, the place looks amazing. I just noticed the new paint," Becks interrupts my very important thoughts.

I open my eyes and stare at the newly painted walls done in a beautiful cream and light sage, with a floral mural painted on the far wall. It came out beautiful despite our inability to afford it since the rent debacle. But we had already paid the company the deposit, which was nonrefundable at fifty percent, so we had no choice other than to bite the bullet and pay the rest. It also complements our new glass cases that are trimmed with delicate gold.

"Thanks. I'm exhausted now. Do you want to come upstairs while I eat dinner?"

"I'll come over tomorrow. I should head back downtown to finish up some work. But I wanted to tell you, you're my plus one this weekend."

That has me sitting up straighter. "For what? And you're just telling me now? The weekend is in two days."

"I only just found out myself. It's this Friday, it's also black tie, but it's for charity, so that's a bonus."

"She'll go," my mom says as she walks out to hug and kiss Becks.

My bestie smirks. "I wasn't giving her much choice, but I'm glad you're here to back me up."

"I'm not going to be here anyway. I'm going to Aunt Liza's house."

"What?" I snap. "Can you stop going there? I don't trust them, especially Amber."

"She's been taking her medicine, and your aunt misses your father. I feel obligated; give it time, and I'm sure we'll drift apart soon enough like we did all those years ago."

I hope so, for Mom's sake.

My aunt is all sorts of fucked up, and her daughter, my cousin, who I am not close with at all, unfortunately, self-medicates for her schizophrenia and multiple personality disorder...or, at times, doesn't medicate at all and has had to be hospitalized on numerous occasions.

There was one time in my life when I can remember she took her medicine religiously, but then she had a psychotic break, and she's never been the same.

"If Amber is there, I want you to promise me you'll leave."

She kisses my forehead. "Only if you promise to go with Becks. You need to get out more."

I glance between the two of them and their begging eyes, deciding there is no way I can say no.

"Fine, send me the details, and let me know which dress I should wear."

Beck claps her hands excitedly. "The dress is covered. I'll bring it over tomorrow. My treat."

What?

I shake my head while Becks's eyes shoot daggers at me. I have plenty of gowns from the galas I had to attend with the ballet, so why should they go to waste?

"Just say thank you, Becks. You're the bestest friend in the whole world for treating me like a queen all the time."

"Thank you, Becks, for being a pain in my ass, and...thanks for the dress. Now I'm leaving. I'll talk to you later."

I kiss Becks and Mom goodbye before limping up the stairs.

My phone blasts through my speakers, and I run over to see Becks calling. "Hello? Please tell me you're running late because I am."

"Of course you are, and you know I'm not, so get your ass downstairs," she snaps and hangs up.

It grates on her nerves when I'm late, so I'm not surprised she's pissed off, but she's bossier than usual tonight.

I powder my nose for a shine-free evening and finish slicking back my hair before taking one last look in the mirror. You would think I'd be sick of my hair tightly pulled back after years of bun-wearing, but you gotta do what the dress calls for.

I spin around to make sure everything's in place. Becks somehow always knows exactly what will look perfect on my body.

It's a dark purple, silk, floor-length dress with a deep slit showing off my long-toned legs—her words, not mine—a high neck and low back. No embellishments or fluff, sexy yet still simple and classic. And, of course, I finish the look with the diamond studs my dad gave me when I earned the role of principal dancer.

Grabbing my clutch, I shut off the lights and lock up but hesitate when I turn the key. Shit…I run in and check the kettle.

It's supposed to shut off automatically. Apparently, that function stopped months ago, and I may have forgotten a few times and left the apartment with it still on. It's hard to remember everything when I'm somehow always running late sprinting out the door, but after my mom freaked out on me the other day, I won't be forgetting anymore.

Hopefully.

I shut it off, turn back, and the letter from building management catches my eye. I tried to hide it, so if it's out, Mom's been sitting here worrying about it. I hide it again in my closet for now; hopefully, she doesn't find it this time.

She's upset, rightfully so, but we have time to figure something out. After all the hell we've been through this year, we'll get through this. The Caldwell women are resilient.

The apartment buzzer goes off, and I press the intercom. "I'm coming down now. I'm sorry! I'm sorry!"

"Yeah, baby, look at you!" Becks whistles over the nonstop, honking from down the street.

What the hell is going on down there?

My nosy neighbor, who sits on her stoop every night, pokes her head around to see what Becks is going on about, so I give a quick wave and run toward the Uber when something almost knocks me down.

"Hey. Watch it!" I stop short. "You're not even supposed to be on the sidewalks, you jerk!" I yell after a biker speeding past me.

What is it, a full moon tonight?

I huff when I get in the back seat. "The city is in rare form tonight. Let's hope it's not a sign of how our night will go."

"It's been a while since we've been out all dressed up together. It's going to be so much fun." She leans over and kisses me hello.

"Hey, Jules!"

Gasping loudly, I throw my hand to my chest. "Holy fuck, Joshua, I thought this was a freaking Uber." I playfully slap Beck's older cousin's arm. "When did you get back to New York?"

"This morning. I just drove into the city. Rebecca jumped in the car and demanded I come pick you up."

"How was Turkey?" I ask. He's been there the last few weeks visiting his in-laws.

"Amazing. We all need to get to Bodrum together. It's fun times."

"As much as I love the chit-chat, this place is close, and I need you to put this on Jules." Becks holds up a mask.

"What in the…"

She shrugs. "I didn't know either. Apparently, it's a masquerade party. I had to pay an arm and a leg to get these shipped the same day."

I take the delicate, ornate mask in my hands and stare with rapt appreciation at the masterpiece. I glance up to see Becks fastening hers around her head, and my breath hitches.

"Becks," I murmur, reaching to run my fingers along her lace and velvet bunny mask. "Will everyone have elaborate pieces like this?" I glance back down to my butterfly mask.

The base is gold, and on one side, it looks like a typical mask hand-painted with purple Venetian motifs. The other side is sculpted into a beautiful oversized butterfly wing, doubling the size of my head, made from purple and gold metal, dressed with small diamonds and pearls.

It's gorgeous.

She helps tie mine securely. "Of course. The person who invited us showed me pictures from last year. People go all out."

"You never did say who invited you."

She smirks. "I know. Let's go, my pretty butterfly. Time for the show."

He's here.

Harrison Davenport is standing across the party in a black *Phantom of the Opera* mask, and I'm doing everything in my power not to pass out right here on the spot.

What is with this man and his power over me?

"Is this a work event?" I hiss at Becks.

She knows I was all flustered over him. Why wouldn't she tell me?

I've been so busy juggling everything and trying to figure out the next steps with the bakery that I didn't even put two and two together that this charity event could be work-related.

"No, well…"

"Well, what?" I snap.

She eyes me with annoyance. "What is your issue?"

"Harrison is here standing across the room with a group of men." I take a deep breath, I don't know why I'm getting so worked up about this, but it would have been nice to get a heads up for fuck's sake.

We both turn toward the guys, and just like at the restaurant, my eyes are glued to him, triggering a rush of heat to spread through my body. I take a deep breath to expel any extra energy because I'm almost positive it's not normal to be this excited over a stranger.

"Oh shit," Becks mutters.

"What? What are you *oh shitting* about?" I asked, panicked.

Her eyes widen. "You need to take a freaking chill pill. You look like a crackhead."

"How do you even know what that looks like?"

She shrugs. "I live downtown."

I roll my eyes, unimpressed. "Spit out why you said it."

"Well." She grabs two champagnes from a passing waiter, one for each of us, before continuing, "Do you see the man in the leather mask that looks like a crow? He's two down from Harrison."

"Yes." It's hard to make him out because his mask covers most of his face, but his green eyes are vibrant and shine against his black face piece.

"Well, he's...a good friend at work and invited me with a guest." She sips her champagne. "I forgot he's close to Harrison and his brothers."

"Why did you hesitate at *good friend*? How good of a friend?"

She clears her throat. "Not great, just friends."

She's lying.

I know Becks better than anyone in the world, and there is only one reason why she would lie to me about him, and I'm scared to even confirm after what she's gone through in her past.

"Rebecca." I drag out her name. "Please tell me he's not your boss."

She cringes and chugs down a massive gulp of champagne.

"Becks," I hiss. "What the hell are you doing?"

She closes her eyes momentarily. "Well, technically, he's my boss's boss, but it just happened, and it's not like last time."

"Fuck," I whisper to myself.

When Becks was an intern in her senior year of college, her boss manipulated her to fall in love with him. He wined and dined her and told her he had recently divorced his wife. He even went so far as to show her an apartment he wanted to buy for them in SoHo.

It turned out he was never divorced or even separated, and on top of that, his wife was pregnant. To say it killed Becks is an understatement.

The wife was the one who found out about Becks, so she did what any other pregnant wife would have done if she found out her husband had a mistress—she went to the office and made a huge scene in front of everyone.

Becks was not only mortified, but she felt horrible. She eventually sent a letter to the wife explaining everything that happened from day one. Then found out the wife divorced that son of bitch soon after, but Becks never fully recovered.

Luckily, her internship was up around the same time, and because of it all, they gave her a raving review.

All I know is if I were her, I would have never been able to stay in that industry, running into the people who witnessed it all. I couldn't handle it.

"Get out of your head, Jules. I promise I'm okay, and it's truly not like last time. We're nothing serious, just fun."

"Are you positive he is what he says he is?" I ask, worried.

"His name is Matteo Moretti. You can look him up if you want. He's not as well-known as Harrison and his family, but you'll find information."

Interlocking our hands, I squeeze gently. "I love you and worry about you."

"I know." She squeezes back.

We turn toward the party, sipping our drinks, silenced by the scene in front of us. "I'm used to bougie galas, but this is different. It's very avant-garde."

"Totally." She nods in agreement as a performer wrapped in ropes drops from the high ceiling. "It's pretty incredible."

The whole vibe of this party is out there, with the outlandish performances and mysterious masks. Electric beats you feel in your core pump through the speakers.

"I feel like I'm at a party with the Life and Death Brigade."

She lifts her drink. "In omnia paratus."

I check her hip lightly. "You jump, I jump, Jack."

"God, I love *Gilmore Girls*. We're due for a binge sesh."

"I'll never say no to that. Do you think someone lives here?" I can't tell if it's unfinished or meant to look raw. All I know is the space is triple the size of any house I've seen in the city.

I might not run in the elite circles, but I've seen my fair share of wealthy places. We were often asked to schmooze with potential donors at their parties when we weren't performing.

"I think it's a work in progress. I overheard someone saying it's two townhouses opened up to be one big house eventually."

God, who needs this much space?

The lights lower, and the music increases as men on stilts walk out, bending down to pass out canapés.

"I'm going to use the bathroom. Do you want to come?"

"I'll wait here or by that bar." I nod toward the corner.

It's the perfect opportunity to be a creepy stalker by myself.

Heads turn as Becks walks away. They always do. She has the curves every woman wishes for, even if her silver Grecian-style dress is flowy and leaves something to the imagination, they're still staring.

Curious, I glance at Matteo to see if he's looking, and sure enough, he's tracking her every move. When their eyes catch, she falters and grins. He smiles back and ducks his head shyly.

Oh.

Oooh.

He likes her.

Feeling like I'm looking at a private moment, I glance back to who I really care about.

Harrison.

While Matteo focuses on Becks, Harrison talks to three other men who look vaguely familiar. It's hard to tell with their masks on.

Maybe they're from the restaurant or my internet stalking. What I can tell from here is they all stand tall and hold a dominant presence about them.

And if they look this good with their masks on, I'd say there is a good chance they're pretty freaking hot, too.

Maybe they're his brothers like Beck mentioned, yet I only

remember them listing one in my— *embarrassed to say*—many, many searches of him, which typically ended with me slamming my laptop closed. I didn't particularly like the feeling I got from seeing every model and beautiful socialite hanging off his arm.

Tonight, however, I see no one by his side.

I take another sip of my champagne and swish the bubbles in my mouth for a quick jolt, reminding myself this is real life.

Him here tonight, in the flesh, feels like a dream. Similar to the ones I've had all week, causing me to repeatedly question what could have been after our last meeting.

Adrenaline courses through my body as I think of all the scenarios that could play out right now. I promised myself if we ever meet again, I would at least have the courage to introduce myself.

As much as I would love to take a risk and walk up to him, it's just not going to happen. Even the new Jules doesn't have big enough balls for that.

He must feel the burning intensity of my eyes on him because he finally turns, and through his mask, his blue eyes catch mine from across the room, triggering my body, tingling head to toe in excitement.

Does he remember?

On instinct, my mouth quirks up on one side in a slight, impish grin. Harrison's head tilts, looking at me with uncertainty. Then I watch his eyes drop the length of my body, clenching his jaw before turning to continue talking.

Huh?

He looks aggravated.

He rolls his neck, and my eyes track down his body to where he's gripping his drink so hard I'm afraid the glass might break at any moment.

He takes a visible breath before turning his eyes back to me, and I'm stunned like a deer in the headlights. Sense finally works its way up, and I turn away from his menacing glare.

Embarrassed that I played out a completely different scenario in my head, I rush over to the bar in the opposite direction and order a dirty martini. I need something much stronger than champagne.

That look wasn't flirty like at the restaurant; it was something I'd never seen before.

The second the bartender places the drink in front of me, it's in my hands and quickly to my lips.

My nose wrinkles, and I place the drink down as swiftly as I picked it up.

Ugh. This is like drinking the freaking ocean.

"Too strong?" a dark voice asks from beside me.

I look up at the man towering over me in a fox mask. "No, too much brine. They were my dad's favorite, but he made them different."

"Ah, I see. You need to ask for it slightly dirty. Though I like it very dirty."

Surprised at his directness, I choke on my drink and raise my eyebrows, causing him to laugh.

"Why a fox?" I ask, changing the subject.

"I like what you did there. Why not a fox? They're sneaky and agile. Sounds fun to me."

"Ah, sly like a fox, are you?"

His dark eyes sparkle. "Exactly." He clinks my glass. "Can I buy you another drink?"

"You mean, can you buy me one of the free drinks?"

His lips twist into a smirk, letting his dimples peek out from his mask. I like this guy. "Touché. Let me be a gentleman and order for you, then."

"Hmm. I believe a gentleman would have at least introduced himself first."

He places his drink down and takes my hand, kissing it as he bows. "My apologies. Let me introduce myself…I'm Leo Morales, pleased to make your acquaintance."

I giggle and open my mouth to say my name but stop myself when a tall shadow hovers over me. How my body is reacting; I know exactly who stands behind me.

Slowly, I turn and look up, coming face to face with piercing blue eyes. My breath catches, and my heart races at a warped speed. I open my mouth to say something, but I'm completely mute.

This is your chance…introduce yourself, you idiot.

Harrison lifts his head to look past me, giving Leo a death stare.

Leo laughs hysterically, punching Harrison on the arm. "See you later, big bro, and you." He looks at me. "Were the highlight of my night. Nice to meet you?"

"Jules," I whisper.

"Goodbye, Jules." He blows me a playful kiss and walks away.

Harrison's eyes slowly drag down to mine, holding me imprisoned by his attention. He takes a deep breath, his nostril flaring slightly, both of us completely dazed. It's then I realize his baby blues that have had me enamored and dreaming about them all week are actually more of an electric turquoise and are heart-stoppingly perfect; I could stare into them all night.

Without breaking our gaze, he lifts his arm to get the bartender's attention, and the scent of his woodsy cologne rolls over me. "Two slightly dirty martinis," his deep, velvety voice commands.

Slight dirty…how long was he standing there?

He extends his hand. "Harrison," he purrs.

He doesn't remember.

3

Juliette

I STAND THERE with my hand in his, completely numb. I thought...was I truly imagining a connection?

A lump forms in my throat, unsure what to say. I'm humiliated.

One side of Harrison's lips lifts, and he raises a brow, waiting for me to answer, completely unaware of my inner freakout.

Snap out of it, Jules, I think to myself.

What does it matter if he doesn't remember? Maybe he doesn't recognize me with my mask on.

Either way, who cares? Now's the chance. Give him something to remember.

A few embarrassing seconds later, I shake his hand, "Hi," I mutter and smile softly, trying to play it cool, which is the opposite of how I feel. "Jules."

His thumb brushes along my skin. "Jules...what a beautiful name for a beautiful girl."

I bow my head self-consciously. "How do you know? I have a mask on."

"True." He chuckles in a deep rasp I instantly love the sound of.

His free hand cups my chin to lift my face, his eyes boring deep into mine. "Though, I say what I mean, Jules. I don't pass along compliments for clout."

I never understood it when I read it in books or saw it in a movie —*the connection between their eyes*—now I do.

When my eyes meet Harrison's, deep inside my stomach, an intense feeling flutters and flips in happiness. They're mesmerizing and completely hypnotize me; for however long I know him, I hope this feeling never stops.

"Well, thank you then," I reply.

"I'm insulted." He bites his lip to hide a smile. "Do you not think I'm beautiful?"

I giggle, unable to hold back my grin. "Beauty to me is not only looks. Sure, you're extremely handsome, but beauty is the whole picture, so I think I'll have to get to know you better before making that assessment."

"Extremely handsome?" His eyes widen. "I'll take it."

We laugh, and the bartender sets our drinks down. Together, we lift our hands to get them, both realizing we're still holding on to one another.

His face drops, pulling our hands apart, staring at his for a second before picking up his drink.

What's that look for?

Without missing a beat, he lifts his drink to cheers me, and we both take a sip, "Better?" he asks.

"Much. Thank you." I smile again. My cheeks are going to burn out of my head soon. "So, were you listening to our whole conversation?" He looks at me confused, "Leo and me. You knew about my martini."

"Oh." He shakes his head, annoyed. "I walked over right then, and he only came over to you to piss me off."

"Why would you get pissed off by your brother talking to me?"

He bends down, and it takes everything in me not to melt to the ground, "Since the second you walked through the door, you've captured my attention. I wanted, no needed, to talk to you.

But my brother thought cutting me off at the chase would be funny."

My heart begins to beat faster. "Is that so?"

"Mmhmm." His eyes quickly glance down my body, and I don't miss it.

I stand a little taller. "So he wasn't flirting with me, only trying to make you jealous?"

He scoffs, "I don't get jealous."

"Hm, sounds like jealousy to me." I shrug teasingly and smirk.

He sips his drink again, seeming to be contemplating my statement, but quickly dismissing the idea. "Do you…" He pauses.

I wait patiently.

Do I what, Harrison?

He points to a seating area completely secluded behind the DJ. "Maybe want to talk some more over there?"

Jackpot.

It takes everything in me not to break out in a massive grin, so instead, I nod eagerly. "Yes, I absolutely do."

He releases a breath as if he thought I might reject his offer, then takes my drink, carrying it to the table for me.

I turn toward Becks, who is now standing with Matteo, motioning toward the seats, and she nods, not giving off much emotion.

I'll unpack that later.

Hours, days, minutes later, who cares? All I know is we've had a thousand drinks, and we're having the best time ever. I haven't stopped smiling or laughing, and he's right there with me.

Harrison Davenport has been completely and utterly unexpected in the best possible way.

He still has this elusive alpha dominance thing going on, even now, with how he's leaning back in the chair—arms and legs stretched wide, commanding all my attention. But besides all that manly hotness, he's also charming, intelligent, and funny in a dry, unbothered way.

He reaches forward, grabs my chair, and quickly pulls it toward him. I squeal loudly with laughter. "Harrison!"

His arm stretches across the back of my chair. "How did you get so far away from me? I like you close."

"Oh." *Swoon.* "Close together sounds good." Like a lovesick puppy, I can't take my eyes off this man. I'm not sure I've ever been so attracted to anyone in my life, and I can't pinpoint what it is.

His flirty smile, big blue eyes, or chiseled jaw? I have no freaking clue, but all of them together are doing all the right things. Even his grown-in stubble is a turn-on.

His hand reaches over, and his finger traces my shoulder. He smirks flirtatiously when he feels my skin pebble under his touch.

"You feel familiar to me," he murmurs.

Hmm, probably because you flirted with me all night at the restaurant. I'm not going to tell him that, though, on the off chance he doesn't remember, and I embarrass myself. Let him figure it out himself.

I sip my water for hydration, "Probably because I'm so likable," I say straight-faced, until he playfully pinches my side, and we both laugh.

"Truth. You are." He nods. "So, you're a baker?"

"A pastry chef whose mom taught her. I work at her bakery." I purposely left out my dancing career tonight. Knowing it's bound to dampen the mood, and tonight is not the night for a pity party.

"Your mom's the baker who owns a bakery, and you're just a poser?" He raises his brows and smiles wide.

"Bingo." I clink his glass. "In France, they separate their bread and pastry shops, but here they often combine them, so my mom did the same. Technically she's a maître pâtissier, a—"

"Master pastry chef," he finishes.

"You know French?" I ask excitedly.

We never speak French at home. Mom taught Dad and me; she even sent me to French school when I was younger, but she wanted to embrace her American life, so we only spoke English.

Unless she's mad…that's a different story.

"I do. As well as German, Italian, and Spanish," he tells me confidently, but not in a bragging way.

"Heute abend war erstaunlich," I whisper.

He holds my eyes, impressed. "You're right, tonight was amazing. You speak French and German. That's unheard of nowadays."

"My mom's from the Alsace region in France. They speak both of those languages. I also know a little Spanish, but that's more of a work in progress."

"Jules?" He turns his head suddenly, giving me all his attention.

I match his position, leaning my head back on his arm, letting my cheek quickly rub against him, and it takes everything in my drunk lust power not to purr against him like a cat.

He takes a breath. "How old are you?"

I don't want to answer this.

"Twenty-four." I cringe.

"What?" His eyes bulge, and he sits up straight. "Fuck."

"What's wrong?"

"I'm thirty-eight. You're fourteen years younger than me. I'm too old to be hanging out with you like this."

Of course, I already knew how old he was, but when he says it out loud, it does sound old. But the hell if I care.

He's too handsome and smart for me to give a shit about something so trivial. And the attraction...there is no denying it. Age doesn't matter.

I shrug. "I don't mind it."

"You should," he mumbles, then leans back, and I place my head back on his arm.

We're both quiet for a beat longer than I like.

"Jules." He sighs.

"Don't, Harrison. Don't ruin a spectacular night over something so insignificant. Who cares?"

He takes a big gulp of his drink. "I should."

I smile wide and position my head closer to his. "But you don't." I turn and kiss his arm.

His breath hitches, and he leans over and whispers, "Do you want to dance?" against my ear.

I frown, not particularly.

Glancing over to the other side of the room, I notice the crowded dance floor. I don't want to share him with anyone else.

Luckily, Becks has wanted to spend time with Matteo, so I've been spoiled all night with it being just us.

"Not there...here." He stands and holds out his hands for me. "Just me and you."

Excitement runs through me. I place my hand in his, and he helps me stand. "Yes, me and you sound perfect."

More than I'd like to admit.

My breathing is loud and labored; his pupils are blown, and we're both completely turned on. Why isn't he making a move?

We've been dancing to countless songs, neither of us ready to stop. It's the perfect excuse to run our hands all over one another and have it be completely appropriate-*ish*.

"Harrison," I moan and squeeze his large, muscular biceps, then run my palms over his broad shoulders.

His knees are bent slightly, so with every sway of our body, his hard erection rubs into me, causing me to see stars and feel shock waves down below.

What is this man doing to me? My heartbeat is in my ears, and I'm going to lose my mind. I'm not sure what magical potion they put in these drinks, but whatever it is, keep it coming.

Stat!

"Fuck, Jules. You feel perfect under my touch." He traces his hands down my back and lightly squeezes my behind, pulling me close to him.

Every few moments, as we glide together, he lets his lips graze the small heart-shaped beauty mark that sits below my ear, and on the last time, I snap.

I can't take it any longer.

"You know, for an older, experienced man, I would have thought you had more game than this," I tease, hoping to push his buttons so he'll finally kiss me.

Or better yet, throw me over the table and have his way with me because it's been too damn long since a man has been inside me.

Scratch that. Now, thinking of it, I'm not sure a *man* has ever been inside of me before. I've only dated immature boys. But now, my body is craving nothing but man, specifically Harrison Davenport.

"What's that supposed to mean?" He grips me tighter, grinding into me.

"I thought you would have at least kissed me by now," I mutter, looking up into his eyes.

He lets me go, and I feel an instant loss, but he quickly moves his hands to my face, cupping my cheeks. "I would love nothing more, Jules. Except I'd rather kiss you for the first time in private."

"Oh. Okay." I lean in, hiding my smile into his chest, then kiss it lightly. "I'll be right back. I'm going to the bathroom."

I wash and dry my hands, then lean over the sink, taking a few deep breaths, needing to recenter before heading back out there. Glancing up at the mirror, I smile, looking flushed and happy...but most importantly, I feel alive.

My mother's words come back to me—*something bigger and better will come along*—and I feel that tonight for the first time in a while.

A loud knock comes from the door, "One minute," I call.

With one last deep breath, I open the door, and for whatever reason, I'm not shocked to see Harrison towering over me in the doorway. His arms spread against the door jams, and without a word, he steps in, wraps one strong arm around my waist, hoists me up in his arms, and carries me down the hall into an unfinished bedroom.

I nuzzle my face into the crook of his neck, peppering small kisses against his skin until he sets me down, letting my body drag along his on the way down.

This is really happening.

The room is poorly lit, but I can make out each inch of his delicious body, especially his big, full lips, that I'm dying to taste.

I reach to untie my mask, but Harrison stops me mid-way. "Don't." His words, as forceful as his grip on my hips. "Here at this party, *mon petit papillon*, you will leave this mask on. Then later, when I have you in bed, withering beneath my touch, you'll take it off so I can see your expression when you come on my tongue. Do you understand?" he says in his deep, authoritative voice.

My breath hitches, and I bite my lip, nodding without an ounce of hesitation. I could tell him I'm not that kind of girl because I'm not, at least, I never have been before.

But tonight, for Harrison, I'm willing to try anything.

"Good girl." He runs the pad of his thumb along my bottom lip, plucking it out from beneath my teeth while my legs wobble from his words.

Our eyes lock, and the prolonged anticipation is almost unbearable. "Please," I groan in desperation, and like he was reading my mind, at the same time, he leans down, claiming my lips.

My heart is pumping against my chest, and every nerve ending is on full alert. Something snaps inside me the second I feel him against me. I lose all control. I'm completely and utterly desperate for him. "Harrison," I moan, grabbing at his lapels to get closer, demanding a deeper kiss.

"Fuck, Jules. God dammit." He barks, pulling me up so I wrap my legs tightly around his core, letting my body take over as it begins to move at its own accord. "Yes, baby, just like that." He grips under my behind, pulling me against his hard length, then recaptures my mouth, more aggressively this time.

He swipes through my lips, twirling our tongues together in a perfect dance as I kiss him back with everything I have. I want to leave him speechless because this is everything I have ever imagined and more.

My hands drag through his hair, and we kiss for a long time…so long I get so carried away that I fail to notice my impending orgasm creeping up as I rub against his erection.

Harrison doesn't miss it. He's pushing and pulling me against him, and the knowing tingling sensation is creeping up hard and fast. Every muscle inside me clenches, trying to hold back, but it's no use. My body is starving for him.

My jaw drops open, panting loudly as he bites the side of my neck, eliciting a loud moan to slip from my mouth. He smiles against me, then lets his tongue peek out to drag up the delicate part of my skin, "Ride me, Jules. Ride me, and let go. I want to hear you scream my name," he growls in my ear.

Oh no. I'll never be able to hold it now.

My hips move with his, bucking wildly, chasing that euphoric feeling as I begin to see stars.

"Oh…oh."

"Say it!" he growls.

"Harrison! Ahhh," I cry into his mouth. "I'm going to come," I moan, gripping his shoulders with a death grip, frantically rolling my hips against him as my body shakes and convulses. I've never felt anything like it before. He is amazing, and now I'm in a complete daze as I come down from my high.

Harrison holds me against his chest, kissing my forehead, which seems too intimate, but I can't deny I love the feeling.

"Harrison?" I mutter.

He slowly and softly places me down on the ground, then cups my cheek. "Yeah, baby?" He smirks.

Bastard.

"I—" I begin to say but get interrupted by his phone's loud ring tone.

"Fuck." He pulls it out of his pocket, and I see the name *Marissa* light up before he quickly answers it. "Hello?" He takes a step back, listening with rapt attention, then drags his hand down his face. "I'm near the house. I'll be home in ten minutes."

What?

He pockets his phone, and his face is full of sorrow. He leans down and kisses my cheek. "I'm so fucking sorry, Jules, I need to leave."

"Now?" I whisper yell.

46

He nods, adjusts himself—*a brutal reminder of what we just did*—and walks in the direction we came in from, stopping at the doorway. "I'm truly sorry. It's an emergency." And without a second glance, he's out the door before I can open my mouth.

What the fuck just happened?

Glancing around the dark, empty room, I suddenly feel more alone than I ever have before, not exactly the feeling you want after you've opened yourself up to a stranger...I don't even know what to do right now.

I'm mortified.

Realizing I can't stay here, I reach for my bag and text Becks.

> Please stay with Matteo, but I need to get out of here now. I'll talk to you tomorrow.
>
> Love you xx

Then I pocket my phone and run far away from this fucking shit show of a party before I have a second longer to think about my actions or how he didn't even ask for my number.

Harrison

I swing open my front door and run up the steps two at a time toward my daughter's room.

Marissa, the babysitter, pops her head out, "I'm so sorry, Mr. Davenport, she just fell asleep. I think she was exhausted from all the crying."

I drag my hands down my face, *fuck*.

"Normally, I wouldn't have called and ruined your night. I know Claudina gets upset when you're gone, but this was more than the last time I was here."

I reach into my pocket and grab cash to pay her, then give her a reassuring look. "You did the right thing. Thank you for letting me know and for babysitting on such short notice."

She smiles a bright, genuine smile, "Any time. I love hanging out with Claud. She's the sweetest little girl. Don't tell the other parents, but she's my favorite in the neighborhood to babysit. If your nanny needs more days off, I'm your girl."

I chuckle at her honesty, though I have to agree Claud is the best. "You got it. Robert, my driver, is out front. He'll take you home, and tell your parents hello from me."

"Sure thing!" She runs down the steps, and when she closes the door behind her, I'm stalking down the hall to get to my girl.

Quietly, I open the door, tiptoe toward her bed, and relax in the chair beside her. Tonight is not unusual, so I wasn't shocked when I got the call; if anything, I should have expected it.

There are only a handful of people Claudina's comfortable with besides me. My brothers, her nanny, Willa, and her grandparents—*on Camila's side.* She tolerates the babysitter enough to enjoy some playtime but begins to freak out when she realizes one of us isn't there for bedtime.

It's why, typically, she's with one of us at all times. However, once in a blue moon, it can't be helped.

Like tonight, Willa was sick, and the whole family got together to support my brothers Leo and Nate, the architects, and their charity Building Unity Organization, which rebuilds homes and run-down towns in both America and Spain, specifically near where the Morales family comes from.

Not that I was doing much supporting hiding in the corner of the room, but—

"Daddy?" my precious girl whispers, then begins to cry again.

I rub her back. "I'm here, angel. Please don't cry."

"I-I missed you so much." She sobs, reaching over to throw her arm around my legs, and it breaks my heart into a million pieces to see her so upset. "I didn't know when you were coming home."

"I'm here now." I lean and kiss her head. "I love you so much, Claudina. You're okay, angel. Back to sleep."

She looks up through her tearful lashes, batting them for attention. "Butterfly kisses first."

I lean down, and our lashes flutter together before she snuggles back under the covers, falling asleep within a minute like all is right in the world.

In her world, maybe. But mine, nothing is fucking right about tonight.

I roll my neck and take a deep breath. *What did I do?*

Claudina will always and forever come first, no matter what. It's one of the reasons I've never had a serious relationship, and never will, or at least not until Claud's much older and can understand that I'm not trying to replace Camila. None of my personal rationale, though, makes the way I treated Jules okay.

She deserves all the respect in the world, and if I ever see her again, I'll make sure she knows how sorry I am.

Until then, I'll accept my punishment and dream of her red plump lips parted in shock and her brown doe-like eyes staring at me with a mix of sadness, horror, and embarrassment as I left her behind without a second glance.

Though out of everything, the fucked-up thing of it all is I called her *mon petit papillon, my little butterfly,* and that name should be reserved for someone special, not a stranger I may never see again.

I could tell myself it was because of her butterfly mask, knowing deep down it wasn't.

"Lauren," I bark, annoyed I have to call for her again. I'm not in the fucking mood today.

"Oh my god, can you stop screaming my name? It's not going to make me work any faster." My lovely yet sarcastic assistant saunters into my office without a care in the world, finally giving me the paperwork I requested over an hour ago.

"Took you long enough," I mutter.

"I'm not a fucking robot, Harrison," she snaps, and I narrow my eyes at her.

"You're lucky you're halfway competent. Otherwise, your ass would have been fired years ago."

She rolls her eyes. "You've been saying the same thing every week for the last ten years. Get a different line." She smugly smiles and slams the door behind her.

Witch.

She knows I'd never fire her. I'd die without her, she's so much more than an extension of me—she probably could do this job better, honestly.

But fuck, does she grate on my nerves.

I hit the buzzer. "What?" she snaps.

"Lauren, I'm not in the mood. Can you please get my brother on the line?"

"You haven't been in the mood for the last two weeks. Frankly, I'm getting sick of it. Which one?"

"Nate, and make it fast. I have shit to do."

Not even a minute later, my phone buzzes. "The better Davenport is on line one," Lauren chirps happily.

The better Davenport, my ass. "Yo."

"Yo? Is that how an Ivy League education taught you to greet your loved ones?"

I throw my head back, groaning, "Can you stop being a pain in my ass? I need help."

Why is everyone getting on my last nerve today?

He chuckles. Dickhead loves to get under my skin. "I just finished a meeting by your office. You want to go grab lunch?"

"Can't. I'm too busy, come here, and I'll have Lauren order us something."

"Dad isn't there, lurking in the halls pretending he still runs the place, is he?"

That makes me laugh, "No, I put my foot down months ago when he was harassing the interns. Haven't seen him since, thank god."

"Good. I'll be there in ten."

My door flies open, and I look up from my computer to Nate yelling on his phone as if I'm not running a trillion-dollar company where people need to concentrate to work. "Run him over with your car if you need to," he shouts before hanging up and dropping onto my couch in the corner.

I raise a questioning brow, wondering what the hell that was.

"Don't look at me with those judging eyes of yours. I'm killing anyone who pisses me off today."

"I spoke to you five minutes ago. You were happy to go to lunch. Now you're a murderer?"

"Not guilty...for now."

Lauren chooses that moment to saunter in with our food, of course, without knocking. "Who's killing who?"

She puts down the takeout bags and walks over to Nate, kissing him hello. "Don't you want to come to work for me? He's probably a miserable fuck to work for, and I'll double your pay."

She turns to me. "You hear that? He'll double my pay."

"Then he'll stab you in the back and murder you." I lean back, stretching my arms behind my head. "Also, do you mind? We need to talk."

She plops down next to Nate. "Sounds important. I'm all ears." Then her phone rings, and she's running out without a goodbye.

"I'm dead ass serious. I want her to work for me. She's probably miserable here," Nate says when she leaves.

"She's not miserable, we're like brother and sister. She won't leave me. If you try to poach her, just see what happens. Now tell me why the hell you were screaming, scaring everyone in my office." I unwrap my sandwich and take a bite of my usual turkey club as I wait for my dramatic brother to spit out whatever he has to say.

"Leo is in Georgia—"

"Nope. Stop right there. I don't want to hear anymore." Not in the mood for his drama.

He regards me with a hard stare. "Don't be such a jerk-off."

"Nathaniel, if Leo is in Georgia, and you were stress yelling, it means it's something about Maddie Grace, and I can't listen to that drama anymore. You want her? Go fucking get her. Otherwise, I don't want to hear it anymore. You've been pining over her from afar for years. Enough is enough already."

He glares with fury as he grabs his sandwich, knocking my water over in the process, and doesn't make one move to clean it up. You can cut the tension between us with a knife. I don't like hurting my brother, but he knows I'm right.

My younger brother is still in love with his childhood sweetheart, and he's letting life pass him by without doing anything about it.

When I can tell he's more level-headed, I blurt out what's been eating me alive all week. "I fucked up two weeks ago, and I can't get it out of my head." I take a deep breath and exhale through my nose. "I dry-humped a girl and ditched her right after."

"First of all, what are you, fifteen? Second, who was she? The hot one from that Friday?"

I nod. "How could you tell she was hot from across the room with her mask on?"

"Masks can't hide that kind of hot." He shrugs. "And those legs. Fuck, they were nice."

And this feeling right now, the burning jealousy coursing through my chest, is why I don't understand anything going on in my head. I don't know this woman from a hole in the wall, yet even having my brother talk about her legs makes me homicidal.

"So you just left her?" His eyes widen, and I cringe.

"Yes, and I've been sick over it since." My stomach has been in knots anytime I think about Jules and the night we had together. If I were any other man, things would have been different with her because *she* was different…the best kind of different.

Maybe it was the mystery of our masks or the forbiddenness of our ages, but something had my walls and inhibitions easily coming down around her, and I'm not sure if I loved or hated it, but either way, she's still affecting.

He takes another bite and mumbles, "So call her."

I stare at him and don't answer. His facial expression at my silence makes me feel like an even bigger asshole.

"You didn't even ask for her number, you idiot. That's a low blow." He shakes his head. "I mean, even if you were never going to call her, you could have at least acted like you cared."

"That's the thing. I did care, and I freaked out."

"You don't normally do repeats with people you don't trust, so does it even matter?"

How could he understand? I barely do. "That doesn't excuse that I left her standing there not even a minute after she was screaming my name. The babysitter called about Claudina crying, and I panicked. I jetted out of the room, barely saying goodbye."

He sighs, knowing I'm fucked. "So why do you need my help?"

"Have your assistant send me the guest list so I can comb over the names."

"What's her name?"

"Jules."

His eyes widen. "Jules, what?"

"No clue." I shrug, embarrassed. I'm never this careless.

"You really are fucked. Lizzy took off after the event. I'll get it to you this weekend."

I glance down at my calendar, and it's blank beside Claud's dance class. "What's this weekend?"

"Seb texted the other day asking to switch his Claudina weekend. He's taking her Thursday."

"I know where my daughter will be. What does that have to do with me?"

"Now you're childless. You can come out for Matteo's birthday."

I shake my head. "Nope, I'm not going out again. I've hit my quota for the month."

He glares at me, "You should be there for Matteo."

I hate that he's right. "Fine."

4

Juliette

"Good morning," I say as I quickly pop into the bakery.

It's my day off, and I'm meeting Adriana, a friend from The City Ballet, for a walk in the park. But first, I wanted to stop in to ensure everything was going smoothly.

Often, I worry about Mom and Alice's niece, Daphne, who steps up to help on my days off. Like me, she's not classically trained and has skills I haven't mastered yet, so I'm excited she's working for us.

Mom, on the other hand, doesn't love the idea. She sees her as a replacement, but Daphne is an asset and a phenomenal baker. I just need Mom to change her view.

"How's everything going, Alice?"

She looks up, and her face is full of worry. "What's wrong?" My stomach plummets.

"Your mom's not having a good morning, Jules, and she won't take help from anyone."

My heart breaks a little. "What's she making?"

"Earlier, she made cupcakes, which you know she hates, so it set

54

her in a mood. Now she's piping out the macarons, but squeezing the bag is giving her a lot of trouble."

Oh, do I ever.

My mother is mostly reasonable. However, there is one thing she loathes most in the world, and she makes it known any chance she gets —baking desserts that aren't gourmet.

For example…cupcakes.

But, considering we're on the path to not one but two popular private schools in New York City, it made sense for the business. All the kids love the addition, doubling our clientele.

"Okay, thanks for letting me know, Alice."

I walk in the back to French jazz blasting loudly through the speakers and observe Mom without her hearing me enter. I glance at Daphne, and she gives me a sad smile, then returns to work.

Mom's face is pinched as her hands shake violently. I can only imagine the pain she's in. She still has some good days, but what I'm witnessing now only reminds me that the bad now outweighs the good, and her time in the back baking with us is dwindling.

The second I see a tear stream down her face, I quietly rush to her and take the piping bag out of her hands. After placing it on the counter, I turn and wordlessly pull her in my arms, hugging her tightly until I feel her breathing calm.

No words are exchanged; if she wants to talk about it, she will.

When I step back, she looks down, and I know something else is up. "What's wrong, Mom?"

She closes her eyes and takes a deep breath. "The building management called for a meeting. They want you to call them back."

This is what has her so worried?

"No, Mom, don't worry. I called them for the meeting." When she looks at me confused, I continue, "Our main goal is to stay here, but we both know we need a miracle. I'm trying to figure something out. Before we start making any decisions, I want to ensure I exhaust all my options with management first."

She pulls me in for another hug. "My love," she whispers. "Strong and smart, just like your father."

I step back and beam. "That's the best compliment you could ever give me."

She smiles warmly, then pushes me toward the exit. "Now, off you go. It's your day off. Daphne can help me with the rest."

I duck under her arm, quickly sticking my finger in the leftover cupcake batter, and moan in delight. God, that's freaking delicious.

"Is that chocolate with orange blossom?" I try and stick my finger in again, but Mom swats my hand. "Hey," I protest. "That was going in the garbage anyway."

"Stop contaminating my kitchen, and of course it is. It's one of your favorites." She kisses my cheek and pushes me toward the door.

"Call me if you need anything at all." I pause at the door, "And go ice your hands, please."

I ask firmly, begging with my eyes, and luckily, she nods in agreement, sadly proving I was right about how bad they are.

"Hey, Willa," I call after my favorite customer when I see her crossing Fifth Avenue into Central Park.

She waves excitedly. "Juliette, I'm so glad I ran into you. I've been meaning to stop by this week."

I kiss her hello. "Where's the little one?"

"She's with her uncle today," she steps back and looks me up and down, "I didn't tell you this when I saw you last, but you look amazing, and this new hair suits you perfectly. You look refreshed."

"Oh," I blush. "Thank you."

"You're welcome. If you're not busy, I have a quick question."

"Sure. What's up?" I ask while directing us away from the crowd swarming in front of The Met and walk us toward the entrance near 79th Street.

"I wanted to follow up on those kid's baking classes you mentioned. No pressure, but any idea when or if you will start them?"

Excitement runs through me; it's something I've been thinking about more and more recently. I wasn't sure anyone would be interested, especially with most of the area leaving for their Hamptons houses soon.

"Do you think I'd get people to sign up? I was worried with summer near, people would be too busy, and they wouldn't be interested."

"Can you do the classes during the week?"

"As if I have a life." I laugh. "I can do them whenever. How about I put out an interest form, and if I get enough responses, we could start them in the next couple of weeks?"

"Yes! Perfect. I'm secretly hoping I can stay and learn something, too."

I chuckle. "The more the merrier."

She glances down at her watch and flinches. "I'm going to grab a cab to get me to the Upper West Side. I'm late for lunch with my granny."

While we hug goodbye, I suck in a breath and freeze at what catches my eye over her shoulder.

Willa leans back with her hands on my shoulder, eyeing me with concern, "What's wrong?"

Completely stunned, I stand there momentarily before shaking off any telling feelings I may show.

I fake a smile, "I thought I saw someone I know." I say weakly and kiss her goodbye before she grabs a cab.

Staring at the now-empty street corner should have me second-guessing who I saw, but my eyes don't lie, especially when it comes to Harrison Davenport.

I have fifteen minutes until I meet Adriana, so I sit on the bench to collect my thoughts and feelings. Taking a deep breath, I run my hands over my face and rub my temples in frustration, then hang my head back against the brick wall that encloses the park.

I hate that this man has such an effect on me.

When I open my eyes and stare at the sky, the calming effect of the American oaks that line Fifth Avenue typically has on me is non-existent, only frustrating me more.

Today was about starting the weekend off fresh; it's why I

suggested a walk in the park with Adriana. Being here always soothes my soul.

I love how diverse the park is. Parts are lively, with music blasting and performers entertaining, and then there are quiet, lesser-known paths and bridges, and even small gardens that people don't know exist, where I like to sit and reflect.

And now it feels tainted because all I can think about is Harrison and the night at the masquerade gala.

The picture I portrayed in my head was that we had some deep, meaningful connection, and then he left me there without a second thought. He didn't even ask for my number. I'm a fool.

Immature, and I need to get over it.

Twenty-four-year-olds in the city have one-night stands and meet guys on a nightly basis without thinking twice about it, except me.

I rarely went out before the accident, and Hunter and I dated for years. Maybe that's why I lack the skills to be okay with casual, but still, deep down, I could have sworn there was something between us.

Or maybe that's the hopeless romantic in me.

Ugh.

Either way, I don't like the lingering unease it's left me with.

The worst part is that I know there's only one thing in the world to relax and reset me more than any walk in the park ever could. The one thing that could make me feel at peace, except it's the one thing I'm petrified of doing.

Dancing.

I'm cleared to dance, maybe not at the high level I used to, but it's been approved. Yet I haven't stepped back into a studio since the day of my accident, and it makes me sick to my stomach, even thinking of taking the steps toward doing that.

Dancing was my life, my whole personality, and going back to the place that no longer feels like home cuts deep, and it's just another reminder of everything that's gone wrong.

Life's been a tumbleweed of bad events for both my mom and me, and I'd give everything to slow down and give us a break.

Dad dying, my car accident, breaking up with Hunter—although that one doesn't seem that significant anymore—Mom's arthritis taking a turn for the worse, now most likely either closing or moving the bakery location after twenty years.

So, when I think of all that, Harrison is not entirely at fault. I've been using that night as an excuse for my spiraling feelings because, let's face it, I wanted to let loose, and I would do it all again if I had the chance.

It was only a minor incident that finally sent me off the ledge, and I was hoping today would be the day I climbed back up and found my footing.

Except I'm realizing today is not that day, so instead of playing the martyr, I'll reschedule with Adriana for next week.

> Hey girl! I'm so sorry to cancel at the last minute. I'm not feeling well. Can we reschedule?!
>
> I'll call you tomorrow xo.

She's most likely on the subway, so I don't wait for a response before throwing my phone in my purse and heading home.

There's only one thing better than getting cozy in your childhood home, on the couch that's formed exactly how you like it, and that's changing out of a dress into oversized sweats.

So it's precisely what I do when I walk in the door—I find my fleece pants and my dad's old sweatshirt before sorting through the basket until I see my favorite wool blanket my parents brought me back from Ireland a few years ago.

I wrap myself like a burrito, then plop on the couch and flip through terrible television and just like that, it's instantly therapeutic.

All I'm missing is some mint chocolate chip ice cream, and I'd be set.

I contemplate between *Gilmore Girls* or *Grey's Anatomy*, and since I promised Becks we could do a *Gilmore Girls* marathon, I pick the latter, knowing McDreamy can make me forget all my worries.

And you know what? Fuck it, I'm going to order some ice cream too.

It's one of the perks of living in New York. Within fifteen minutes, I will have my favorite mint chip ice cream from downtown to uptown, hand-delivered for five extra dollars.

And not any ice cream. Mouth-watering homemade ice cream with large dark chocolate chunks made with fresh mint from the owner's garden. No fake flavoring, and it's the best thing in ice cream history.

After one-and-a-half bowls, I somehow got five episodes into season one, where Derek and Meredith just got caught having sex in his car, and it does the opposite of what I wanted. Visions of Harrison and our reckless yet equally exhilarating night together flood my mind, and although I feel foolish for how it ended, the way I felt with him makes me smile for the first time all week.

My phone buzzes on the coffee table, so I lean over and see its Becks. "Hey," I answer and pause the show, then put it on speaker so I can cozy back under the covers.

"Are you avoiding me?"

Leave it to her to cut right to the chase, but she's not wrong. I have been.

Not once in our friendship have I ever lied or hid my feelings from Becks. She's always been my lending ear with no judgment. So, I'm unsure why I've been throwing myself into work instead of talking to her. I've felt out of my element lately, and after my out-of-character humiliating performance at the masquerade party, I've been avoiding her like the plague.

I'd rather not go into detail, so I tell her, "I've been busy." Then she falls quiet. "Becks?"

She takes an audible breath. "I have to go," she replies flatly and hangs up.

Wtf?

I remove my arm from the blanket to redial her, but she sends me to voicemail. Seriously? I have all day. I'll keep calling her until she answers.

"What, Juliette?" She sighs.

"Mind telling me why you just hung up on me?" I sit up, annoyed.

"Don't play dumb. You know exactly why I hung up." She covers the phone and mumbles to someone. "Listen, I don't have the time to play games. Tell me what's going on. Otherwise, I need to get back to work."

Crap. I can tell by her tone she's pissed off, which doesn't happen often, or at least not directly at me. "I'm really sorry, Becks."

She speaks, but it's hard to hear her. I can tell she's outside. There is loud honking and chatting in the background. "Hold on a sec." I wait, and then the background noise silences. "What's going on, Jules?"

"I'm sorry for avoiding you, truly. I'm feeling a bit out of my skin lately. Come over later, or let's get dinner tomorrow so I can make it up to you."

"You're free tomorrow?"

"Yeah, I miss you," I tell her truthfully. Now that we're talking, I wish she was here so I could tell her everything I've been feeling.

"I miss you too, Jules. I don't like feeling cut out, especially by you, so since you're free, you can make it up to me by being my side-kick tomorrow."

"Okay, no problem," I tell her quickly, knowing it will make me feel better after avoiding her if I do something for her. "Where are we going?"

"Remember I told you about that new rooftop bar in SoHo opening? Tramonto? Their launch is this weekend, and it's Matteo's birthday."

Ah, fuck.

"Oh, come on, Becks, haven't I hit my quota of wing woman this month, and if it's Matteo's birthday, Harrison will be there."

"He won't be. From what I've gathered from Matteo, he doesn't go out much either, and he'll have his daughter this weekend, so he can't come. I'm just excited I finally get to have you as my wingman. You could never go out like this before."

"Okay," I finally give in, unable to come up with a reasonable argument for why I can't go besides wanting to cozy up with Mom and watch a movie. "I blew off Adriana today. Do you think we can invite her too?"

"I'm sure it will be fine, and maybe I'll invite Carrie. Her mom is finally flying in from Vancouver for the summer to help, and I think she deserves a night out."

"Perfect, send me the details. Love you."

"Love you too."

I bounce on my feet as we wait in line to get into the club to meet Becks. It's chilly for a May night; luckily, it's invite-only, and the line should go quickly.

"Can you believe I'm at a club? At midnight, nonetheless." I smile over at Adriana, who understands my former life more than anyone else in this whole place. Although Adriana is also a professional dancer, her schedule is much less demanding since we held different roles in the company.

Carrie frowns. "Do you not like to go out? You're twenty-four. Live it up, girl. Trust me, the never-ending energy ends eventually. I'm not much older than you, and I still had to nap in preparation for tonight."

"Oh, it's not that. My former profession had me tied down. I didn't have much of a life, but I was okay with that; it was my choice. It just feels strange now."

Carrie flinches. "Shit, sorry, Juliette. I forgot. Becks told me about the accident."

I wave her off. "It's fine, just adjusting to all the changes."

"Well, since I put my foot in my mouth, let's change the subject to finding me a man tonight."

My eyes widen. "Yeah?"

Adriana high-fives her. "Well, I second that. I need to find a man, too. I would die for a boyfriend."

"Well, let's not get crazy." Carrie laughs. "My divorce isn't even finalized, but god, just a kiss sounds nice. I'd even take some dry humping on the dance floor at this point if I had to."

Adriana whips her head toward me and widens her eyes.

Carrie looks between us. "What?"

Adriana smirks unapologetically. "Ask Jules."

"Next!" the bouncer calls.

Saved by the bell.

The muscular bouncer, busting out of his suit, marks off our names and sends us into a cool, modern, all-glass elevator with sweeping city views.

"So spill it." Carrie waggles her brows.

Not sure how much I want to share, I go with the CliffsNote version. "I met a guy, and we hit it off, but he had to leave abruptly. End of the story."

"After she had an orgasm up against a wall, dry humping," Adriana whispered-laughs.

Who let her pre-game? The sweet girl who teaches little kids to dance has a blabber mouth after a few drinks.

Carrie gasps.

"That's what I get for letting my guard down."

"What do you mean?" Carrie asks. "It's not your fault he had to leave. Is it?"

"I know, it's just not my typical MO. I'm the responsible, good girl. Though, sometimes, I crave adventure, you know?" I snigger. "Maybe break my pathetic two lovers count."

"Hey!" Adriana cuts in.

I scrunch up my face. *Shit.* "Sorry!" Adriana has only had sex with one guy, and she's not even sure he broke her hymen, so she always jokes about that, saying she's still a half-virgin.

"Long story short, I thought he could be my one-night-stand hall pass, but then I felt a connection with him that I shouldn't have. Maybe tonight I'll meet someone completely forgettable and have a whirlwind fling."

The elevator doors open, and the beat of loud music pumps through the space.

"Holy shit. This place is sick," Carrie cries.

My eyes bulge at the beauty before me. "This is really out of this world." I point toward the balcony. "Look at those views."

"Yeah," she murmurs and drops her head, checking out an attractive man walking by.

I laugh loudly. I'm glad she came along. "Not those views... although he was freaking hot. But look." We make our way through the crowd and head outside.

I can see why it's called Tramonto, the Italian word for sunset.

"This city still surprises me. Especially when it's lit up like this," Adriana mutters, lost to the breathtaking view.

She's originally from the Midwest and still gets awe-struck at the best city in the world. I've lived here my whole life, and I'm still impressed every time I see it like this.

There's a wrap-around balcony, and we're far enough west in SoHo to have unobstructed views of the Empire State Building and the Freedom Tower.

"Hey, bitches!"

I'd know that voice from anywhere. "Hi, babes." I turn, and a broad smile creeps the width of my face. "You're fucking hot as hell. I thought there would be work people here."

I found out Matteo is part owner of the club; it's how Becks got us all on the list, and she mentioned some of her coworkers would be here.

"Fuck 'em. I'm a lonely analyst; none of them will know me." She spins around to give us a good view of an itty bitty leather skirt with a matching crop top and sky-high leather boots.

"You're like a sexy dominatrix." I slap her ass. She laughs and fluffs up her blue and now purple-streaked hair.

"But seriously, Matteo said it would be fine tonight since it's unrelated to work, and no one would care," she says, kissing the girls hello, then pulling me in for a tight hug. "Thank you for coming," she whispers in my ear. "Now, let's get a drink and dance."

I grab her hand and interlock our fingers while she drags me toward the bar. "Hey." She looks over her shoulder. "I'm sorry for being MIA."

She picks up my hand and kisses the back of it, and just like that, all is forgiven.

"Everything is on Matteo tonight since it's his place, so take advantage," Becks calls over the music when we head back inside.

I glance around the club while we wait, and I'm suddenly self-conscious. This place oozes wealth—both décor and people. "Do I look okay? Everyone in here looks like models."

Becks doesn't respond with anything but an eye-roll, then hands me a gin and tonic. "Let's go dance near those guys." She points to a group of men leaning against the wall.

Holy shit, what do they feed these guys? They're a whole different level of *fine*.

"Matteo won't be jealous?"

She smirks. "Oh, he will. Italians are crazy possessive, but you know me, I love to play games." She clinks my glass, and we all dance for hours.

Harrison

"I ordered Claud a new life jacket for the boat. She's going to freak out. It's pink with sparkles." Nate announces as his eyes scan the room, checking out every attractive girl who walks by.

Which isn't hard, almost every woman here tonight is a ten.

He's going to have slim pickings, though. He refuses to even look at a brunette and will only hook up with blondes and, occasionally, redheads. Tonight's about ninety percent brunette, which is unfortunate for him.

And if I had to take a wild guess, he's already slept with half the blondes here tonight since we all run in the same circles.

"Did you hear me?"

My eyes drop to my empty negroni; I've been gulping them down like water. I hold the empty glass up to our waitress to order another, "I did, but I don't like to think about my angel being away from me for two weeks."

He slaps me on the back. "It'll be fine."

"Uh-huh," I dismiss him. "How about her?" I jut my chin toward a beautiful blonde with killer tits, Nate's kryptonite.

"Nah, I think I know her. You go." He pushes my shoulder.

Eh. "Not for me." I haven't had an appetite for anyone but a beautiful brunette, and it's pissing me the hell off. My usual hook-ups that I keep on speed dial haven't even been doing it for me.

And they always do it for me.

I need to get over the idea of her and get her out of my head, but fuck it. She's always lingering in my subconscious…her and her lush lips. Especially every morning in the shower, jerking off, wishing she was there on her knees with them wrapped around my cock. All red and swollen.

I adjust myself like a teenager. It's the new constant state I'm perpetually in.

Horny, hard, and frustrated.

"Not for you?" he scoffs. "She's fucking hot, or are you still butt-hurt about that chick from my charity event?"

"Fuck off." I grab my new drink and chug half of it.

"Lizzy's back tomorrow. She'll send you the guest list."

I sigh and take another gulp. "Don't worry about it. What's the point anymore?"

"Why not? Clearly, she's doing it for you. I've never seen you like this before."

I shrug. I have nothing to say.

He knows I don't date.

"Wait a second," he walks around to sit next to me, glaring at me with concern. "What is this about? Tell me why you're not pursuing her."

Again, I don't answer.

"Harrison. Don't tell me you're still keeping your promise to Seb?"

"Just leave it, Nate."

The group of girls dancing in front of us moves over, and my eyes narrow in on the one front and center.

Shit. She's stunning.

Tall, with toned legs, and a tight white dress showing off her every curve. She throws her head back and rakes her hands through her hair, moving with ease as the song continues.

She turns to the side, and I see her wide smile, laughing at whatever the other person is saying next to her. The song switches, and she tosses her hands up, swiveling her hips to the beat.

It's the first time I've reacted to someone since meeting Jules.

"Are you listening to me?" Nate snaps.

"No." I'm too engrossed in the scene before me, and then it clicks. I know her.

"Who are you staring at? The hot one in the white dress?"

I nod. "We flirted a few weeks ago at Labo. Remember the night we all went there for dinner?"

"Yeah. I don't remember her, though."

"You guys left, and I ran into a client and stayed for drinks. We were pretty much eye fucking each other all night." She feels so familiar, and we barely talked.

I bite my lip as she shakes her ass. Clearly, my body is on the same page.

I'm fucking turned on.

But at the same time, I don't stop thinking about Jules, even as I watch the goddess right in front of me.

Fuck's sake.

I lean down and bury my head in my hands. Most guys would love to have this problem.

Me? Not so much.

"What's with him?" Leo asks Nate as he walks up to us, Matteo by his side.

I shake his hand and wish him a happy birthday and congrats on the club investment. He's been working the room the whole night, and I've barely gotten to talk to him.

Nate points to me, "Did you know this idiot hasn't dated anyone in all these years because of that dumb promise he made Sebastian?"

"What? Seriously?" Leo looks flabbergasted, "That's idiotic. If you met someone, he would understand if you talked to him."

I raise a sarcastic brow. "Really?"

Nate chimes in, "Probably not easily. The bastard's a hard-ass. But you make it like he rules you. Talk to him like a grown-ass adult. You're thirty-eight, for fuck's sake."

"I promised for Claudina, Nathaniel."

"Don't give me that crap," he says at the same time that Leo shakes his head, annoyed.

They can give up the idea of me talking to Seb. I'm not ready to date anyone seriously anyway; my life is Claud and Claud only, and on top of work, that's already enough.

I sip my drink and scan over the dance floor for the girl from the restaurant. Where'd she go?

Ah. *There she is*. I lean back and take her in.

"What even brought this up?" Matteo asks.

"He's lovesick over that girl from the Building Unity party. He's been miserable ever since."

"Who? Jules?" Leo frowns. "I thought you hit it off. She seems like a good girl." Regret swirls in my stomach. "I mean, if you're not going after her, put me in, Coach, because she's looking fine tonight."

That snaps me out of it, "Tonight? What are you talking about?"

He looks at me, confused, and points to the girl in the white dress. "Jules? Matteo's girl is her best friend. We were talking to them earlier."

I stand up in a hurry and quickly pace over to the edge of the dance floor, ignoring my idiot brothers laughing behind me.

My overexcited dick, which has been rock hard from the start, knew exactly who he was looking at the whole time. *Jules*.

And then it hits me—she said her name was Juliette that night at Labo. How fucking stupid could I be?

Jules…Juliette.

What the hell is her deal? Did she know it was me all along and not say anything? It was public knowledge that it was a Davenport/Morales event.

Crazies are part of the deal when you're as rich as us. Women, and even men, will do anything to get close to you because of the money you have, but I never got that vibe from her.

Besides one slip-up years ago, I'm usually a good judge of character.

So why didn't she mention anything? What is this girl playing at?

She spins and pushes her hair off her neck, and there it is. *Bingo!* Her heart birthmark.

I see red.

Fuck motherfucking fuck.

I stride with purpose across the crowded dance floor, not giving a shit who I barrel into on my way.

"Jules," I bark. Turning blindly, she stumbles, and I catch her around the waist. I lean close to her ear. "Or is it Juliette?"

Her eyes widen, and recognition is plastered all over her face.

Gotcha.

5

Juliette

"W-Wᴀᴛ ᴀʀᴇ ʏᴏᴜ ᴅᴏɪɴɢ?" I stammer, trying to break away from Harrison's firm grip.

His normally turquoise eyes are dark, with a sharp gleam staring lethally into mine. He takes a deep breath, flaring his nostrils, and I notice his mouth clamped tightly shut and a small muscle flicker along his jaw. "Harrison?" I murmur.

He takes another breath and straightens us out, never removing his hand from my hip.

"We're going to walk over in that corner and talk. Do you understand?"

Shocked at his tone, I nod and comply easily.

"What's wrong? I don't understand." I look up at him, concerned. This is an entirely different man than the one I spent hours with that night.

"Stop it, Juliette. Don't try to act innocent now."

"Innocent? I'm so confused. Can you slow down? You're hurting my leg," I cry.

He narrows his eyes. "You're fine. We're almost there."

"No, seriously," I snap. "My leg."

He stops abruptly, and his face falls, looking my body over. "What's wrong?"

"It's fine mostly," I mumble. "I was in an accident, and I still get nerve pain."

He leans down, picks me up bridal style, and storms off toward the corner. I don't protest for even one second. I love the feeling of being in his arms.

Even if he is acting like a lunatic.

Unable to help myself, I nuzzle my head into his chest and place my arm around his neck to steady myself. I feel him take a deep breath and sigh like he can breathe now that we are connected, even though I know that sounds insane.

For me, when my hands meet his skin, my body burns; something deep inside me stirs, begging me to lift my head and kiss his sharp jaw and those luscious lips. Harrison's presence makes me feel feral with need, something I've never experienced or knew I had in me.

When he places me on the floor, his hand returns to my waist, trapping me against the wall. My stomach flips with nerves, and I open my mouth to talk, but nothing comes out. I'm so out of sorts I don't know what to do.

"So, let's start from the beginning," he growls. "How long have you known me for?"

"What?" I question, completely confused.

"Maybe I should ask in French. *Depuis quand tu me connais?*"

"Is this a trick question? The first time I ever saw you was at the restaurant."

He huffs out a laugh and smirks sarcastically. "There it is. *The first time*. Then how many times after that?"

Okay, what is he insinuating?

Because now I'm starting to get pissed off at his tone, and I am usually the epitome of calm.

I put my hands on my hip and plaster on an unimpressed resting bitch face.

"Harrison, I don't know where you're going with this, but spit it the fuck out. And I don't like the tone you're taking with me."

"Don't tell me what tone to take, Juliette. What is your deal? Your goal?" He commands, "Because clearly, you kept your identity a secret for a reason."

My eyes widen in shock, "Oh my god, are you joking right now?" I laugh in his face. "My identity? Who am I, Jason Fucking Bourne?"

"Dead fucking serious." He yells and squeezes my hip, reminding me his hand is still on me.

I push with all my might and fling his hand off.

"You're not who I thought you were," I poke my finger into his chest, "But I shouldn't be surprised." I shake my head, disappointed he's like all the rest of the wealthy, entitled New Yorkers.

He narrows his eyes and glares at me. "What the hell does that mean?"

"It means," I poke him again, raising my voice, "That I had no ulterior motive. I was embarrassed, Harrison. That's why I didn't say anything."

He looks at me, and I look down, annoyed at myself for admitting that.

I don't know how long we stand there, but eventually, he lifts my chin so I look directly at him. "Why would you ever be embarrassed?"

I shake my head and take a deep breath to calm my nerves. "It's dumb now, looking back, but the second I walked into that party, I noticed you, Harrison. Even with your mask on, in a crowded room, I knew it was you." I take a breath. "So you can imagine my excitement when the hot guy from the restaurant comes over to the bar thinking he recognized me back until I said hello, and you introduced yourself. I felt embarrassed you didn't remember me." I shrug.

"Jules."

"You don't have to say anything, Harrison. We were wearing masks. Of course, you wouldn't. I felt too stupid to mention it at the time. Then you left me so…" I shrug.

"I see. But to be clear, I didn't want to leave."

"It's fine—"

"Don't interrupt me," he snaps. "Because it is *not* fine, Juliette. It was a shitty thing to do. I had an emergency I needed to attend to, and I panicked. Looking back, I should have handled it differently. For that, I'm sorry."

He takes a dangerous step closer, trapping my body against the wall.

"The fact you thought I didn't want to stay is ludicrous." I shrug, mortified by my insecurities. I'm sure strong, successful older men like Harrison are completely turned off by women like me, who have no control over their emotions. "Does this feel like I don't want you?" He grinds his groin into my stomach, and his hand darts out to catch me as my knees buckle.

"Harrison," I whisper.

My arousal sweeps in and the air swirls around us. Feeling him against me instantaneously instills confidence in me; the connection between us is palpable, literally.

"Before I knew it was you tonight, my body reacted to watching you and only you on the dance floor." He lifts me by my hips, and my legs quickly wrap around him, squeezing him tightly. "Make no mistake, I wanted you before I saw your face tonight, and now that I know it's you, *mon petit papillon*, I don't want you. I *need* you."

The tone of Harrison's voice should frighten me, yet instead, it electrifies me deep in my core.

He cups my cheeks and darts his tongue out to swipe around my parted lips. A small part of me is saying this is too much, and I should run, but my body says no fucking chance. This man is waking up every good feeling in my body, and before I can think about it for a second longer, my mouth parts, and a heartbeat later, our tongues collide.

This man can kiss like nothing I've ever felt before. Starting slow and sensual, quickly turning wild and frantic, like we can't get enough of one another.

Desperately, I push myself flat against his muscled chest, feeling his hard erection that has my head spinning in circles. He moans loudly at our connection, dragging his lips away to ravage my neck with hot, open-mouth kisses and bunching up my dress to palm my behind, pulling me aggressively into him.

My fingers are threaded through his hair, tugging on the ends as my sex sparks with excitement every time his thick cock rubs against my soaked panties.

My god.

He releases one hand to run up the side of my body, cupping my breast and running a thumb over my nipples.

I whimper, and he tugs tightly, making me clench hard below.

Oh shit, this can't happen against a wall…again.

I pull back, panting loudly. "Harrison. We're in the club."

"No one can see us," he murmurs against my neck, then bites down, and I almost combust.

Some inner strength I didn't know I had helps me unhook my legs and drag them back to the floor.

He's breathing just as heavily as I am, his eyes completely blown wide and wild. "I need you. Give me tonight."

"Just tonight?" I ask without thinking. Why would he only want tonight?

A look, maybe regret, passes over his face. "It's all I can give, Juliette. I'm not someone who can give more than that." He doesn't explain. Instead, he leans down and kisses me hard with suction. "But I can promise you it will be the best fucking night of your life."

Say yes!

"Oh god, I can't even think when you kiss me like that."

"Don't think," he traces a finger over my already soaked underwear. "Feel."

My hips swivel, and he grins, knowing exactly how much I want this.

"Fuck," I whimper.

"Yes, exactly. Let's fuck."

"Don't be so crude." I laugh.

"Oh babe, you have no idea. We have one night, and you'll never be the same again."

His eyes hold mine, and nothing in me can say no to this man, and he knows it.

This is what I wanted, right?

To live life, let loose, and feel alive, even if it's for only one night.

"Okay." I stand on my tippy-toes and kiss his jaw. "Take me home, Harrison."

"Best words to ever leave your mouth, Juliette."

He interlocks our fingers, pulls me toward the exit, and I freeze. Crap, I need to find the girls.

"What?"

"I need to tell my friends where I'm going. I'll be right back."

He rolls his eyes, unimpressed, and adjusts himself. "Be quick." He pats my ass as I run off.

I tell the girls. Carrie high-fives me, and Becks doesn't look happy.

"What is it?"

"You're going to get hurt, that's what. This isn't like you."

I cross my arms, annoyed. "So what? Can't I live a little? God, I was stuck in my Hunter bubble for years, and for once, there's a man who makes me feel exhilarated. I want this."

She kisses my cheek. "Okay. Then have fun and make the most of it." I can tell by her expression she doesn't mean a word of it. She worries about me too much.

While walking through the crowd back toward Harrison, my stomach knots with anxiety. What if I can't live up to his expectations?

Oh god, imagine I'm the worst he's ever had?

There's no denying the sexual chemistry between us, and my body, so far, knows precisely what to do. But I'm so inexperienced it's not funny.

Looking back, Hunter was the worst lover. Harrison has turned me on more with his kisses than Hunter ever had in the four years we were together.

I'm so out of my league.

"Hey," Harrison says, and I snap my head up before almost running into him. "Ready, babe?" He reaches out and takes my hand.

You can't like it when he calls you pet names...especially when he calls you his little butterfly.

It's one night only.

"Yup," I smile wide, masking all my worry while he leads me down the elevator and outside.

Cameras flash, causing Harrison to curse under his breath and pull me along swiftly to a waiting black car. He gets me in first, then slams the door behind him.

"Fuck, I'm sorry." He sighs, then looks down at my leg and rubs where I did earlier, "Are you okay? I had to get you in the car quickly."

I reach over, palm his nape, and rub his jaw with my thumb. "I'm okay. Don't worry about it. Does that happen a lot to you?"

"Sometimes. I mostly stay out of it. Tonight was a big club opening in the city, and they knew many influential people would be there. I should have taken you out the back, but I wasn't thinking clearly. Obviously." He smiles, raking his eyes down my body, then does some magical move that has me in his lap. "They'll get a more interesting picture of someone else, or they'll list it as 'Harrison and Friend,' so don't worry."

I don't tell him they will most likely know who I am if they decide to post it. However, we're not getting personal tonight, so I'm not bringing it up. Instead, I take advantage of this new position that gets me up close and personal with his strong features.

I trace his jaw with the tip of my finger and lean in to kiss him lightly.

He cups my face and runs his thumb along the apple of my cheek, "Something is playing in my mind. What did you mean before when you said I wasn't who you thought I was?"

Ah shit.

I hesitate, and he lifts a brow.

"You came over guns blazing, and I knew you felt like you deserved answers." I shrug. "I didn't appreciate the entitlement, especially because your behavior seemed so different than the man I spent hours with."

"Jules, baby." He sweeps my hair off my face and tucks it behind my ear. "I know this sounds pretentious, but because of who I am, people try to take advantage of me every day. I can't afford to take any chances."

"That makes sense."

"And that man you spent time with at the party, he's..." I sit and let him get his thoughts together. "He's someone I don't get to be often. Only in the privacy of my own home, and even then, if I'm working, so not much."

"So, are you pretending to be someone else? I don't understand."

"Not at all. I'm the head of my company, and my line of work is cutthroat. I'm aggressive and, at times, abrasive." He shrugs. "I get what I want when I want it, and that's why I'm one of the leading CEOs in my industry, and I will never apologize for it." He kisses my fingertips and continues. "At the party, we were secluded in the corner, and I'm sure the free-flowing drinks factored in. I let my guard down for the first time in a while. You got lucky to see that side of me." He winks.

"Lucky, huh?" I roll my eyes and smirk, and something tells me I'd like both sides of Harrison.

"You're here, sir," his driver says, breaking me out of my dirty thoughts.

"Thank you, Robert," Harrison replies while helping me out of the car.

We walk past security with his arm slung around my shoulders, leading me into the elevator. The sexual tension in the air is thick; you can almost hear it crackling between us, making my sudden nerves skyrocket in tandem with the climbing elevator.

Becks was right; this is so out of character for me.

What have I gotten myself into?

The elevator dings, and the floor-to-ceiling windows momentarily stop my worried thoughts.

"This is incredible, Harrison."

"Mmhmm," he responds. "Would you like a drink?"

I nod. "A water would be lovely. Thanks." I walk around, and although the penthouse's view is impressive, it lacks any personality.

Usually, I would think that's normal for a bachelor, but I know he has a daughter he's yet to mention. There are no pictures of her or a trace of another person living here at all. "Did you recently move in?"

"What? Oh." He pauses, and I watch his face change; then it hits me. I may be naive about many things, but I'm not stupid.

I take a step back, suddenly feeling cheap about this whole situation.

"No. No." He panics and rushes toward me. "Let me explain, please."

"I'm not the type of girl that does things like this...I should have known better."

"Juliette," he says firmly, and I snap my head up. "This is not where I live. But I promise you I've never been here with another woman."

I narrow my eyes. "I'm sure you say that to everyone."

He raises an unimpressed brow and lowers his voice. "Are you calling me a liar?"

Before I can tell him no, that I'm just freaking out, he has his phone dialing a number on speaker.

"Who are you calling?"

"My brother."

The phone picks up, and you can hear loud music blasting through from the other end. "Sorry bro, if your old dick can't get up, I have nothing to help you. I'm like a fucking stallion."

Harrison groans, pinching his nose, "Nate, shut the fuck up. You're on speaker phone. Can you please tell Juliette whose place this is?"

"Oh fuck. Sorry, Juliette! It's my place—have fun, you two." Then he clicks off.

I smirk at his brother while Harrison takes a step closer into my personal space before I can remember I was *attempting* to leave. "My brother recently bought a new place around the corner, along with all new furniture. He kept everything here because he's deciding whether to rent or sell it."

"Okay?"

"I'm an extremely private person, Juliette. I don't allow anyone but my family and close friends in my house. It's nothing against you."

Everything in my body tells me to shut up and not ask anything else, but I can't...I need to know. "So," I look down and wring my hands. "If you've not brought anyone back here before, where do you normally go?"

"Jules," He sighs but continues, albeit reluctantly. "Normally a hotel. One of my other brothers runs The Valencia Hotel Group, so I have complete discretion. Is that all?"

"Your brother on the phone wasn't surprised we were here."

"Is that a question or statement?" He smirks. "And no, he wasn't. He's been teasing me relentlessly about you all week."

"Me?" I squeak and widen my eyes, surprised.

He takes one more step forward so our chests touch and cups my cheeks with his strong hands. "Yes, you. You've been on my mind every day, Juliette. I can't stop thinking about your big doe-like eyes or these pouty lips." He traces his thumb along my bottom lip, plucking it from between my teeth. "And I especially couldn't stop thinking about your long, toned, sexy legs wrapped around me. It's all I think of every night, alone in bed."

My breath catches. *Oh god.*

He tightens his hold on my face and turns my head to kiss me with everything he has. It's deep, passionate, and completely unhinged. "Do you feel the tension between us?"

I whimper as an answer. Of course I do. The chemistry between us is like nothing I've felt before.

He stares at my face with hunger, darting out his tongue to lick his bottom lip, and with every swipe, my arousal builds. I finally snap and decide to go all in.

Fuck all the rest of it.

It's what I wanted, I remind myself once more...I can be carefree, just for tonight.

"Are you in or are you out, Juliette?" he whispers.

I don't hesitate. "In." *So in.*

He leans down, picks me up, and slams our lips together as he walks down a long hallway, then kicks open a door, and we fumble into the room.

"Oh my god." I laugh. "Did you just break the door?"

"Who the fuck cares," he growls and places me down to tug off his shirt, and I almost die on the spot.

His body is what every girl dreams of.

Tall, tan, and toned muscles, with a dusting of hair that trails down his body over his defined abs.

I reach forward, and my palms skim over his broad, bare shoulders, following the small goose bumps that rise under his skin.

He's the type of man you read about in books or visualize when you're alone. Men like Harrison are not supposed to be real.

But yet, here he is, sex personified…and I'm living out every girl's fantasy.

"This needs to come off now." He grabs the hem of my dress, pulls it over my head, and curses loudly.

"Are you kidding me right now?" he says more to himself while he traces his fingers over my lace lingerie.

It's not often I splurge, but there's something about putting on lingerie for yourself and feeling sexy.

It's empowering.

Tonight's bra is see-through, with light pink hand-stitched rosettes and a white lace trim. The panties are a matching pink lace. Innocent with sex appeal.

His eyes trap mine, and my breath falters. "You're beautiful. So. Fucking. Beautiful." He cups my breast, and it's as if he's lost in his own world.

It shouldn't, but tonight feels more intimate than it should. If he hadn't mentioned one night, I would have sworn this could be the start of something extraordinary.

Maybe because it's more than just sexual chemistry, it feels different. We spent that night together at the party, completely enamored with one another, talking for hours.

And tonight…I feel that spark ten times more than before.

Harrison kicks off his shoes, unbuckles his pants, and begins to pull them down, along with his briefs.

Thump…thump…thump.

My heart is in my throat, and my sex is on fire.

Everything about this man is a turn-on. I can almost smell his desire from here as I watch this perfect specimen in front of me take the most enormous cock I've ever seen in his hands, tugging at it with hard strokes. It's long and thick, with dark trimmed public hair at the base.

My mouth falls open, and I stand there in shock.

With every stroke, the head begins to swell, and I've never seen anything more erotic in my life.

When I realize I'm practically drooling, I slam my mouth shut, and the fluttering nerves take over my stomach.

Harrison steps into me, his cock pressing against my stomach. I can feel his wet pre-ejaculate spread across me when he lightly pumps his hips, reaching around to unsnap my bra, "That's better," he whispers softly against my ear. "After I fuck you, I'm going to fuck these." He pulls my nipple hard in the best way.

"Harrison…" My voice trails off.

"What is it?" He pauses. "Why are you suddenly nervous?"

"I've only been with two people," I blurt quietly.

Way to ruin the moment…how lame can I be?

"What?" He leans back. "Two?"

I shrug, embarrassed. "I told you…I'm not that type of girl."

"Fuck."

Oh no. "I-I—"

He pushes me onto the bed and crawls up my body, coming nose to nose, with a cocky grin plastered on his face, "You have no idea how sexy that is to me, do you?" He smashes his lips against mine. "And fuck, there's something inside me wishing there weren't even two people at all," he mutters. "You taste good, Jules. I love kissing you."

"Mm, I thought you didn't get jealous?" I mumble against his lips.

He pulls back, and his eyes rake down to my chest, and his cock jumps slightly in appreciation. "I'm not." He reaches out and cups both my breasts. "Or maybe I am only with you. When I realized it was you tonight, even though I was pissed, I still lost my mind when any other men looked at you on the dance floor in that white virginal dress."

"Virginal dress?" I giggle.

"Yes. It's going in the trash after tonight." He leans down, taking one breast in his mouth, and he begins sucking hard.

My eyes close, and a loud moan slips through my lips as his teeth scrape across my pointed nipple.

"So sensitive," he groans, then trails his open-mouth kisses down my stomach and along my waistline. Spreading my leads wide, he's able to position his body between them, continuing his kisses down to my inner thigh.

My breaths are deep and fast, and I quiver with an unfamiliar desire. It's taking all my might not to arch my hips into his face.

His lips trail over my small red scar, still not fully healed, then moves over to where the second scar takes up a majority of my hip.

I close my eyes and suck in a breath. I was hoping he would ignore them. They're an insecurity I'm not ready to explore, especially against his flawless body. Thankfully, he doesn't pry, but before returning to his mission, he kisses them again and whispers, *beautiful* against my skin.

There's no time to think about his actions because his head leans forward to my sex, inhaling deeply before closing his eyes and letting out a loud guttural groan.

Holy. Fucking. Shit.

I clench on instinct, and he doesn't miss it. His nostrils flare in appreciation, and I can tell he's beyond turned on by it.

His fingertips brush against my center, and his eyes snap to mine when he slides two thick fingers inside me. "Clench again, baby," he demands.

I do. Twice. He hisses his approval each time, then begins to really work me with his fingers, in and out, in and out.

"Such a good girl," he growls, then adds a third, picking up speed.

My legs drop wide and open for him as my arousal echoes through the room. I'm wetter than I ever thought possible and can feel the evidence dripping down to my behind. My body starts to shudder as the oncoming feeling of the most intense orgasm I will probably ever have creeps up my spine. I reach out and try to grab on to something. The sheets, Harrison...*anything.*

He drops his face and licks up my whole center, then focuses on my clit, over and over with his thick tongue.

"Oh…ah. I'm going to come."

I wish I could hold it. I want this feeling to last forever.

My god, please, don't let it stop.

"Is this how you like it, babe?"

"I don't know. Yes?" My head flies back, and I see stars, oh yeah, just like that. "Yes, this is exactly how I like it."

"You don't know?" I don't answer, too lost to my pleasure. "Juliette," he growls against my clit, and it vibrates deep into my core. "Answer me."

"My ex didn't like going down on me. Now shut up," I arch my back, and he laughs darkly, rubbing his fingers against my g-spot, and sucking my clit hard between his lips.

I cry out, and my body starts to convulse violently as my orgasm rips through me. My toes curl, and I grab Harrison's hair, rocking my sex into his mouth until the very last second. Then I collapse, and I think I've gone to heaven.

I should feel embarrassed that it took less than a minute, but I have zero ability whatsoever to care, especially when I can see how turned-on Harrison is.

He sits up in a rush and quickly tears open a condom. I'm enamored as I watch him roll it on. Why does this all feel so new to me?

There's something about being with this man that makes me feel like I'm experiencing sex for the first time.

Or maybe, in a way, I am since he's the first experienced person I've been with.

"Your ex is a fucking prick, by the way. Though I'm happy he missed out on the most delicious pussy on the face of this earth."

"Oh god. You have a way with words." Then my eyes bulge as he lines his dick up with my opening and slowly starts to enter me.

He smirks, and I want to slap it off his face. "You'll be fine. I'll go slow."

Will I be? Because I'm not so sure.

6

Juliette

"MY INSURANCE CARD is in my bag if I pass out and you need to take me to the hospital," I tell Harrison, half serious.

He chuckles. "What would I say? Excuse me, doctor, she couldn't take my giant dick in her tight young pussy."

"Shut up," I laugh, which *barely* distracts the burning pain and pressure radiating through my lower half.

My mouth hangs open, and I squeeze my eyes shut tight. Harrison leans over, stilling inside of me, as the mood changes as he kisses my lips. "Jules, look at me," he whispers. "I won't hurt you, I promise."

"I know," I kiss him back, and we stay like this in each other's arms until my body begins to relax.

"Juliette, tu t'en sors bien." He murmurs, telling me I'm doing great, and it's the hottest thing listening to him speak to me in French. "Let me in." He reclaims my lips with a surprising tenderness as he slowly pushes in deep.

He's patient, gradually pulling out, then in, letting my body adjust with each stroke as I try to control my erratic breathing. When he feels I'm ready, though, it's game on, and all hell breaks loose.

Pent-up feelings from the last few weeks come out in spades, and we can't get enough of each other, kissing frantically, sloppy, and oh, it's so hot. His hips veer back before slamming back into me until his balls hit my backside, then he starts to ride me with punishing thrusts.

"I've been dreaming about this tight pussy since the night at the restaurant," he grinds out, his hooded eyes locked on mine, while he leans back and grabs me behind my knees to spread me out wide.

"Trust me, I've been dreaming about it, too. You feel so perfect, Harrison." I cry out in pleasure.

Something in me has snapped, releasing a side of me I never thought I could show…and tonight, I'm letting it all out.

"Your leg okay?" he grinds out.

"Yes. Shut up about my leg," I cry.

He reaches around and slaps my ass. "Do not tell me what to do," then slams in hard and hisses loudly, nearly breaking me in half.

I've had sex, I've made love, but I've never fucked, and I think I'm addicted.

That or I'm already addicted to Harrison, which can't happen.

"So I shouldn't tell you to fuck me harder and that you feel so good stretching me wide?" I scream, and his hips take on a mind of their own, hitting just the right spot. Our skin slaps together, and our loud, labored breathing echoes through the room. That alone is enough to set me over the edge *again.*

His eyes squeeze shut while he keeps his demanding pace. "Oh fuuuuuuck," he moans loudly. "Not yet, fuck, Juliette."

Seeing him unhinged, knowing I did this to him, is more of a turn-on than anything else.

I clench hard, now pushing him over the edge. I have this innate need to make him come and come hard.

He tips his head back and tightens his jaw before letting go of my legs and falling forward to bite my neck. He slams into me one, two, three more times, then we both scream out together, and I can feel the telling jerk of his cock as it releases.

He falls to the side, picks up my slumped body to lay on his chest, and kisses me affectionately. I break it and snuggle into his neck, knowing we can't kiss like that if he wants me to leave here without a broken heart.

"And to think...that was round one," he mumbles as he strokes my hair.

"What?" I snap my head up. The crazy thing is, I can't tell if he's joking or not. "My body is out of commission, Harrison. As it is, I won't be able to walk for a week."

He chuckles darkly. "And I thought the perk of being with a younger woman was that she would be able to keep up with me." he yawns, then laughs.

"This is beautiful," I trace the large pink butterfly that is tattooed over his heart.

He removes my hand and then pulls the blanket over us. "Thanks." He kisses my forehead, his lips lingering a few seconds while wrapping his arms around me. "Goodnight, beautiful Juliette."

Goodnight.

Harrison stands at the end of the bed, buttoning up his shirt, his face void of emotion.

"What's wrong?" I croak, sitting up to drink my water.

He jumps, startled. "I didn't know you were up. It's later than I expected. I need to leave."

My stomach sinks to the ground. There's something in his tone I don't like. This is Mr. CEO, who was at the club last night, not my Harrison.

He passes me my dress. "Oh, okay." I scamper out of bed.

"You can stay if you want, but I figured you'd want to leave too."

Suddenly feeling awkward, I run into the attached bathroom to change and quickly splash my face with water to wipe off any mascara residue. I'd rather not look at myself in the mirror, but I also don't want to look like a ho walking out in broad daylight in an itty bitty dress and mascara down my face.

I open the door, and without looking at Harrison, I reluctantly put my shoes on my swollen feet. You'd think this would be the easy part since my feet are no stranger to pain and misery after years of pointe shoes.

Harrison stands there with his hands in his pockets, rocking back and forth, impatiently waiting for me.

"Ready," I whisper.

Wordlessly, he escorts us to the elevator, where it's there waiting for us.

Same elevator, same feeling of nerves.

"If I could stay, I would," he murmurs, staring straight, not making a move to look at me. For some reason, I feel as though it's deliberate. Afraid I might see a sliver of emotion.

The doors open, and I step out. "It's fine, Harrison. I know what I signed up for. One night, right?"

He flinches at my words, but it's the truth, isn't it?

Even if I hate the stupid truth.

I feel myself getting emotional, so I quickly walk out to the curb and throw my hand up with gusto.

Where are all the freaking cabs today?

"Jules," Harrison places a hand on my back, and I freeze, causing him to step back. "Let me take you home, please." I don't respond. "Juliette," he says my name more firmly, so I look into his eyes and clench my jaw.

You. Will. Not. Cry.

He looks me over, and something passes over his face that I don't understand. Not regret...maybe sorrow? I haven't known him long enough to decipher.

A cab turns the corner, and I quickly shoot my hand up again to extract myself from this situation. In no world do I want to leave this man, but if I stay for even a second longer, I'm going to be a blubbering mess.

Harrison stands silently, and since he's not making demands, I know he's as uncomfortable as I am.

The cab pulls up, and he opens the door for me.

And with my heart in my throat, I place my hand on top of his, then stand on my toes to kiss his cheek.

His hand shoots out, and he smashes me to his body, holding me in a tight embrace, letting down his steely armor. "I wish things could be different," he mumbles, and I take a step back.

"Me too," I gulp. "Thank you for the best night, Harrison." I give him one last peck, get in the cab, and once the door shuts, and we veer into traffic, I finally let the tears go.

"Eighty-Sixth between Park and Madison," I tell the cab driver, and when we're halfway down the street, I can't help myself. I look back, and Harrison is still there, crouched over on the bench with his hands on his face.

I knew he felt it, too.

Something in my gut told me this was all wrong, but he gave me no other choice than to leave.

Harrison

One Month Later

"Hi, Daddy!" Claudina skips into my office, her pigtails swinging side to side as she drags a large bag behind her.

For a second, I freeze, getting a flashback of her mother, Claud's twin, wearing the exact hairstyle when we were younger.

"Hi, angel." I hold my arms out, and she drops her bag to run full speed into my embrace. "How was your day?"

She climbs into my lap as I minimize my screen and open a blank document, knowing she's two seconds away from clicking like a little maniac on the keyboard.

"We had the best day. We went to the American Girl Doll store to get Samantha's ears pierced, and now we have matching earrings." I noticed her new star studs immediately. "Then we went to that one playground in the park where the older kids climb the rocks."

"Heckscher Playground," I remind her. Though I know she knows the name, she can't pronounce Heckscher, and it bothers her, so she pretends she can't remember.

"Yes, that one. Oh…" She jumps off my lap, rummages through her bag, and holds up two bottles of my arch nemesis. "Uncle Sebby bought me nail polish. Can I paint your nails? Pleaseeeeee, Daddy?"

"Claud," I groan. Of course, I'm going to say yes. But I have to push back a little.

She giggles. "Pretty please with a cherry on top?" She holds the bottles up high, "Look, hot pink!"

Oh, joy.

"Fine. But what do I get for it?"

She taps her finger on her chin. "Hmm…" She pretends to think, then throws her body back into my lap and kisses me a million times. "You get kissy monster time!"

"Okay, okay." I laugh. "I'll do it."

"Yessss." She drags out the *s*, shrugging her shoulders excitedly. "Uncle Sebby even let me paint his."

"What?" I widen my eyes, shocked. "He did?"

"Yup. Because he was in trouble," she whispers.

I smirk, wondering what my brother could have done to warrant a punishment from Claud. "What did he do?"

She looks over her shoulder, then leans into my ear. "He yelled at a little boy on the playground and made him cry. It was very mean."

"Excuse me, little one, that was between me and you," Sebastian says as he enters my office.

She laughs loudly. "Oops."

One thing my brothers and I have come to realize is you can't do anything without the others knowing. Claud is a blabbermouth when it comes to her uncles, *just like her mom.*

"Hey, angel, can you go out to reception and hang with Lauren while I talk to your Uncle Seb quickly?"

"Okie dokie, artichokie," she says and gives me a thumbs-up.

Claud leaves her nail polish on the desk to torture me, then skips out of the office.

"Sebastian," I warn.

"Don't give me your shit, the dickhead pushed her down the slide."

I run my hand down my face, too tired for this. "You can't call a little kid a dickhead either. Am I going to be getting a call from the parent?"

"Well, if you do, you can tell the husband how the wife wanted to apologize for her son's behavior on her knees." He raises a brow and sits down in front of me.

I change the subject because Sebastian's going to do what Sebastian wants to do when it comes to protecting Claud. "How was Dubai?"

"Complete shit."

My cell rings. "It's Leo." I put it on speaker.

"Hey, fucker." He pants into the phone.

"What the hell are you doing?" I ask.

"Jiu-jitsu," he grits, and then I hear a bang and a loud oomph from across the line.

I look up at Seb, and he's shaking his head, already annoyed. "That's your brother," I say.

"Debatable," he replies dryly.

"Is that Uncle Sebby?" Leo chuckles.

I throw my head back and laugh loudly. We have no clue why Claud started calling him that, and he would never deny her anything, so he goes along with it, but when Leo busts his balls about it, it's the best.

"Can you hang up on that jerk-off?"

"What do you need, Leo?" I ask, hearing a lot of moving around and men groaning, "And did you need to call in the middle of your new hobby?"

"Don't you have a business to run?" Sebastian asks dryly.

"Don't you?" Leo counters.

Seb closes his eyes, annoyed.

"Time out, guys," Leo calls out to whomever he's with. "I was calling to let you know of the change of plans for Mom's birthday. She wants to cook brunch this weekend instead of going out."

That doesn't surprise me. We all would prefer to take her out and treat her, however knowing her, she would rather the whole family be at the house to move and talk freely.

"I'm not shocked. We'll see you there." I hang up, and Seb is looking at me deadpan. "What?"

He widens his eyes and shakes his head. "Just trying to figure out how me and him are related."

Yeah, they couldn't be more different, but also, their relationship couldn't be stronger.

"I have a meeting with Matteo in five minutes, and then I need to drop off Claud at her baking class. Anything else?"

"Kicking me out so soon? Nice." He leans back and crosses his legs. "Next month, I need to fly back to Dubai to sort out permits because we've been having problems building the new hotel. The next full week I have with Claudina is the same week they want me to fly out. I'm going to switch with Nate this week and bring her out east so she can swim."

"Nate was okay with it? He's been pumped to get her out on the boat. Went on and on about some pink life vest."

Seb smirks. It's rare, but if it has to do with Claud, the grump is a softy. "I saw it. It's so sparkly they'll see her in space. She'll love it. He's fine with the change. They have some boating competition near Sag Harbor in August, so it works out for him."

I make a note of it in the calendar so I don't get confused, not that it matters. As long as she is with one of the four of us or her grandparents, I know she's safe.

Nevertheless, I like to stay on top of it, especially for Willa, since she sometimes travels to help.

"And Leo is still taking her the week after you?" I grumble, annoyed, while Seb confirms.

I know Claud looks forward to this time with her uncles. She spends weekends with them throughout the year, and they often take her to school in the morning or surprise her at pick-up if they can fit it into their schedule, but typically, we spread out the full weeks they take her in the summer.

This is the first time it will be back-to-back, and it's killing me a little on the inside that she won't be home with me for two weeks in a row. There is no way I won't be making surprise visits to see my girl during that time, since my stomach is already in knots just thinking about her being gone.

I won't be able to deal without her.

Seb's texting on his phone when I pull my attention back to him, and I stare at him for a minute while contemplating if I should ask him what's been eating me alive all week. "How's the new therapist?"

He stills, dropping his phone in his lap, then crosses his arms, glaring at me. "None of your fucking business, that's how."

"Actually, it is my business when my brother stops talking to me and the rest of us for two months." It's harsh to say, but hiding doesn't help.

The five-year anniversary of Camila's passing snuck up on us quickly, and it was a tough time, to say the least. Still, to this day, Sebastian handles her passing the worst of all of us—or at least the worst on the outside.

We've all taken on different ways to cope and honor her life—Rosa and Javier, Camila's parents, honor her through Claudina. They do all Camila's favorite things so Claud never forgets.

Rosa cooks all of Camila's favorite foods. Together, they watch her favorite childhood television shows and visit all her favorite shops and museums.

Nate loves to sit around and share his favorite stories, and Leo masks his pain with humor. For me, I internalize my feelings the most, but it's my job to protect Claud.

That's how I honor my best friend—I be the best fucking dad I can be for that little girl.

I promised her I would live for Claudina, and that's what I do every single day of my life.

Then there is Sebastian, who is completely unpredictable, and this year hit him harder than ever. He was suddenly busier than normal, not returning our calls, and would only talk to Claud.

The second I heard he would be missing her dance recital because he got pulled away for work, I intervened, knowing that was a lie, and if he was lying to Claud, things were worse than we imagined.

I tracked his phone to one of his LA hotels and found him so fucked up on booze he could barely function. Sebastian is a social drinker at best, so it only confirmed how bad he really was.

I forced him to go back to therapy and used Claudina as the driving factor, which might have been manipulative, but it did the job, and to me, that's what was most important.

It struck him hard, and he made an appointment the next day.

Sebastian stands up in a rush, and the seat nearly falls over, lowering his voice to a deathly level. "I didn't come in to get the third degree, and I don't need some fucking quack to tell me I'm fucked up because my sister died of fucking cancer." He takes a deep breath. "And maybe you should take a good look in the mirror before you start pointing fingers at other people."

I veer back, "What the hell does that mean?"

"It means you think because you hide your feelings that you're so much better than the rest of us," he screams. "Let me tell you, brother, you're not."

"That's bullshit," I snap, annoyed, then slam my fist on the desk. "And don't project on me because I love and care for you. I'm allowed to fucking worry, Sebastian."

The buzzer on my phone goes off. "Yes?"

"Shut up, you two." I can tell the phone is muffled by the sound of Lauren's voice, "Claud can hear you yelling, and you're frightening her."

"Fuck. Thanks for the heads up."

I hang up, staring at Seb breathing erratically, and decide to take the high road and calm down, lowering my voice. "All I asked was how the new therapist was. Not what you talk about or how you're feeling."

"I'll see you Sunday." He dismisses me and walks out, slamming the door behind him.

That went well.

Fucking shit. I run my hands over my face and only have myself to blame for bringing it up today of all days.

I've been on the phone with the board all morning, and on top of that, my Chief Legal Officer, someone I trust most in my company, just informed me he is retiring in the new year, elevating my stress levels even further.

If Claud weren't in the other room, I'd be reaching for that thirty-year bottle of scotch staring at me from the bar, but she is, and she'll unwind me better than any liquor, so I buzz Lauren to have her come back in here.

Her sweet giggle alone will calm some of my nerves in seconds.

"Matteo is walking down the hall for your meeting; I'll send her in in a little." She says. Then, two seconds later, he's walking through my office with a wide smile stretching his face, and I'm not sure if I want to slap it off or be thankful for the mood shift in the room.

"Way to knock," I mutter and pull up the board documents we go over for the next twenty minutes. "Do you have anything else to add?" I ask, valuing his opinion.

Matteo was a friend of Nate's when we were younger. Then, one day, his family abruptly moved back to Italy, and we never heard from him again. Nate tracked him down once he got older, and the rest is history. Now he's my Global Head of Real Estate, and he's a fucking brilliant investor.

He's texting with a passion on his phone. "Matteo," I snap, not in the mood today.

"Sorry." He puts his phone away.

"Who were you talking to?"

"No one," he answers too quickly.

I stare at him, wondering what's wrong with him, and it hits me: he's talking to Juliette's friend.

"Was that that girl?" Fuck, I can never remember her name.

He rolls his eyes, "Becks, your employee who you can't remember? Yes, that was her."

"Don't remind me that she works for me and, technically, you." I think for a second. "And don't make me regret not having a no fraternization rule in the handbook."

"Yeah, yeah," he dismisses me to text again.

"So…" I lean back in my chair and don't finish my sentence.

There's no point.

"So?" He lifts a brow. "So, have I seen her? Is that what you're going to ask me? *Again?*" I don't answer, and he breathes, annoyed, "No, I haven't seen Juliette. Well, besides on FaceTime yesterday when she was with Becks."

I sit up taller, and he laughs. "You're a fucking idiot. It's been a month. A MONTH, and you're still obsessed. I don't understand why you can't see her again."

Of course, he doesn't. How could he understand something I don't even comprehend?

All I know is that I'm so fucked over her that even a month later, I'm still thinking about our time together…*every night.*

I couldn't stand it anymore, so I forced myself to go out with Rachel, someone I've had a casual relationship with for years. We're both similar—single parents that aren't looking for anything other than a good time.

We got back to her place, and I freaked the fuck out when she went in for a kiss. I didn't want her lips anywhere near me. I went home, and within minutes of thinking of Juliette I was hard as a fucking rock.

In the thirty-eight years of my life, I've never thought about a woman like I have about Juliette, and I barely know her.

And that scares the shit out of me.

I feel Matteo's eyes on me, and I hate myself right now, but I have to ask, "How did she look?"

"She's beautiful, Harrison. You already know how she'd look. Although she's not my type, she's still hot."

Not his type?

He doesn't like perfection?

What's there not to like?

Her long, endless legs or big, wide, curious brown eyes encased in the longest, thickest eyelashes I've ever seen?

The light dusting of freckles on the back of her shoulders or her red, lush, pouty lips?

The way her skin feels like silk under your fingertips, or how perfect her laugh is when she throws her head back, stretching out the length of her neck that begs you to sink your teeth in?

Fuck.

I bring my fist to my mouth and bite my finger out of frustration.

"You're torturing yourself, Harrison. Why don't you come with me—"

There's a knock on my office door, interrupting Matteo, and by how soft it is, I know it's Claud. "Come in," I call.

"Daddy, can I sit in on your meeting?"

I roll my lips to suppress a laugh. She once heard me ask Lauren to sit in on a meeting to take notes, and now she asks every time she's here.

"Sure. Would you like to be my assistant?" She holds up her note-book and nods her head eagerly. This kid is too much. "Come here," I pat my leg.

"Assistants don't sit on the boss's lap, Daddy," she states seriously. Then, after giving him a high-five hello, she climbs into the chair beside Matteo and crosses her legs.

"Some do," Matteo mumbles under his breath, and I stifle a laugh.

"They better not be in my company."

After five minutes of talking about nonsense since our meeting was over before Claud came in, and there was nothing else we needed to discuss—*besides Juliette*—we say our goodbyes to Matteo and Lauren for the day and head to Claudina's baking class.

"There it is!" Claudina points to the bakery excitedly. "Wait until you see what I can do. Today, we're making sugar cookies and deco-rating them with icing and sprinkles. I can't wait to show you." She says, swinging my hand exaggeratedly.

"We're early, Claudina. Let's wait outside," I say, but she's already trying to open the door.

"No way, we need a good seat," she explains, so I help her open the door to Le Petit Boulanger, and in an instant, Claud drops my hand to run across the shop into the arms of the one person who's been keeping me up at night...Juliette.

What the actual fuck?

Juliette

The bakery's front door opens while I'm crouched down, putting away supplies. Even without the view of the door, I can already tell by her enthusiastic footsteps and giggles it's my favorite girl.

I shouldn't have a favorite in class, except there's no denying it. Plus, I've known her longer than all the others. "Hey, sugar plum," I laugh, using Claudina's nickname as she piles into my body with a huge hug. "Where's Willa?" I look around her and freeze in place.

What's going on?

I stand and whisper, "Harrison?"

His furious eyes bore into mine, "What the fuck is going on here?"

"Daddy!"

"Come here right this instant, Claudina," Harrison demands, holding his arm out.

Daddy.

I look between Claudina and Harrison, bewildered, and then it hits me. "Claud, is your daughter?"

"Claudina Rosa Davenport," he snaps, "I said come here right now."

She lets go of me with confused eyes, glancing between Harrison and me, then runs over to his side, looking up at him with worry. "Why are you yelling?"

Without taking his eyes off me, he puts a protective arm around his daughter, "What are you doing here?"

I narrow my eyes but stay absolutely silent. I think I'm in complete and utter shock.

He takes a deep breath, controlling his anger for his daughter. "Claud, please sit over there for a moment." He points to the table in the furthest corner.

"But, Daddy—"

"No, buts! Do as you're asked." She looks at him briefly, then her bottom lip quivers. Harrison doesn't miss it, either. He crouches down on one knee and takes her into a tight embrace. "Everything's okay, angel. Please go take a seat, and I'll be right there." She nods, mollified, and runs off.

His attention is back on me in a millisecond, and neither of us says a word until his eerie voice splits the silence. "You need to explain how you know my daughter right now and do not lie."

I shudder inwardly at his cold demeanor, fear knotting my stomach.

What is he implying?

"Juliette!" he demands, snapping me out of my trance.

"This is our bakery," I spit out on a shaking breath. "The one I told you about, she's been coming here for ages with her nanny."

He steps toward me, and for the first time in his presence, my body is screaming at me to step back, only he's too quick, standing so close I can feel his hot breath as he speaks.

"Look me in the eyes," he murmurs through a clenched jaw.

Something in his voice has me obeying his command, and my eyes snap to his furious ones.

"Why are you acting like this?" My voice trembles with hurt and confusion. His formidable appearance falters, but he shakes his head and yields his mask just as quickly.

"You're telling me you had no idea Claudina was my daughter, and this was a complete coincidence? You happened to run into me not once, not twice, but three times within weeks of each other, and now my daughter is acting like she's your best friend?"

I'm so taken aback by this whole situation; my brain is slow to comprehend his words today.

Is he trying to say...

"Are you insinuating that I planned this? Who do you take me as? What type of person do you think I am?" I feel the back of my eyes fill with tears, mostly out of frustration but also hurt that someone I thought I had a connection with would think I was conniving and manipulative.

Harrison shakes his head, and I can tell he's just as confused as I am.

He opens his mouth to speak, but nothing comes out, so he spins on his heels, grabbing Claud to leave, then pauses on the door's threshold, turning back to glare at me.

"I don't know who you are or what you're playing at, Juliette. I will only say this only once—stay away from my daughter."

His harsh words knock the air right out of my lungs, and I stand there staring at the now-empty doorway in complete shock.

7

Juliette

"I'm sorry, Ms. Caldwell. I wish there was something we could do. This is business, not personal." Larry from the building management company says, looking me square in the eye.

I direct my glare up to the ceiling instead of at the man in front of me, who's breaking my spirit left and right.

After going over the bakery finances and the rent increase, there is no way we will be able to stay afloat for long. We will likely have to make some hard decisions in the near future, even though I promised Mom I would figure this out.

The worst part is that if we need to give up the bakery, it will be rubbed in our faces daily since we live above the space. I can't imagine Mom ever wanting to move.

Or at least, I hope not.

Eventually, I'll need to find my own place again, but Mom should stay, mainly because that's our family home. I grew up in that apartment, and Mom and Dad lived their whole lives there.

There are too many memories to leave behind.

Luckily we're rent-controlled; legally, they can't raise it above a specific price, so it gives me peace of mind that I'll never have to worry about her living situation.

Now, I'm trying to process how I'll handle the next steps, and I'm wishing I had brought Becks to the meeting. She would know what to ask, or at least could have been my voice so I could sit here and hide my emotions silently.

I swallow and clear my throat. "Thank you for your time," I say as I stand up and rush toward the door.

"Ms. Caldwell?" I pause with my hand on the doorknob. "It was a pleasure having you as tenants. Your dad was a lovely man. I'm sorry to have heard of his passing."

This man does not deserve my voice any longer or to speak of my father, so I whip open the door and stroll out with my head held high.

The sudden mention of my dad has given me a burst of resilience, along with a jolt of anger. Larry's company is taking away Le Petit Boulanger, my mother's pride and joy, and the gift my dad was so proud to give her.

I fucking hate Larry and his dumb company.

I stride down 57th Street on a mission to get to Becks' office, not caring that my feet are burning from a newly formed blister or that I'm bumping into half the suits rushing to lunch.

"Hi. How'd it go?" she answers on the first ring.

"Not one bit good." I grit out. "I'm so angry, I could burst."

She chuckles at me, losing it.

"It's not funny, Rebecca!" I raise my voice, causing some heads to turn my way, but who the hell cares? It's one of the good things about living in New York.

Nothing fazes anyone.

"There she is, my little fart."

"Um, excuse me?" *Did I hear her right?*

She laughs again. "Yeah, you're silent but deadly."

"Oh my god. I hate you, and I can't even laugh right now because

I'm so furious." I pause and take a deep breath, suddenly over-whelmed. "And so incredibly sad, Becks. Can you imagine how Mom will feel when she finds out? She said if she loses the bakery, it'd be like losing Dad all over again."

She sighs, hiding her emotions better than I am, although I know she's feeling this just as much. Becks grew up in that bakery, too. "Did he say who was buying the property?"

"No. It's confidential for now." I use air quotes even though she can't see me. "Please tell me you can grab lunch with me before I lose my mind. I'm only a few blocks away."

"Yeah, I need to finish one thing. Can you give me fifteen? You can come up and wait in the lounge area if you want."

Yeah, no thanks. I'm never stepping foot in that company and risking a run-in with her CEO after the other day.

"Honestly, I'm going to keep walking around the area. I have too much pent-up anger to get rid of before I explode."

"All right. Please do me a favor, take a deep breath and calm down. You're being a bit extreme and scaring me. Oh shit, I have to go." She says, then hangs up.

Calm down?

How the hell am I supposed to do that?

Ugh. I hate when people tell me to calm down; it makes me feel the exact opposite. Like, does she think I want to be so worked up?

My phone dings with a message from Willa, and I almost drop it from my shaky hands.

> Hey, girl! So, I'm not sure what happened, and I'm trying to get to the bottom of it. Unfortunately, Claud can no longer attend baking classes.

What? I stop dead in my tracks.

"Watch it!" someone yells from behind me.

I'm so bummed, but between you and me,
her dad was being an asshole. He's super
protective. But I have no clue what this was
about.

Is he kidding me?

Today is not the day to fuck with me, Harrison Davenport.

Something comes over me, and I see red, so I turn around and march into Becks's office building.

"Hello, welcome to Abbott. May I help you?"

I smile, probably looking marginally deranged, "Hello. I'm here to see Harrison Davenport."

"I don't see any guests in the system, miss."

"Oh, that's because it's a surprise visit. You can tell him Juliette, his *friend*, is here to see him."

The security officer looks down at my shaky hands before taking my ID from me. I need to get a handle on myself before he escorts me out of here.

"Hi, Lauren? It's Derrick from lobby security. I have a Miss Juliette Caldwell here. She says she's a friend of Mr. Davenport's, and she'd like to see him."

He covers the receiver. "She's checking," he says, then lifts the phone to his ear again, nodding to whatever *Lauren* is saying.

"This way, miss." Derrick leads me to the elevator, which promptly shuts behind me.

The sound of it closing is like an instant shock to my system, snapping me back to reality.

Oh. My. God.

What the hell am I doing?

I need to get out of this elevator right this very moment!

"Where are all the buttons?" I mumble in a panic and run my hands all over the elevator walls. Why does everything have to be so freaking high-tech? It's all digital, and I can't change the floor number.

I frantically look through my bag for my cell phone to call Becks for help. I'm not sure what the hell she can do, considering she doesn't work for the elevator company, but maybe she knows about some magical emergency stop button somewhere.

No service.

Great, just fucking great.

The elevator zooms to the top floor, and I can feel my pulse pick up. Maybe if I pass out, I'll forget this is happening. I'd never have that kind of luck; instead, the doors are going to open any second now, and I have to hope I don't throw up from nerves.

Breathe, Juliette, breathe.

When the doors open, I'll stay here until they close and bring me back down.

The perfect plan. I think to myself until the doors open.

There stands the most beautiful man I ever laid eyes on, in his dark navy, perfectly tailored suit and crisp white shirt, who's staring back at me like he can't decide if he wants to kill me or fuck me.

Even though I'm so angry with him, I'd gladly pick the latter to avoid Harrison's wrath.

My body stays still while my brain tells me to speak up and tell him I've made a mistake, but I stand there like a statue until he steps into the elevator and cups my elbow to pull me out.

There's no chance to protest or run. I can feel all eyes are on me as my heels clickety-clack down the hall while Harrison pulls me along, leading me into his office.

He locks the door behind us, silencing me when I open my mouth. Then, grabbing a remote out of his drawer, he presses a button to frost the glass of his corner office. All while leaning his behind on his desk, crossing his legs and bulging arms, dominating the room.

He lifts his chin in my direction, "You may speak."

I may speak?

Who does he think I am, his puppet?

Suddenly, my lingering anger, which hasn't diminished at all, ramps back up, and I cross my arms exaggeratedly to mimic him.

"I received a text from Willa telling me Claudina will no longer be taking baking classes. Is that true?" I ask with a surprisingly steady voice.

He raises a sarcastic brow, without answering.

I purse my lips, annoyed. "I was right all along. You're not who I thought at all. What kind of father pulls their child from something she truly loves and is great at?"

His face falls, quickly turning deadly while stepping in my direction. I move back *or try* but realize I'm still standing against the glass wall.

"A father." He lowers his deep voice. "Who protects his daughter at all costs from crazy stalkers and people wanting to take advantage of her privileged family."

What? This again?

"Listen here, you pompous asshole. We went over this the other night at the bakery. I didn't know who Claudina was." He stares at me, reading my face. "I'll have my mom teach the class or Daphne, the other baker. Claud's so happy there. Don't punish her because of me."

He shakes his head slightly. "And why should I believe you?"

"I googled you," I spit out. "There are no pictures of her anywhere. Which I'm sure is deliberate, and you're well aware of. So tell me, how the hell am I supposed to know who she is?"

"How do stalkers know anything?"

I throw my arms up in the air and lean forward, raising my voice. "I am not a stalker!"

His lip twitches.

I narrow my eyes, confused.

"I know." He lifts one side of his mouth into a sinister smirk. "I think we need a time-out."

"You know what?" I step to the side when he advances toward me again.

"I know you're not a stalker, Juliette *Caldwell*. You came in here guns blazing, and I reacted. Let's start again." He widens his eyes, matching mine.

"I never told you my last name."

"No." He laughs. "But you did tell Derrick downstairs." *Oh.* He shrugs. "And I guess you could call me a bit of a hypocrite because I kind of stalked *you*."

"What is going on right now?" Am I in the Twilight Zone?

He reaches out, sweeps my hair off my face, and tucks it behind my ear. "God, you're beautiful."

"Harrison," I snap, ignoring every nerve ending sparking my body alive from his slight touch. "What do you mean you stalked me? Are you having some mental breakdown?"

"I couldn't get you off my mind. It was driving me insane. Then I walked into that bakery, and there you were, *mon petit papillon*."

My heart flutters at my moniker. "I don't understand. Why were you so angry then?"

"Because when in life is anything that much of a coincidence? Do you see how I would take it in my position?" I nod because I do, and I thought the exact thing myself once he left. *What are the chances?* "To be honest with you, at first, I was freaking out, unsure of your intentions."

"And now?"

He shrugs. "I'm not sure you're as much of a threat as I thought."

"Are you on drugs?" I ask semi-seriously. "Ten seconds ago, you accused me of being crazy."

"You know," he says, ignoring me while boxing me in, placing both hands against the glass on either side of my face. "My sweet Juliette is a turn-on. But demanding, Juliette, she is fucking hot."

I duck under his arm and walk around his office, not trusting myself around him.

The second I lock eyes with his, I'll be done for.

"Harrison," I warn, pausing behind his desk to take in the unobstructed view of Central Park. Seeing the park from the south entrance is not the view I'm used to, but it's still remarkable, if not better. "Back to you stalking me."

"I made Matteo do inconspicuous digging while hanging out with your friend." His voice lowers from right behind me. "Then, I may have also googled you."

"Why did you google me?" I can't help asking. "You said one night. What would it matter?" I whisper.

His body presses up against mine. "Turn around," he demands. His breath tickles the back of my neck, eliciting a sheet of goose bumps to pimple over my skin.

I close my eyes and melt into his chest as his lips brush against my ear. "Juliette." My name rolls off his tongue, this time using a French accent, while he combs his fingers through my hair. Tugging at my roots in a punishing grip, he pulls my head back at an angle to look down on me from behind, causing a traitorous whimper to slip through my lips. "Kiss me," he demands, and like always, I don't think or hesitate.

I obey.

My body is in complete control and begs to feel his lips against mine once again. My chin tilts up in a welcoming motion, and without hesitation, his full lips are sealed against mine in an instant.

My arousal sweeps in as his hips surge forward, pressing his hard-on into my backside. Instinctively, I push back, rotating my hips against his groin, provoking a loud moan to escape him, echoing through his office.

Our mouths hang open, and our tongues collide just as his phone goes off. It's like a bucket of cold water splashed in my face, bringing me back to reality.

What the hell is wrong with us?

I extract myself from his hold and high-tail to the exit.

"Jules, wait." He spins me around, and I shake my head furiously.

"I can't," I murmur, then run out, not caring one bit how many eyes are on me this time.

I burst through the front door back onto 57th Street and finally pull in a full breath, taking out my phone to see five missed calls from Becks and a new text.

Hey, I tried your cell first. But I got called into a meeting, and I won't make lunch. Sorry, love you! We'll talk later, I promise.

And don't forget, if Italy wins tonight, we're going out with Matteo for the semi-finals on Sunday… AND don't worry, it's with his home friends, not work friends.

I breathe a sigh of relief.

As much as I wanted to see her, there was no way I could keep it together after my little performance back there.

And after crying in her arms for the last month, I think she's had enough of my drama.

Harrison

"Grammy!" Claud screams as she runs up the brownstone steps into Rosa's waiting arms. "Happy, happy, birthday!" Claud squeals, hugging her tightly.

"Claudina, Grandma's on the phone. Give her a second," I call out.

"Oh, you shush up. She could interrupt the President of the United States if she wanted to."

I follow them into the house and store Claud's luggage in the front closet for Sebastian to take. They're leaving straight from here for the Hamptons after brunch.

"Happy Birthday, Mom. Who's on the phone?" I ask and kiss her hello.

"My other favorite son," she mutters.

Nate and Leo scream *Jackson* simultaneously from the other room.

"Tell that asshole to call me back," I yell loud enough for Jackson, one of our other best friends growing up, to hear without even thinking.

The second the curse slips through my lips, I realize what I've said and wait for a slap to the back of my head.

I may be thirty-eight, but Rosa Morales will still put you in your place if you disrespect her in her house.

When nothing comes, I count myself lucky and run out of there like a little kid in trouble, following Claud into the living room, where she's already climbing over the back of the couch onto Nate's head, trying to reach Skye, her true love, Nate and Leo's german shepherd mix, who they rescued last year for Claud.

They live in the same building and share all the responsibilities.

Leo tickles Claudina relentlessly once she falls onto the couch; you can barely hear her giggles over the TV, blasting the replay of last night's Yankee game.

"Hi, Dad." I raise my voice and grab the remote to lower the volume, then slap my brothers on their backs as I walk past to sit in the corner. "Where's Seb?"

"Just left a job site. He's on his way," Nate replies.

He's been nonstop lately. "How many hotels are under construction at the moment?" I ask Javier and Leo.

Javier is officially retired, but before handing it off to Seb, he built The Valencia Hotel Group from the bottom up and takes pride in still knowing all the ins and outs.

Leo designs all the new buildings, as one of the family architects, making sure he's still part of the family business.

"Four," Leo answers, as he stands up and spins Claud around in a circle, Skye following along in case anything happens.

She's fiercely protective over Claud, no different than the rest of us.

"Five," Javier interrupts.

"Until the permits come through, I'm not counting Dubai, Dad."

Javier shrugs. "It will all work itself out. You kids know what you're doing."

I glance at Leo as he smiles softly in his father's direction.

Complete, utter support and unconditional love are what you would call the epitome of the Morales family.

Somehow, I was fortunate to be part of it all growing up, and for my daughter to be their blood, I know every good trait she has comes from them.

My parents don't have a parental bone in their body—do they love us? In their own way, yes, I think so. But any affection and encouragement came from my chosen parents or my grandparents.

My grandma and grandpa's names were listed on school documents and legal paperwork, and my grandfather is the only reason I run Abbott today.

When I was younger, I thought I would run the hotels with Seb. I quickly realized my future was with Abbott to keep my grandfather and forefathers' legacy alive once he passed because, knowing my father and his zero moral compass, he would have disrespected and ruined all the hard work my grandfather put into that company.

My father was CEO for a short time when I was younger and thought he could win over the board and have me voted out, but they saw through his phony exterior.

Since my grandfather appointed me CEO when I turned thirty-five, the board trusted him and his judgment and didn't hesitate to name me CEO when the time came.

Since then, my father has sulked around, and our already limited relationship has diminished further.

Because you know…it's hard to be a billionaire with nothing to do, so why not blame your son?

Either way, it would always be my future—I would never let my grandfather down. Although I rule with more of an iron fist than he probably would like, other than that, I've kept the integrity of what his grandfather started to build in the nineteen twenties.

Rosa walks in and comes straight to me. "I didn't give you a proper hello." She unties her apron, then whips me with it in the side. "And watch your mouth in this house."

"Sorry," I tell her, then take her in a tight embrace. "How are you, Mom?"

Seb walks in behind her, and she grabs him, so we're all hugging in a weird cuddle, but I'd never pull away from her. "Better now that all my kids and granddaughter are here." I bend and kiss her cheek, and then Sebastian does the same before she walks off and sits on Javier's lap.

Still, to this day, they are madly in love.

"Brunch is almost ready."

Claud pauses, then runs toward her grandparents, not wanting to miss out on all the attention.

She climbs on their lap and sits between them, snuggling to get comfortable.

"You look pretty, Grandma." Claud smiles and runs her hand down Rosa's dress. Claud's right, she looks gorgeous, but it's not a surprise when her doppelgänger is Sofia Loren.

"Thank you, sweetie." She pulls Claud onto her lap and then leans closer to Javier.

Usually, I love the love they share with Claudina, but now, looking at the three of them like a small, loving family causes a knot to form in my throat.

Am I doing her a disservice by not introducing that kind of affection into our house?

There are plenty of single-parent homes where the child does fine. I know this, but I've been actively choosing not to bring a woman into our home. *Is that different?*

If it weren't for Rosa and Willa, she would have no women influences in her life being brought up by four men.

It also doesn't take a scientist to figure out why my thoughts have shifted lately. Even from a few encounters, Juliette Caldwell has left her mark.

"What did you do this morning?" Rosa asks Claud.

"I danced for Mom and told her all about my week," she tells her as she pets Skye. Oblivious to the instant silence in the room.

Rosa or I frequently bring Claud to Central Park to visit Camila's memorial stone that's laid in the ground along the Gilder Run pathway, where Camila often ran.

My brothers disagree with us.

They think, in a way, it's morbid that Claud goes as often as she does.

Rosa senses the tension, so she asks Claud what dance she did for her mom and requests her to perform it for all of us.

Thankfully, it distracts us for the next half hour.

"Hey," I catch Seb as he starts packing up his Range Rover, "We good?" I ask.

He nods but gives me nothing more. Not that I expect him to elaborate.

"I—"

"Harrison," he warns. "I said we're good, leave it at that."

"Well, as your older brother, I can say whatever I want."

He looks at me deadpan. "You're five days older."

I shrug. "Older is still older."

"What are you, two six-year-olds?" Nate calls, though I ignore him as a tutu-clad Claudina comes barreling toward the car, doing pirouettes in between her skips, which gives me a semi-heart attack, though thankfully she makes it to me accident-free.

"Okay," I bend down so we're eye to eye, trying to keep my voice even, "You'll be good for your uncle, right?" I brush her brown syrup-filled hair back from sticking to her face.

"Uh-huh." Claud nods with enthusiasm. All she cares about is leaving so she can swim in the pool and run in the yard with Skye, who is going out east with them for the week.

"And you'll call me if you need me at any time. I don't care if you have a bad dream in the middle of the night. I will always have my phone on."

"Daddy, I know. I know."

I kiss her forehead, then her right cheek, her left, then her forehead again for good measure. "When did you become so mature?"

She replies in giggles.

"I love you, my precious angel. I'll miss you."

She throws her arms around me. "I love you more. Will you visit after work one day?"

I glance up at Seb, and he nods.

Although we all pitch in and care for Claud together, when one of the brothers has a designated week, I try to give them alone time since I see her the most.

Except with this being two weeks, one with Seb and one with Leo, there is no way I'll be able to stay away.

"I'll be there and show you who the best diver in the family is."

She giggles again. "You're the best, Daddy."

Reluctantly, I release her before I don't let her go at all. "I'll call you later to say goodnight."

She waves goodbye and climbs up to buckle herself into her booster seat.

"It feels like Thanksgiving when you need to unbutton your pants from being so full," Nate says to Leo while they give their baby, Skye, some love before she jumps in the back with Claud.

"I know. Mom's french toast will do that."

"Are you going like that, or are we changing before the bar?"

Leo looks between them. "We do look douchey to go to a hole-in-the-wall pub, but I don't think we have time."

"Where are you two going?" I interrupt them.

It's Sunday afternoon; typically, it's my day with Claud. I'm not sure I want to go home and think about how the house is so empty.

Leo smirks. "Out."

"Out where?" I ask, already annoyed. Why is he being so elusive?

"To the pub for the Italy-Brazil game—we're meeting Matteo."

"Oh, I'm coming with you guys. I can't sit at home right now."

Nate's eyes sparkle like he knows something interesting.

"What is it?" I ask.

"Matteo texted and might have mentioned a brown-haired beauty is in attendance."

My eyes bulge. "What the hell? And you weren't going to tell me?"

"We thought you might be off her after her little stunt in your office." He waggles his eyebrows like a dickhead.

I stare at him like I want to kill him. "Fuck off, let's go."

Leo hits Nate in the arm to get his attention. "I've never seen the man move so fast to get somewhere in my life," he murmurs, and Nate bursts out laughing.

"Wow, what a comedian," I mock.

But also, get me to the goddamn bar, *now*.

Juliette

"Why do you keep staring at your phone?" Becks yells over the rowdy Italy fans.

They just scored the first goal of the game, only five minutes in, and the fans are going wild.

I look up and know she's going to be pissed. "I think I should leave and go back to the bakery."

She pauses mid-sip, then puts down her beer. "What? We just got here."

"Alice said they're busy. I feel guilty sitting here having fun with you while they're up to their necks with customers."

She twists her hips so we face one another on this crowded bench where we're squished between Matteo and his brother.

"You're allowed to take time off, Jules. When was the last time you took a day?" She stops me with a head shake. "That was rhetorical because I know it's been ages. You work six days a week in the bakery, and then on the one day a week it's closed, you teach baking classes. It's been almost a month working seven days a week."

"They need my help," I say weakly. She's right, I have been working constantly, but I can't tell them no. "Let's not talk about this now."

We've been busier than ever because of a viral video someone posted of our croissants. It's great for business but not for work-life balance.

"If you don't want to discuss it, we can chat about your little rendezvous in my office building." She wiggles her body in excitement.

Last month, she didn't want me to talk to Harrison; now she's excited about me being naughty.

"Let's not." I widen my eyes for effect. "If you drop it, I'll stay, okay?"

"I love Inès, and I know she has difficulty trusting people in her bakery, but you need to hire more help or close an extra day. It's not fair to you."

"I don't mind. I want to help."

She shakes her head, annoyed. "They take advantage of you. Alice shouldn't text you that they're busy to guilt you into coming back. You deserve a day, so take it."

I think about her words.

They don't take advantage...or at least Mom doesn't. If she heard Becks, she'd be devastated.

I think.

In a daze, I stare out into the bar, watching all the patrons laugh and let loose, enjoying their favorite soccer team. I lean back in the booth and sip my drink, and I admit, I feel relaxed.

Even with the blasting televisions and loud cheering, the excited energy in the room makes me feel good.

The front door flies open a little harder than the person probably expected, and a group staggers in. The people break in different directions when an expensive pair of loafers comes into view, closer with each step.

With a mind of their own, my eyes drag up legs that fill out perfectly fitting jeans. As they rise higher, I gasp, taking in a deep breath.

It's Harrison...*and I can't stop staring.*

And if I had to make a bet, with how he looks, every woman here is staring, too.

My chest burns at the idea...no.

He's mine. *No, he's not.*

His dark honey-blonde hair is swept back, in a bit of disarray from the burst of air conditioning that blasts everyone with arctic air as they step over the threshold.

His square jaw is covered in a light shadow of stubble, and his eyes, like laser beams, stare right through me.

Of course, he watches me ogle him, and by the way that his lips are lifted in a cocky smirk, he's enjoying himself.

I reach over and squeeze Becks's arm. "Ow, Juliette...*oh shit.*"

"Did you know?" I mumble under my breath, not taking my eyes off as Harrison finally approaches our table.

"No. I'll kill Matteo for you."

Dear god, his muscles.

"Lucian, move," Harrison demands to Matteo's brother, who's next to me.

"No," I warn. "You sit over there. Don't you come closer."

His eyes twinkle, and he warns Lucian again without taking his eyes off me.

Lucian moves at lightning speed, and Harrison slides into the booth.

Breathe, Juliette.

Harrison leans over, bracing his hand high on my thigh, kissing me right below my ear, on my beauty mark. "Hello, beautiful Juliette."

He says hello, and I'm melting into a puddle.

8

Juliette

"Jesus, Harrison. You can't kick someone out of their seat like that," I snap.

He leans back, uninterested. "I can do whatever I want, especially when I see him staring at you with *the* eyes."

"Eyes? They *are* what you normally use to look at people with," I snark.

"Don't be smart. He was checking you out, and I wasn't having it," he says, then shakes his head as if he wants to forget all about it. "Enough about him." He lowers his voice while reaching over to tuck my hair behind my ear, letting his fingertips linger in a feather-like touch along my skin. "God, you're beautiful."

My body quivers, and I suck in a breath, casting my eyes down so he can't see the effect he has on me.

"Harrison," I whisper. "What are you doing here?"

"I needed to see you." He matches my whisper and lifts my chin to look me in the eyes. "I don't like how we left off the other day. I wanted to talk to you…about everything."

I avert my eyes again and nervously pick at my newly painted red nail polish.

Looking at him this close-up puts me in some weird trance. I lose my mind every single time I'm around him. He completely overwhelms me.

Couldn't Becks have fallen for anyone but Matteo? I'm worried I won't be able to handle these run-ins anymore because all I want to do is lean into his touch and bask in this feeling he provokes from my body, but I know I can't.

He's the one who told me it can't be more and freaked out instead of explaining.

So why is he doing this?

"There's nothing left to say," I tell him, then think. "Will you let Claud come back to classes?"

"Yes. She's away for two weeks with her uncles. When she's back, she'll be in attendance."

"Two weeks?" I snap my head up. "That's so long."

His jaw clenches. "I don't even want to talk about it because, trust me, if you think it's long, it feels like a lifetime to me."

He looks sad and somewhat vulnerable; it's a different side of Harrison than I've seen before.

"I'll look forward to having her back. Besides that, there's nothing left to say. I understand now why you reacted the way you did. Let's leave it at that." Harrison's face softens as he replies, except I can't hear him over the crowd cursing and groaning over a lousy call in Brazil's favor. "I couldn't hear you." I raise my voice.

He throws his arm over my shoulder, pulling me tightly into his side, leaning down to speak into my ear. "There is more I need to talk to you about, regarding us. Leave with me. It's too loud in this place."

Us?

The warmth of his body pressed against mine and his woodsy cologne that invades my senses makes it hard to think.

My vagina and my heart think leaving with Harrison sounds like the perfect plan.

However, for the first time, when it comes to this man, I need to think with my brain, so I move back, pushing his hand off me.

"You can't touch me anymore," I mutter, instantly hating the words.

Apparently, Harrison hates them too because his face falls deadly, leaning back slightly. "You don't mean that."

Of course fucking not.

I take a deep breath, nodding, then quickly shake my head, unable to lie to either of us. "I'm not made for random hook-ups, Harrison. I could have gotten over our night together, but then the kiss…it's too much for me. I'm not made for teasing."

"Juliette," he croons. "Please, take a walk with me. I'm not teasing you. I would never do that, to you at least." He smiles softly and instinctually lifts his hand to cup my cheek, then pauses, unsure of himself.

Knowing I'm giving him mixed signals, I still lean my head over so my cheek presses against his skin.

My eyes close on contact as he brushes the pad of his thumb along my cheek—this shouldn't feel so perfect. "I haven't stopped thinking about you, Jules. You're on my mind constantly."

I peek up at him, his eyes telling me he's sincere. Still, what does that mean?

"What is it that you want to talk about?"

He leans forward when the bar gets loud again. "I want to see you again. One night wasn't enough."

My breath picks up, and my heart beats rapidly against my chest. "Just one more night?"

Don't get your hopes up.

"No, baby, at least I hope not. That's up to you. It's what we need to talk about." He leans forward, and our lips meet for a quick kiss.

God, I could kiss his pillowy lips for days.

I feel myself falling down the Harrison rabbit hole quickly, and I need a second to think. "I need to use the restroom." I point so he can let me excuse myself.

He leans back and intertwines his fingers behind his head. "Go ahead." He smirks.

"I'm not crawling over you," I complain, and he shrugs unbothered. "And stop being all flirty."

He sniggers, and I know my comment has only egged him on more.

I turn my other way to come face to face with Matteo and Becks somewhere between making out and groping one another after they had way too many tequila shots.

"Harrison." I drawl.

He lifts one brow and widens his thighs slightly.

Fuck's sake, he's really not going to move.

"Fine," I fake annoyance.

I shimmy over, then straddle him, using his shoulders as leverage. My body stills, and unsurprisingly, his hands reach out, grabbing my hips, pulling me toward him, smooshing our chests together.

"You have no fucking idea how amazing you feel against me." He mumbles more to himself. "The perfect fit."

He lifts his head to look at me, where I hover slightly. His turquoise eyes gleam, burning with desire, trapping me in place.

Every single muscle in my body tenses with expectation.

"You need to stop," he growls, and I pause to realize I've gotten carried away, and my hips are moving without my permission.

God, one minute, I'm telling him he can't touch me; the next, I'm on his lap in the middle of a crowded bar.

Who am I? I think for the millionth time since meeting Harrison.

"This is your fault," I scoff teasingly. "You make me do crazy things."

He playfully slaps my ass, then lifts me off his lap onto the bar floor. "Be quick," he warns, then reaches forward to pull down my jean skirt that's risen. "Better."

I roll my eyes, then walk through the bar and stand off to the side to get my bearings. I don't actually need to use the bathroom, I need a second to think, and I can't do that when he's in my presence.

I straighten my jean skirt and re-tuck my white T-shirt that's gotten skewed from the straddle session.

"Juliette!" a voice I recognize instantly yells through the crowd.

You've got to be kidding me right now.

Not knowing which direction his voice is coming from, I turn left, hoping to avoid him. "Hey, wait up," Hunter says from behind me, swiftly catching up.

Fuck.

"Hi, and bye." I push through the crowd, trying to make my way back toward the table.

I have no interest in stopping for him, but of course, he follows me, and I realize if I don't get him to leave me alone, there is a good chance Harrison will kill him if he sees him following me.

The man swears he's not jealous, yet I've never met anyone more green-eyed in my life, and I've known Harrison for about two point two minutes.

A burly man cuts in front of me, and I stop to tell Hunter to back the hell up, but he slams into me, causing me to stumble forward.

"Shit, sorry," he apologizes as he grabs my arm, catching me before I fall. His eyes roam over me. "Jesus fucking Christ."

"What?" I panic.

"You just…wow, you look amazing. Your hair…everything."

His eyes linger on my bare legs longer than acceptable, and it's insane how even though we spent four years of our lives together, he's like a stranger, and I don't like the feeling he's giving me.

"You okay, Jules?" I whip my head to the side and realize Hunter is still holding my arm.

I rip it away.

"Everything's good, Leo. I was heading back to the table," I reply, ignoring Hunter.

Leo places his arm around me, holding me tightly to his side, and glares at Hunter, "I suggest you keep your hands to yourself."

"It's fine. He was only helping me," I cut in, trying to defuse the situation.

"What's going on over here?" My now favorite deep, gravelly voice booms over the televisions, glancing down at Leo's arm around my shoulder.

"This guy had his hands on your girl. It's all under control now. Right?" Leo lifts a questioning brow toward Hunter, who is wide-eyed, staring at Harrison, as he removes Leo's arm and pulls me into his chest.

The reasonable part of me should be worried about what the guys will do with Hunter, but all my silly brain can think of is how Leo called me Harrison's girl.

Though, apparently, so is Hunter, "Your girl?" He glares between Harrison and me. "How old is this guy, Jules?"

I tense, and Harrison's arms tighten around me.

How fucking rude.

"Excuse me?" I stand up straighter and raise my voice. "That is none of your business."

Hunter puffs out his chest, and I can tell by years of experience he's ready to go on the defensive.

"I beg to differ, considering we only just broke up. You can't expect me to stand here and believe you're with this *man*."

I look at him deadpan. "We broke up six months ago. Apparently, since then, you've lost the ability to comprehend time."

Leo ducks his head and chuckles beside me.

Harrison finds none of this funny. I can feel his anger vibrating through his body. I'm shocked he hasn't said a word.

"Oh, you've got to be fucking kidding me!" Becks barks in anger. I look over to see Matteo and who I assume is Harrison's other brother, joining us, crowding Hunter into the corner.

"Rebecca," Hunter nods his head.

"Fuckface," she growls. "Why don't you scurry back to your friends and leave Juliette the hell alone." Her voice rises, and I can tell by the high-pitched tone she's drunk. "Better yet, go back to Hoboken. You're not wanted in a New York bar."

"All right, all right," Matteo says, laughing, pulling her back.

Hunter looks between all four Andonises, scowling at me with disgust. "Since when do you drink at bars? What happened to you?"

"That's enough." Harrison's lethal voice cuts in before I can defend myself. His body cords with anger as he lets go of me to take a meaningful step toward Hunter. "Do not speak to her again unless spoken to. I think you've said enough for a lifetime, so turn the hell around before you regret your next fucking move."

Harrison pivots and strides in my direction, not once glancing back at Hunter, though I sense his fury is in full force.

He bends down as he wraps a possessive hold around my shoulders to speak for only me to hear. "We're leaving now." His words leave me with no room to disagree, not that I want to.

We walk back toward our table so I can grab my belongings; our friends follow, leaving Hunter in the dust.

"You're in big trouble, mister," I tell Matteo as I say goodbye.

"Bros before hoes," He laughs and immediately tells me he's kidding. "To be honest, I never expected him to come. I've known Nate since we were kids, and I can count on one hand the number of times Harrison has come along with us for a Sunday Funday."

Over the last month, I've gotten to know Matteo—even though Becks still swears they're casual—I've become fond of him, and I can tell he truly cares for Becks, even if she doesn't want to believe it.

"You're sure you want to leave with Harrison? I'll go if you want to head home. I wouldn't blame you after that run-in." Becks says.

I kiss her cheek, assuring her I'm okay, and tell her she should stay. Then wave goodbye to Matteo's brother and Leo.

Harrison intertwines our fingers and leads us out of the bar; a voice calls out for us when we're not even two steps outside.

"Oh, you've got to be fucking kidding me," Harrison grumbles.

"Hi, I'm Nate." Harrison's brother reaches his hand out to shake mine. "Harrison's younger brother and much, *much* better-looking Davenport."

He winks, and I giggle at his playfulness. From one sentence, I can tell he's different from his brother. He still has a serious edge, but he's definitely more easy going.

"It's nice to meet you, Nate. I'm Juliette."

His lips lift into a mischievous grin. "Oh, trust me, I know who you are."

It's the first time I've had a good look at him.

I'd like to know what the hell their parents were taking to produce these two. I may be biased toward Harrison, but there's no denying Nate is just as handsome.

They're similar in looks, with the same killer eyes and broad shoulders.

Nate is tall enough I need to look up to him, though shorter than Harrison, with a more slender build. His hair is darker, with a slight curl, and his uninhibited smile could charm any woman's pants off, I imagine.

I glance over to Harrison, who's shooting daggers in my direction. Clearly, I've been caught checking out his brothers, and I can't help but egg him on, so I waggle my brows.

He turns his attention back to Nate. "Great, you met. Now fuck off."

"Don't be so rude," I chastise. "Jealous of your own brother. What next?"

Nate throws his head back and laughs loudly. "Oh, I definitely like you. You tell him who's boss."

Harrison, Mr. CEO, is here, and I can tell he's about to lose his shit on Nate, and for some reason, it makes me laugh even more.

"What the hell?" he retorts.

"You're so high-strung. You need to calm yourself down."

He lifts one brow. "I know a perfect way to calm down, and it includes you on—"

"Aaaaaand, that's my cue." Nate kisses my cheek goodbye, promising to see me soon, and runs back into the bar.

Harrison's face drops the second Nate is gone, taking my hand back in his, directing us down the street, not saying a word.

His stressed-out energy is swirling around us—I think the whole city block can feel it. There's no way he could genuinely be mad. *Could he?*

"I was only playing around, you know that, right?"

He stops at the corner and turns toward me. I'm unable to read his face.

"Does my age bother you?" he asks, clenching his jaw. His nostrils flare slightly as he takes a deep breath.

Oh.

He's pissed about what Hunter said.

Brazenly, I step closer and link his arms behind my back. On my tippy-toes, I raise mine over his shoulders so we're as close as possible.

"Have I ever given you that impression? Because not even a small part of me is bothered by it." I kiss his neck. "It's kind of hot that you're an older, sexy man."

Harrison needs no other confirmation. He drops his head and kisses me with urgency. It's exactly the reassurance he needs.

However, it also sparks hope that if this bothers him so much, maybe he does want more from us.

Our kiss is all suction, no tongue, as he presses my body against his. I go weak in my knees, but he has me tightly pressed against his body so that I don't fall.

"You drive me completely insane, Juliette Caldwell," he murmurs against my lips, then pulls back. "And apparently, you make me feel young again. Making out on a street corner." He shakes his head as if he can't believe it.

He hails a taxi and opens the door like a gentleman, closing it softly behind me before running to get in on the other side.

"Seventy-Eighth and Park," he tells the cabbie.

"I thought you had a driver?"

He drags me over to the middle so we're touching, then buckles my seat belt.

It takes everything in me not to make a joke about him taking care of me. But I think twice about it, knowing the age issue is too fresh.

"I gave him the day off." He pauses. "I was supposed to be home. This pit stop was unexpected."

I roll my lips to hide my smile, staring straight ahead.

"What is it?"

"Huh?"

He narrows his eyes. "What's that little smirk for?"

Shrugging, I try to play it cool. "Nothing."

He sighs, exasperated. "Juliette."

Turning my head toward him, I smile at how irritated he is. He riles up so easily.

"I like that I was your pit stop." He rolls his eyes as if annoyed I called him out on it.

We drive up the FDR, hand in hand, in a comfortable silence, heading to, I assume, his house. Though he once told me he brings no one there, so I'm not exactly sure where we're going.

"So." He side-eyes me. "That was your dickhead ex who didn't know how to please you?"

I close my eyes and hit his arm. "Shh. Are you crazy? He can hear you." I gesture toward the driver.

Harrison chuckles. "He has headphones in."

Oh.

"In that case, yes. That was him." I give no other information. No part of me wants to discuss Hunter.

"Huh."

"What?" I stare at him. "What is that *huh* for?"

"Nothing. I'm just surprised. He doesn't seem your type."

He knows nothing about me. "I don't have a type. Clearly."

"It's not older, good-looking businessmen?"

"Right this second? Definitely not," I hiss, annoyed. For no reason other than that, he's being cocky and knows he's right.

"Really?" he questions, then grabs my hair and positions my head to kiss the side of my neck. The tip of his tongue glides to my ear, where he bites down, prompting instant shivers and goose bumps up my body. "No attraction at all?" he mocks.

He positions my legs over his lap, out of view from our driver.

"Harrison," I warn as his hand creeps up my inner thigh.

"So you're telling me, if I pushed this skirt up and ran my fingers over you, you wouldn't be soaked through?"

"No," I lie right through my teeth.

His eyes hold mine. "Are you sure about that? "

"*Huh*," I mimic him. "Didn't take you for one to fish for compliments."

His fingers make it to the cusp of my skirt. My mouth hangs open in anticipation of one of probably the naughtiest things I've ever done.

The car comes to an abrupt stop, and I groan in protest.

Harrison chuckles and swipes his card to pay. "Next time. Come on."

He helps me out of the back of the cab, then lets his eyes roam down my body. "How tall are you?" he asks.

"Five six." I frown. "Why?"

He shrugs. "You seemed taller."

Men.

"That's because all the times I've seen you, besides the bakery, I was in four-inch heels."

The wind picks up at that moment, whipping my hair in front of his face.

Harrison reaches out with both hands—I ignore the warmth shooting through my body as our skin touches—and pushes my hair behind my ears.

"Better," he whispers. "Your face is too perfect to hide, especially from me."

"I beg to differ. It's probably you I need to hide from the most."

With his hands still cupping my face, he leans down and lightly kisses my lips. "Let's go."

I glance around the penthouse in complete awe.

It's stunning.

Lived in, yet contemporary and well-designed, not to mention the kitchen is to die for. Top-of-the-line appliances and enough workspace on the thickly veined marble island with a waterfall edge to do some serious baking on.

"It's beautiful here, and so much more lived in than the last place you took me," I joke. "Is this your home?"

"It is. Would you like a glass of wine?"

I wasn't going to drink today, but maybe one glass will help my nerves. "Sure. Could I please have some water as well?"

I want to wander around and take it all in. I see a baby picture of who I can only assume is Claud in the corner, but I stay close to Harrison instead.

His demeanor changed the second we entered his private elevator. I think he's uncomfortable with me being here. Which makes sense based on what he's told me, so instead of wandering around, I lean on the counter and take in the rest of the kitchen.

"I don't know why I thought maybe you would live in a town-house, not a penthouse. Though I have to admit this place is bigger than most houses."

He passes me my wine and clinks my glass, smirking. "What?"

"Nate and Leo are building me a house. You've been there." I narrow my eyes, confused. "At the BUO event."

"Still have no clue what you're talking about."

"The masquerade party, Juliette."

"Oh." I scrunch up my nose, embarrassed. "I was invited last minute, and then I was so distracted with you once I got there that I never found out what the charity was for. I know that's terrible."

He chuckles softly. "Building Unity Organization was founded by my brothers to build up towns and villages that need assistance."

"Oh." I gulp my wine back, even more embarrassed now. "That's amazing and something I probably should have paid more attention to. So, are they both architects?"

His eyes linger over me briefly before answering. "They are. A bit attached at the hip, those two. They were in the same classes in college, had an internship at the same firm, and now own one together."

"That's impressive." I think for a second, unsure if this is an appropriate question, but it's been on my mind. "Can I ask you something?"

He leans back on the counter and crosses his legs at his ankles, and for a second, my brain fizzles. He takes a long sip of his wine, his eyes never leaving mine. "Sure."

"You refer to Leo as your brother, is he…"

"My brother. That's it," he says in a harsh tone.

My stomach drops. "I'm sorry. I shouldn't have asked." I sip my wine again; at this point, one glass won't cut it, and we've only been here for five minutes.

He shakes his head and runs his hand down his face. "No. I'm sorry for snapping. People don't always understand our dynamic. Frankly, it's none of their business."

I step up and sit on the stool to get more comfortable. "You don't need to explain. It was nosy for me to ask."

"Nate is my biological brother," he begins anyway. "We aren't close with our parents, and now, looking back, we were probably craving some attention."

"Understandable."

He nods. "My grandparents were around but older, so from a young age, Nate and I gravitated toward spending time with Leo, Sebastian, and Camila's family."

"Sebastian and Camila? I didn't meet them, right?"

"No." He pauses, hesitating for a second, then continues. "Seb was at the masquerade party but had to leave early. So anyway, Rosa and Javier Morales took my brother and me in like orphans. Ever since then, they've been Mom and Dad. And Leo and Sebastian are as much my brothers as Nate; there is no difference in my eyes."

I wish I were standing next to him to hug him. I couldn't imagine not having loving parents, but I do know what it is to have a chosen family.

Becks is that for me.

I didn't miss how he skipped over whoever Camila is, but I've already pried enough, so I'll leave it.

I search my bag, take out my phone, and then pass it over to him once I've opened the right screen.

"I have this saved on my phone and send it to Becks periodically. I'm not sure who said it, but I think you can appreciate it as much as I can. Maybe even more so."

He takes my phone and reads it out loud. "*Family isn't always blood. It's the people in your life who want you in theirs. The ones who accept you for who you are. The ones who would do anything to see you smile and who love you no matter what."*

He slides the phone back across the counter, and I see his thoughts racing. "You send this to Becks? She's your chosen family?"

I nod. "How you found solace in the Morales family. She found it within mine."

He stands straight and heads to the fridge, pulling out two blocks of cheese and some crackers, then places them in front of me. "So you're the one with the loving parents?"

Suddenly, I feel awful.

Here I am boasting about my family when he just told me he didn't have a great one.

"Don't," he warns. "I can see where your thoughts are going, don't worry. Be proud that you don't have shit parents."

Without invitation, I lean over and cut myself some cheese, place it on a cracker, and drizzle it with the honey Harrison passes me.

"Becks's mom loves her in her own way," I tell him. "Her dad left them when she was younger, and something changed in her mom. She became a bit... promiscuous. Always bringing men home when Becks was there as a kid. I think it's how she coped with losing her high school sweetheart. So Becks often stayed with us."

"That's tough."

My head dips in a quick nod. "It is. They still have a relationship, and honestly, I love Becks's mom; she just had her priorities backward for a bit."

I take another bite of cheese, then freeze. "Are you not eating any?"

"I am," he cuts himself a piece, takes a bite, then offers it to me. I lean forward and decide to tease him in an effort to change this serious mood around.

My lips linger around his fingers, sucking slowly.

I'm not sure where all this confidence is coming from, but my motto lately is 'fake it till you make it.'

Harrison pulls his finger out and stalks around the counter; his eyes return to me the second he's in front of me, lifting me from the stool and placing me on the counter.

He steps between my legs, and I grab my drink and bring it to my lips. I needed to do something distracting before he has the chance to kiss me.

There's no denying it's what he wants. I can see it in the crazy look he has in his eyes. He was about to go in hard and quick.

An awkward silence falls over us while I sip the rest of my drink. "So why did you bring me here, Harrison? What's changed?"

"Are you suggesting there are more things to talk about than other people's shitty parents?" he jokes.

"God, I'd hope so. I think we're a bit more interesting than that." I grin. "Tell me something else."

He kisses my forehead, then leans back, staring at me. The mood changing instantly when he whispers, "You're the only woman I've ever brought to my house."

What?

He mentioned he doesn't bring people here, not that he *never* has.

"Never?"

"Not once," he says with meaning.

I stare wide-eyed and in complete shock.

"Come, let's talk outside." He refills my glass of wine, then takes my hand to lead me out toward the terrace.

"Oh my freaking god, Harrison," I turn toward him and smile. "You get this view every day? It's amazing."

He walks up behind me, trapping me with his arms on the railing in front of me. "It's a good city."

"The best," I mutter.

All I want to do is lean my head back and bask in the warmth of his body, but I know once I give in, we'll never talk.

"Have you always lived in the city?"

I nod. "All my life. Above the bakery, actually."

He leans down and kisses up my neck. I give in. My head falls back, and I close my eyes to the overwhelming feeling.

"I know we need to talk," he mutters against my skin. "The problem is I can't help myself around you. I'm addicted."

I feel the exact same way.

He pulls back too soon, then directs me to the lounge chair made for two people, with his hand splayed across my lower back.

Harrison's phone rings, and without hesitation, he picks it up. "Angel." His voice lowers to a soft hum.

A high-pitched *"Daddy"* screams over the line, causing me to chuckle.

Harrison rolls his eyes and whispers sorry. "I'm going to take this inside. I'll be right back."

The door is left ajar, so I hear a lot of what Harrison says, and it's just another piece of the Harrison puzzle—the soft, loving father piece, and it makes me want him even more.

I close my eyes, listening to him laugh, letting his guard down with Claud as the soft breeze hits above the city. All while I cross my fingers, hoping that whatever he wants to talk about has something to do with him wanting *more.*

9

Harrison

I'M COMPLETELY and utterly fucked over Juliette Caldwell.

After hanging up with Claud, I stepped back onto the terrace and have been standing here in silence since, watching the hottest woman I've ever laid eyes on.

She's curled up, sleeping peacefully.

Jules is unassuming but equally gorgeous, and I have a feeling she has no idea the power she has over me.

The last few times I've seen Jules, she was done up and dressed to the nines, but today, her face is void of makeup, showing off a small dusting of freckles and all her natural beauty.

My eyes have been glued to her, never wanting to look elsewhere.

The fucked-up thing of it all is there is only one word that comes to mind when I stand here and watch her.

Mine.

One single word that feels so right when I think it, yet I know I have no right to claim it.

Though, deep down, something's telling me I might be wrong.

Why else would I bring her here without even a thought? We pulled up to my building, and the second we walked through the doors, it hit me like a ton of bricks.

Never once since the day Claudina was born has another woman stepped foot in this house.

My stomach clenches, and for the first time, my thoughts tonight go to Camila and her crazy idea of naming Claudina after a butterfly so she could be here in spirit.

I never believed in all that mumbo jumbo—I put it off as her being sick and out of it.

But now, with Jules…if this is what she was talking about, I'm fucked.

I can't have Jules forever.

I can't.

Shaking my head, I rid myself of any thoughts about going down that path—we've just met for fuck's sake.

The sun's setting and the wind picks up, so I grab a blanket, walk over to cover her as I sit, and pull her into my arms.

I tuck a piece of hair behind her ears and softly kiss her plush lips.

I wasn't kidding before…I'm utterly addicted to her.

"Baby," I whisper when she starts to stir.

We need to talk, but also, a part of me wants to Rapunzel her ass so she never leaves.

I stop mid-thought.

Yeah, I'm going to need to stop watching so many Disney movies with Claud.

Slowly, her eyes open. She flutters her dark, thick lashes until her big brown eyes stare at me in shock. "Did I fall asleep?" She croaks, and instead of moving, she snuggles into my side.

I squeeze my arms around her tightly and kiss the top of her head. "You did. You look tired. Are you okay?"

"I've been working a lot at the bakery. Long hours and early mornings are finally catching up to me I guess." She pauses and chuckles to herself. "Which I'm sure you're familiar with. Running your own company on top of caring for Claud."

Claud.

There's a shit ton we need to discuss, and it keeps piling up.

I think of her working at the bakery, standing on her leg for long hours. She hasn't told me yet, but I found out about her accident when I was searching her background.

A big part of me wants to know all the details, but I know she has to tell me in her own time. So instead, I ask, "What's your favorite thing to bake?"

"Hmm," She thinks, smiling to herself. God, she's so refreshing and different from the typical women I see. "Probably éclairs because they're my mom's favorite. Well, they were until I began experimenting with flavors. I think I gave her about a hundred and ten heart attacks already."

"She didn't like them?" I frown.

"Mom is old school. She thinks classics should stay classics, but it's hard for her to say no to me, so she lets me do what I want. My cousin from France was in Paris last month and stopped in one of the new éclair stores that have been popping up all around Paris. It's the only thing they make with fun flavors. I think it would be a nice addition to spice up the shop." She pauses and looks up at me, and I almost lose my breath at her beauty. "Sorry, I'm rambling."

"I could listen to you talk for hours," I tell her truthfully.

She snuggles back into my chest. "I see Swoony Harrison is in the house tonight."

"Swoony Harrison?" I chuckle.

She shrugs. "You have a lot of personalities. Grumpy Harrison, Jealous Harrison." She looks up and widens her eyes. Waiting for me to protest.

I won't.

She's got me...I'm fucking jealous, and I'm owning it now.

"Go on," I say dryly.

"Sweet and Swoony."

"I'm not fucking sweet, Juliette," I say unimpressed.

"To Claud, you are, and don't try to lie. I heard you on the phone."

"I'm not going to be a dick to a five-year-old." I scoff. "And she's my daughter."

Sweet. I've never heard of such a thing.

She pinches my side playfully and continues. "Demanding Mr. CEO."

"That's a good one," I mutter.

She shakes her head. "Of course, you'd think that."

"So, which one's your favorite?" I ask curiously.

She scrunches her face in disgust. "I don't want to say."

"What? Why not?"

She flips her body so she's lying facing the city view between my legs. I pull her closer to my chest, fix the blanket to get comfortable, and circle her with my arms.

"Well, of course, I like Swoony Harrison, who wouldn't?" She shrugs and runs her hands up and down my legs. "But is it terrible to say I like you when you're jealous?"

"Well, obviously, I'm not going to say it's terrible since you're describing me."

"I've never had anyone be possessive over me. I like that you want me all to yourself." She pauses. "Harrison?"

"Yeah, baby?"

"Can I ask you something?" She whispers.

"Go for it."

"This is off-topic, but it's been playing in my mind." She thinks for a minute. I can tell by her hesitation how her hands stop and go on my legs she's nervous to ask. "I know all of our run-ins were crazy coincidences. But why is it you automatically thought I was a stalker? Why wouldn't you assume it was because Becks and Matteo being together, putting us in the position of seeing one another? It's what I thought."

"Would have made logical sense, wouldn't it?" I murmur sarcastically. I hate that my life's a three-ring circus. I also know I need to be honest with her. "Before Claud was born, I was dating a girl who I didn't know as well as I thought I did. It was before I became CEO, trying to prove I deserved this position. She didn't mind my long hours, and it was nice to have someone to come home to because, I had no time to date. It was either that or do what all the rest of the industry does—pay for high-class prostitutes."

From her side profile, I see she scrunches up her nose at the idea, and I chuckle, "I'm not saying I did, but it's what most people do. You have needs, you want them met, but you have no time. It's convenient."

She shakes her head in disgust. "This would be a great time to skip forward."

I smirk. "Then things turned ugly, and she became an entirely different person. It was right before Claud was born. I ended up needing to get a restraining order against her."

"You did?" Her voice raises in shock.

"Mmm hmm. It's why I don't do relationships. I made a promise to wait until Claudina's older to ever date seriously. I don't want to fuck up and bring the wrong person home."

She reaches over to grab the wine she hasn't touched to take a sip. She's trying to hide her feelings.

But I don't miss it, she's pissed.

"Don't give me that look, Juliette. Claud will always be my number one priority."

"Why am I here, Harrison?" she snaps, putting her drink down with force. "And do you truly think I'm the type of person who would want to come before your daughter?"

"All right, calm down for a second."

She whips her head around. "Word of advice. Don't tell a woman to calm down. It will have the exact opposite effect."

I move her hair over to one side and kiss her neck, trying to distract her from spinning out of control—just another part of her I'm obsessed with.

Something about the curve of her neck turns me on.

"I told you, Juliette. One night wasn't enough."

"And I told you, I don't want another *one* night."

I sit straighter, annoyed. "Will you let me finish?"

"Fine," she huffs, and I take a deep breath.

I saw this going differently.

"Day in and day out, you're on my mind. Ever since the masquerade party—"

"Not the restaurant?" She raises a brow.

"No. I wasn't wasting precious time thinking about a stranger, Juliette."

Her face falls. "Oh."

Fuck.

"That came out wrong." I take her hand in mine. "I *did* think about the insanely hot girl from the restaurant. Just not in the way I do now. You consume all of my thoughts."

"I'm waiting for you to get to the punch line."

"Why are you so defensive? Where's my sweet Juliette?"

"Back at the restaurant," she deadpans.

I squeeze her hand in warning and clench my jaw, so I don't snap at her snarkiness and continue. "I don't want it to be one night. I—"

She waits patiently for me to finish, but when I don't, she asks, "You what?"

"I want to be with you...but I can't promise a future... " I trail off, hating the words. In another world, this outcome would be completely different. "In my life, right now, I can't commit more. One night is usually good enough, but with you, deep down, I knew it never would be." I search her eyes. "Say something," I whisper.

"So what does this mean? I'm not made for one-night stands. That night nearly broke me."

"What?" I ask, horrified.

She maneuvers our hands so our fingers interlock. "I'm not telling you this to make you feel bad. I'm an adult and made a decision to sleep with you. In the future, I'll never do that with anyone again." She thinks. "But...I'm not sure I want something so serious either. I do need commitment, though."

"What do you mean? How is that different?"

She faces me fully. "You're busy with your job and Claud. But if I'm sleeping with you, I need to know I'm the only one." She pauses to look me in the eyes. "After a long, stressful day, I don't want to come home and worry about what or who you're doing."

That's an easy answer. "I wouldn't want to be with anyone else.

Exclusivity is a no-brainer for me, baby." She chews on her bottom lip and taps her fingers quickly against my thigh. "What is it?"

"How does this work?" she asks uneasily. "Do I sit around and wait for you to call me?"

I lean forward to capture her back into my arms, bringing her close to my chest. "I think we just see when we're free and go from there."

She hums to herself. "Okay."

"You're not very convincing. Tell me what you want."

"I don't know…our schedule is all over the place. Maybe we can check in periodically." She shrugs. "Something to know we're still… whatever we are."

"Try to keep me away." The words slip out easily.

"So, is this considered…friends with benefits?"

Laughter rumbles from my chest. "The way you say it, you'd think you were the old one."

Her head tilts to the side, looking up at me, her eyes sparkling with humor. "How the hell should I know? You know I'm inexperienced, and you're not old." She hits me in the leg. "And don't look at me like that."

"Like what?"

"Like it turns you on that I'm inexperienced."

"Okay." I grin, and she playfully hits me again, a ghost of a smile passing over her lips. "I can't help it. It does turn me on." I reach down and pull her hips back so she can feel my hard-on. "I'm in a perpetual state of discomfort because I think about fucking you all day, every day, like a goddamn teenager."

Her tongue peeks out, seductively licking her lips before leaning into me to lick up the side of my neck. "Now, *you can* fuck me all day, every day."

I inhale sharply. *Fuck me.*

This girl surprises me at every turn.

My hands travel up and down her body, pushing the blanket off for easier access.

Untucking her shirt, I run my hands teasingly along her lower belly, then up to cup her breast, which fit perfectly in my hand.

"Harrison," she moans. The husky rasp of her voice is a straight shot to my balls, the best aphrodisiac in the world.

"I want to take my time with you, feel what's mine." I pinch her erect nipple and squeeze. "This is mine for however long I want. Is it not?" I growl.

Forever crosses my mind. But that needs to stay buried deep down.

"Yes," She breathes, subtly rocking her hips, begging for my touch. "Yours."

I reach my free hand up, taking her chin between my fingers to have her look ahead of us. "All these people out there in the city, watching us, are jealous you're not theirs."

"Oh my god," she cries, moaning simultaneously. "They can't see us, can they?"

"Who knows?" I tease—of course, they can't.

I'd rather kill myself than let another man or woman look at Juliette. She doesn't need to know that, though. The thrill of it all is getting her hot for it.

Juliette Caldwell is mine and for my eyes only.

"Now sit back and let everyone enjoy the show."

Juliette

One Hour Later

The smoldering flame of desire burning in his eyes has my hips swiveling with a mind of their own. Forward and back, over and over, onto Harrison's hard cock, which has me stretched out to the max.

With each pass, the need for this man naturally guides my body to find its release.

Every touch, gaze, or whispered word causes a tingling pleasure that I can't control even if I try. I'm completely lost to the sensation, and Harrison's lust-filled eyes tell me he's right there with me.

A sheen of perspiration layered on our skin, mixed with the small amount of rain that's fallen, helps glide our chests together, rubbing my sensitive nipples he played with for the last hour against the light dusting of his chest hair.

His strong fingertips dig into the flesh of my behind, as I use his shoulders for leverage as he begins to bounce me up and down with force.

Something inside me snaps...I want to blow his mind, so I take over and ride him like I'm born for it. Deep and hard, no holding back.

My mind wanders to the heated scene that we played out earlier. My back to his chest, my thighs spread wide. One leg over his forearm, his thick fingers parting my center for all the Upper East Side to see, teasing me until he finally let me come.

"Harrison," I whimper. "Ohhh. This is so so good."

"Yeah, Jules, baby. Just like that," he cries as he lifts me, slamming me down one last time.

"Ahhh," I gasp, our eyes never leaving each other as my lingering orgasm finally bulldozes right through me.

No sooner than I've even come down from my high, Harrison flips me around onto my hands and knees, plunging into me with a guttural groan that could be heard citywide.

The air leaves my lungs as his massive cock hits me deep, causing me to fall forward from the force. I almost face-plant, but just in time, Harrison grasps my hair and fists it tightly, pulling me up, not losing his stride as he rides me with hard, punishing hits.

Dear God...this man.

My gaze pulls to our reflection in the floor-to-ceiling window, and the image has me wide-eyed and turned on to the next degree.

I've never seen anything like it...raw, unrestrained, and totally fucking hot.

"Look," I tell Harrison.

His eyes snap up, and I can tell by his strained expression and contracted muscles that he's about to lose it.

Releasing my hair, he takes hold of my waist and widens his knees. His hips swivel to hit that perfect spot with each go, keeping a steady but powerful rhythm as we watch together, in awe, him taking me from behind.

The sound of incessant moaning and our bodies slapping together echoes off the terrace walls, and all too soon, I begin to feel a deep burn starting in my toes again.

Harrison lifts one leg, places his foot down for leverage, and really lets me have it, not holding back now. I've never had sex like this in my life. Where he could break me in two, but in the best possible way ever.

Abruptly, the sky opens, and rain begins to pour down on us.

Time feels like it slows down while my greedy eyes continue to watch our reflection, just as Harrison roars in pleasure, throwing his head back and letting the rain run over his body.

His hair slicks back, and rainwater travels down his corded throat, trickling onto his muscular chest as he wildly cries out my name repeatedly into the night sky, just in time for my insides to spasm alongside him.

We stay like this for a second, both our chest heaving, before he drops to the side and pulls me into his chest.

Immediately, he wraps his arms around me, kissing me with passion and emotion.

"Jules," he mumbles softly against my lips, then pulls back to look me in the eyes.

My heart beats wildly against my chest. Something I'm not sure he's ready for passes between us.

He says he doesn't want more than casual. I may be young and inexperienced, but I know what he tells me is a lie.

Whether he knows it or not, sooner or later, he'll figure it out, and I hope *we* can handle it...*together.*

For now, I'll wait and take anything I can get from him.

The sky illuminates as lightning hits, and soon after, a loud boom of thunder rumbles over the city.

Without hesitation, he jumps up and leans in to pick me up. I don't protest because I know he won't put me down.

Somehow, with magical muscles, he leans back down, me still in his arms, picks up our important belongings, and runs us into the house.

We leave a trail of water as he walks the hall with me in tow before entering a sleek, all-white, and gray marble bathroom that's the size of my bedroom. I glance down at his chest to his butterfly tattoo and wonder the meaning behind it.

Earlier when I put my hand on it, he nonchalantly removed it, like he did the first night we were together.

"One sec, let me grab a clean towel," he says, placing me on the ground, then searches the linen closet.

He bends and starts to dry up my legs…I feel it before he sees it, and it's clearly not rainwater.

I look down as he pauses once he gets closer to my private parts. "I'm on birth control," I whisper.

His body is frozen, and his eyes widen as he takes in the come dripping down my inner thigh.

Neither of us remembered a condom.

I pull him up and cup his face, pressing my lips to his, kissing him to distract the freakout he's about to have.

It must work because condoms are *forgotten* two more times after.

It's late.

Claud called Harrison a while ago to say goodnight, and Becks texted me numerous times. They all went out after Italy won and are only getting home now.

Thank God we left the bar when we did. I would have never been able to handle a long day out drinking like that.

Becks is also now in love with Nate and Leo, so she thinks Harrison's not as bad as she thought. For once, her opinion wouldn't have mattered, though I'm happy she's getting on board.

"I should go," I say reluctantly, not only because I don't want to leave the beautiful man lying beside me but because my body is screaming in soreness.

"No, stay." His eyes beg me.

Curling into the curve of his warm body, I place my head on his chest and ask, "Are you sure?" I don't want him to feel obligated.

He nods without hesitation.

"Okay, the bakery's closed tomorrow, so no early morning for me. I'll need to call my mom."

"What? You're joking," he sniggers. "I know you're young, but fuck, you need to call her and tell her?"

"I live with my mom, Harrison," I mumble into his manly scent. God, everything about him drives me crazy. "It's just the two of us, so it's common courtesy. She was expecting me home hours ago."

"You still live there, above the bakery?"

I pause and take a big gulp, pushing my emotions down. "Last year, I moved downtown, and then my dad passed away soon after. I broke my lease and moved back home to be with Mom. She needed me more than I needed my independence."

"Oh, Jules, baby," he whispers but doesn't extend his apologies other than tugging me tighter into his body, which I appreciate. "Were you close?"

"He was my best friend," I murmur, my voice catching. "Sorry. Normally, I love talking about him. Lately, it's been harder than ever."

He runs a soothing hand up and down my spine, lingering his lips against my temple. "Any particular reason why?" he mumbles, and when I don't attempt to answer, he tells me. "We don't have to talk about it. Death is never easy."

He's right, it's not, but I tell him what's wrong anyway. "I was at a place where talking about him brought me peace, and sharing our memories was therapeutic. I never want him to be forgotten." I pause to get the right words. "I often think people are selfish after a loved one dies."

"How do you mean?"

"Well...we sit depressed instead of celebrating their life. They died, not us, and we should honor them, so for the past year, I have tried my best to do that. Until recently...since we found out the rent for Le Petit Boulanger is being raised substantially by new owners." A despondent sigh slips through my lips. "I know this normally wouldn't seem like a huge deal for some people, especially for renters in the city. However, for Mom and me, it's much more than that. My dad rented the space to start the bakery for my mom twenty years ago. He surprised her, paying the first few years upfront, and on top of buying her all brand-new, top-of-the-line appliances, he had it decorated to match her favorite patisserie from her hometown. She's been baking there ever since, so being kicked out has drudged up a lot of old memories for us."

His hand stills. "Twenty years. Jesus, I'm sorry, Jules."

"Yeah, it's a shit situation. Soon, I'll meet with a realtor to look for a new storefront if that's what Mom wants. Just another thing to add to my ever-growing list of things to do." I complain, then remember something. "It's why I went a little psycho the other day and barged into your office. I had just left a meeting with my building management company, my emotions were high." I cringe, thinking back on that day.

His eyes light up. "You'll hear no complaints from me, that was fucking hot."

"Of course, that's your answer."

"What about your apartment?" He asks.

"We're rent-controlled."

He's quiet momentarily, and I wonder what he's thinking about.

"Seemed like your dad truly loved your mom, surprising her with the bakery and all. Either way, it's still a great memory."

My lips pick up in a huge smile, while I lean back to look at him. "You have no idea. They were so in love. Until the day he died, everyone around them, even strangers, could feel it."

He smiles tenderly. "How did they meet?"

"Ah, this is my favorite story to tell." I lay my head back on the pillow and look up at the ceiling, imagining my dad telling me their story like he always did before bedtime. "My dad was on a European ski trip with his friends from New York. It was late at night, and they were detoured off the highway in France. Of course, they ended up getting lost since this was way before reliable GPS, so they drove until they hit the next town to find a small bed and breakfast." I close my eyes and picture them together. "My dad walked in and looked across the room to find my mom checking in. She was there for her cousin's wedding weekend...anyway, my dad said it was love at first sight. He knew the second his eyes landed on her." Harrison's thumb startles me when he wipes a few happy tears from my cheeks.

"And let me guess, the rest is history?"

"Not quite...they had a bumpy road ahead of themselves. They spent all night together that first day they met, drinking and laughing at the town bar. Two days later, my mom brought my dad to her cousin's wedding, and he ditched all his friends, which they weren't so happy about. Mom says this is when she fell in love, so not love at first sight for her, but almost. My mom's family loved my dad and were supportive from the start, but not my dad's side."

Harrison frowns. "Why not?"

"Sooo," I drag out. "You probably know my family." His brows furrow. "Do you know the Archibald family?"

"As in the Archibald Oil Company?" His eyes widen. "Yes, Juliette, the whole world knows them."

"Surprise." I throw my hands up. "Technically, I'm an Archibald. Not that I've met any of them besides my one aunt and cousin."

"I don't understand." He looks at me confused.

"After the wedding, my dad returned to New York with my mom and confessed his love for her to his parents. They were not happy, to say the least. You can imagine the rest, so my dad picked my mom over their billions and had his last name legally changed."

"Holy shit, how did I not know this story?"

"Seriously? You know better than anyone that money can bury any story. Though if you do a deep dive on the internet, you can find it."

He shakes his head like he can't believe it. "So then what?"

"My dad was one of six children. Four of them picked the side of their parents, and one of them, my aunt, changed her name along with my dad. She was the outcast and saw it as a way to escape from her family but still be connected to my dad. She later got married and changed her surname again."

"This is a wild story. So you've never met your family at all?" He sits up, wholly intrigued, making me laugh out loud.

I've known the story my whole life, but from the outside looking in, it is pretty unbelievable.

"Nope, not beside my aunt. Though…" I think back to one memory I've never forgotten. "Maybe we ran into my grandfather and uncles once when I was younger. I can't remember the exact details, but I do remember thinking the one guy looked just like my dad. He shuffled us out of there so quickly, I never thought to ask him about it."

"So your dad gave it all up for your mom," he says more to himself. "What a great story to remember him by."

I can feel the tears again, so I change the subject. "So, how about your parents? I know you're not close, but are they in love?"

In a dark, sardonic way, he sniggers. "Definity not."

Oh. "That's sad."

"It's more surprising, only because my dad grew up in a house similar to you. My grandparents loved each other unconditionally."

Grinning, I say, "Well, that's a better story."

"My grandfather was quite the romantic, too. It's where my company name came from—Abbott. It was founded in the twenties by my great-great-grandfather. When my grandfather took over, he renamed it to my grandmother's maiden name."

"That's sweet and very progressive of him."

"It was." He leans over, kisses my lips, and confirms, "So, you'll stay tonight?"

Propping myself up on my elbows, I glance at the clock. "Yes. Mom's probably already sleeping, but I should still call her."

"There are a few things I need to do for work if you don't mind. Since it's way past dinner time, we can order food and eat in my office while I finish."

"It's eleven o'clock on a Sunday," I mumble.

He smirks, "Yes. But some insatiable younger woman kept me on my toes all day, and I didn't finish what needed to be done for an important meeting tomorrow."

Harrison helps me out of bed, and I don't miss how he glances down at my scars. I can tell immediately that he knows what happened.

The look in his eyes changes from wonder to sorrow, and I can't deal with it.

He mentioned the other day he looked me up, and I know from experience that you don't even have to type my whole name out in the search bar for all the articles to start populating.

It's why I hate bringing up my accident.

"Not on the table for discussion," I say with meaning. His face drops, but I know he's dying to know more. "Not tonight, Harrison. It will ruin the rest of the evening."

He pauses and nods. "Okay, beautiful. Whatever you want."

10

Juliette

"Juliette." Harrison's strong, warm hand strokes my bare back, "Baby, it's time to wake up," he whispers against my skin, peppering me with soft, minty kisses.

Snuggling closer into the pillow, basking in the scent of Harrison, I ignore him, needing just a little more sleep.

He's a machine.

It's the only possible explanation as to how he's already up, showered—I turn my head, peaking through one cracked eye—dressed and ready to go by the looks of it.

"It's too early, Harrison," I mumble into the pillow. "I'm too tired to move. What time is it?"

"Six thirty." He lifts the blankets off me and slaps my naked behind. "I've been up for an hour. I already worked out and read the newspaper."

"Good for you."

He chuckles. "Are you cranky?"

"Yes. Why are we waking up so early? You said you didn't have to be in until nine."

"I know." He picks me up from my comfortable position. I'm entirely naked…not that I have an ounce of energy to care, and like it's the most natural thing in the world, I wrap my legs around his waist, secure my arms tightly around his neck, and bury my head deep into the crook of his neck.

God, he smells good.

"Did you just smell me?"

"Yes," I tell him truthfully, and he chuckles. "So tell me again why we're up?"

He turns and kisses the tip of my nose. "I wanted time with you before we left and didn't want to rush. I thought we could have breakfast together."

Oh.

I smile to myself as he sits me on the counter and takes out a spare toothbrush.

"You know…" I laugh, waking me up a bit. "You're so concerned about our age difference, yet you're being very dad-like right now."

He shrugs. "I like taking care of you. Open." He holds out a toothbrush.

"Give that to me. I can brush my own teeth, Harrison."

He stands there, back straight, all demanding, giving me a challenging look. "Open."

"Fine." He puts the toothbrush in my mouth and starts brushing, and I can't help but laugh. "Stop, you'll choke." He chuckles at the ridiculousness of it all.

"You're lucky I'm too tired to fight you this morning," I mumble around the toothbrush.

"I would have won anyway," he states confidently. "Spit." I comply as he hands me a towel.

I wipe the excess off my face. "Thanks."

"Well, I can say confidently this is another first for me. Brushing a woman's teeth." He shakes his head like he can't believe it. "Let's go."

He lifts me off the counter and takes my hand. "Harrison, I'm not eating naked."

He stares at me long and hard like he wants to fight me on it, but that's where I draw the line. He must be on drugs if he thinks I'd do that…especially with him fully clothed.

"Fine, here." He hands me a robe from behind the door. "Your clothes are still drying."

He guides me down the hall, and I stop short at the one door that looks entirely out of place in his home.

"Is this Claud's room?" I ask, even though I already know the answer from the pink paint and ballerina pictures pinned on the door. "Can I see it?" His body tenses, and I realize I'm overstepping. I'm not even sure why I asked. "Come on, let's go eat," I tell him and try to pull him down the hall, covering up my intrusion attempt.

He shakes his head, and I see the wheels turning—to open or not to.

"Harrison, it's okay. She's off-limits, and I overstepped." I tug on his hand. "Come."

He shakes his head again, then opens the door. "You're right, she is off-limits. It's why I've never brought someone back here. But you're different…" His voice fades off. "And you know Claudina already."

Different? Different how?

Every single inch of me wants to overthink this…but I'm trying to act fucking cool.

Instead, I focus on the masterpiece in front of me.

"Oh my god," I whisper in awe as I step inside. "So this is what it's like to be a rich kid who loves ballet?" The second I say it, I turn to tell him I'm joking.

I'm already walking on thin ice and keep opening my dumb, rude mouth.

He raises his hand to stop me. "It's fine, Jules. I know you mean nothing by it."

Yes, this room is completely over the top, one hundred and fifty percent, but it still makes me extremely happy.

I've always pictured the little girls of these penthouses having modern, boring rooms, but that's not the case here.

I feel like I was shot back in time to my childhood. Only this is on a much grander scale—all pinks and purples, tutus and leotards, everything a five-year-old would love.

I spin around as if I'm a child again and stop to see Harrison intently staring at me.

"Sorry." I chuckle, for fuck's sake, Jules, get it together today. He's going to think I'm insane. "Harrison, it's amazing in here. She must love it. This is every child's dream room." I walk over to the corner of the room. There's even a wooden doll house that's as tall as me, which too is, of course, pink.

My head is on a swivel, taking in every part of this until I stop dead in my tracks.

What the…

Harrison must sense something's off and is at my side within a second. "What's wrong?"

I suck in a breath and clench my teeth together so hard I think they might crack. It's the only thing I can do to keep the tears back.

From my peripheral vision, I can see the panic on Harrison's face, but I don't have the words…not yet.

"Juliette…please."

"That's me," I whisper, pointing to the collage of pictures tacked on the board. "It's fine. I'm fine." I shake myself out of the daze. "It hit me hard because it's the first time I've seen pictures from that night." He shifts his gaze, and his eyes stay anchored on the pictures until I explain. "The photographer took these in motion. I know it's hard to make out my face but trust me, it's me. No one does fouettés like that." *Or did fouettés.* "They were my specialty."

"When was this taken?" he asks in a lowered voice.

"Six, no…wow, over seven months ago." I pause, still not ready to talk about it, but I want to give him something. "It was the night of my accident," I admit. "It was the opening night of the performance, and the last day I ever danced professionally."

He steps behind me and takes me in his arms. I appreciate him not prying for more information. I'm not ready to relive that story yet.

"Do you want me to tell her to take it down?"

"That's thoughtful, though I doubt I'll be in this room often, so no.

Thank you." I turn and kiss his chest, and we stand like this for a while, with me in his arms.

"You know…I consider myself a good dance dad, but I have no idea what a fouetté is."

Laughter breaks from my chest, I can't contain it.

Happy he broke the silence and awkwardness, but also, the way he seems so genuinely upset is heartwarming.

"Don't worry, the move is way too advanced for Claudina. You shouldn't know what it is," I tell him as he maneuvers us from the room. "Actually, I've been meaning to speak to Willa about something, so I might as well tell you."

He shuts the bedroom door, and we continue down the stairs toward the kitchen. "About dance?"

"Yeah. I know Claud is determined and wants to be the best she can be, but—" I stop when I see his face morphing into protection mode. "Don't get defensive. I'm trying to help."

He bites his bottom lip, grinning. "Sorry, you're right. Go on."

"Thank you." It's killing me inside, not to mention that he said I'm right, but I won't push it this morning. "She's only five, correct?" He nods, confirming. "Well, I think she's super advanced for her age. I know it's silly, but when you see a child with a raw talent at five, you watch them closely."

"She dances for you?" His face lights up.

"All the time, I love it. I'm telling you this because I've seen her obsessing over pirouettes…the wrong way. She mentioned YouTube."

He nods, pouring himself a coffee and me some green tea. "Yes, she started self-teaching."

"Try and steer her away from that. She'll start learning them next year, and if her technique is wrong, she'll fall behind because they'll have to correct her form first."

He sips his coffee, eyeing me over his cup. "Thank you, I appreciate it."

"I can help her," I say, surprised at myself, yet I also one hundred percent mean it. I haven't wanted anything to do with dance since the accident.

"Thanks—" His phone beeps, and he curses. "I have to make a call in my office. It can't wait, and it might take a while." He pauses and stares at me. "I can have Robert take you home now, but...if you want...you can come hang out with me." He shrugs like he's suddenly shy.

I think it's hard for Harrison to be vulnerable, and I can see it on his face that he wants me to stay.

I want to stay, too.

"Sure, what's another meal in your office browsing your boring books." I laugh loudly when he tickles my side.

"Mr. Abdullah, the funds we manage on your behalf—" Harrison takes a deep breath, looking up at the ceiling in frustration. I've come to the conclusion he hates being interrupted on his calls. He starts pacing with annoyance. "Yes. The returns have been exceptional over the last five years, and we see additional investment opportunities over a broad array of asset classes."

I zone out for the rest of what he says, too lost in how sexy he looks behind his desk.

Somehow, even his deep, velvety voice has my lower half tingling from the familiar, dominating tone he's using.

God, I could stare at him all day.

His head snaps up, looking at me with narrowed, suspecting eyes.

Holy shit, did I say that out loud?

I bite my lip hard, afraid a moan might slip through, as I watch Harrison's blue eyes rake over every inch of my body, lingering at my slightly parted legs. My thighs snap shut and squeeze tightly as wetness starts to pool between my legs.

His nostrils flare, and he reaches down to adjust himself. That move alone has me wanting to do something I've never done before.

"Agreed. When will you be in America next?" Harrison asks his client, never taking his eyes off me.

This man makes me crazy with lust, and if you had told me what I was about to do next, even one month ago, I would have laughed in your face.

As seductively as possible, I stand and lower my robe, letting it slowly slide down my arms to expose my naked body. When I have his full attention, I stride over to where he stands.

He covers the phone. "What are you doing?" he hisses.

Ignoring him, I advance around his desk to stand before him.

Without hesitation, he reaches out and palms my breast with his one hand, positioning it up so he has easy access to lean down and take my nipple into his mouth, sucking with a deep pressure.

My mouth hangs open as my knees buckle, and before I have a second to do what I came here to do, he pushes me back onto his desk.

He stands between my legs, which dangle off the edge and pushes them open wide. Without even a warm-up, Harrison drives three of his thick fingers into my sex and begins to pump me so hard that the sound of my wetness echoes through the room.

Harrison, I mouth.

He glances down and watches as he takes his fingers all the way out, then slides them in again, in and out, over and over. "Yes, agreed. The sooner, the better." He answers his client without missing a beat.

This. Was. Not. The. Plan.

My back arches off the desk in pleasure as his pistol pace picks up. I'm about to orgasm embarrassingly fast. *Again.*

He puts the phone between his ear and shoulder, all without ever removing his fingers, drops to his knees, throws my legs over his shoulders, and sucks my clit *hard*.

My body convulses, and my sex clenches as he begins to really eat me, lapping me up like I'm his favorite meal.

Trying my very best not to make any loud noises, I look up and scrunch my face, squeezing my eyes tight as my body starts rocking against his face while my orgasm rips through me, contracting, squeezing his fingers tight.

His eyes snap to me, and his tongue flattens to lick me from bottom to top one last time.

Fuck me.

I lay still for a second more to catch my breath, all while he answers more of the client's questions. Then I push off the desk and drop to my knees. He might have taken over momentarily, but I'm going to finish what I came over here to do.

When recognition hits, he helps me, unbuckling his belt when I can't do it quickly enough. I unzip his pants, pulling them down for access.

"Yes, I can make Bermuda work. We're flexible and here to please you."

I can't hold back my giggle, and then he palms his face when he realizes what he just said.

"Shut up and suck my dick," he whispers, causing me to laugh out loud again. "Stop it." He grins, trying to hold back his own laughter.

He grabs the back of my head, then pushes his brief-covered groin in my face. "Suck." His voice darker now than before.

The swollen tip of his cock, that's leaking pre-come sticks out the top of his briefs, and it's a quick reminder of how big this man is.

I pull his briefs down and suck in a breath, swallowing the lump in my throat.

You can do this, Juliette.

He reaches down and begins to stroke himself right in front of my face. I cast my eyes up, knowing the innocent look I'm giving him is turning him on more than ever.

The head of his cock hits my mouth a few times until he presses into my parted lips, demanding me to open wide.

Salty liquid hits my lips, and I push his hand away, suddenly desperate to show him I can please him as much as he does me.

I've never wanted anyone in my mouth more than Harrison, so like him, I'm going in for the kill. Opening wide, I hold him at the base, take him in as deep as I can go, and gag.

"Yes, I'm still here." He coughs, covering the crack in his voice. "Okay, yes. Send us the dates, and we'll meet you there," he spits out and slams the phone down onto his desk.

"Holy Mother of God, Juliette," he roars loudly in the room, only egging me on.

My eyes close, and I concentrate on doing this right and remind myself this is for him, and I can't come right now, even if pleasing him on my knees is the biggest turn-on in history.

I drag my lips up, sucking, with my tongue flattening on the underside, then lick around the head and cup his balls before taking him all the way in my mouth again.

He hisses sharply, then grabs my hair, pulling it away from my face in a punishing grip. "Such a good girl, look at you taking my cock down." I choke when his hips press forward, hitting the back of my throat. "Fuck yeah, baby, take it all."

My hand drops from his dick, and I steady myself on his thick quads as his pace picks up.

I'm sucking hard, and on instinct, he begins to ride my face. Not even seconds later, I can feel the swell of his cock. "Oh, Julessss," he cries.

"Come in my mouth," I surprise myself by saying around him. It's like those words put him over the edge, and he comes in a rush right down my throat. "Fuck, fuck, fuck."

Without any hesitation, I drink him all down, then look up and lock eyes with him as I lick up every drop dripping from my lips.

His chest is heavy as he picks me up off the ground and kisses me hard against the mouth. We stay like this until I feel his erection grow again against my stomach.

"Get on the couch, on your back. I want to look you in the eyes when I fuck you this time."

Harrison's getting re-dressed, and I burst out laughing. "Oh jeez." I chuckle.

"What?" He looks around, then down at himself, and unties and rips off his tie. "This is all your fault."

I can't control myself. I almost fall off the couch, dying of laughter. "Imagine I didn't notice, and you went to work with come all over your tie."

"Fuck's sake, don't say that." He pretends to shiver, then turns to me, holding up two ties. I point to the pinkish-colored one.

"Let's go, you sex maniac."

We're about to pull up to my building when he finally gets off the phone.

"I'm sorry, babe. Monday mornings are crazy."

I squeeze his hand, the one that hasn't let go of mine from practically the second we woke up, to reassure him it's okay.

"It was quick, Harrison. It's fine." I could have walked home. He lives close by, but he firmly objected.

Not that I'm complaining about spending more time with him, even if he's working—morning rush hour and getting stuck behind a garbage truck turned a five-minute commute into fifteen.

"What will you do for the rest of the day?" he asks.

There's no way I can tell him my actual plans…that would mean I have to admit I used sexual activities and casual banter to hide the fact that after seeing Claud's room, I'm not all right and feel like I'm dying inside.

So, I go with what I typically do.

"Usually, I have physical therapy for my leg on Mondays. But it's canceled today. Other than that, I normally walk in the park, be lazy, and catch up on the sleep and television I've missed throughout the week. And at four, I have the kid's baking class I teach."

His eyes travel down to my legs. "I didn't—"

"Harrison, I told you. If it hurts, I'll tell you. I'm fine."

"Okay." He nods, mollified for now. However, I can see his lingering concern. "I'm jealous of your relaxing Mondays. Today is going to be insane. I already have a headache, and I'm not even in the office yet."

His phone chimes with a text, interrupting us.

"Work?" I ask sarcastically.

"No." He pauses. "It's Sebastian, which reminds me, I wanted to mention something quickly."

"Okay. Go ahead," I say as we pull up to my apartment building.

"Give us a moment, please, Robert."

"Of course, sir." Robert, his driver, gets out and waits for us on the sidewalk.

"Come here," I scootch over, though he has other plans, and picks me up, placing me on his lap. "I don't like you being so far away." He sweeps my hair off my neck and kisses my heart-shaped beauty mark.

"Harrison," I warn. "Don't get distracted."

"Don't ever stop me from kissing you." He squeezes the inside of my thigh, kisses me again to show me who's boss, then leans back to look me in the eyes. "Leo and Nate know about you, and that we're…"

"Know that we're having sex?" I raise my eyebrows playfully and he chuckles.

"Yes, that. Which is fine, but if we're ever out together or you see me and Sebastian is around, it's best that we keep this between us."

Confused, I ask, "Why?"

"This has nothing to do with you, and I don't want you to think that. It has all to do with Seb. He's very protective over Claudina, maybe even more so than me, and the people entering her life. Normally, he doesn't care about what I do on the side, but if he finds out you're someone who is in Claud's life, even in a small role, he will not make it easy on me and honestly, the other brothers for knowing."

I push back a piece of rogue hair that's fallen over his eye. "That seems a bit intrusive, no?"

He smiles sadly. "He has a right in a way, and there's a lot more to the story I'm not going to get into right now. But sometimes, it's easier to appease him than push him. He's been traveling more than ever lately, so I rarely see him and can't imagine it being a problem. He's only in New York for Claud."

"Okay," I tell him easily. I would never want to get in the middle of brotherly drama.

"And I'm sure I don't need to say that Claud can't—"

An annoyed feeling takes over. "Don't even say it and insult my intelligence, Harrison. I think we have a bigger issue if you need to tell me not to say anything to your five-year-old daughter." I spit.

"All right, all right. Stop being so defensive, and let's end today on a happy note."

Shooting him a look, I tell him truthfully, "You're the only one I'm ever like this with."

Displeasure crosses his face. "What? What are you talking about?"

I think for a moment, "I'm not sure it's a bad thing. I enjoy the back-and-forth between us." His knitted brows tell me he's not sure he should believe me. "I'm being serious, Harrison. You're challenging and demanding, something I'm not used to. But it's who you are, and…I like you," I tell him with a half shrug.

He cups my cheek in a surprisingly tender way. "I'm not too much for you?"

"No, because what also comes along with your prickly side makes me laugh like I've never laughed before, even if you're not trying to be funny. In the last twenty-four hours, I've gotten more of an ab workout than I have in ages." I shoot him a subtle wink, and he lifts my hand to kiss each knuckle.

Leaning in, he turns his head to skim his lips along the sweep of my cheek until he meshes our lips together.

"I don't want to leave you right now," he mumbles against me, then audibly swallows before saying, "It's a new feeling for me, Juliette."

Leaning back, I look him in the eyes and smile. "I had the best night."

Overcast skies have the outside suddenly looking dark and dreary, and I can tell it's about to pour again soon. "I'm not in the mood to get soaked. I should go."

"What if it's a different type of soaked?" he asks dryly, and I laugh, swatting his chest.

"See…laughing." I smile again in an overly exaggerated way.

"You don't have to walk me," I tell him when he attempts to get out of the car. "There's a good chance my mom is looking out the window since a brand-new Bentley is idling outside."

"This car is typical for a businessman on the Upper East Side, Juliette."

"You're right, but it's not when your mother is nosey and is going to wonder who's dropping her daughter off from her wild night out." As I say it, I duck to look out the window and check—luckily, I don't see any lingering shadows.

Harrison taps the window, signaling to Robert he can open the door, then takes my face and kisses me one last time. "I'll speak to you soon."

Soon.

I know we made no promises, but suddenly, I hate our arrangement, and the expression on my face must tell him everything I'm thinking.

When I'm about to put the key in my door, he lowers his window and calls out my name.

"Not soon—tonight, beautiful." Then his car drives off and *soon* goes from being my least to most favorite word.

However, my happiness quickly dies the second I step over the threshold into my apartment.

The world around me seems to fade, and it's as if my body knows home is a safe place to let down my guard and unleash the emotions I've been holding in for the last two hours.

When my mom sees my distraught face, her forehead creases with worry, and she's up, off the couch, taking me in her arms, engulfing me with the comforting scent of my father.

"Come, my love," she whispers, guiding me to the couch, keeping her arms wrapped tightly around me.

Laying in my mother's comforting embrace has my silent tears quickly turning into sobs. Long overdue tears for a life I no longer live, one I've never fully grieved, pour out onto my mom's shoulder while flashes of me dancing on stage come back in full force.

I miss it terribly.

I miss gliding through the air, freeing my body of gravity.

The accomplishments and ability to push myself to be greater.

But most importantly, I miss being me.

My heart shudders with sadness, and I know I need to move on, but when? When will this feeling of sadness and failure go away?

"Juliette, please, are you okay?"

I take a deep, shaky breath, and when I'm calm enough to get words out, I explain what happened with as little detail as possible. It poses a bit of an issue, but Mom never pries. She holds me, rocking me back and forth when more tears come.

She never tells me I'm overreacting or all will be okay; this time, she knows I'm hurting, and reassuring words won't do anything to help.

After many more tears and thoughtful words from Mom, I regroup my thoughts and think long and hard about my future, but like always, I come up blank.

Maybe I'm not ready to move on, but what I do know is this morning, looking at those pictures of me was like ripping off a Band-Aid.

It had to be done to heal.

I guess the fancy new haircut didn't relieve me of all my problems after all.

11

Juliette

MY EYES ARE CLOSED as I let the warm shower water trickle over my body in a relaxing, therapeutic way. My favorite sandalwood candle that reminds me of Harrison's cologne is lit, with eucalyptus hanging from the shower head.

I needed this.

After watching a movie with Mom and an afternoon nap, I decided, for now, that I need to be happy with what I *do* have in life rather than dwell on what I'm missing.

I do this sometimes...let myself feel the loss of my situation and then remind myself how lucky I am to be alive.

"You only live one life, Juliette. Live it up, laugh it up...either way, don't fuck it up," my dad would say, and my mom would yell at him for cursing.

He'd smile and shoot me a playful wink.

My mom is alive and, for the most part, well.

My best friend is happy for the first time with a man and is working herself to the bone to become a kick-ass girl boss one day.

The bakery is thriving. We might be moving locations, but our pastries and bread are well-liked and lucrative enough to live a decent life.

"Juliette? Are you in there?"

My mom interrupts my thoughts, and I throw my head back on the cold tile wall and groan. "Yes, Mom. I'm in the shower."

"Are you feeling better?" she calls over the running water.

Is she serious right now? "Yes. I'll be out in a minute," I call back.

"Well, I'm going to go to the community garden. Did you want to join me?"

"Mom, please give me a moment. I'll be out in just a second."

She closes the door, and I let out a loud sigh. It's been a year since I moved home and about three hundred and sixty-five days of interrupted alone time—in the shower, my room, even masturbating.

Yes…masturbating.

Can you even imagine?

Luckily, that time, my hand was under the blankets, and she had no idea what was going on.

Don't get me wrong, I love my mom to pieces, and on mornings like today, when I needed her to console me, I've never felt more grateful. But, simple day-to-day boundaries continue to be broken, and I think it's time we have our own space.

When we find the new place for the bakery, I'm hoping the realtor can find me an apartment nearby. That, however, will stay a secret until the time comes. She won't mean to, but she'll guilt trip me, and I'll end up staying another year.

I step out of the bathroom, and my heart leaps out of my chest. "Hi." My mom is standing right next to the door.

"For god's sake, Mom. Give me a second to breathe."

"Sorry." She smiles. "Did you want to come with me? Ted Edelman said the tomatoes are all coming in."

"Oh." I frown. "I wanted to go and check it out, but I should get ready for class and make sure the cakes the kids made last week are thawed and set up on their stations. We're practicing piping skills today."

"We can go after the morning rush tomorrow," she says, kissing me goodbye, then promises to stop by class on her way home.

The door to the bakery opens, and I turn to see Claud skipping through the entrance...alone.

"Sugar plum. What are you doing here, and who's with you?" I ask, confused.

She giggles at her nickname I gave her during the winter, when she danced in *The Nutcracker*, and runs toward me.

"Juliette." She hugs me tight.

"I thought you were in the Hamptons. What are you doing here?"

She bounces in my arms. "I'm back just for class."

My eyes widen in shock. "You came all the way back to the city for baking classes?"

"Well." She looks down and lowers her voice. "I didn't mean to cry. I know crying is for babies, but I saw it said Monday on the calendar, I got upset that I was missing class."

I frown. "Who told you crying was for babies?"

If Harrison told her that, he'll be getting a swift kick up his behind.

"Liam," she whispers.

My anger flares. I hate Liam's mom, and my irrational side now hates Liam too, but I remind myself he's just a kid.

When he comes to class today, I'll make sure to have a word with her.

"Well, don't listen to Liam. I cry all the time," I tell her truthfully. I cried for hours just this morning.

Her brown eyes widen with acknowledgment. "You do?"

"Of course, we all do. Did Liam say anything else to you?"

She thinks for a second. "I don't think so."

Thank god. I'm not in the mood to start shit with a parent today.

I stand up and take her hand to walk her toward the back of the class. "So you got upset, then what happened?"

She gives a half shrug. "Uncle Sebby said he doesn't like seeing me sad, so he brought me to class. He's going to drive us back later."

Oh, Claudina Davenport has her uncle wrapped around her little finger.

"Okay, well, don't listen to Liam anymore. Grab your apron, then take a seat, and we'll wait for the rest of the kids to get here."

"Okay…Juliette?"

"Yes, sweetheart?"

"I wanted to see you today too." she declares, smiling and walks off.

This could be a teachable moment—I could easily cry happy tears from her words.

Later, I have to remember to tell Harrison what an excellent job he's doing with her. She is always kind and thoughtful, helping other kids in class.

Turning around, I gasp out loud startled by the beautiful man in the perfectly tailored suit and tie I picked out this morning standing in front of me.

"Oh, hi." I smile, trying to act cool. I wasn't expecting to see Harrison again today.

I thought I'd meet this Uncle Sebby, who I assume is Sebastian, the one who's not supposed to know I exist.

"Bonjour, ma belle Jules," he says through a smirk. "How's my girl's day going?"

My heart and insides somersault at his words, but I quickly remember that I'm in fact, not his girl. "I'm Fine."

His brows furrow. "What's that look for?"

Shrugging, I say, "No reason."

"Juliette. I don't have time for games. I came to see you, and now you're giving me the fucking shrug off."

I know I am.

"Watch your mouth here," I chastise.

"Explain what the attitude's about." He crosses his arms.

I step closer and lower my voice. "In the bedroom, I can be yours, but that's the only place I'm your girl."

"You're not my girl?" he challenges with a deathly tone. "So it'll be okay if I ask Melody's mom out for dinner tonight?"

What the hell.

He wouldn't.

I take a deep breath through my nose, trying to calm my nerves. "Don't be a dick, Harrison."

"Well, don't say dumb fucking shit, Juliette," he snaps.

"Juliette, my love," Mom calls as she walks out from the back, and I freeze, realizing Harrison is about to meet my mom.

Holy crap.

He knows exactly what's going on through my head right now, so he plasters the widest, fakest smile on his face as she walks over.

"Oh, hello." She stumbles, her eyes widening when she takes in all six-foot-four of Harrison.

Way to be cool, Mom.

"Inès!" Claud jumps out of her seat to come to say hi.

"Oh, there's my favorite girl." She picks up Claud and puts her on her hip like a baby.

I think my mom likes her better than me at times.

"Mom," I whisper. "Other kids are here now. You can't call her your favorite."

"Well, I'm not a woman who lies, and this class is your thing, not mine. So why should I care?"

Harrison chuckles. Of course, he would be amused at something like that.

"Inès Caldwell." My mom sticks out her hand, introducing herself.

He picks it up and kisses the back, and I want to roll my eyes all the way out of my head.

"Harrison Davenport." He points to Claud. "I'm Claudina's dad." Then he turns to me, those blue eyes sparkling. "And a good friend of your daughter." He raises his eyebrows, and Mom doesn't miss it.

Oh…he's dead.

She looks between us a few times, and I can tell by the look on her face she's putting two and two together.

"Anyway," I interrupt her mental assessment. "Claud, it's time to take a seat." I take her from Mom, put her back on the floor, and then turn around. "Was there something you needed?"

She pulls out her calendar. "Alice and Daphne have a family wedding this weekend, so I will need you to work both Friday and Saturday. I know you were off, however, we'll need coverage."

"And they only just told you?"

She shakes her head. "They said they told me, but I don't have it anywhere on the calendar."

She flips the calendar page to the following week, and my stomach drops.

It's another six days straight working, plus Monday's class I teach the kids.

Mom's oblivious to everything and continues to tell me the days I need to work and cover for the others.

"Okay, Mom," I tell her and kiss her cheek before she says goodbye to Harrison, fawning all over him and then walking off.

Harrison goes to say something when the alarm goes off, and the kids cheer, ready for class to begin.

———

Harrison stands up and follows me around the class. "What are you doing?" I ask, narrowing my eyes.

He's like a little puppy at my heels.

"Which one is Liam's mom?"

So, he did hear our conversation earlier. I wasn't sure. I give him my most serious face. "Do not say anything. I will."

"Juliette," he warns. "She is my daughter, and I will handle it how I see fit."

I put my hands on my hips, annoyed at his tone.

I don't know why I'm getting pissed off at everything he says today.

"Yes, but it happened in my class, so trust that I will handle it. If it doesn't get resolved, then you can say something," I tell him, and to rub salt in his wound because he was giving me attitude, I add, "Plus, she didn't even tell you. She told me."

"If I promise not to say anything yet, will you point her out so I can quietly stare daggers at her?"

I shake my head, chuckling. "You're crazy, you know that? She's not here yet. Their nanny dropped Liam off, and his mom will pick him up later." I turn toward the kids. "Everyone, Alice is in charge. I need to get more sprinkles in the back."

Cheers for more decorations rock the room while Harrison huffs his disappointment about Liam's mom.

Of course, he follows me in the back, then pushes me against the wall, trapping me in with his arms.

"What are you doing?" I cry.

"Kissing you. What does it look like?" He takes my face in his large hands and then smashes his lips against mine.

God, he feels incredible.

I pull back, mortified my mom might see. "My mom has cameras back here, Harrison."

He shrugs like he doesn't have a care in the world. "She seemed to like me. She won't mind."

"Also, we're supposed to be incognito. We shouldn't be kissing here."

"No one is coming back here," he says, irritated. I know he's angry that I'm denying him. "And what the hell was that all about earlier? You covering those girls' shifts."

I roll my eyes. "Don't start. You sound like Becks."

"Don't start that attitude again, Juliette. I see you limping. Call your mom and tell her no." He begins kissing up my neck, then my lips. "And how will I ever see you if you're working every day starting at four in the morning? I'll never get my fill of you."

"Harrison. Don't tell me what to do, and we haven't even set a date to see one another again." I try pushing off again.

"Stop pushing me away, I'll take *my girl* when and where I want." He kisses me again, and I melt into his words.

Pathetic comes to my mind.

Who am I kidding? I couldn't care less because, once again, I hear his demanding tone, and my body submits, getting lost in an abyss of Harrison Davenport.

"Daddy? Juliette?" Claud's meek voice comes from the other side of the door.

I move faster than the speed of light and jump back, irrationally worrying she can see through a wood door.

I throw a box of sprinkles and glitter dust at Harrison, and without missing a beat, he swings the door open. "Got the goods, angel."

"Yessss!" She goes on her tippy-toes to look. "Can I use the pink shimmer first?"

"We have to share," I remind her. All the girls in the class go nuts for these metallic shimmers.

"I will," she singsongs then skips off.

I grab the other box of supplies and follow Claud. "*I'll take my girl when and where I want,*" I mock, teasing Harrison as I walk by.

"I'd slap that ass right now if I could," he mumbles under his breath.

"Oh, here's Liam's mom now," I say as her usual immaculate self walks through the door.

Harrison's body freezes. "I'll handle her. Don't worry about it."

"Do not say anything yet."

He'll be scaring off the bakery clients.

I drop the box off for Alice to distribute evenly among the tables, and I glance over at all the creations my little bakers are making.

Some are meticulous, like Claud, and some like to Pollack it up. That wouldn't fly in traditional French baking classes, but I encourage the kids to use their imagination.

When I see Harrison approach Liam's mom, Rachel, I stalk over there to diffuse Harrison's wrath.

"Harrison, I haven't seen you in weeks. Where have you been, hon?" she whispers so no one can hear.

Harrison ignores her, but they're obviously familiar. "Rach, is Liam your son?"

"Yes? Why, what has he done now?" She rolls her eyes like she couldn't be bothered.

Now I feel bad for Liam.

"What has he done?" Harrison's voice lowers. "He told my daughter crying was for babies, making her feel as if her emotions are less than valid and that she would be made fun of if she expressed herself in that manner again. And I don't appreciate—"

She cuts him off and tosses her hair back flirtatiously. "Oh Harry, they're just kids."

"Harry?" I accidentally say out loud when I wanted to say it in my head, but my big mouth opened up instead.

Harrison whips around, and guilt is written all over his face.

"Jules, this is Rachel, Liam's mom," he spits out fast, stumbling over his words.

"I'm aware, Harrison, her son is in my class." I turn toward Rachel. "Nice to see you. Now, can the two of you please speak outside? I don't need unnecessary tension in my class." I open the door and gesture for them to leave.

Rachel's mouth opens and closes like a guppy, whereas Harrison's face is a sheet of shock.

"Jules—"

"Outside, Harrison," I snap, then close the door behind them.

Don't let it hit you in the ass on the way out.

I roll my shoulders and walk back toward the kids since they're the ones who matter most right now.

Not freaking *Harry and Rach.*

"My little bakers," I call out. "Who wants to vote for what we bake next week?"

Me, me, me, me, me, rings out, and I smile as I roll out our board to write down next week's ideas.

Harrison

Fuck.

I watch my beautiful Juliette through the window. She rolls her shoulders and stands a little taller before returning to the kids.

She's smart, my girl.

She caught onto Rachel within seconds, and I can feel the jealousy radiating off her from here.

Between the two of us and our jealousy, we have some serious issues for two people who aren't in a long-term relationship.

"Ugh!" Rach says, speaking up.

"Listen—"

"Please don't tell me you're fucking the baker. Is this why you haven't called me back? And what is she, twelve?" Rachel scoffs loudly, staring at me while I watch Jules.

I was going to try to reason with her, but my hackles went up the second she uttered those words.

"Keep your goddamn voice down, people know who I am in this neighborhood, and they're going to think I'm a fucking pedophile. She's twenty-fucking-four."

She shrugs cockily. "If it walks like a duck and talks like a duck."

"Still the same old Rachel, a fucking bitch."

Rachel is for a good time only and has been a super bitch since the day I met her. We sat next to each other at a dinner party, bonded over being single parents, and that's about it—once she's annoyed, she doesn't have one nice bone in her body.

"Same old one you love to fuck. Does miss little sweet thing know how much you love fucking my ass? I can already tell she's too sweet for that." She laughs loudly. "You probably have sex in silence, staring into each other's eyes. Although…"

"Although what?" I snap, annoyed at myself for engaging.

"She's probably flexible because of her failed dancing career. I bet you could do a lot with that."

How the fuck does she knows about that?

I take a deep breath through my nose before I lose my shit. "She didn't fail. She was hit by a fucking car, you heartless witch."

I also want to tell her that Juliette is the hottest fuck I've ever had and the most genuine person I've ever met. She should try putting the two together, but that would mean I give away details about Jules, which won't happen.

Jules is all mine. No one has the right to know anything about us.

My phone rings, and Seb's name illuminates the screen. I've never been so happy for someone to interrupt me because I could tell you right now if Rachel were a guy, she'd be out cold on the ground.

"Get out of my face, Rachel, and tell your son to keep his mouth shut. Otherwise, I'm going to the school and making a formal complaint."

She screams something unintelligible as I walk away to answer. "What's up?"

"I grabbed what I needed from my office, and I'm on my way uptown now. Is Claudina almost done with her class?"

"I could have brought her to you. I have to return to the office for a late meeting," I tell him.

"I'm going to wait until traffic dies down. We'll have dinner at Mom's, and then we'll leave. She'll sleep in the car."

I look at my watch, and it's almost five…he's right. If he leaves now, it will take him over three hours instead of two. "Class is over in ten minutes. Meet us in front, and I'll have her jump in your car."

"Okay. By the way, have you spoken to Nate today?"

My steps falter at his tone. "No? What's wrong?"

Seb sighs. "Leo and Nate were working from home this morning. Nate had to run back to his place to copy some documents. Leo didn't realize how much time had passed, and his phone was on speaker while talking with Mason."

Fucking shit.

"Let me guess, it's about Maddie Grace?"

"Of course. While Mason was home this weekend, he saw her go on a few dates with the same guy, and Nate lost it. I don't understand what the hell the problem is. He loves her. Why is he sitting back and waiting around like a jerk-off?"

"I don't know. I know he was waiting for her to finish school, but after that, I have no fucking clue." I sigh loudly. "I'm going to give him a call before her class lets out. I'll see you in a few."

I hang up and then call Nate. "What?" he snaps.

"What's going on? Seb just called."

I hear him pacing back and forth. "She's dating someone. I don't know what the fuck to do." His voice catches, and I feel bad for my little brother.

He wanted to let his sheltered southern country girl thrive on her own before going back to her, now it might be too late.

"Why have you waited so long to get her back?" I never understood.

"I went and saw her." He lowers his voice. "A little over a year ago, she made it very clear to me that I hurt her too deeply. I thought I could be selfless and give her up so she'd be happy without me."

What? "What kind of bullshit is that?" I shout.

"I don't know! I have to go." He hangs up, and I'm left standing there shocked.

When did he see her?

And then it hits me...the conversation right before with Seb was the most cordial we've had in a while. He sounded like himself again, and I'm hoping it's because this therapist is finally working.

I catch a glimpse of the kids packing up from across the street, so I have no time to think about either of my brothers right now.

"Let me see, angel." I peek over Claud's shoulder.

"Daddy! You scared me. You can't creep up on people like that." She laughs and then goes on to tell me about every piping tool she used to decorate the cake and how she learned to transfer the different frostings to the piping bags. "Can we bake something when I come home from the Hamptons next week? I could teach you a lot, you know." Her eyes suddenly sparkle with excitement. "Or when you come to the Hamptons to visit, we can all bake together. Uncle Sebby loves raspberries, and you love blueberries, and last week we made berry tarts. I know how to make them, or I can ask Juliette for the recipe, and you can help me read it, or—"

"Okay, anything you want, Claud." I don't like interrupting her, but when she gets excited about something, she can go on forever, concocting a whole bunch of ideas, and we don't have time to sit here forever.

"Promise?"

"Of course, angel." I kiss her and tell her it's time to leave and to say thank you to Juliette for the class.

Jules nonchalantly glances up at me with judging eyes when Claud says goodbye, and not me, but what she doesn't know is that I'll be back the second Claud is in Seb's car.

There is no fucking way we're ending the conversation like we did.

After waving off Seb, Claud, and a happy, tail-wagging Skye, I'm back watching Juliette's every move like a lion stalking his lioness.

She is oblivious to my intrusion as she turns up the music and moves around to the sounds of Coldplay's "Something's Just Like This" with ease, cleaning up the bakery.

It also gives me time to look around Le Petit Boulanger and take in a piece of Jules. It doesn't surprise me that the place oozes femininity.

Jules might be a spitfire when I piss her off, but from what I've learned in this short amount of time is that she is soft, caring, and does things with a feminine flair.

The way her mom, Inès, spoke and conducted herself, I get the feeling Jules got it from her.

She picks up a drawing one of the kids drew, and from here, I have no freaking clue what it is, but she chuckles, folding it nicely, and stores it in her bag.

When she turns and lifts her head, she gasps loudly, throwing her hand to her chest. "Harrison! What the freaking hell?"

"You're lucky it was me and not some serial killer. I've been watching you for a good five minutes without you noticing. You need to be more aware of your surroundings." I don't know why I say it. I already know she's going to lose it on me.

She takes a deep breath through her nose and points toward the door. "Get out."

"Juliette."

"No. Better yet, *Harry*, why don't you go spend time with Rach."

I bite my lip to hide a smile. There she is—my beautiful, jealous girl.

Whereas this would turn off most guys, it's the complete opposite for me. Something deep inside me gets joy from knowing she wants me and needs to take possession over me as I do her.

Not forever.

Thinking that makes my stomach turn with disgust. Jules deserves more from me...she deserves forever. But I'm a selfish bastard who wants her, even if I can't give her forever.

I prowl toward her, and she backs up. "Don't give me that look, Harrison."

"What look, baby?"

She narrows her eyes. "The *I'm going to pounce and take what I want look.*"

"You're mistaken." I take a step closer, and when I realize she's trapped and can't move, my body rejoices at my triumph.

Once I'm close enough, she'll soften and melt into my touch.

"Harrison," her husky voice quietly slips through her lips, and I need to ignore my body's reaction for now.

The second her voice lowers to that sexy husk, my dick jumps in excitement.

Every. Single. Time.

One more step, and I'm towering over her. I don't miss the slight shiver her body releases when our arms brush.

I feel it, too, baby.

She tries to straighten and hold her stance; she has no idea what she does to me. To say it's a turn-on would be an understatement.

There are rarely any genuine connections made in my world, and people typically cower at my glare. Having money and power makes people do funny things around you.

But not my girl.

If there ever was one, she is what I would consider the perfect woman.

Strong, sweet, and spirited as hell, wrapped up in the perfect fucking bow.

Leaning close so we're eye to eye, I tell her, "First, I'll only ever take what you give me. Second…" I cup her cheek and smile on the inside when she doesn't move away. "You got the look wrong. That look was saying how fucking hot it was you seeing you jealous over me."

Her eyes flare with embarrassment, but she doesn't back down. "I'm not jealous, Harrison. I don't appreciate her blatant flirtatious attitude, and you say nothing about it."

"Sounds like jealousy to me," I goad.

She crosses her arms, aggravated. "And I don't like having restrictions."

"Now I'm lost."

"If the roles were reversed, you would have lost your mind without caring who was around. What if I did that today, and Claud overheard? Or Sebastian, who I assume was the one who picked up Claud." Her cheeks redden, and her eyes flash with a mix of anger and hurt.

Fuck.

"You're right." She is…I would have lost my shit without thinking of the consequences, which is new for me. "Do you want me to call her to come back so you can go bat shit crazy on her?" I smirk, and she hits my chest.

"I'd rather you lose her number." She looks down and lowers her voice. "You said no others when we're together."

"Baby." I palm her nape, bringing our faces closer together to kiss her lightly on the forehead. "She is in my past and staying there. I promise."

"Okay," she mumbles.

"Hey." I lift her chin. "I'm a man of my word. If we're monogamous, that's the end of it. You never have to second guess me."

My stomach hollows, making me sick even thinking of being with another woman right now.

"Harrison." Her big brown eyes study mine, which are hostage to hers.

"Tell me you'll go out with me tonight."

"Oh…"

"Tell me."

A few seconds pass as her eyes flutter with mixed emotions.

"But, what if people see us?"

"It's a date. They don't know what happens after."

"Harr—"

"Tell me." I kiss up her neck.

"Oh my god, you're insufferable. You're like a big baby."

I bite down, drawing a soft moan from her parted, plump lips.

"Well?"

"Fine." She gives in and finally tilts her head so she can kiss me.

That's it, baby, don't deny me what's mine.

"And you'll sleep over again," I demand against her mouth.

She shakes her head. "I can't. I need to be up at four."

"Not a request. Pack a bag, Juliette." I lean down, kiss her again, then step back. If I don't stop now, I'll never make my meeting. "I don't care if you need to be up at one in the morning. I want you next to me until the very last second." She stands there shocked, like she wants to fight me, but knows she wants to be there just as much as I need her there. "I'll pick you up after my meeting at seven."

Without waiting for an answer, I walk out, fearing what my mouth might demand next.

12

Juliette

My phone dings with a notification. "Can you check that for me?" I ask Becks, who is currently spread across my bed with her laptop working, as I get ready for my date with Harrison.

Just the thought of Harrison makes my heart race eagerly.

It's been only two hours since I've seen him, and already, my body is excited for our night together.

"Harrison says to wear flats," she reads aloud.

"What? Why?" I look down at my white fitted dress that I planned on pairing with a small block heel—anything to give me more height next to him.

"I'm not Harrison," she answers dryly. "Do you want me to ask him?"

"Yes, please." I sit down and open my makeup bag.

Only mascara and a bit of lip gloss for tonight, maybe some blush. Then, I brush out my curled hair so it becomes waves.

She snorts as she reads the message that comes through, then hands it to me.

Because I said so.

"Is he all demanding in the bedroom? It's probably so hot," she says, leaning back on my pillow and smiling at the ceiling.

"Matteo strikes me as someone who would be nothing short of demanding."

Her smile widens. "Oh, trust me, he is, but Harrison is my boss. It's all taboo and shit."

"Matteo is your boss," I deadpan.

"Barely. Harrison is like the big-time boss."

I ignore her ridiculous rationality and text back Harrison.

Not good enough. If I'm wearing flats, is this place casual?

Yes.

How casual?

Juliette, baby, I'm trying to be calm, but I don't have the time to talk about a woman's wardrobe right now. I need to finish work, so I can pick you up. Be ready in thirty minutes.

Ugh! He's so frustrating at times.

Yet still, my body yearns for the next thirty minutes to pass quickly so I can see him again.

I rummage through my closet and find what I'm looking for.

"I thought he said to wear flats." Becks looks me up and down.

Propping myself up on the wall with one hand, I bend and put on higher heels than I was planning. "Do you do everything a man tells you?" I lift an accusing brow.

Until Matteo, she would have slapped someone if they had sent a text like Harrison. She likes it in the bedroom, but outside of it, she's the demanding one.

She grins. "Touché. What if he wants to take you rock climbing?"

Chuckling, I think of Harrison coming over in his suit to go rock climbing. "Can you imagine?"

"No." She laughs. "Definitely not."

"Do we even have somewhere in the city to rock climb?"

"Fuck if I know, do *I* look like I go rock climbing?" she asks, and I think about it.

"Yes, actually, I can see you buying a whole new outfit to go. You're very adaptable."

She picks up her phone and types quickly. "There's one in Brooklyn. Should we go?"

"Oh my god. I can't with you." I shake my head in amusement, then spin around. "How do I look?"

She grins, her eyes dancing amusingly. "Like your ass will be red from disobeying."

The old Jules would have been completely turned off by spanking. Now thinking about Harrison smacking my ass like he did while taking me from behind, and the feeling it elicits within me, would have me thinking otherwise.

Becks's phone rings, and she doesn't realize it's on speaker. "Hi, Indie baby." A soft but deep voice with a slight Italian accent purrs.

My eyes widen like saucers. *Indie?* I mouth.

She quickly switches it off speaker and gives me the middle finger.

The front door closes, so I leave the bedroom to give her and her Italian lover some privacy.

"Hi, Mom," I call out.

"My love, can you help me with these bags?"

I round the corner to see her almost toppling over from carrying the groceries I ordered.

"What are you doing?" I cry. "You're going to hurt yourself. I would have picked them up if I knew they were delivered."

She waves me off. "Oh, nonsense. I can pick up some groceries, Juliette."

I let out a sigh of disappointment, and I hope she hears it. She's going to drop the bags and hurt herself if her hands or knees give out, and then what?

She trips down the steps?

"I don't care if I'm wounding your pride. I don't want you hurt, don't you understand that?" My voice catches, and she doesn't miss it, whipping around to apologize, taking me into her arms.

"I feel okay today, Jules." She hugs me tighter.

Earlier, I was thinking of moving out. Now, this makes me rethink everything. What if I weren't living here?

She'd be too stubborn to ask for help.

She pulls me back and looks me up and down. "You're going out again?" she asks with not one ounce of judgment.

If it were up to Mom, she'd have me on dating apps, going out every night.

"Yes." I pause, knowing I need to tell her I'm not coming home but cringing on the inside, thinking about it. "And I'll be sleeping out, too. I'll go right to the bakery in the morning."

"Oh?" She beams. "Would you be sleeping over at a very handsome *older man's* house?"

"Mom!"

She shrugs. "I'm just stating the facts. And he's a dad."

"It's not serious. We're just having fun."

"Mmm," she says, staring at me like she knows I wish it were more than that.

"Jules," Becks screams from my room. "Hottie Harrison texted he'll be here in five minutes."

"Oh, for god's sake," I mumble. "Don't even say anything."

Mom pretends to zip her mouth and throw away the key.

I walk back to my room to grab my purse, overnight bag, and a light sweater in case the air conditioning is on too high at the restaurant, to find Becks lying on her stomach, back to work.

"How's Matteo? You seem to be getting along well."

"It's not like that."

Pausing mid-step at her tone. "What do you mean?"

"He's not always around, or in New York. It's not serious."

Huh. "Where does he go? Does he work from another office?"

"I'm not sure," she says dismissively, typing furiously on her laptop. My phone dings and I know it's Harrison telling me he's downstairs.

Becks hands me my phone without looking, so I take her face and squeeze it while kissing her cheek hard.

"Ugh. You're like the grandmother I never had. All you're missing is the red lipstick that never comes off."

I laugh and slap her bubble butt. "Bye. Love you."

"Love you more. Have fun."

I say bye to Mom and hear her yell down the hall as I open the front door. "Rebecca. Are you staying for dinner?"

"Yes. I'll be out in twenty minutes when I'm done with this spreadsheet," she calls back. A pang of jealousy hits quickly, followed by guilt that I want to be with Harrison over staying here.

I take the elevator down to the lobby and walk out the front door. My breath catches, and the strange tingling sensation I get whenever I see Harrison grips my body like a vise.

He's on the phone and doesn't see me at first, but when he turns and our eyes lock, every inch of me has to hold back from running into his arms.

Harrison Davenport is perfection in his crisp navy suit.

The tie is gone, and the top two bottoms of his shirt are undone with a white neatly squared-off pocket square tucked in.

He holds his arm out for me when I get closer, wrapping it tightly around my middle.

"I have to go," he says into the phone before pocketing it and lifting me off the ground, pulling me into his chest.

"Jules, baby," he whispers and smashes our lips together on the busy sidewalk, kissing me with a passion that takes my breath away.

My arms wrap around his neck, and one hand weaves through his hair as his lips open, dipping his tongue in, exploring mine with a tenderness that I feel in my toes.

When I remember there is a good chance Becks and my mom are watching from the window, I lean back, then burrow my face in his throat, smiling broadly against his skin.

"What?"

"Don't look, but Mom and Becks are most likely watching."

He chuckles. "So I shouldn't let you go and broadcast my raging hard-on for them to see."

"Oh god." I laugh. "Could you imagine?"

"No." He smirks, loosening his grip so I slide down his body right over his hard length. "Don't make that face."

"What face?"

His large hand palms my cheek, holding it gently. "The one where your eyes glass over whenever you're turned on."

My lips part, and the air leaves my lungs.

No words come out.

I am turned on.

His other hand runs down the hollow of my back as he whispers, his breath hot against my ear, "Let's go, baby, before we never make it to dinner."

His hand travels further down my behind, then laces our fingers together before he turns sideways to inconspicuously fix his massive *issue.*

He turns back, raking his eyes over my body, and pauses at my feet.

"What the fuck?"

"What? These went better with the outfit?" I retort sarcastically.

He purses his lips, and his nostrils flare. A clear sign he's annoyed.

"I asked you to wear flats."

"No, you demanded."

He stands there staring at me, then takes his phone out of his pocket and dials someone on speaker.

"Yes, sir?"

I instantly recognize it as Robert's voice.

"Change of plans, please come pick us up to go to the restaurant." He says all that through gritted teeth.

"No problem, give me ten minutes."

We stand there in a silent debate for five of those ten minutes.

I can't look at his eyes, so I stare at his big red lips while biting my tongue so hard I'm surprised I'm not bleeding out by now.

That's it. I can't take it anymore.

"What was the plan?"

"Don't worry about it," he snaps and stretches his head out into the street, looking for Robert.

He said ten minutes, you big idiot.

I teeter back and forth on my heels as a muddled mess of emotions runs through me.

A small twinge shoots into my leg, and I rub it out with my knuckles.

He looks me over and scoffs loudly before turning his attention back to the street.

What the fuck is his problem?

"Why did you make that sound?"

He looks over his shoulder. "If you don't want to take care of yourself, why should I bother?"

What is this man talking about? "Can you stop talking in riddles? What's the issue, Harrison?"

I see him debating whether he wants to talk to me, but his pride loses this time. "You're rubbing your leg. You may not want to talk about it, but that doesn't mean I won't make sure you're taken care of. You were rubbing your leg, and earlier, you were limping in baking class, too."

"I know." He's right. I was in a lot of pain toward the end of class. "I had Becks massage me, and I iced it on and off for an hour."

He scoffs again.

"Stop with the fucking scoffing, Harrison," I snap in frustration.

"Then why are you wearing those fucking death heels?" he booms.

I pause, taken back by his anger.

…And then it hits me.

This goddamn, moronic, idiotic, amazing, perfect man.

If I didn't already have feelings for him, this would do me in.

I lower my voice. "You didn't want me to wear them because you thought they would hurt my leg?"

He doesn't answer. Instead, he fiddles with his watch and fixes his cufflinks.

He won't look at me.

I walk up to him, so close we're touching.

"Tell me, Harrison," I whisper.

He audibly gulps and nods his head.

"I know you like taking walks, and it's a beautiful night. But there was no way I was letting you walk there with those fucking things on."

My heart swells, nearly exploding out of my chest.

"I want to walk with you," I tell him, squeezing his hand tightly.

"No, it's too late. Robert will drive us," he says with finality, but not on my watch.

I walk to the side where my bag is and unzip it, finding my flats.

"What are you doing? I said it's too late."

I ignore him and use his shoulder to balance myself while switching my shoes. Then, pack my heels away.

"Okay, I'm ready."

"Jules—"

"Please, Harrison," I beg. "I want to walk with you." He stares at me. "Please. Call Robert and tell him."

He picks up his phone, and I bounce on the spot.

"I'm sorry, Robert, Juliette is having some sort of brain aneurysm today, so we will indeed be walking."

He stares at me as he talks, and I twist my lips to hide my smile.

Robert chuckles. "No problem."

"Actually. Are you close by?"

"About to turn down her street."

"Perfect, I'm going to drop off her bags in the car so we don't have to carry them around."

After doing that, Harrison takes my hand in his, interlocking our fingers.

"Come on, you pain in my ass."

I don't want to bring it up again, but I need to say something.

"Hey." I grab his attention. "Next time, talk to me. We could have saved a lot of time if you weren't making demands."

He looks down at me quickly before needing to maneuver around a woman with a double-wide stroller. "It's who I am, Juliette."

"Well, can you try to be less with me?" I look at him. "I know it's who you are, Harrison. Trust me, from the first day I saw you, I could tell exactly this is how you would be."

He smirks. "How?"

"You have an air about you. You command a room even if you're not talking."

"You're great for my ego, babe." He rubs his thumb along my skin. "I'll try, Juliette. But I am who I am."

"I know." I stop walking and step to the side so we're out of the way of others. I go up on my toes, and he meets me halfway so I can kiss his lips. "I would never want to change you. Only sometimes the demands don't always need to be so intense."

He kisses me again. "Let's go. We're almost there."

"I didn't even ask what we were eating."

"Mediterranean. If that's not okay, there's an Italian spot one block over. I'm telling you though, this place is amazing."

"Really?" I squeal with excitement. "Mediterranean is my favorite."

He chuckles at my excitement and looks around as we walk down 76th Street. "I grew up on this block. It's weird. It doesn't feel like home."

"Which one?"

He points to a beautiful brownstone with marble stairs. The curtains are open, so I can easily see in, and there's no mistake that it is designed with precision.

"My parents still live here, but I haven't been back in years." He glances up one last time, and we continue walking.

"Do you feel at home when you go to the Morales's house?" I ask, hoping somewhere is home for him.

I can tell by his smile he does. "Definitely. I don't knock or call before. It's the house where anytime you show up, you're welcome with open arms."

"I'm glad you had them." Then I think of something. "Isn't it crazy how big this city is? We've lived ten blocks or less apart, including your new home, our whole lives, and we never even knew it."

"Juliette."

"What?" I shoot my eyes to his when I hear the odd tone of his voice.

He laughs, not in a ha-ha way. "There's also another very good reason we didn't run into each other."

"I'm not catching your drift."

He rubs his hand over his forehead and shakes his head like he can't believe it. "When you were born, I was starting high school."

"What?" My eyes widen. "Oh my god." I throw my head back and laugh. "When you put it like that, it sounds creepy as hell."

"Please don't remind me." I can't stop giggling, and he can't stop shaking his head. "Let's go, we're here."

I'm not sure if it's because it's a small, intimate restaurant, or he doesn't care, but Harrison's holding my hand over the table, and he has been for over an hour now as we've chatted away.

He even tried to fight me on it when I pulled away to eat.

I won.

"You know, you've told me about your dad tonight. But I just realized I know him as Dad. What's his name?"

I grin ear to ear, thinking of Dad again.

Harrison has asked me questions all night to get to know me better, from my favorite flower to how I take my coffee. I didn't have an answer to this since I mostly drink green and herbal tea. Most importantly, he's taken a genuine interest in my dad.

"He was named after his great-grandfather, Reginald Nelson. He hated them both, so he went by Reggie."

"Typical old money name."

I take a sip of my Diet Coke. "You would know." I look at him wide-eyed, wondering if he's kidding with that statement.

"Yes, but not like the Archibald family—"

"Shh!" I cut him off. The Upper East Side is big, but when you don't want people to hear or see, they somehow always do. "Tell me what you do for fun. I know you said you were a bad kid, always getting into trouble with Sebastian, but what do you do for fun now."

He sips his wine, which I forced him to order. Why should he have to suffer if I'm the one who can't wake up at four and handle one ounce of alcohol?

"Honestly, my life revolves around Claud. We take a lot of walks in the park, similar to you. There's a lot, and I mean a lot of ballet talk, and now baking is a hot topic." He rolls his eyes, but I can tell he loves it.

He would do anything to make her happy.

"What if she's away with Leo or one of the other brothers for a week?"

"I keep myself busy. I catch up on work. I make dinner plans with people I haven't seen in a while, and in the summer especially, I play a shit ton of golf, but mostly sit and miss Claud. That sounds pathetic, but she's an extension of me."

"You're a good dad." I smile. He reminds me so much of mine.

He takes another sip. "I hope so. I try my best."

"From what I've seen, from her both in and out of baking class, she's well-mannered and sweet to everyone. She genuinely cares for others. I think you're doing an amazing job raising her."

Every cell in my body is screaming to ask about her mom, but I know in my gut that if I do, the night will be ruined.

Harrison's blazing turquoise eyes hold mine across the table, and they glow with a deep appreciation. "That's the greatest compliment anyone has ever given me. Thank you, Juliette."

I wave my hand in front of my face. "You're going to make me emotional. Tell me something else you like to do."

He smiles softly, squeezing my hand in his. "How did I get so lucky to meet you?"

"Harrison," I whisper, my heart catching in my throat. I can feel my emotions barreling through me quickly. *Too quickly.* I try to change the subject again. "Tell me what you like."

He pauses and thinks. "I love watching sports with my brothers, we're big into baseball and football. In the winter, I enjoy skiing. Claud, not so much, but she does it."

"Oh, that's a dream of mine. I was never allowed to ski. Actually, there was a whole list of things I couldn't do as a professional dancer. Since that's off the table, I hope to one day tick some of them off my list."

"Because of getting injured?"

"Exactly. Also, I was on a semi strict diet. I ate a lot because I was burning so much of it off, but I ate healthy, and rarely let myself cheat, otherwise I wouldn't feel my best. I love eating whatever I want now."

"Like what?"

I scrunch up my face, embarrassed. "One thing I haven't eaten yet that I'm dying for is a dirty water dog."

His face is a sheet of surprise, and a bit of disgust. "A hot dog is what you're excited for?"

I bite my lip and nod, unable to hold back my smile. "Don't make fun of me. I always loved them as a kid. If I had one, I'd want a million, and that's a no-no in dance."

Harrison's quiet, staring at me. "Do you miss it?"

I take a deep breath. "It's a complicated answer, but yes, every day."

His face drops. "Every day?"

I cast my eyes down and draw imaginary circles on the table with my free hand as I think.

"It was my whole life. Moving my body freely while connecting with it in such a deeply emotional way was exhilarating. I will always miss dancing." I pause for a moment. "I was fortunate to move my body like that. But I don't miss the people and the politics behind it. That's like any job, but sometimes it was hard for me to separate the business part from the creative part, if that makes sense."

"It does. You know Claud pretty much wants to be you when she grows up."

I huff out a laugh. "Oh, trust me. I know. She tells me, or anyone who will listen how she will be a real ballerina when she grows up."

He squeezes my hand. "Well, I hope soon enough you'll be able to feel that freedom again, even if it's not through dance."

I gulp down my unease and hope he's right.

"Where's Robert?" I ask as we exit the restaurant and begin walking uptown toward his penthouse.

"He dropped off your stuff at my place, and I told him to go home for the night. I thought you'd want to walk again."

"You're right." I put my hand in his. "Summer nights like this are perfect. The rare absence of humidity is the biggest bonus, though. Otherwise, my hair would be five times the size."

"Normally, I have no idea what women are talking about, but humidity I get. Claud's hair is unmanageable in the summer."

Frizz is just a normal thing for us New Yorkers.

We turn off Lex toward Park Avenue to escape the honking and outdoor chatter of all the restaurants, walking in a pleasant silence until someone screams Harrison's name from behind.

"You've got to be kidding me," Harrison grumbles and turns us around. "Do you have a tracker on me or something? You don't even live up here," he calls out to Nate.

Nate jogs the rest of the way to us, and to be honest, he looks like shit.

I'd never say so, but he looks so much different than he did yesterday afternoon.

"Dad's at the Yankees game, and there was a leak in their bath-room, so I left Leo at the bar to fix it for Mom."

"Why didn't she call my guy?" Harrison asks.

Nate rolls his eyes, and it reminds me so much of Harrison. "Some of us can handle things without paying for them," he says, then turns to me. "Hello, Juliette, you look beautiful tonight."

"Thank you, Nate." I smile and lean into Harrison's hold.

"I haven't even checked the score. Who's winning?" Harrison asks, and Nate freezes, looking between us.

"What?" I ask.

Nate smirks and shakes his head in disbelief. "Harrison loves the Yankees and has alerts on his phone with constant score updates. You must be pretty special for him to ignore them." He winks in my direction, while Harrison grumbles something under his breath.

Nate's phone rings and Leo's name lights up.

"Fuck. He's going to kill me. He's still sitting there, and it will take me twenty-five minutes to get back downtown."

"Wait," I say, shocked. "You left Leo at the bar and came all the way uptown to help your mom, just to go all the way back there?"

"Of course," he says easily.

I look between these men like I can't believe my ears.

Harrison gives me a look like he knows what I'm thinking. He's aware of how close I am with my mom, and it's so rare for grown men to treat their moms right that it warms my heart.

These men are billionaires, yet they come rushing home to fix a leak.

"All right, we're getting out of here. Juliette has an early morning. Go drown your sorrows."

Nate lets out a manic laugh. "Oh, trust me, I have been. Soon, I won't give a shit if Boston wins over the Yankees because I won't be able to remember." He leans in to hug Harrison. "Love you."

"Love you too," Harrison says.

I stand there staring at them, and I think I might cry. I don't know why seeing these two say I love you is getting me emotional.

But it is.

Nate blows me a kiss and jogs past us to grab a cab.

These two are freaking swoony.

"What was that about? Him drowning his sorrows," I ask as we begin to walk again.

"Girl troubles."

Oh. "Does Nate have a girlfriend?"

"No, he wishes. It's a long story, but he found out today that his childhood sweetheart is dating someone."

"Oh, that's sad if he still has feelings for her." Then I think about what I read online. "You're the older brother?"

"Yes. Sebastian and I are the same age, and Leo and Nate are the same age but younger." He points to his building. "We're home."

We wave to the doorman, and then, as we enter the elevator, my mouth opens, and the yawn I've been holding back escapes.

"Sorry," I mumble into his chest, melting tiredly into his arms.

The doors open. "Come on, baby. It's time for bed. You're exhausted."

Harrison's lying behind me, spooning me, naked in the dark.

His strong hands have been incessantly running over my body, feeling each inch of me as if he's trying to memorize my every curve.

Once in a while, he'll leisurely trace my areolas and run his fingertips over my nipples before sliding them down through my wetness. Torturing me as he glides past my clit, to continue his journey elsewhere, all while I try my hardest not to fall asleep.

My eyes are heavy, and I've given up trying to keep them open. His teasing is pure agony, but it's also the most relaxed I've felt in a long time.

Tonight, when we arrived back at his home…it was different.

He undressed me, admired my delicate white lace lingerie, then took me in his arms and kissed me long and hard before laying me down to hold me to his chest.

I've never felt more adored in my life.

"I had the best night—" I yawn mid-sentence, just as his hard length rubs through my soaked center.

"Go to sleep, baby." He kisses my temple.

My mouth hangs open, and I shake my head. "Keep going," I breathe into his forearm, which I'm using as a pillow.

"Is this mine?" he whispers huskily against my ear, and I shiver from the pure rawness in his tone.

He takes my leg and puts it on top of his large thigh, then presses the head of his cock into my entrance teasing me further.

My eyes flutter behind my eyelids, lost between sleep and pure bliss.

"Yours," I whimper so softly I'm not sure he heard.

His breathing is deep, picking up a quicker pace as he slowly enters me.

Each movement is unhurried and deliberate like he's trying to keep me in a state of sleepiness.

I can feel myself drifting.

"And if you fall asleep?" he purrs.

"I'm yours. Yours to take."

Those were the last words I remember, and there's no telling if I was dreaming of the most magical orgasm of my life or if he fiddled with my body, keeping me in a half-conscious state until I came.

Either way, it was the most sensual and stimulating feeling my body had ever felt.

My eyes open two minutes before my alarm goes off, so I lean over and shut it off, then stand up and stretch.

I look down, and a sleepy smile stretches my face when I see the dried come on my inner thigh.

Guess it wasn't a dream.

What the hell was last night?

And why do I want it to happen tonight?

"Harrison." I lean over the bed, whispering against his lips.

His arm shoots out and pulls me back onto the mattress.

"Mmm," he groans as he pumps his morning wood into my leg.

"Down, boy." I push off him before he makes me late. "I'm going to go."

He opens his eyes, and I stand there mesmerized by them. "Kiss me goodbye," he mumbles.

I kiss him, then kiss him again.

God, he's so addicting.

He takes my hand in his as I stand again. "At the end of the week, I have a black-tie event. You'll go as my date."

"Is that a demand?" I lift a brow.

"Yes," he grumbles, trying to reach out and smack my ass.

"Bye, Harrison. Have a good day."

"You'll come," his throaty morning voice calls out.

"We'll see."

Of course, I'll go.

And he's right. Knowing him and the way he makes my body feel whenever he's near, I'm sure I'll *come* too.

13

Juliette

TODAY IS NOT the day to be running around sweating…or to be late.

In my defense, it's not entirely my fault.

The subways were backed up, and every taxi from here to Queens was taken. Uber was ten times the normal price, and though I considered paying for it, they were all too far away, which never happens in the city.

What else was I to do other than to jump out of the delayed subway and haul my behind to Becks's apartment, where I'm getting ready for the black-tie event tonight with Harrison.

Unlucky for me, though, today is the Fourth of July, and it's almost ninety degrees out. I can feel the sweat dripping down my back.

On top of that, I cut through Washington Square Park, which happens to be one of my favorite places to people-watch, and just my luck, I run right through about fifteen teenagers smoking weed, and now I'm pretty sure I reek.

Or maybe I am even slightly high. Contact high is a real thing, right?

I buzz Becks's apartment, panting like crazy.

What the hell is taking her so long? I buzz again.

"The buzzer up here isn't working. Give me a minute, and I'll come down and get you," she screams out her window from the third floor.

I look up and tell her to hurry up. Suddenly, I have to pee like a racehorse and start fidgeting to hold it in.

"Where the hell have you been?" Becks snaps as she opens the door for me.

Ignoring her, I throw my garment bag in her arms, then run past her up the stairs.

Her landlord has been *fixing* the elevator for two years now, so there's no other choice.

Who would have thought taking the stairs would feel rebellious? I easily envision Harrison being mad if he saw me running around the city and then up three flights of steps.

Harrison still doesn't know the whole story, only what he's read online, yet he is so protective about my leg, and I can't say I hate it.

I run into the bathroom, and when I'm done, I wince at the girl staring back at me. I guess I wasted an hour curling my hair before I got here because now, there is no way in hell it's staying down.

Ugh. What a frizzy rat's nest.

I crack open the door as I get undressed. "Hey, Becks?"

"What's up?"

"Bring me my face wash, please. I'm going to jump in the shower quickly. I'm sweating in places I shouldn't be."

"Hi, Jules!"

"Hey, girl," Adriana and Carrie call out from Becks's bedroom.

"Hey! I'm sorry for being rude. I'll be five minutes tops."

"Can you ever be on time, like even once? How are you going to be ready in time?" Becks scolds me as she hands me the bottle.

Why is she always on my case? "It's not my fault, Rebecca. I would have been here forty-five minutes ago on a normal day, but nothing has gone my way."

She gives me a look like she doesn't believe me. I'm not in the mood for anyone's crap right now, or maybe it's because I hate the way she can see right through me.

After the quickest shower known to man, I stand in the bathroom, leaning back into the wall, taking deep breaths to reset myself.

I rub my temples with a deep pressure, hoping that will help. Instead, I feel the sensation of hot tears trickling out of the sides of my eyes for no other reason than stress.

The truth is, Becks was right. It wasn't just transit issues that made me late.

I had a meeting with a realtor who didn't give me much hope for our budget, and an hour before that, Mom called from my aunt's house to tell me my cousin Amber was home and not acting herself.

Which is not helpful since I don't know what "herself" means anymore since she stopped taking her medication. When I begged her to come home, she said she was afraid to leave my aunt alone until my uncle came home.

Thankfully, she texted soon after that she was leaving.

Let's not forget earlier this morning, one of the largest and most expensive mixers we own decided to stop working during our mid-morning prep.

Now, I need to get ready for a black-tie event with Harrison on about three hours of sleep and a confused mind.

I was ecstatic all week for tonight, but now that it's here, I suddenly feel overwhelmed with emotions.

This past week has been a dream. Harrison, in my eyes, is perfect; he's a little grumpy and a lot bossy, but I love every part that makes him who he is, which leaves me falling for him…hard.

There is no doubt in my mind or heart that he feels more for me, that it goes far beyond casual. The problem is he's more stuck in his head than I am. He has a daughter, and for that reason alone, I will never push him into anything more than he is willing to give.

Claud will always come first to him, as she should.

My best friend was the queen of casual until she met Matteo, which I still haven't figured out; nonetheless, she's been noncommitted to almost everyone she's ever been with. I know the signs and the actions, and it's completely different from how Harrison has acted over the last week.

To most, a week is not a long time. But…it hasn't been *just* a week.

It's been a week with a man who has been possessive over my every move, obsessed with my well-being, and now my mom's after I told him about her arthritis.

He insisted I sleep every night in his bed in his home, a home he'd never brought another woman to.

One day, he sent me flowers at the bakery and Mom red-light gloves because he read they'd be good for her.

Another, he had lunch delivered when he knew I'd be running from the bakery to physical therapy and back in a short amount of time. And, of course, he made time out of his busy day to call to make sure I ate said lunch.

"Juliette? What the hell are you doing? You're going to be so fucking late," Becks barks and opens the door without knocking.

Jeez, she's like a freaking drill sergeant today.

She looks down at my now slumped body, and not because I'm naked, but because she can see the worry in my eyes.

"I'm not having some sort of breakdown," I tell her. "I'm just extremely stressed and overtired. Sorry."

She comes in and shuts the door before sitting next to me, wrapping her arms around me.

Yes, I'm still naked, but we're sisters. Nothing fazes us.

"Is this about Harrison?" she asks quietly.

"Yes, but also I'm nervous about the bakery. We've been lucky with low rent, and I'm only realizing that now that I'm seeing market prices for other spaces." I take a deep breath, then continue. "What if we can't find anywhere in the neighborhood and lose our loyal customers? I truly don't think we'd make it in this economy." She holds me tighter and says nothing because she knows it's true.

After a while of silence, she breaks it. "And Harrison?" I shrug. She won't understand. "You're in your twenties, Jules. You're finally able to live and let loose. Don't sacrifice your life again."

She still doesn't get it.

Becks has always supported me and cheered on my successful dancing career, but it doesn't mean she understood it. Though she is no stranger to hard work, she never got the strictness that went along with my career.

"I didn't sacrifice my life. I loved it. I could have been partying and living it up. But *I* chose not to do what everyone else was doing. That would have never got me to my end goal." It's what *I* wanted. "My dedication might have seemed like a burden to most people our age, but to me, discipline and dedication would reward me in the end. Never did I think it would end so early."

She turns toward me. "You're right. I'm sorry, I just…" She trails off, and I can see her contemplating her next words.

"You just what?"

Her eyes connect with mine. "You're going to be mad at what I say next."

I roll my eyes. "Great," I mutter.

"I'm worried that now you don't have dance, you're romanticizing your life with him."

"What? I wouldn't do that," I say, and even to my own ear, I sound like a liar.

She stands. "I need to finish packing, but I love you. Just think about it. Your whole life has been romanticized. You're a fucking ballerina, for god's sake." She smirks and shakes her head. "And you're the girl who wants what your parents had. You're ready to get married at twenty-four and have kids. But remember, sometimes, men mean what they say, and a future might not be on the table. It's not always meant to be."

My alarm goes off, meaning I should be getting dressed, which clearly isn't happening.

I can't answer her right now. I'm afraid what she says holds some truth. "I should call Harrison to tell him I'm running behind."

"Okay." She kisses my forehead. "Come out soon. The girls and I need to leave shortly. And put some clothes on, for fuck's sake." She laughs and leaves me.

"Hi, are you okay?" Harrison picks up right away.

I cringe—shoot. "Ah, aren't you in an important meeting? I was going to leave a voicemail."

"You're important, Juliette. What's wrong?"

That means he is, and I'm interrupting. "I'm running late. Is that going to be okay?"

"Hey, take over," he says to someone. I hear him walking, and I know he's left the meeting.

Shit.

"Late because it's you, or late because I hear something else in your voice."

"Why does everyone say I'm late? I was on time yesterday."

He chuckles. "Five minutes late is not on time, Jules. Anyway, talk to me, baby. What's going on?"

I place the phone on speaker, then stand up and put on the sweats Becks brought in for me.

"It seems silly now when I interrupt you dealing with your super successful company. My issues are minuscule compared to yours, but I had a stressful day, and it's hitting me I guess. I needed some time. I'm getting ready now, though. I promise."

"Don't do that," he bites. "Don't—"

"I won't. I won't," I cut him off, not wanting to get into an argument over the phone. "My issues are important too, I know. I'm sorry. Let's not make it a thing. I need to get ready."

"Okay…" he sighs. "Matteo is leaving now to get the girls, and I'm going to leave with him and get ready with you."

I pause mid-step. "You don't have to do that."

"I know I don't have to. But I want to."

"But you have the mid-year—"

"Juliette," he sighs. "I said I'm coming. End of story."

Then he hangs up without saying goodbye.

———

"Hi, baby." The deep, dark rasp I love has my head snapping up.

His lips twist in a cocky grin, and I giggle. Unable to help myself, I drop my blush, jump up, and run into his arms.

It's like an instant mood booster being wrapped up in his arms, my body pressed against him.

I kiss his lips, but it takes him a second to kiss me in return, which is totally unlike him, so as quickly as I kiss him, I pull back and realize what I've done.

I lean away and drop my feet to the ground. "I'm so sorry, Harrison. I lost my head. I forgot everyone was here."

Turning around, I find Adriana and Carrie staring at us with slack jaws. Becks looks concerned and Matteo, amused. *Fuck.* "I'm sorry," I say again, whispering this time, then drop my head, embarrassed.

"*Mon petit papillon,*" he murmurs for only me to hear.

I stand frozen.

Since getting together, he hasn't used that name, and I hadn't realized how much I missed it.

He lifts my chin and looks me in the eyes. There's a war going on in his, but his gaze is still unwavering.

"Fuck it." He cups my cheeks and smashes his lips to mine with such passion that it shocks me to my core.

He doesn't hold back, opening so our tongues slowly dance together, and when I let out a soft moan, he breaks our kiss, stretching his mouth into a smile against me.

"We can kiss in front of your friends. It's Sebastian I need to worry about. That's it," he whispers against my lips.

"Okay," I reply and pucker my lips for one last kiss.

He kisses me back, then trails his plump lips along my jaw, dipping his head to linger against my beauty mark, nuzzling his face in my neck until I pull back.

His eyes glow with an inner fire I'd never seen before; this is how it's been all week. Discovering sides of each other that are new and exciting but equally frightening because the more I learn about Harrison, the more I want from him.

"Okay, then. You two, nice little show, but our plane's leaving soon, so we need to get out of here," Matteo says, breaking up our private moment.

Wait.

"Plane?"

Carrie nods and shimmies her body all around. "A free vacation and we're taking a PJ, as the rich kids like to call private jets. What is this life?" She chugs the rest of her drink, and her infectious attitude has me smiling ear to ear for her.

She deserves it.

Everyone says goodbye, so I step to the side quickly and take Becks in a tight embrace, lowering my voice. "The other day, you seemed okay with Harrison. Now you're not again?"

"I'm not sure how I feel, honestly. He's different than Mr. Davenport, CEO, and I can see he cares about you. But...please be careful."

I kiss her cheek. "I will." I step back to see her face. "And Matteo?"

She shrugs, similar to the other day. "I told you, it is what it is. I'm having fun for now."

"Nantucket for the Fourth of July via private jet is the epitome of fun. I'll give you that." I lean in and hug her again. "Love you."

She slaps my butt. "Love you." She winks. "Laters, baby."

I climb out the window onto the fire escape and wave to the girls as they leave. "Have fun!" I call out. They're all a little tipsy, singing Journey's "Don't Stop Believing" as they make their way into the waiting car.

Harrison helps me step back into the apartment, then runs his hand down my back and over my behind. "Did she just slap *my* ass?" he growls, and I laugh out loud.

We do slap each other on the butt a lot, I realize, but it's all for fun. Becks's butt is also the most perfect round bubble. I can't help but slap or squeeze it.

"She slapped *my* ass. She also quoted Christian Grey."

His face says it all. "You don't know who Christian Grey is? From *Fifty Shades of Grey?*"

He looks at me deadpan.

Then I think about it for a moment and decide against suggesting we should watch it; he'll get some crazy idea I like being flogged, which I most definitely do not, or at least, I don't think I would.

"Harrison?" I call from Becks's bedroom.

"Yeah, baby?"

He steps into the room, and I turn around. "Can you zip me, please?"

His fingertips run along my bare back before leaning down to place barely there kisses along my spine, following my goose bumps up the curve of my neck. "Avec plaisir." *With pleasure.*

He turns me toward the mirror, watching both of us as he slowly slides the zipper up.

He kisses my neck again. "Ich mag dich mit ein wenig makeup auf."

Switching to German, he tells me he likes me when I wear a little amount of makeup. "Ich weiß" *I know.*

I lift my arm above my head to rub my fingers over his stubbled cheek. "Du siehst sehr gut aus in dem Smoking." *You look very handsome in your tuxedo.* "It reminds me of the masquerade party."

He kisses the back of my head. "I loved spending my time with you that night. You were so intriguing. I should—"

He stops mid-sentence. "What's wrong?"

"I think the zipper is stuck." I turn around, look in the mirror, and see for myself that it is definitely not stuck. I turn my back toward Harrison. "Try again, please."

"Jules."

"Try again, please." I raise my voice, he tries again, and it won't zip. I wrench away and dig into my garment bag. "I didn't want to wear it anyway. This one is better." I take out a gold slinky dress that shines if you move right.

It's better suited for the Fourth of July.

He sits in the corner chair quietly, not saying a word when I slip it over my head. No zipping required. "This is better, no?" I ask, then put on my heels.

He stands when he sees I'm just about ready. "Hey," he says softly.

Don't be nice to me right now, or I'll start crying.

"It's fine, Harrison. What did I expect? I used to work out six days a week, eight to ten hours a day when I was a ballerina. Now I limp around, testing out éclair flavors and eating macarons or a croissant or two every morning."

Some people may look at me, not understanding, because they'll see a somewhat petite, lean, and toned body. Muscles from twenty years of dedication don't fade overnight, but that doesn't dismiss the changes my body has gone through and my feelings about them.

Women's bodies change for many reasons, including injury like me, age, and motherhood, to name a few, and that's okay.

It's part of life.

But I have the right to be affected by not fitting into my favorite dress or the new stretch marks on my behind. I like and appreciate my body.

I was too skinny.

This is better…healthier…just different.

However, it doesn't make it any less shocking when something changes, even for the good, like the fact that I suddenly grew boobs at twenty-four.

Harrison interlocks our fingers and guides me out of the room, and before we leave, he stops me at the door.

His eyes hold mine with understanding as he speaks with a gentle but meaningful tone. "To me, Juliette, your body is perfect, however, I would never, and will never, dismiss your feelings. For whatever it's worth, your body doesn't define you. This"—he points to my heart—"and this"—then my head—"define you. Your kind heart and intelligence are the important bits. Well, and these too"—he traces my lips, smirking.

I stand wordlessly. I'm sure he can hear my quick beating heart pound against my chest.

With his hand cupping my face, his thumb sweeps across the apple of my cheek, and he says, "Now it's time to get the fuck out of this weird apartment."

I burst out laughing, so happy he changed the subject.

He looks around. "It's a fucking shoe box. Am I not paying her enough? What the fuck is up with this place?" He fakes a shiver, cringing.

"Don't be snobby, Harrison."

"Juliette. Let's be serious, this place is out of a scary fucking movie. What the hell is that lamp? It has fake fucking blood on it."

I throw my hands over my face and laugh, like a full-on belly laugh.

When I calm myself, I tell him the story of Becks high on shrooms while she was in college. "She called me, and I had no idea what the hell she was saying. The next morning, she called me again, with no recollection of talking, and while I was on the phone, she walked into the living room of her townhouse she shared with five other girls and started screaming. I was so nervous, I couldn't make out one word she was saying." I shake my head at the memory. What an idiot she was. "She took pictures and sent them to me. The whole room was filled with all this weird furniture. More than what's here—the other roommates took some too. None of them remember how it got there, so now, it's just a part of their history. She'll never be able to give it up."

He looks at me like he wants to call me a liar.

Trust me, I know it's the craziest freaking story on the planet.

"You know what…if Seb and I weren't so out of control in college, I would think this was a prank." He shakes his head, chuckling. "Lock up, and let's get out of here, babe."

"Look." Harrison hands me his phone as Robert drives us through the city, somehow getting us to the event on time.

I take it, and instantly, I'm smiling. "Why is she so stinking cute?" I zoom in on Claud's face covered in flour. "What is she baking?"

"No clue. Nate sent it to me, saying to send help," he mutters as he leans over me, smiling at the phone.

"Look at her smile. She's so proud." I hand it back to him. "Is it hard not being with her on a holiday?"

He sighs. "Extremely. Though I have a brown-eyed beauty keeping me company." He kisses my head, then sits up. "Her uncles like having time alone with her, without me there, so I have to suck it up. I'll see her soon." He pauses. "I told you I'll be there for three days next week, right?" His tone is apologetic, though he should never feel bad for seeing his daughter.

Still, I swallow the lump in my throat and nod.

It's three nights, and I shouldn't feel any type of emotion over it, although after spending the whole week with him, every night in his bed, I already know I'll miss him terribly.

The rational part of me...which is a very, very small part, knows this is good for us because once Claud comes home, things will change drastically, and I won't see him anywhere near the amount I do now.

With his arm around my shoulder, he pulls me in closer to his chest, and I lean my head on his shoulder. "What are you thinking about?" I mumble.

"That it's nice to be able to talk to you about Claud. She's normally off-limits."

"On dates?" I ask, holding back a disgusted shiver, hating the very idea of him ever with another woman.

He shakes his head against mine. "No, she's off-limits to everyone who is not close to me. I pay a lot of money to keep her out of any articles, even if it's not gossip, which is why you couldn't find a picture of her. Even colleagues and employees know not to ask about her. They are very aware my personal life is just that, personal. That's why I have a side entrance into my office building leading straight into a private elevator to take her to the top floor. You know, a different elevator than the one you used," he says, his chest shaking against my cheek, thinking he's funny as shit.

I'm not amused.

"Don't remind me of that day. I'll never step foot in the vicinity of that building again," I grumble. What must his coworkers think of the crazy lunatic girl showing up there unannounced?

Then I think of something.

"If Claud is so private, why can we talk about her?"

He stills under me, and I can feel him thinking. "Well, you knew her before me, and...I trust you."

I quickly sit up to look at him, surprised by his admission. "You do?"

A tingling sensation creeps up my arm as his fingers trail sensuously over my skin. His eyes are cast down, deep in thought, but when he finally looks up, he nods, full of meaning. "I do, beautiful."

The car comes to a stop before I can say anything more, though I'm not sure what there is to say.

Harrison Davenport, Mr. Elusive, as many articles have named him, trusts *me*.

That's a big freaking deal.

"Hey." I snap my attention back toward him when I feel his hand creeping up my inner thigh. "Kiss me one more time before we get out of the car."

"Oh, yeah." I frown. "I forgot the rules."

"We're not going to stay long, I promise. Trust me, there is no way I'll be able to stay four hours next to you without touching you freely or kissing you."

I smile at his honesty. "That's because you show affection through physical touch. Haven't you noticed? You almost always need to be touching or kissing me."

He thinks about it and shakes his head. "No, it's because you're so fucking hot that I can't keep my hands off you. Now kiss me before I make you."

Harrison

She's beautiful. My eyes have not left Juliette for one second tonight.

And I'm not the only one.

The moment we walked through the doors, everyone's line of

vision, both men and women, trailed her as she gracefully glided through the room. I shocked myself when I felt pride versus jealousy that she was on my arm tonight and no one else's.

Jules has me so crazy over her; two times tonight, people have had to repeat themselves because I can't pay attention to anything or anyone but her.

Our situation has me feeling utterly confused and out of my mind lately. I've never felt so conflicted about what to do as I do now.

You've never cared about a woman before like you do her.

Juliette has weaved a path through my complicated life, and everything in me screams to keep her as mine.

Because that's what she is, *mine*.

I remind her of that every day.

Only then does my conscience kick in, reminding me of my promise to my brother.

When Claudina was born, it was clear I would be her father and sole caretaker, even if deep down, Sebastian would have loved to take on the role if he were in a better place mentally. When the decision was made, he asked one thing of me…to make Claud my world.

I promised him that Claud would be the only one in my life until she was older, that I would focus on her and only her, and that I wouldn't let another possible threat into her life, as I almost did with my ex.

Until this point, I haven't even considered breaking my promise.

My client walks away, so I turn and watch Jules as she throws her head back, laughing freely as the woman in front of her tells a story.

Everything about her is beautiful, including the small things, especially how she articulates herself and genuinely cares for others. She is utterly enchanting.

Juliette Caldwell is one of the special ones who is good down to the core, and I'm positive I don't deserve her.

Sipping my scotch, I reach my hand out and rub along the curve of her back.

In slow motion, she turns her head toward me. Her face lights up, and her broad smile stretches, reaching her eyes.

"Hi," she mouths, then reaches back to squeeze my forearm, shooting me another whisk of a smile before continuing her conversation.

She hugs the older woman goodbye, then sips her drink while her grin returns as she stares at me like I'm the center of her universe.

I know the feeling, baby.

I take her hand and guide her toward our seats. "Who was that again?" I ask. "She looks familiar."

"Mrs. Windward. She is a major donor to The City Ballet. We became close, and she often visited the bakery until a couple of months ago. I wondered what happened, but she moved to the West Coast to follow her daughter since she recently gave birth." She links our fingers together, then pulls them back quickly.

"What are you doing?" I growl, grabbing her hand again.

"You said we couldn't touch, Harrison. For god's sake, get your story straight," she says with an irritated, mocking tone.

"You know I meant we couldn't touch how we normally do. I can hold my date's hand, Juliette." I step forward and cup her cheek, ready to kiss her without thinking, to show her I don't care what people say anymore, but then I see him.

Fuck.

Goddamnit, Sebastian.

"Hey, Jules, baby." I lower my voice. "We need to get out of here."

She stills, looking at me confused. "What's wrong? I was only kidding about the hand-holding."

My heart breaks in two that she thinks this is because of her.

No, my beautiful girl, it's because my life is complicated, and I can't have you as mine as I thought.

"Seb is here, and I don't want any issues between him and me. I thought he was with Claud and my brothers. He must have come back for the event. I'm sorry I dragged you here."

Her eyes narrow, and her lips pucker with annoyance. "So it's okay when you bring other women as your date, but when it comes to me, I'm not good enough?" she retorts in a cold, sarcastic tone.

Usually, I love her sass, but we don't have the time right now.

I bend so we're eye to eye. "No, Juliette. It's the complete opposite. I haven't given two fucks about any of the other women, but one look at us…one glance at how I am with you, Seb will know, and I don't want to waste a night with you fighting with my brother instead."

Before she can answer, I escort us out of there while thinking how to save our night.

As we wait for Robert to pull around, Jules is silent, so I take the opportunity to text Lauren to help execute my plan.

After Lauren confirms, I text Robert and instruct him to take the long way so there is time to make it perfect.

Tonight was a harsh reality check that I won't be able to give her a future, but I'll do whatever it takes to make the ending of the night what my girl deserves.

14

Juliette

CONFLICTING NERVES SWIRL around my stomach as I sit in the back of the car in an unusual silence. Typically, I need to stop myself from rambling. Even when Harrison is his stoic self, I feel a level of comfort between us that has me letting my guard down.

Tonight, though, I'm as quiet as a mouse, trying to process my mixed emotions.

He senses my hurt, but he's done no wrong. He warned me this would happen.

I know, though, by how he's holding me and continues to blabber on about random, pointless information in a fast, nervous chatter, he's worried about asking me if I'm all right.

Only, I'm not sure if I am…

It's as if my heart let me down.

It beats rapidly day and night for this wonderful man who feels so much more than casual to me, yet I know deep down it deceived me.

He warned me about this, too…that there's no future between us, yet my heart tricked me into believing he'd want more if he spent time with me. I know he has genuine feelings for me too.

"Jules," he whispers my name, finally giving in to the urge to talk. "You're so quiet, baby. What's wrong?"

"I'm fine, Harrison. Just ready to go home."

His body stills, and he leans back to look at my face. "You want to go home?"

I can sense his twinge of disappointment, but honestly, I'm not up for anything else. "Yes."

He settles back into his seat, still facing me. "Why?"

"I don't blame you, but what happened tonight does not sit well with me." I pause, thinking of my dad. He wouldn't like this, I know it. He continuously encouraged me to stand up for myself, so I pull strength from him to open my heart and speak from it. "I deserve more than to duck and dive out of a beautiful event because you can't be seen with me. I should be more than someone's dirty little secret."

A flash of surprise and hurt crosses his face. "You're not my secret, Jules. It's just Sebastian—"

"You don't need to explain. I know you've told me this, and I agreed. It still doesn't make me feel any different."

"I'm going to make this up to you. It will be the best night." He kisses my forehead. "I promise."

If I had any self-preservation I would object and ask to go home again, yet even knowing how this will end, I want to soak up every minute I have with him, knowing my heart will most likely suffer the consequences.

To distract myself from my warring thoughts, I take my phone out of my bag to check on Mom and see I missed a message from the realtor.

I sigh, not wanting to look at this.

"What is it?"

I show him my phone. "The realtor is sending us spaces within our budget, but it's nowhere near home, and with early mornings, it's going to be too far of a trek for Mom."

"And you."

I shake my head. "I'm going to move out once we settle on a place, to wherever it is. I can't live with Mom forever, even though she'd love me to."

"What? You're moving?" His voice is odd—something in his tone I can't decipher.

"There's no other choice if we need to move the bakery downtown."

He stares at me like he doesn't understand, then clears his throat. "Can I ask you something?"

"Of course."

He takes a deep breath. "I know we still haven't discussed it, but it's public knowledge that you were hit by a taxi. Didn't you receive a settlement from the city or cab driver?"

I lean back and close my eyes while answering something I've been at war with for months.

"Long story short, no. The cabbie has his own insurance that I would have needed to go through, and if I had done that, his premiums would have skyrocketed. My accident was just that, an accident. He was swerving because of another idiot, not because he was being reckless. However, his insurance company wouldn't see it that way." I pause to gather my thoughts. "I wouldn't want to ruin his life because of that. If I had sued, Mom, the bakery, and I would have been set. We could have stayed right where we are now. But to me, that money would have been tainted. He is an immigrant with few job opportunities and many young children who rely on his paychecks. I could survive without them. He couldn't."

I open my eyes to see his shocked face. "I remember reading about this now."

I nod, knowing most of the city has read the articles. "My insurance covered my surgery and physical therapy, the small bills I had, the cab driver insisted on paying out of his pocket. It was cheaper than him being sued. He's checked on me many times since the accident. He's a nice man."

"Jules…" He sighs. "You were born in the wrong world, my sweet girl. You're too kindhearted and caring."

"That's kind of you to say, Harrison." Then, the car stops in front of an unfamiliar building. "Where are we?" I ask, realizing just now we've been in this car for a very long time. That's what happens when I'm with Harrison—I lose sense of everything, even the most minor things like time.

"I wanted to end the night on a good note." His face is sheepish. "But if you'd rather go home, we can do anything you want."

Knowing I can not deny him and that deep down I don't want to, I opt to stay.

Robert opens the door, and I smile at Harrison. "Show me a good time."

———

Harrison walks up to the front desk. "Hello, we're guests of Mason Cunningham. He should have left my name." He passes over his driver's license, and I do the same, and then they scan our faces.

Jeez, who the hell lives here?

I don't even do this much in Harrison's building.

"Yes, sir. You're both all set. Please use this key to enter the main door and then this key to access the elevator. I assume you know the code?"

"Yes. Thank you." Harrison takes the cards, then swipes the first one, causing two twenty-foot mahogany doors to open to an expansive lobby.

It's sleek, modern, and sexy as hell. Where the hell am I right now?

"That wasn't the lobby?"

He chuckles. "No, it was the check-in area."

My eyes are probably embarrassingly wide as my head is on a constant swivel. Who the hell has a check-in area before the lobby?

"Where are we, Mars?"

He smirks and squeezes my hand. "I'll tell you when we get upstairs."

We take an all-glass private elevator up to the penthouse, surprise, surprise.

Harrison knew the code off the top of his head for the elevator, and now he enters a different one to enter the apartment.

"Harrison, this is unbelievable." I spin around. "How is this possibly better than your place?"

"Um, thanks?" He laughs, and I can tell he's not insulted because he knows this place is out of this world.

"Whose place is this, and why are we here?" He's looking around nervously toward the staircase off to the side. "What is it?"

"Nothing, sorry. I thought I heard something." He opens the wine fridge and grabs a bottle of vintage Dom Perignon and two glasses. Then he leads us toward the backdoor to a small terrace, which I'm shocked is smaller than Harrisons, though the East River and Brooklyn views are to die for.

He pours two glasses, turns on some music, and then it hits me…

He's familiar, making himself at home. Was that whole thing in the lobby an act?

"Oh my god. Is this your fuck pad?"

He gives me a funny look. "What the hell are you talking about?"

I wave my hands around dramatically. "I don't know. You're familiar here helping yourself to thousand-dollar bottles of champagne. You know the ways through secret freaking passageways. Maybe your alter ego is this Mason guy."

"Secret passageways?" He lifts a sarcastic brow, and I see he's trying to hide his laughter. "We went through a set of doors," he deadpans.

I widen my eyes. "Well, you're not denying it."

He places our glasses down on the table, grabs me by the waist, and pulls me into his chest.

"Come here, you crazy lady," he says, then smashes his lips to mine. "God, you're hot when you're all sassy. I told you before I used my brother's hotel in the past"

"Harrison," I growl, swatting at his chest. "I don't want to hear about that."

He smirks. "When I said Mason Cunningham, it didn't ring a bell for you?"

I think…and think some more. "Yeah. No clue."

"I can't wait to tell him that one. Mason Cunningham is a star quarterback. He won two Super Bowls in a row."

"Wait." I think. "The guy who was dating Marisol Herrera, the supermodel?"

Harrison throws his head back, laughing so loud it echoes through the night sky.

"What?" I ask.

"I'm just loving that you have no idea who he is and only know him because of his ex."

"Ugh yeah, have you seen his ex? Actually, don't answer that." He bites his lips and waggles his brows. "What?"

"Nothing. I find it amusing when you call me jealous…pot meet kettle."

"Oh, shush. Now, how do you know Mason?"

Before he answers, he pulls me over to the balcony to take in the view and hands me my glass. "Cheers, baby. Happy Fourth of July."

"Cheers—" Then it dawns on me. "We're going to be able to see the fireworks from here, aren't we? That's why we're here?" I ask excitedly.

He leans down and brushes his lips against mine, then stands back up and fixes my hair behind my ear. "We are, but not from here. Mason has a huge rooftop that you'll see after this drink." He sips his champagne and continues. "Mason is more Nate and Leo's friend since he's their age, but we're all close, it's the kind of thing where their friends are my friends. He's originally from Georgia, but they met at summer camp when they were younger."

"Ah, those rich kid camps where you slept there all summer and went horseback riding and took classes like pottery?" I ask playfully.

When I first started seeing Harrison, I was embarrassed to bring up our clear differences. But now, it's fun to tease him.

"Yes. Exactly that. However, Mason did not grow up privileged. He had gotten a scholarship to go because they have a well-known sports center."

"Huh, I wish I could picture him. I'm going to google him when I get home." The second I say it, the fire in Harrison's eyes burns wildly. I put my hands up in defense. "Not like that, crazy. So that I can put a face to the name."

"Let's not."

Hmm…if he's that worked up, that means this Mason guy is hot, hot.

His phone pings, and he picks it up quickly. "Claud or the Yankee score this time."

"Smartass." He sniggers. "No. But, good guess." He places my glass down, then his, and interlocks our fingers together. "This way, baby. Time for a surprise."

A surprise?

He walks back into the penthouse and up the smaller staircase off to the side that he was staring at before.

We get to the top, and he opens two large glass doors that lead us to a ginormous rooftop overlooking the same view of the East River. We haven't even stepped toward the ledge, and I can already see why up here is better. You have a full view of the Brooklyn and Manhattan Bridges. I bet if I walked around the side, I might be able to see the Statue of Liberty, too.

"Harr—"

"Mr. Davenport." An unfamiliar voice calls, causing me to jump.

Where the heck did he come from?

A man around my age is standing there off to the other side of the rooftop, holding a tray with two glasses of champagne.

And then I see candles…*a lot of candles.*

I'm not even sure what is going on yet, but the tears start welling up in my eyes. "Harrison," I whisper and lean into him, burying my head into his muscular chest. "What is this?" I squeeze his hand tightly.

"Come and see for yourself."

He leads the way toward the waiter, who passes Harrison and me another glass of champagne.

"Thank you," I say shyly. I'm feeling very overwhelmed right now.

Harrison hands him something, which I presume is a tip. "I know you were hired for the night, but you may go. I'll take it from here."

We both smile and thank the waiter. Then, as he leaves, neither of us misses it when he looks me up and down. Harrison stiffens in my arms and starts to turn us. "Harrison," I beg through clenched teeth. "Don't."

He doesn't listen.

Instead, he lets me go and walks toward the guy. Standing right in his face, he lowers his voice to a deathly level. "Word of advice if you want jobs like this again, you keep your fucking eyes to yourself."

I can tell by the waiter's shocked, wide eyes that he can't believe he got caught. I'm also shocked that was all Harrison said.

"Yes, sir. I'm sorry." He scurries away while Harrison walks back to me.

I love this side of him too much to scold him; he's what I want—possessive and jealous, and Harrison knows it.

He runs his hand down the length of my spine, then presses my lower back to gently guide me forward toward the glowing light, where more candles and flowers come into view.

Thousands of peonies fill the entire side of the rooftop.

My heart beats wildly as I stand there, shocked to the core.

Oh no.

When I barely start to wrap my head around the idea of us never having a future, he does this.

What does it mean?

Harrison has made it clear, on many occasions, that he's never had feelings for someone enough to do anything romantic for them. Yet, this is the most thoughtful, over-the-top, romantic thing anyone could do, especially because he remembered my favorite flower.

Becks might tell me I romanticize my life, but how can I not when there is a man who makes me feel like a princess? *No, a queen.*

I continue my inspection, taking in the rest of the space. There's a small bar in the corner, with bottles of champagne lined up. Next to that is a table for two, with silver platters, surrounded by more candles.

My breathing is coming out in fast succession through my nose as I try to calm my nerves. I'm afraid if I speak, I'll burst.

"Beautiful?"

I look up into those dazzling turquoise eyes, and I'm done for. "Harrison," I choke, not able to get anything else out.

He spins me around so he can hold me close to his body. I turn into him, then lift my arms so he'll pick me up. I need to be as close as possible.

As he lifts me, I kick off my shoes, then wrap my legs around him and bury my face into his neck.

When I get my breathing under control, I can finally speak. "How, why?"

He leans back, and when he knows I'll hold on, he lets go to hold my face in his palms. "The second I knew I'd disappointed you, I want to prove that you're worth more than being a secret."

A warm glow flows through my body while hope blooms. *This is more...it has to be.*

Then something comes to mind. "You didn't know we were leaving early, though."

"Lauren is a miracle worker. Robert helped, too."

I freeze. *Who the hell is Lauren?*

"Lauren is my assistant, Jules. She has connections all over the city and helped execute my plan."

I cringe. "Did I say that out loud?"

He kisses the tip of my nose. "No, my beautiful, jealous girl. But it was written all over your face."

"Oh..." Crazy thoughts start to circulate. Like, what does she look like?

I need to get a grip on this newfound jealousy and quickly. It's not a good look.

He walks us over to the table. "The fireworks start soon. Let's eat first so we can enjoy the show." He pats my behind, so I unlock my legs, and then he gently puts me on the ground, on the other side of the candles.

He looks down, narrowing his eyes. "What's wrong with your leg?"

"God, do you miss anything?" I huff. "It's just sore from a long day on it."

He bends to rub his hand up and down the side of my leg. "I'll massage you later. Do you need a painkiller?"

"No, it's only a little sore. I'm okay for now." I pat his cheek affectionately. He's a pain in my butt sometimes, but at least he cares.

He pulls out my chair for me to sit and refills our glasses. "What a gentleman." I smirk. "Thank you."

"Bon appétit."

He sits down, then leans over and picks both silver lids off our plates simultaneously, pulling a gasp right from my chest.

Blinking slowly, I adjust my sight to ensure I see this right.

Oh, Harrison Davenport, what are you doing to me?

I shake my head in disbelief, then push back my chair and round the table. I pick up my gown and straddle him so we're face to face, then kiss him tenderly. "Our dinner is hot dogs," I whisper with tears in my eyes.

He reaches up and traces the pad of his thumb along my cheekbone. "It's what you've always wanted."

I stare at him with an expectant look. "So you got me hot dogs and champagne?"

"Yes," he replies, not elaborating, but his steady eye contact and emotion-rich voice speak volumes.

I steeple my hands and press my fingers to my lips, wondering how I got so lucky. Never once would I have thought the older, dominant man in front of me would have turned out to be the one I'm falling madly in love with.

Or maybe I did because from the first night I saw him across the bar, he had me completely enamored before even speaking two words to each other.

Earlier, I thought my heart was playing tricks on me, but maybe it's just been as confused as I've been.

After all, my heart's never felt love like this before.

"Are you going to eat on my lap, baby?"

"I am," I say with reverence. "It's exactly where I want to be right now."

Both literally and figuratively, I want to live in this moment for as long as possible.

My body shivers in pleasure with each pass of Harrison's leisurely exploration.

"You cold?" he mumbles into the back of my neck, tickling my skin below his lips.

"No. I need you inside of me, Harrison. Please," I beg over the loud explosions of beautiful fireworks in front of us. "If you don't stop, I'm going to explode along with the show tonight, not you."

He nips at my skin, then trails wet kisses along the sweep of my neck; at the same time, I feel him shifting his body to pull down his pants.

Arching my back, I make room for him, then when he's ready, he grabs my hips and slowly guides me over his waiting cock. His swollen head coaxes me wide, causing my eyes to scrunch up at the burn.

"Easy, Jules. I didn't warm you up enough tonight," he warns, but my body isn't listening.

I use my muscular thighs to take over and sink down onto him.

"Fuck," he hisses, and at the same time, I throw my head back onto his shoulder, moaning loudly from the intense, overwhelming sensation.

He's massive, and it wouldn't have mattered if he warmed me up more or not. It's still the same feeling every single time we have sex.

Once I'm open for him, Harrison begins to move, and naturally, my hips rotate in sync with his.

"That feels good, baby," Harrison mutters as he pumps me with unhurried thrusts.

He wraps his thick corded arm around my middle to hold me

against his chest while his other hand has a tight grip on my hip, guiding me exactly how he wants it.

I lift my arm up and around his head, then turn into his neck, kissing him with an open mouth, peeking out my tongue to trace up along his skin just as he loves to do to me. Then I cup his cheek, turn his head, and kiss his red, plump lips with all my being.

The familiar burn starts to creep through my body, and I'm ready to let it go. It's been lingering in my core for the last thirty minutes as Harrison teased me for what he called delayed gratification.

"Harrison," I moan breathlessly against his mouth.

In front of us, bursts of colors are gaining momentum as they release into the sky.

"They're almost at the finale," Harrison calls over the increasingly loud booms. His hand snakes down between my legs, and I cry out in pleasure as he rubs my clit in a deep, pressured motion. His hips begin to pick up the pace, thrusting harder as the crescendo hits. "Yes, Jules. Let it go and show this city that when you explode, you're more beautiful than any of these fucking fireworks." He growls in my ear just as I scream my release, and my sex spasms around him, milking his own right out of him.

The telling jerk of his cock has barely finished when he flips me and glides me back over him, entering me quickly before he goes soft. Our eyes lock, and the same affection I felt earlier passes through us.

I cup his cheek and smile softly. "Harrison."

"I know, baby. I know," he whispers, then leans in and kisses me with a less animalist passion than usual.

This kiss is unhurried and full of warmth, and for the first time, we didn't have sex…we made the best kind of love.

———

"Eat up."

I look down at my pancake stack and can't possibly eat one more bite without bursting out of my pants.

I shake my head. "I can't. It's too much."

Harrison frowns and looks at my plate. "You never eat lunch, and you're always starving." He pauses to think. "I'll have Lauren send you something later."

"Don't you dare make your assistant send me lunch, Harrison. I'll die a million deaths of embarrassment."

He looks at me deadpan. "Dramatic much?"

"I'm not kidding. Don't do it. Go to the Hamptons to see Claud and pretend I eat three meals daily."

He looks down at his overly expensive watch. "I should get going to the office to get this meeting out of the way. Already as is, I'm going to hit bad traffic."

"Why don't you take a helicopter? Wouldn't that be quickest? It's not like you can't afford it."

He chuckles through a sip of his coffee. "I thought about it. I love driving, though, even if I hit some traffic."

After paying, he walks me a few blocks to the bakery.

I was able to get Daphne to open so I could enjoy a morning with Harrison before he left for the next three nights.

He tugs my hand to get my attention. "Can you do something for me?" He kisses the back of it, and with his lips pressed against my skin, he looks me in the eye. "When I'm gone, I want you to ask your mom for a day off. You more than deserve it, and everyone's back, so she has coverage."

I nod. "Okay." Then smile wide.

He has no idea. Mom already gave me the rest of the week off after today. So I'll have plenty of time to rest and recuperate.

He wraps his arms around me. "You already have off, don't you?"

I smile and nod again. "Yup. After today, I have off until I teach class on Monday. So when you get home, we'll have the last three days uninterrupted besides your work."

"That sounds perfect. I'll try to shift things around so we can spend all the time together." He pauses and thinks. "What will you do when I'm gone if you have off?"

"Number one priority is getting back to my morning routine of walks in Central Park. There's a music installation of classical composers at The Met I'd like to see, and I'm sure one night I'll grab dinner with Becks."

"Mmm," he says, unimpressed.

I roll my eyes, and he calls me dramatic. "What is it, Harrison?"

"Nothing. Just be careful, please. The only times I've ever seen you drink a lot is with Becks."

His phone beeps. "Shit. This meeting just got moved." He calls Robert to get him now.

"If you want to wait, I'll go to The Met with you." He leans down and brushes his lips against mine.

I'm going to miss kissing him the most. We're both addicted.

"You hate classical music."

"Yeah, it's shit." He laughs and shrugs. "It puts me to sleep. What can I say."

"It's fine, I'll go with Mom," I tell him, and then we stand looking at each other for a few moments.

Something's been on my mind the last few days, and I can't hold it in any longer. "Harrison?"

He runs his hand down my face, cupping my neck. "Yes, beautiful?" I lean into his hold, hoping I never have to forget this feeling.

"What happens when Claudina comes home?"

He stills and sighs, taking a deep breath like he's relieved I asked it. "I don't have the answers for you, Juliette. I wish I did because, trust me, I've been thinking about it too."

Robert pulls the Bentley up to the curb, and the mood is gloomy. Maybe it was the wrong time to bring it up, but I couldn't stand holding it in a moment more.

We kiss goodbye, and then Harrison takes a step back. "We'll figure it out, baby. Okay?"

I nod. "See you in three days." I wave and blow him a kiss.

Once he's out of sight, I turn and bump straight into my mom.

"Are you okay, my love?"

I shrug because I genuinely don't know. "I have a bad feeling."

"No negative energy, Juliette." She hugs me tight, then leans back to look me in the eyes. "Harrison is a good man. Before I knew anything about him, I could tell just by how he was with his daughter. So if there is a way, he will make it happen."

"I hope you're right," I mumble.

She rubs my arms affectionately. "I don't know if it's an easy journey between the two of you, but a rocky journey to the end is better than no journey at all."

15

Harrison

I TURN down the music and dial Matteo. "Hello?" his voice comes over the car speaker.

"Hey, can you do me a favor but keep it between us?" I ask.

"Yeah, no problem."

"You can't tell Becks. It's nothing bad, but until I have answers, I don't want to mention it."

"Well, how about you tell me first, and then I'll see if I can keep it from her."

What?

"That defeats the whole fucking purpose of me saying to keep it a secret."

He laughs over the line. "True. Okay, fine. I won't say anything."

This idiot is making me nervous he's going to slip, but I have no other choice.

"Can you look into who is buying Juliette's building?"

"Yeah. No problem. What's going on?"

I rub my temple with my free hand, unsure. "Something feels off with how the building management is handling it. I could be overreacting, but I'd rather make sure." I hear him typing, probably already looking into it. "How's Tramonto doing? Killer season for rooftops."

"It's doing great. We couldn't have asked for a better opening. Damn, sorry, my four o'clock is here. I've got to go. I'll look into this and get back to you ASAP."

"Thanks, appreciate it. Talk soon."

The large, weathered mahogany gates to our Bridgehampton home open as my car pulls up. The sensor is broken, one of my brothers must have seen me on the security camera and opened it.

It feels nice to be back here. It's been a while since we've all been together.

Usually, we all come out to the house as much as possible, but work has been crazier than ever for both Seb and myself.

Nate and Leo built this house from the ground up three years ago, so they like to be out here even more now to enjoy their handy work.

We chose to be inland over the beach to get fifteen acres for Claudina to enjoy running in the grass, using the tennis courts, pools— whatever her little heart desires.

This, of course, piqued people's interest. No one understood why four billionaires would share a house. There was even a goddamn article written about it as if they have nothing else in the world to report about.

Either way, it will never change, If we're out here with Claudina, none of us would want to sacrifice our time with her. Plus, who the hell needs that much space? We could all have five kids, and still share.

The guest house alone has three bedrooms. It's typically where Leo stays since he's the one who brings women home on a regular basis, and there's no fucking way he's coming into the house with Claudina there.

As I make it down our long, tree-lined drive, I see my angel standing at the end, jumping up and down once she spots my car.

I beep the horn, rev the engine, and fly down the rest of the way.

She cups her mouth and yells, I can't hear her over my V12 engine, but it's cute to watch her get excited.

The second the car turns off, she's running down the porch front steps right into my arms. I spin her around as she squeals. I hadn't realized how much I missed her until now.

It was an odd feeling the past week and a half having Jules with me every night. She made me forget a lot about my reality—not that I would ever forget about Claud—but she made me feel alive, more than I have in a long time, and tricked me into thinking maybe there's a possibility for a life outside the one I live.

My stomach twists.

It's the same one I get whenever I think of her…or of the what if *she was* my reality. Only I need to stop my thoughts from wandering too far because lately, it's all I've thought of.

A life with Jules.

It feels like it could be perfection but completely out of reach.

Claud lifts her head from my shoulder and scrunches her face. "I don't like when you drive that car."

"Oh, angel, I know. It was the only car for me to drive from the city. I'll drive the Jeep while I'm here."

Claud is the only person I'd happily trade my Bugatti Mistral for. The Bugatti is a two-door convertible I got for fun. Not for my daughter.

There is no way in hell she'll ever be allowed in that thing.

"With the sides off?" Her eyes jump in excitement.

"Only near the beach or town when we're driving slower," I remind her.

She jumps down and takes my hand to drag me toward the house. "Or you can drive Uncle Leo's new car. I think that's my favorite."

I look around the driveway and spot the brand-new custom Land Rover Defender.

"Did this just get delivered?" I ask her.

She nods. "Yesterday. We rode to Grandma's for breakfast, and he let me blast all my favorite songs."

"That's because he's a good uncle. Where is he and the rest of your uncles, anyway?"

"By the pool. Will you change right away and come out to swim? I've been waiting all day for you."

I pick her back up and squeeze her to my chest. "I know I'm sorry, Claud. I got stuck in a meeting, and then it was too late. Traffic was terrible." I kiss her forehead and put her back down. "I'm here for three days, and then you come home three days after that."

"Okay!" She smiles wide, then does a pirouette before taking off toward the backyard.

Seeing her do that reminds me of Juliette and what she suggested.

I don't think Claud will be too happy, but I hope she'll listen if I tell her Jules said so. Naturally, my thoughts go back to my Juliette and how I'm not the only one with a soft spot for her. Claud adores her too.

"Fuck. I needed this." I lean my head back on the lounge chair and bask in the sun after three hours of switching on and off between diving competitions and cannon balls.

"Same. We've been traveling nonstop. I'm exhausted," Nate says from beside me.

"When do you leave again?"

"Next week. I'm not back until it's my turn to take Claud." He shakes his head, annoyed. "I think it will be my longest time away from her."

I lift my beer to my lips but realize it's empty, and I have no strength to walk the two feet to the outdoor bar for another one.

"She'll miss you, but honestly, two weeks away from home is a lot. She's missed several dance classes, and although she seems okay, I think it will take her a while to acclimate back to city life."

The back door opens. "Ah, yes. Leo, coming in clutch." I take the beer bottle from him. "Thanks."

"Daddy! Look at me," Claud screams. I look up and see her getting set up in the first position. "Are you watching?"

"Yes, Claud. We're all watching." I tell her. Then she jumps, *or rather sautes*, five times, and on her fifth, she jumps forward into the pool.

Skye gets soaked, and I think she's had enough, so she takes off and jumps up to lie between Nate's legs.

Claud swims to the top and over to the steps. "Did you see? Pool ballet is soooo cool."

"The coolest." I give her a thumbs-up while she runs over and does it again.

Laying back down, I think how I miss being out here all summer. The smell of freshly cut grass, drinking around the pool, barbecues, and bonfires.

Work has been insanely busy, and I'm still a new, young CEO; I want to prove that I deserve the position, so I need to be available in the city.

"Let's do a bonfire on the beach by Mom and Dad tomorrow night," I tell Leo, knowing he'll set it all up.

My phone pings, and the second I see her name, I can't stop the smile stretching my face. I turn, and Nate and Leo are staring at me, unsurprisingly.

"You better turn into the world's best actor in about two minutes. Seb was finishing up his call when I came out here."

"No clue what you're talking about." I put the phone down even though it's killing me inside, not knowing what she said...what if she needs me?

Goddammit, I lean back over and grab my phone. I have no restraint when it comes to Juliette.

> Thank you so much, Harrison. I love the new lingerie. It's too expensive, but I appreciate it nonetheless. It's exactly something I would pick out. xx

I know it is.

After I dropped off Jules the other day, I was late for my meeting because I passed La Perla. Staring at me in the window was the most delicate-looking lace bra and panty set in lavender and ice blue that was almost silver.

With her love for beautifully designed lingerie, I knew I needed to get it for her.

> You're welcome, baby. What are you doing?

Thinking of you xx

Following the text is a picture of her butterfly mask on a shelf in what I presume is her room.

> You were so fucking hot that night, but I think you'd be hotter if you wore it while I watched you take my cock like the good girl that you are. Will you wear it when I fuck you, beautiful Juliette?

Of course. I'd do anything for you ;)

> Anything, huh?

Within reason...

> You just opened up a door of opportunities for us, baby. You have no idea.

Like what, H?

> H?

Quicker to type out, I guess.

I like it.

Why I like that she has a nickname for me, I have no clue.

H it is... so back to what you were saying.

Eager, are we?

Let's call it curious. I like thinking about us together.

What are you doing right now?

Laying in bed...all alone.

"Are you fucking kidding me?" Nate snaps from beside me, looking down as my hand adjusts myself.

"Fuck off," I grumble, ignoring him.

Trust me. Tonight will be misery without you.

So you're alone...

Yes.

Suddenly, I'm in her bedroom with her.

Her raspy voice breathes out a yes, and even though I'm not actually there, I can hear it like I'm right next to her in bed.

I envision her lying down, her dark hair splayed out on her pillow, her plump lips parted, while her breath comes out quickly like it does whenever she's turned on. Her long, thick lashes flutter as her big, brown, willing eyes stare back at me, begging me to touch her.

But I'm not there.

And besides me, there is only one other person that can touch my pussy…

> Jules, baby. Touch yourself. Tell me if you're wet.

H…

> Do it. Now.

Okay. But, H… I'm talking to you. Even without hearing your voice, I already know I'm wet.

Fuck.

> Do you want to play, beautiful?

Play?

God, her innocence gets me every time.

"Daddy?"

Shit. "Yes, angel?" I throw my phone down guiltily as if suddenly Claud had x-ray vision to see through the back of my phone.

"What's for dinner?"

I chuckle. "Why are you hungry?"

She brushes her wet, long, dark hair away from her face for me to see her wide smile. "Yes, starving."

"Uncle Seb is going to barbecue. Why don't you tell him to hurry up with his work and grab yourself a snack for now? I cut up some fruit for you in the fridge, and Willa sent over a loaf of your favorite banana bread." Her eyes widen with excitement, not for the fruit but at the prospect of having a cheeseburger, then she takes off running toward the house. "Dry off before you go in the house, Claudina!" I yell after her, probably too late.

H... I'm waiting. Not so patiently.

Tonight, Juliette, when I FaceTime you, I want you naked, on your back, legs spread open and ready.

I put my phone away, smiling, thinking of her shocked face.

Jules, although she is opening up much more, talks a big game. I'm not sure if she's trying to please me or trick herself, but she's still my innocent girl who is finding her sexuality more each time we're together.

Nate says something quietly to Leo, and I hear my name in passing. "What?" I ask.

They pause and look up. "I haven't seen you smile like that in a long time, and come to think of it, you're not as grumpy as normal," Nate says. "She's good for you."

Before I can answer, the back door opens, and Seb stands there looking ridiculous. He has a shirt and suit jacket on, with his board shorts on the bottom.

Leo lifts his hand to block the sun, staring at Seb. "Fuck, you're a big motherfucker."

Seb smirks, and I can't hold in my laughter. Leo lacks a filter more than half the time, but he's not wrong.

Seb is the tallest and most muscular one out of all of us, and in the shadow of the sun, he's a fucking giant.

"Anyone need another beer?" Seb asks as he walks over to the bar, taking off his suit top.

"Me," Nate calls.

Seb clearly was on a video call, so they didn't see his bottom half, which reminds me of a story. "Did I ever tell you guys about the time one of the board members started getting naked on a call?"

"No." Leo chuckles.

"Mark, who has to be reaching eighty-five easily, never knows how to set up his video calls properly. One day, the whole board was on, and he was dressed similarly to Seb. Then he gets up to grab a file, and he's fucking commando."

"Buck naked?" Nate asks, laughing.

"Wrinkly balls and all." We all burst out in laughter, and I shiver in disgust. "I don't know why I brought that up. I'm getting flashbacks now."

"Worst fucking nightmare," Leo mutters.

"How many times are you naked on your calls?"

"Never, but I want to be. You have no idea how many times I think about jerking off while on a call with Jasmine. She is so fucking hot I don't even listen to her half the time she's talking. I stare at her lips moving, imagining them around my dick."

"You're a dirty bastard." Seb laughs.

"Who's Jasmine?" I ask.

"Our Miami liaison," Nate answers. "And she's a fucking smoke show."

Seb hands Leo his beer. "I can top Harrison's story," Seb chimes in. "One of our vendors thought because everyone had their camera off, and he couldn't see them, that his was off, too. So he set his laptop up on the bathroom counter and then began to get undressed in front of us. He was on mute, so he didn't hear us screaming his name to stop. Then he stepped into the shower and stood there full frontal with his hard-on hanging between his legs."

"Bullshit." I laugh.

"Swear it. He was definitely about to jerk it until finally, someone called him. Luckily, his volume was turned up."

"Hi!"

Seb's eyes widen, and he looks at me in horror. We really need to be better about censoring ourselves. Claud loves to pop out of nowhere. "Hi, princess." He picks her up and snuggles her. "You want me to start grilling soon?"

"Mmmhmm," she says around a mouthful of banana bread. She's a bottomless pit. She could always eat. "Will you make me a cheeseburger and grilled corn, please?"

"Of course, is that it?"

She narrows her eyes, thinking. "Well, what are you having?"

"Steak and some grilled veggies. Grandma made us both macaroni and potato salad. She also made a watermelon feta salad."

She scrunches her nose at the watermelon salad. "With that green stuff in it?"

Seb chuckles, then throws her up like she weighs nothing.

Claudina is growing by the minute, but in Seb's arms, she looks minuscule.

"You mean mint? Yes, but I can take it out for you."

"Okay!" She giggles as he throws her up again. "Can I have a little of all the food?"

"You're going to eat the vegetables?" I ask, doubtful.

She nods enthusiastically. "I love asparagus now. Do we have that?"

I look at her with a wary expression.

"Mom made it the other day, and she ate it all," Leo tells me.

Claud jumps out of Seb's arms. "Oh! Then, can we all bake something for dessert? Pleaseeeee? I want to go home on Monday and tell Juliette everything I baked here."

"She doesn't stop talking about her baking teacher. Have any of you met her?" Seb asks.

Nate chokes on his beer, and Leo chuckles.

Fucking idiots.

"What?" Seb narrows his look between the three of us.

I'm not answering this. I don't want to lie, but I can't tell the truth either, so I turn and give them a look to help me.

"We've all met her at one time or another. She's fucking hot, is all," Leo says, his eyes shining bright as I give him a death stare. He leans back in his chair, crossing his legs, loving every bit of this. "Like ten out of ten hot."

"What's hot mean?" Claud asks.

"It means she's beautiful," Nate interjects.

Claud nods, smiling as she agrees. "Yeah, she's sooo pretty, and guess what?"

"What?" Seb says.

"She used to be a ballerina, just like I'm going to be."

"Hmm," Seb says, running his teeth along his bottom lip. "Maybe I need to stop by and see the infamous Juliette." His eyes widen. "You know, so that I can see what the fuss is all about. Do a little inspection of my own."

"Definitely. Do it." Nate nods his head encouragingly.

Then, when Claud is not looking, Seb whispers, "She single? I bet she's bendy as fuck."

"Oh yeah, she's single. No commitment in sight," Leo adds, smirking, and my breathing picks up to an ungodly pace.

I'm going to kill these two with my bare hands.

"So, baking. Yes, right?" Claud interrupts, thank God, jumping up and down.

Nate groans, "Not again, Claud."

She puts her hands on her hips, walks over to Nate, and then points at him. "You're the one who tripped. You can't blame anyone but yourself."

Why does she sound like she's fifty-five scolding her child?

I love seeing her like this, though. Claud is often soft-spoken and shyer around her peers, but she lets her true self shine when she's comfortable.

"What happened?" I ask.

She rolls her eyes. "Uncle Nate broke an egg, and it fell on the floor." She throws her hands up. "Juliette tells us to keep everything clean. If you do, it helps with accidents, andddd I told him that. Then he slipped on it, and when he grabbed the counter, he hit the bowl of flour, and it went everywhere."

Leo, Seb, and I can't control our laughter, and when we calm down, I look around at my brothers. Although, at the moment, I'm murderous and wish they would disappear from my sight for their comments, I couldn't be happier to be here with them this week.

Suddenly Claud sucks in a breath and points.

The four of us go entirely still.

I roll my lips and turn, watching Seb lock his jaw and run his hands over his face.

"Fuck," he breathes out, holding back all his emotions while the rest of us watch in silence as a colorful butterfly flutters around and lands on his shoulder.

She's here.

Never one to miss out on the fun.

My phone rings, and I smile when I see my girl's name light up. "Hi baby, I'm leaving soon to see you."

"Harrison," she purrs. "I'm so excited you have no idea."

What the. "Are you drunk right now?" I look at my watch. It's one o'clock on a Friday.

"Mmm. Maybe?" She hiccups. "I went to brunch with Becks and Adriana. Becks took a personal day."

Then I hear loud bursts of laughter coming from somewhere nearby, including men.

"Who is that, Juliette?" I snap into the phone.

"Who?"

Then I hear the voices again. "The fucking guys I hear in the background."

"Oh." She giggles but doesn't answer.

"Juliette, so help me, God, answer the fucking question." I clench my jaw from really losing it. I have no patience left in me after the last few days.

Fucking Nate and Leo were egging Seb on about Juliette, and I couldn't say a thing about it.

"What was the question again?" She laughs, then covers the phone. "It's Harrison," she tells someone.

"Juliette," I shout out of frustration.

"Oh yeah, sorry. I don't know who the guys are. They keep trying to talk because they're sitting next to us. They're from Australia. How cool is that?"

I close my eyes and take a deep breath. "Stop talking to fucking strangers, Juliette. Especially men. What did I tell you about going out with Becks?"

Becks is a good friend. I can tell she cares for Juliette deeply, but unlike Juliette, she also has a wild side.

"I rarely drink. I'm just having fun. Don't be such a stick-in-the-mud," she sasses while the voices and the music get louder, so I can barely hear her. "I'm going to go outside. Hold on."

"Oh my god, what the hell, you jerk!" she yells. Then I hear a big thud, and Juliette begins to yell out in pain.

Panic rushes in. What was that? "Juliette, what's wrong?" I yell down the line while she's yelling hysterically. "Jules, baby, please talk to me."

"Hello?" Becks says down the line in fear.

"Becks," I snap, pissed off at her. "What the hell is going on?"

I can hear a tremble in her voice. "Some idiot kicked out his leg and tripped Juliette. But Harrison—"

"What? What is it?"

She lowers her voice. "I'm scared. She's crying a lot and holding her bad leg." *Fuck!* "Should I take her to the hospital? I'm so worried."

I roll my neck a few times to calm myself. Making Becks more stressed out is not going to help the situation, even though I want to strangle her at the moment.

"Help her up, and call her ortho doctor first. Then put her on the phone."

"Okay. Okay," she says nervously.

She puts down the phone, and I hear Juliette's shrieks as Becks helps her.

"Just hold on, Harrison. Give her a second," Becks says.

I look down at my hand, and it's shaking from nerves. I've never felt so uneasy and helpless in my life.

You know what?

I put the phone on speaker, then go to my texts and ask our company pilot if he can bring me back to the city. He's in the Hamptons with his helicopter, and I could be back there in no time.

I hear a rustling on the phone, and my girl's voice comes through. "Harrison? I'm sorry," she sobs. "It wasn't my fault, I promise."

"I know, baby. What hurts?"

"I don't know, my whole leg." She starts to hyperventilate, and I think I'm going to have a full-on panic attack if I can't get to her soon.

"Jules, I'll be there shortly. I'm going to take a helicopter. Can you please have Becks call your doctor?"

"She's on the phone with Mom now to get the info," she whispers. "I'm sorry." She cries again.

"It's okay, beautiful. You're going to be okay." I say to soothe her, not knowing if that's the truth at all.

"Daddy!" Claud's voice suddenly booms through my open window from the backyard. "Daddy! Help me!" She screams louder than I could ever imagine possible from her, and then one second later, I hear Nate's voice screaming at Skye.

"Daddy!"

I sprint down the stairs, realizing once I get to the back doors, I ran so fast to Claudina on instinct that I dropped my phone upstairs, but Jules is in good hands with Beck.

I hope.

I slide the glass doors open. "What's going on?" I scream in distress, feeling completely out of my mind.

Claudina stands there, shaking down to the core in Leo's arms. Once she sees me, she screams my name and runs for me.

I pick her up and cradle her against my chest, and I can feel her pulse thumping hard against mine.

"Is Skye okay, Daddy? Please tell me she's okay." She blubbers through her tears.

I look around, and I turn Claud's head so she doesn't see Skye in Nate's arms, full of blood.

"What happened?" I mouth to Leo, but he doesn't answer, paying full attention to his dog, full of worry.

When Nate approaches, Leo gets up and grabs his car keys.

"Claud, sweetheart, Skye is okay, but we'll bring her to the doctor just incase. But she's okay," Nate reassures her as he passes.

"Okay," she whispers into my chest. "I love you, Skye. Thank you for saving me."

I rub a soothing hand up and down Claud's back. "Angel? What happened?"

She tightens her hold around my neck and begins to cry again. "This is all my fault."

"What is Claud? Talk to me, please. Daddy is getting nervous."

"I was playing fetch with Skye." She sniffles and wipes her runny nose on my shirt. "And I accidentally threw her ball near where the fence is broken."

This still doesn't explain why she's so shaken up, and Skye is covered in blood.

"Then what."

"She couldn't find the ball, so I was helping her when all of a sudden, I looked up, and a huge buck was standing there staring at me. It was so scary. That's when I screamed for you, I think I scared the deer, so it started running toward me. I started screaming more, and Skye saved me and attacked the deer to stop it."

You've got to be kidding me. Three weeks ago, I told our maintenance guy that the fence needed to be fixed. The second I'm back in the city, he will be hearing from me, and he'll be lucky if he has a job anymore.

This situation could have been worse for Claud had Skye not been there to protect her, and I can only hope that Skye is okay.

She might not live in our house, but she is Claud's pride and joy, and it will devastate her if she doesn't pull through.

I walk us back into the house and bring Claud to the couch to put her down, but she starts screaming, furiously shaking her head. "No. No, I want to stay with you."

"Okay. Calm down, angel. You can stay with me as long as you want."

She tightens her grip around me. "I want to go home today, Daddy. Can we, when we know Skye is all right?"

I blow out a breath. "Okay, angel. We can go home. I need to grab my phone upstairs. Can I put you down, or do you want me to carry you there and back?"

She thinks about it momentarily. "You can put me down if you promise to come right back."

"Of course, Claud. We can watch a movie after until we hear from Uncle Nate or Uncle Leo." I kiss her forehead, then run upstairs to grab my phone.

I call Juliette, and it goes straight to voicemail. On my way downstairs, I try two more times. Nothing.

Then I text Matteo for Becks's number.

Again nothing.

What the actual fuck is going on? I need to be one hundred percent present for Claud right now, and I won't be able to do that if I don't get a hold of Juliette.

"Dad! It's been more than a minute."

I suck in a deep breath and wonder if I'll ever get a break in life.

Then I text Jules to see how she's feeling and head back to my precious girl.

Juliette

"Come on, Jules lay down. You need to sleep," Becks begs me. "You're exhausted, and you need to elevate your leg."

Luckily, there was no real damage to my leg, only bad luck the way I fell. Now it's mostly swollen and sore.

"What if he calls while I'm sleeping? I don't want to miss it." I've been waiting for Harrison but haven't heard back.

We played phone tag earlier, and then it completely stopped. I thought he'd be knocking on my door like a madman soon after.

Yet…nothing.

"Jules," she sighs. "He's not calling babe. He would have already."

My heart drops, and I feel sick to my stomach. "I don't understand. He was so concerned earlier, and now he's not answering his phone or texting me back." For the twentieth time today, I feel the tears prick the back of my eyes. "What if something happened?"

I can see Becks is annoyed, but she's trying to keep it together for me.

"Matteo lands in Italy in one hour. I'll have him reach out to Harrison and all his brothers the second he does. Okay?"

"Yeah. Okay," I whisper, and then she props my legs up.

She gets in next to me and hugs me tight. "I set my alarm in case I fall asleep and miss when Matteo calls."

I love her.

"Thank you." I squeeze her arms.

Where are you, Harrison?

Please be okay.

16

Juliette

"I'm sorry you wasted your time, but I'm not moving or commuting to Brooklyn," I explain to Barbara, the realtor, in the kindest voice possible.

She is trying. I'll give her that. This space is unbelievable, except I'll never get Mom here, and to be honest, I don't want to leave the city and live in Brooklyn alone.

Her face drops, exasperated.

Nothing she's shown me in the last two weeks would work besides this place.

In Brooklyn.

"The train ride is almost the same as it is to go downtown. Remember that this neighborhood lost their beloved bakery, so they're looking for another one. You would have instant customers."

The way she says *you would* has me freezing in place, and suddenly, I'm in another world having a revelation.

You would have instant customers…not Mom or anyone else.

Me.

My stomach twists, and I can't decipher my feelings.

Working all together in the bakery Mom created has always felt familiar to me. When I had time off, I often worked there during my teenage years, so it only felt natural to step in when my career ended.

Now that it's all changing, it's hitting me that this is my new life. One I never saw for myself or ever imagined. *One I'm not sure I truly want.*

I should be grateful I had something to fall back on and that I'm getting to take over the business my mom put her heart and soul into. Even more so that she trusts me with it.

When did everything in my *new* life start to fall into place without me realizing it?

The more important question is…is it falling into the right places?

My phone dings, and I rush to open my bag, leaving my thoughts behind. When I see it's a text from Becks, my stomach drops, and my heart aches from disappointment.

Just another thing to add to the list of confusions.

My contact with Harrison has been minimal since my fall at the boozy brunch that Becks dragged me to.

He apologized and explained what happened to Claud. I knew something was off that day, and thankfully, everything turned out fine. I'm okay, Claud's okay, and her beloved Skye is making a speedy recovery.

My leg might be okay—my heart—not so much.

With Claud home now, sleeping at Harrison's is out of the question, and he has wanted to spend most of his time with her since she's been gone. On top of that, he had a business trip that's been planned for a while.

We've tried to make plans, however with our conflicting schedules and the need for our "relationship" to stay semi-private, we've seen one another twice in the last three weeks, and recently, the phone calls and texts have diminished as well.

Of course, I knew this was coming; I just hoped it wouldn't.

"Are you okay, Juliette?" Barbara asks, and I realize I'm still standing there quietly, staring at an unlit cell phone.

Dropping my shoulders, I swallow my feelings and nod. "Yes. I have to get back to the bakery, though," I tell her, making plans to see more places next week before leaving.

Deciding I'm not ready to go home, I walk toward the East River and admire the skyline of the greatest city in the world, my home, and take a moment for myself.

I'm trying my hardest not to focus on the fact that I'm standing directly across the river from where I had the most amazing date of my life only a few weeks ago.

I lean my head back to let the sunshine warm my face, let my thoughts run free, and suddenly get an idea. Instead of returning to the bakery, I lie to my mom for the first time and tell her we're still looking at spaces, then get an Uber to Westchester and visit my father's grave.

"Juliette, my love," Mom whispers as she opens my bedroom door. I know I need to get up to open the bakery, but I can't move this morning. My body is tired, my head hurts, and I'm feeling completely out of my skin…a shell of a human.

I need to get out of this funk soon—I'm sick of crying and feeling sorry for myself.

It's freaking exhausting.

She walks over and sits on the side of my bed, brushing my hair back from my forehead as she looks down at me, watching closely as I hold Dad's sweatshirt to my chest.

Closing my eyes so she doesn't see my pain, I pull my knees to my chest and bury my head in the sweatshirt, inhaling the scent of my father to comfort me.

I miss you so much, Dad.

Since visiting his grave at the beginning of the week, I haven't slept much. Last night, though, for no particular reason, was worse than the others.

I stayed up and talked to him for hours, wishing he was here with me, needing his advice and comfort.

God, even one hug from him would make me feel whole again.

I scrunch my eyes, not wanting to think like this anymore, but at the same time, I can't stop. I want this nightmare to end, for him to come home where he belongs.

With me and Mom.

Over the past year that he's been gone, I've never missed him more. I feel sick to my stomach that I have to live the rest of my life without my best friend.

I open my mouth to talk, but the tears blinding my eyes choke me up, and I can't get out the words.

Mom maneuvers herself against my pillow, then pulls me down so I can lay my head in her lap as she lightly strokes my hair. She's been doing this since I was a little girl, and I'll never be too old for the comforting gesture. "Have you spoken to Harrison?" she asks softly.

I shake my head. This isn't about him. *Not entirely.* I feel so out of my element in every aspect. I needed the comfort of my dad, even if it was a stone in the ground or a sweatshirt around my body, but unlike other times since his passing, those comforts weren't enough, and now I'm stuck in a perpetual state of hopelessness.

"I miss him so much," I sob. "It's not fair. Why did he have to die?"

My mom stills, I can feel it under my body, then lets out a long-winded breath. It's hard for her, too. She doesn't like to talk about it, but I can't hold this in any longer.

"Is this why you've been crying all week? I've given you your space because I thought it was about Harrison."

I nod into her lap. "I'm sorry. I didn't know you could hear me. I…" My voice trails off, unsure how Mom will take this, admitting this to her.

"What is it?"

"Please don't be mad, but I went to Daddy's grave. I needed to feel close to him. I think the mix of my grief and the lack of communication with Harrison has made me begin to lose it."

She pulls my ponytail, so I looked up at her. "Ow. What the heck?" I narrow my eyes. "Why are you smirking?"

"I visit your father all the time. Why would I be mad?"

I sit up in a rush. "You do what?" I ask in disbelief. "I always tell you when I go, except this one time. Why would you keep that from me?"

"Because look what it's done to you. Am I sad? Am I depressed? Yes, I lost the love of my life, and I will never love again. But when I visit his grave, I leave it there. Otherwise, I'd never move on with life. I think of him every day. How you talk to him often, though, like he's still here, would kill me slowly. We mourn in different ways, and every time we've ever gone to his grave, you regress into a deeper depression, and I don't like seeing you like that. So stick with your talks at night, and I'll visit him. What's not okay is to sit here and cry for days on end." She widens her eyes. "Do those words sound familiar?" she accuses, then stands up. "Come on."

I stand up and throw my arms around my mom. "I love you."

"I love you too, my love." She hugs me tightly, then leans back and kisses my cheek.

"I'm sorry, we're going to be so late."

"I texted Daphne last night to cover for you. After you're showered and dressed, we'll stop down to make sure everything is okay, and then I'm taking my sweet daughter out to breakfast."

Standing there, dumbfounded, I'm wondering who this person is and who has abducted my mother.

She walks out of my room, then turns back. "Chop, chop!"

"Are my eyes swollen?" I ask as my mom holds the bakery door open for me.

"Yes."

The French, they don't mince their words. "Thanks," I mumble.

"Oh, there she is!" Alice calls.

I look up and freeze.

Oh no.

Today is not the day to mess with my emotions.

Harrison walks over, kisses Mom hello, and then turns toward me.

"Hi, beautiful." His deep, familiar voice mutters as he leans down and kisses my cheek. Nothing slips by him, though, so the second he's up close, he narrows his eyes in confusion while he stares at my face. "What's wrong?"

"Allergies," I lie.

His nostrils flair at my easy lie; he's never been one to miss something about me, and he knows allergies are not what is causing my red face.

As I walk past him, the heat from his body trails behind me. "Juliette."

Rounding the counter, I use it as a shield. "Did you need something, Harrison? I'm about to grab breakfast with my mom."

His face falls, and then he shakes his head, hesitating momentarily. He might be taken aback by my stark tone, but today, I am on the brink and will break if he says anything nice to me or anything at all.

"No, I don't need anything," he says, though the hitch in his tone tells me differently.

Chancing a glimpse up at him, something I was attempting to avoid, not wanting to get sucked into his power over me, I see a different man standing in front of me than I'm used to.

Still perfectly put together in his dark, expensive suit, fitted to his muscular physique, but the dark circles and the beard stubble he typically only leaves for the weekend is telling me maybe he's not okay either.

"H…" I whisper.

"Can I get a box of your favorites to bring to the office? It's Lauren's birthday."

I pause with my hand outreached.

Feeling like a complete fool, I pull it back slowly. "Sure. No problem."

I make the box with neither of us saying a word to the other. You can cut the tension with a knife, not just from us. I can feel Mom and Alice watching our every move.

"Tell her I say happy birthday." I fake a smile and pass over the box, then wave him off when he tries to pay.

His chest expands while he takes a deep breath through his nose, then hesitates in front of the counter before attempting to leave. He turns back halfway, not looking me in the eyes. "I miss you too, you know," he mutters, then walks out without a second look.

"Are you okay?"

I jump at my mom's words. "No." I shake my head. "I'm not."

Harrison

"Happy birthday." I throw the box of pastries on the table next to Lauren's desk and continue to my office.

I'll properly wish her a happy birthday and give her the real present when I calm myself. I can't handle her third degree this morning.

After I slam my door shut and sit at my desk, my door creaks open. I should have known she would barge in. "You've been crankier than normal all week, and then you mentioned you were stopping at the bakery. I wanted to check on you." She pauses, looking me up and down. "Are you okay?"

I shake my head, annoyed at myself. I'm a fucking douchebag.

"Come here." I hold out my arms and wrap her in a hug. "I'm sorry. You shouldn't have to deal with my shit today. Happy birthday, Lauren."

She rubs my back, then steps back, smiling. "You pay me well to deal with your shit."

"True. But today, you're off the hook." I wink.

She rolls her eyes, as usual, then goes and sits in my chair, forcing me to sit on the couch.

"How are you really, Harrison? You don't look like yourself," she asks, swiveling my chair.

Roughly running my hands up and down my face, I lean over, resting my elbows on my knees.

"Fucked up the ass, to put it lightly." I laugh sarcastically.

Lauren knows all about Jules. After the date she helped me set up, she wouldn't leave me alone until I spilled my guts, and now that I have, she's relentless.

"How was she when you saw her this morning? I thought you were going to ask her to breakfast."

Beautiful as always, except so fucking sad looking. "She had plans with her mom, but she had been crying, and it killed me leaving her there like that." I take a deep break, then lean back. "Seeing her like that makes me physically ache."

"Harrison, look at me." Reluctantly, my attention moves toward her. "Do you love her?"

I blow out a breath, thinking about this, and shrug. "I'm falling for her hard. But the shit thing about it is I can't go on like this anymore."

She stops swiveling, looking at me with confusion. "What do you mean?"

"I either need to talk to Seb or completely end it with her. It's not fair to either of us to string this along if I keep us in the dark. No matter what bullshit I said, she and I always knew, this was never casual. From day one, she was always more, *always mine*. But my complicated life is stopping us."

"Option one should be your only choice. Don't let this slip away. You said she's amazing with Claud, and I've never seen you talk or act like this over a woman."

"Claudina's obsessed with her. If Jules was around more, in a more permanent way, I already know she'd be thrilled. A big part of me knows it would be good for her, too."

She gets up and places her hand on my shoulder, giving me a serious look. "I think you have your answer."

"There she is! The birthday girl," Leo announces, and Lauren is instantly engulfing herself in his arms.

"Hey there, handsome." She laughs as he kisses her cheek and then hands her a card.

"From Nate and I." He smirks.

"Where is that hottie?"

Thankfully our floor is key access only—our conversations always sound inappropriate.

Lauren has been with me since day one, and she's formed a unique, different friendship with each of us.

"He's in Dubai with Seb, working on the new hotel, and I leave for Copenhagen in about five minutes."

She opens the envelope, looks up, looks down, and then squeals so loud I'm sure my eardrums have burst. "Holy fucking shitballs! Thank you, thank you!" she yells and starts running around in circles until her ankle almost gives out from the heels she can never walk straight in. "Is this real life?"

"Let me see." I hold out my hand and smile when I see it's something to do with the Broadway show Hamilton.

"Leo. Two premiere seats and dinner with the cast. How the hell did you even pull this off?"

He waggles his brows. "I have to keep some secrets to myself."

She looks at me. "How will your present ever top this?"

"Maybe I didn't get you anything."

Now I'm going to tease her and wait to give her the Chanel bag she's been dying for, for years.

She widens her eyes. "Don't even joke like that."

"Hey, you look like shit," Leo chimes in, glancing over my face.

"Yeah, he's about to go off the deep end. You better be ready to resuscitate because I draw the line at doing mouth-to-mouth with him." She sticks out her tongue and fakes a gag.

"Yeah, thanks a lot. Get back to work," I snap. "Actually, both of you get the fuck out. Playtime is over."

She salutes me, then leaves.

Leo stands there staring at me with a pensive look on his face.

"What?" I demand.

"Could this possibly have something to do with Jules?"

"Not this fucking crap again, Leo. You know my deal with Seb. I'm trying to work it out, but mind your business."

He takes a meaningful breath. "Unfortunately, it is my business." He puts his hand in his suit jacket and pulls out a pink envelope.

I step back. "What is that?" I ask although I don't need to. I recognize it right away.

He doesn't need to explain.

I've given one to Seb when he hit rock bottom, and I have a stack for Claud for when she's older.

Leo places it on my desk. "Love you, brother, but it's your time for one." Then, he walks out of my office without another word.

Fuck.

Slowly, I step closer to the envelope like it's going to bite me, and then eventually, I sit and pick it up, staring for what feels like forever.

The envelope burns a hole through my skin, and as bright as I am, I feel foolish. I should be running to read her words.

I buzz Lauren. "Yes, Mr. Davenport?"

My stomach drops. "Is my father here?"

"No."

"Then why did you call me Mr. Davenport? You stopped doing that ten years ago."

"I know I just wanted to annoy you. What's up?" She chuckles.

I pinch the bridge of my nose, for fuck's sake. "I'm locking my door. Hold all my calls unless it's from Claud or someone's dying." I hang up before she can pry any more information from me.

Slowly, I open the envelope, careful not to rip it. I look inside, it's another envelope.

And in a very familiar cursive, it says—

To my beautiful baby's daddy and the love of my life.

Love of her life?

What the hell?

I quickly open the second envelope, and find a two-page letter. Thankfully the first two words ease my confusion.

Just kidding.

Fuck it. I get up and pour myself a hefty glass of scotch. I don't give a shit how early it is. I'm standing by the old saying *it's five o'clock somewhere* because I have a feeling I'm going to need it.

Then I begin.

Harrison,

Did I get you there for a moment? I mean, I do love you, but not like that. Incest is totally not my thing, even if we're not blood-related. A brother is a brother.

Anyway, if you're receiving this letter, it's because you've found your one, someone who has captured your heart. Did you feel the butterflies in your stomach? I hope you did. They're magical.

Leo is under strict instructions as to when it's the right time to give you the letter. So, let me guess...you're struggling.

I know you better than you know yourself. Better than Nate, Leo, or even Seb, and somewhere deep in your core, you're worried about introducing a woman to Claudina, someone who could possibly be a permanent fixture in your life, in Claud's.

You are, aren't you? It's that, or you're worried Seb will flip out.

I already know the two of you will be so overprotective of Claudina that you'll probably be overbearing at times, but it's out of love, and that's what counts.

There's another thing I know. Sebastian will never ever be okay with introducing another mother figure to Claud. It's the reality of who he is, and that's not fair to you. You can't live a life of seclusion. It's not what I want, Harrison. For you, or Claudina.

That was another criterion Leo had, by the way.

First... Does Harrison need guidance? Is he confused?

Second... Could Leo see this woman being the mom to my sweet little girl?

And before you get yourself into a tizzy, think for a moment.

Doesn't Claud deserve a mom? A woman who will guide her through life with all that you can't relate to.

Although Mom and I fought like cats and dogs, I would have never wanted to grow up without her. She was my best friend, and I want that for Claud too.

I'm sure Claudina looks up to you like you hang the moon. I did when I was younger, and god, do I wish I could be there to see you two in action. A daddy and his little girl is the most precious thing in the world. But it's nothing like having a relationship with her mother, and I took that away from her by dying.

It's the cold, hard truth, but again, a reality.

I will always be her mother, and she better know all about me! But, Harrison, she needs a mom if you can give her one. And since you're reading this, both you and Leo think this woman is pretty spectacular.

Let yourself be free of confusion and find your happiness.

It would make me so, so happy, wherever I am, if you could figure this out. If you love her, truly love her, I'm sure Claudina will love her too. If she's anything like me, she'll love all the things you love.

It's okay to be worried about it, but don't let this stop you...please. I beg of you.

Don't wait or waste time, Harrison.

Love is an extraordinary feeling.

You deserve to love and be loved, not just by Claudina. But by someone who loves you back, who will call you out on your demanding ways but will stick by you because they know you're loyal to a fault and would do anything in the world for them.

The first day I ever felt true love was when we were at the ultrasound appointment, and the tech asked us if we were ready.

I wasn't...I thought I was, but I could have never been prepared for the overwhelming sensation of emotions that rushed through my body.

The very second the heartbeat monitor made the first beep was the exact second I fell in true love for the first time in my life, and I wish I had lived longer in that joy.

So don't let it pass you by.

Hold on to it tight and let in all the love.

I love you.

Always and forever,

Camila

I slam my empty drink onto the table and clench my jaw, breathing heavily as I try to calm my emotions.

Goddamnit, Camila. How did you know?

She's not even here and yet knows exactly what I'm going through. It's been like this my entire life, but now I'm unsure how to handle it. *I wish she was here.*

I want to honor her…so fucking badly.

However, she doesn't know what her brother went through. She knew Seb would have a hard time, but I'm not sure she could have ever imagined the hole he went down.

Would she still push me toward this if she did?

And if I go against Seb…would we still be bonded?

Juliette

"Okay, little bakers, before you leave, I have homework for you this week," I announce, followed by instant groans.

"Homework?" one of my little girls whines. "But it's summer!"

"What if I told you that this homework had a prize?" I widen my eyes to sweeten the deal, looking around at each student, then freeze when I see Harrison standing next to Claud and Willa.

Quickly, I attempt to hide any emotion and continue. He might have ruined my weekend when he didn't answer any of my messages or phone calls, but I won't let him ruin the joy I get from this class or the happiness of the children.

"Next week, I want you to bring in a story. You can write it, draw it, perform it, I don't care. I want you to tell me what you loved most about class and what your favorite thing we baked was. Then, I will randomly pick a winner from whoever participated in the homework assignment. That person gets to choose our final dessert the week after, which sadly is our last class of the summer session." I pause while the kids animatedly express their displeasure over ending class. "We'll make it the best class yet, and instead of one hour, it will be two hours. The first hour, we'll bake. The second, we will have a pizza party to celebrate."

Excitement echoes through the room as I say goodbye, trying my best to ignore Harrison until I hear my name slip from Willa's mouth.

So I walk closer as I begin to wipe down the tables, pretending I don't hear anything.

"Claudina loves Juliette, and I trust her, and I think you might too."

"Willa," Harrison's deep voice snaps with a warning tone.

Willa doesn't know about me and Harrison…well, not exactly.

I never told Harrison, but once we were out together, Willa was at the same restaurant. She's never mentioned it, and neither have I, but we both know what he and I were doing.

A week later, Willa was at the party brunch and overheard me talking about him to Adriana in the ladies' room.

Again…we never mentioned it.

"I'm just saying you don't have much of a choice. Someone needs to watch Claud while you go to Bermuda. I can change my schedule if you need—"

"No," he cuts in. "You're not doing that. I appreciate it, but you're not missing the birth of your niece because of a last-minute meeting I need to attend."

"Well, what will you do then?"

Attempting to get closer to listen, I bang my knee into the corner of the table.

"Ah." I scrunch my eyes up. Lord, that's worse than hitting your funny bone. I rub my knee and notice Willa and Harrison staring at me.

"Are you okay, Juliette?" Willa asks while Harrison stares down at my leg, his nostrils flaring. I rub my knee and fake a smile. "Yup. Just clumsy."

Harrison's phone rings. "Shit," he grumbles, then looks at me, then Willa, and I know he wants to say something. But he can't. "Claud, let's go, angel. Something important came up, and Daddy needs to leave right this second."

My phone buzzes on my nightstand, and I turn to see it's Harrison. When I notice the clock says midnight, I pick it up straight away, worried.

Hi, baby. Are you up?

Yes.

My phone rings a second later, and Harrison's name flashes.

"Hi."

"Jules." He sighs, his voice husky. "It's good to hear your voice, beautiful."

"Are you okay?"

"Yeah." He hesitates. "I'm really stressed at the moment and needed to talk to my girl."

His girl?

I've always loved hearing him say that, but now it feels like a slap in the face.

"Jules."

"I'm here. Obviously the line's still on," I snark.

"What's with the attitude?"

"I'm just thinking how I don't feel very much like *your girl* lately."

He sucks in a breath like I've hit him with the worst possible insult. "Don't say that. I'm trying to figure it all out, Jules. Please be patient with me. I…"

His words trail off, and something about his tone has me concerned. He doesn't sound okay. "What's going on, Harrison? Talk to me."

He lets out a long, frustrated breath. "What isn't going on?" I hear him maneuvering himself in bed, so I give him a moment. "Everything is going on. That's the problem. I barely have time to think. I'm at the office nonstop, and I'm exhausted. In my five years as a father, if I'm home, I have breakfast with Claud. It's our thing. My nights, and even hers with her activities, are unpredictable, so I wanted one stable thing in her life. Already three times this week, I've missed it with her, and it's killing me inside."

His hurt pulls at my heartstrings. Harrison is a good dad, it's one of the things I'm most attracted to when it comes to him. "You can't do it all. What you need are some days off, which you tell me all the time."

He chuckles sarcastically. "Maybe soon. I came by the bakery today to see if you wanted to get dinner. I'm sorry for not getting back to you this weekend. I was working out some personal issues. If you can't tell, I'm going a little insane. That idea blew up when one of my clients demanded a meeting, telling me my employee was underperforming for him."

"Dear Lord. You don't need some days off. You need a whole vacation."

"Tell me about it. On top of that, one of my high-wealth clients only informed me yesterday afternoon that he's in from Saudi Arabia for one day, and I need to fly to Bermuda to meet him tomorrow morning. Which is a fucking nightmare because I was going to have Claud in the office tomorrow. Willa is away."

This is what he and Willa were talking about, where he dismissed her when she suggested me. I'm not telling him I already know. Screw that, let him have the guts to tell me he doesn't trust me. If he says that, though, it's highly likely I'm going to lose my ever-loving shit.

"Well, who will watch Claud while you're away?"

"I have no other choice at this point. She'll come with me and stay with my CTO's wife and kids while I'm at the meeting."

I let out an audible huff, downright insulted. What a joke. "No other choice?" I snap, no longer able to hold back. "You can think of me when you want me to suck your cock, but I'm not good enough to be considered to watch your daughter."

"No, no," he quickly cuts in. "It's not that. It's just—"

"It's just what? You once told me you trusted me, so clearly, that was a lie. I love Claud, and we get along amazingly. So this can't possibly be because of you and me," I retort sarcastically, knowing that's exactly it. "Can't you separate the two?"

"It's overnight…"

"So?" I raise my voice. "You would rather have her be with a strange woman all day than have her stay with me? And does she even know these freaking kids? Is she comfortable with them?" Even though he can't see me, I shake my head. "You know what, I need to go, Harrison."

"Jules, baby," he murmurs.

Then I think of something, "And I can't believe you're making her miss her dance surprise."

"Shit. I thought that was next week."

"No, they moved it. Remember?"

"Fucking hell. I completely forgot." He pauses. "But you remembered," he whispers.

"Of course I did. She's been looking forward to it for weeks."

Claud's summer dance program is ending, and they are having an end-of-summer surprise for the dancers and their parents or caretakers.

We both go silent again, which gives me a second to think. He really does sound stressed, more than usual. "Harrison, I could help. This has nothing to do with us. It's all about Claud. Neither of you can miss tomorrow, and I'm off for the next few days."

"I used to know your schedule," he says quietly, more to himself, then surprises me. "Juliette, would you please watch Claudina while I go away for work?"

"I'd do anything for Claud. Of course," I tell him truthfully and without hesitation.

17

Juliette

IT'S EARLY, and although I would have preferred to walk, Robert picked me up five minutes ago and is dropping me off at Harrison's.

My emotions are completely out of sync with my body. It's why I wanted to walk, to take a breath, and maybe even detour through the park quickly to center myself.

I'm not sure what changed; I used to feel at home coming here to spend time with Harrison, but now, I feel like a stranger, like I don't belong.

No matter how I'm feeling, I'll keep it to myself today. I'm here for Claud, and Claud only, and my mind will stay focused on that.

Suddenly, my door opens, and I let out a small shriek. "My god, you scared me half to death."

I was so lost in my head that I hadn't realized we pulled up to the building.

"By opening the door for you?" Harrison asks sarcastically, letting out a low chuckle, then reaches to help me out of the car. He pauses in front of me, cupping my cheek. "Good morning, beautiful Juliette."

"Morning," I murmur, slightly dazed by his good looks and blue eyes.

He smirks playfully, then bites down on his lower lip as he rakes his eyes down my body, spotting my tight yoga pants.

This is weird…usually, he would be all over me.

He takes my bags from Robert, then interlocks our fingers and leads us to the front. "Good morning, Ms. Caldwell."

"Good morning, Freddy." I smile brightly at Harrison's doorman. "I told you, call me Juliette. And I have something for you." I grab one of my bags from Harrison and hand it to Freddy. "They're for you and Suzette. I remember you saying she loved rose flavor, and I happened to have made rose macarons yesterday. I also added the pistachio and blackcurrant violet ones you love."

He pats my shoulder in appreciation. "You're a good kid. Thank you so much."

"Anytime." I wave goodbye as Harrison leads us to the elevator. He's quieter than usual. "What's wrong?" I ask, looking up to find him staring at me with bewilderment.

He cups my cheek again and *again* doesn't kiss me. "You're a good person is all."

I turn into his palm. "Because I gave Freddy desserts?"

"Do you know how many people are allowed to call him Freddy?" He doesn't let me answer. "Zero. Not one person, and I've been living in his building for fifteen years."

Huh.

I shrug. "Being nice goes a long way."

The elevator doors open, and he leads me in. "I never got to thank you last night for doing this. It means a lot. Be prepared. She just woke up, and it's still early for her. Don't be surprised if she's shy or quieter than normal."

"Okay." I smile, imagining Claud, all sleepy and snuggly. She's already cute as can be, but I'll bet she's even more adorable this early in the morning. "I never asked where your brothers were."

"All are traveling overseas and would have never made it back in time. Rosa and Javier are in Spain visiting family. They go the same week every year, and Willa's sister is giving birth today." He pauses, his face growing serious. "She's never slept over with anyone who wasn't family or Willa, and even then, it's very few and far between with Willa. Maybe once or twice ever."

I rub his arm in comfort. "It's going to be okay. You can FaceTime us every second you're not in your meeting, and please tell me if there is anything I can do to ease your mind."

"A lot of updates and pictures would be great. I'm not sure. This is all new to me, and I'm trying not to think about it. Otherwise, I might be staying home and blowing a huge deal for us."

The doors open, and the highest, most excited screech I've ever heard rings through the penthouse. Then Claud is off the stool, running toward me.

I raise a brow. "Shy and quiet?" I mutter as Harrison shakes his head, amused.

"She's comfortable with you."

"Good morning, sugar plum."

She barrels into my legs, hugging me tightly. "I'm so excited you're here. We're going to have the best girls' day."

Harrison's body goes rigid beside me, so I glance over, giving him a questioning look. He shakes his head and looks the other way.

What the hell was that about?

Claud keeps chattering, unaware of her father's mood change. "Can we have a tea party after dance class today? Or even a spa day? I went to a spa for a birthday party, and it was sooo fun. It was for little kids, though," she giggles. "And Dad let me rent some new movies. There are so many cool things we could do!"

"Whatever you want to do, Claud. I thought we could make dinner together, too, since we normally bake together."

"Yess!" She jumps up and down. "Let's make whatever your favorite dinner is," she exclaims, then pauses. "Well, as long as it's not salmon. I hate salmon."

Her excitement makes me laugh. Today is going to be entertaining. Exhausting but still fun. "I don't like salmon either."

She lets out a dramatic breath like she was scared I would say it was the best thing created.

Harrison is in the corner getting his personal items together. When he messaged that Robert was picking me up, he told me he would need to leave immediately.

"What are you doing?" Claud walks over to inspect.

"I'm leaving. You're still okay with this, right?" Harrison whispers, crouching down to look her in the eyes. "If you're not, it's okay. Just tell me now."

"Are you kidding me? I'm soooo excited." She puts her hand in mine and swings our arms eagerly. I look down, not able to keep the smile off my face. "I was asking because you didn't give Juliette a tour." She huffs, annoyed, sounding more grown-up than she is.

Little does she know, I know this place like the back of my hand.

Harrison chuckles. "You can do it later. Come here, my precious angel," he says, opening his arms.

She flings herself into him but keeps her hand in mine. Harrison glares at us, not missing her attachment.

Is this weird for him? I unlock our hands, feeling like I'm overstepping, and then walk into the kitchen while they say their goodbyes.

Right after, Harrison runs up the stairs, Claud following behind him. He's late, so he's hustling.

"Daddy! What the heck are you doing?" she cries.

"Claudina, I told you to stay in the kitchen."

I hear her tears from here. "Don't take those down. They're my favorite ballerina pictures. What are you doing?" she screams again.

The second the words are out of her mouth, I'm up the steps, racing toward her room.

"Claud, it's fine, angel. I am going to have them cleaned."

"Harrison. No."

His head snaps toward me, and I'm shaking my head frantically. "No. It's fine, I'm fine."

"You're not, though," he whispers. Claud's head is bouncing between the two of us.

"Come on, sugar plum. Daddy will put them back while we go downstairs." Luckily, she listens, sniffing and rubbing her eyes.

I turn back and mouth to put the pictures of me back in their place.

Warmth runs through me at the idea of him protecting my feelings, but taking pictures off a little girl's bedroom wall also puts it into perspective that something needs to change for me.

Harrison returns to the kitchen, saying goodbye to Claud one last time. I can see he's struggling, but he'll be in trouble if he doesn't leave now. "Bye, angel, finish your breakfast. I need to speak to Juliette before I leave," he tells her, then points to the foyer.

When we're out of earshot of Claud, I quickly ask what's wrong, hoping he hasn't changed his mind.

He lifts his muscular arm, reaching into the closet to grab his bag. I watch in awe as his biceps contract against his tightly-fitted shirt. I'm surprised they make shirts that can even fit him.

What do scrawny men do, swim in their shirts?

Who am I kidding? He gets these professionally made to fit him perfectly...and that they do.

"Jules."

Rolling my lips, I attempt to hide my smile. "Sorry."

He laughs it off, but I don't miss the flex he does. His phone dings a few times in succession. "Shit. I need to go, but quickly. Are you sure you're okay? I'm sorry. I should have thought about it earlier."

"Yes. Albeit thoughtful, it's unnecessary. You need to go."

He blows out a ragged breath. "I know. I know. You have her doctor's number and all the brothers in your phone. Obviously, it goes without saying, you only call Seb if literally no one else in this whole city doesn't pick up."

"Harrison. Goodbye." I push him out the door, but before I can close it, he turns back, and his eyes hold mine.

Just a short time ago, this moment would have gone much differently.

The familiarity of it has a knot twisting in my stomach, and at the same time, warmth grows below at the numerous memories of me up against the wall as I attempted to leave for work. Harrison would have never let me leave without a proper goodbye.

Now, though, we stand silently as lingering unspoken feelings pass between us. Both of us are in limbo, unsure how we proceed, and I know if I were to look in the mirror, my face would be full of insecurities.

Harrison steps forward and cups my cheek. "Will you call me tonight?"

"I told you. FaceTime us when you are done with your meetings."

"No." He leans down, lightly pressing our lips together. "I want to talk to my Jules later when Claud's asleep."

My Jules.

"Okay," I mutter as he presses forward to deepen the kiss.

I still. Shaking my head while he frowns in question.

"What are you doing?" he growls. "I want a kiss goodbye."

"Claud—"

"Is eating breakfast, and the sooner you give me those lips, the sooner I can leave."

He sinks his fingers through my hair, moving my head to the side, and runs his tongue along the length of my neck.

God, have I missed that move.

"Now." He bites down on my ear. "Kiss me."

His lips are on me, and I can't deny him when he's like this. "You're so bossy," I mumble around his sexy smirk.

"Nothing new to you." His tongue delves in just as his phone dings, and we both know it's time.

"Bye, baby." He brushes his thumb against the apple of my cheek, catching my eyes once more, wordlessly looking as if he's trying to tell me something I've yet to solve.

Doesn't he know I freaking suck at puzzles?

"Stop wiggling." I laugh.

Claud shakes her head. "I'm too excited. What do you think the surprise is?" She whispers.

She's different here, more reserved.

I'm unsure if it's because of ballet or if she's always shy in front of the other kids, but she's holding back, even with her dancing.

"I have no clue. When I was your age, I never got any surprises at dance school."

She leans back, resting her head on my shoulder. I'm sitting criss cross on the floor of her ballet studio with the other adults. Claud decided to sit in my lap instead of with the children.

I snap a selfie of us and send it to Harrison. He hasn't missed a beat of our day with the number of pictures I've sent.

"It's so cool you're here, Juliette. It's fun at baking classes but double fun at dance class." I see her smiling wide in the mirror across the way. My face mimics hers.

I tickle her side, causing her to laugh out loud and for me to get a side-eye from some of the uppity moms. "Are you saying the dance studio is better than the bakery?"

"Yes," she hiccups through her laughter. "My mom would love to be here too if she could. I think she'd like you."

What?

Ah. What the hell do I say back to this?

Why can't her mom be here?

Oh. My. God. *I'm going to kill you, Harrison.*

"Where is your mom, Claud?" I ask hesitantly.

She turns her head, smiling brightly. "She's everywhere."

Um, what? "Claudina, what does that mean?" I ask as she sits up quickly. "Claud?"

She shushes me and points. "Look, people are coming."

My head is spinning a million ways, and there's no doubt my thoughts would go down a rabbit hole if the door didn't open to my worst nightmare.

My breathing picks up, and it feels impossible to let the breaths out of my chest that's tightening at a hurried pace.

Claud turns toward me. "What's wrong?" she mutters softly. "Jules?"

I swallow the large lump in my throat and fake a smile. "Nothing's wrong, sugar plum."

She narrows her eyes. "But you made a funny noise."

"I know. I'm sorry," I mumble, lost in hell.

I've never used so much restraint to hold back my emotions—my tears, anger, and, most of all, my vulnerability.

If I didn't have this little angel to care for, I'd be running out the door.

Later…later, I'll let all my feelings run wild.

Claud's ballet instructor steps into the corner of the room and sweeps a hand behind her. "For the end of the season surprise, I welcome you, principal dancers from the New York City Ballet."

Hunter and Annalise, my archenemies, step up and wave excitedly to the children. Behind them stand eight other dancers I've worked with for the majority of my career.

Besides Hunter, I haven't seen anyone since, especially Annalise… my replacement.

Hunter falters when he spots me. His face drops with perplexity.

No. No. No.

"Hunter McMillon and Annalise DeCampo are partners who lead in—" The words begin to dissipate as I force myself to go somewhere else—reminding myself to breathe and that I'm fine.

It's all fine.

Be strong for Claud. Don't have a panic attack.

"Juliette." Hunter's voice is too soft, too familiar. "Are you okay?"

My eyes shoot open, not realizing I had squeezed them tightly shut.

I can't speak.

My heart beats wildly against my chest.

"Answer me. You're scaring me."

Claud turns in my lap and grabs on to me tightly; that move is the wake-up call I need.

"Fine. I'm fine."

"Jules?" Claud whispers in my neck. "I want to go home."

"No, sweetheart," I choke out. "I'm okay. I'm sorry. I wasn't feeling well, but I'm much better now."

"Are you sure?"

"I am." I kiss her forehead. "Thank you for caring. You're a sweet girl, Claudina." I maneuver her so she can see the dancers again.

Annalise comes over to us, up on point, and I know Claud is probably wide-eyed in awe.

Discreetly, she runs her fingertips along Hunter's arm as she settles next to him. Hunter's eyes shoot to me. If I were more with it, my eyes would be rolling.

I couldn't care less about them as a couple, but as dance partners, it makes me sick to my stomach.

"Juliette, what a surprise," Annalise's annoying, nasally voice mutters through a fake smile. "Or maybe not. You can't be a dancer anymore because of your *disabled* leg, so you what...come here and watch little kids dance? That's kind of creepy." She turns toward Hunter. "Right, Hunter, babe?" Hunter shoots her a look to shut the hell up. She misses it, though, and continues talking. "I mean, we all feel bad for you, but god, Juliette. Have some self-respect," she mutters with disdain, hoping others won't hear.

Except I can already hear the whispers, wondering what we're saying and who I am.

The tears burn, but I will not let them drop, not in front of her, Hunter, and especially not in front of Claud.

I'm stronger than this.

"Enough, Annalise," Hunter snaps, then turns toward me. "Are you okay?"

"Fine."

"Jules, I know what *fine* means."

"Whatever. Can you get her out of my face?"

His shoulders drop, and he nods, then turns back. "I'm sorry, by the way. For the bar and today. She's still jealous of you."

"I thought ballerinas were nice. You're nice," Claud mumbles. "She was very mean. I don't like her."

"Me neither, Claud."

She's an ex-professional ballerina.
I feel bad for her.
Why is she here?
Poor girl.
Who does she know here?
She was dating the blonde.
Who is better? Her or Annalise?
Hit by a taxi.
Poor girl.
How terrible.
She probably wasn't good enough.
What does she do now?
It's pathetic she hangs around here.
How do you come back from that?
Poor girl.
Poor girl.
Poor girl.
Poor girl.

All the mumbles of the last half of the class play through my mind like a broken record as we make dinner and eat dessert. As we paint our nails and watch *Beauty and the Beast*, and now as I tell Claudina a bedtime story.

I'm hanging by a thread, but I will not ruin this night for Claud, and the only thing that's helping me is telling her my favorite story.

My parents' love story.

Claud yawns big, one that stretches her face. "This is about Inès and your dad?"

"It is. Did you like it?"

"I did. Maybe you could tell me again sometime?"

I kiss her forehead. "I'd like that, Claud. Good night, sugar plum."

When I get up, I strategically look in the opposite direction of my framed photos in the corner.

Claud calls my name as I shut the door. "I'm sorry that girl was mean to you today," she mutters, then rolls over and closes her eyes.

I shut her door, then, as if my body knows it's had enough, it gives out, and I drop to the ground. My head falls forward, and I let the tears flow freely down my face.

Poor girl

Poor girl.

Poor girl.

Covering my ears, I beg the murmurs to stop. I knew this day would come when my haunted troubles would come to a head and would bring me down.

I've had enough.

Make it stop.

Please...make it stop.

Harrison

Somewhere in the distance, an irritating bird chirps repeatedly over Mr. Abdullah's voice, dragging on about his new private plane and his fourth wife. It's driving me up a fucking wall.

The rest of the senior management team laughs, kissing his ass, which is what they get paid for when he's around, considering he's our biggest client.

It's a good thing they are because I couldn't be bothered.

My mind is on my two girls in New York, having the time of their lives.

As promised, Jules has been sending me nonstop pictures of her and Claud, and I've never been fucking jealous of my daughter until now.

I should have known Claud would be loving herself sick. Not once did she cry, that's never happened in the history of me leaving for a trip, and it's clear as day it's because she adores Jules as much as I do.

I flip over my phone when it buzzes across the boardroom table to see Matteo texting.

> Hey. I just landed from Italy and wanted to update you before I'm inundated with work. I think you may be right about the building purchasers.

> It's a shell company with a name I'm unfamiliar with. And at this point in my career, I've heard them all. Unless it's a foreign company, I'm unaware of it.

> Also, why would they want to buy a few buildings on a random Upper East Side block?

> I'll keep digging. My brothers are still in Italy and using their international connections to find out any info they can.

> Something's definitely off.

Fuck. I knew it.

> I need this information ASAP.

> On it.

I slam my phone down, and all eyes snap toward me. I put my hands up in apology. "Sorry. Please proceed."

We're heading to a late dinner, and a dark shadow of unease falls over me. Call it a sixth sense, but Jules doesn't answer her phone, and I can't stop thinking that something is wrong. The whole thing is making me feel uneasy.

"Mr. Abdullah," I call out ahead. "I'll meet you all at Harry's restaurant in a few minutes. I need to make a call." I hold up my phone, then step aside toward Hamilton's Harbor and call her again as I stare out at the dark waters, running my hand through my hair.

Pick up, Juliette.

It rings out again, and typically, I wouldn't think twice. Jules wakes up early, so most nights, she's passing out by eight or nine. Tonight, though, she would have called or at least texted when Claud went down.

I'm an idiot...how the hell did I forget this. I open my newly installed security app and turn it on to the penthouse.

They only installed the system two days ago, which completely slipped my mind.

The second it's loaded, I click on Claudina's room, and my shoulders drop. I let out a breath of relief when I see Claud spread starfish in her bed.

I never told Jules where to sleep, so I check all the bedrooms and the living room.

Nothing.

Then, her favorite place, the balcony, and my study.

Still nothing, until I click on the one labeled Hallway. My breath snags in my chest, and a wild, nauseating sensation tears through my body.

I fall forward, catching myself on the guardrail, frantically redialing Jules.

What the hell is going on?

Putting it on speaker quickly, I switch back to the security app, and I can see her phone vibrating beside her. She doesn't attempt to make a move to answer.

Pick up. Pick up.

Not even a sudden move to look at her phone.

Show me your face, baby. What's wrong?

Her knees are pulled to her chest, and her head is bowed, so I can't see her beautiful face, but there is no mistake she's crying. Her whole body is heaving up and down.

Show me your goddamn face, Juliette! I yell internally, willing her to fucking listen.

This is the exact reason I kept my pilot on standby.

I'm coming for you, baby.

Fuck the meeting, fuck everyone else.

My girl needs me.

I tear through the penthouse, and thankfully, she's not in the hallway anymore. I find her curled up, sleeping on the couch, with the warm blanket she loves from my room wrapped around her like a sheet of armor.

The barely there dusting of freckles along Jules's cheeks has disappeared behind red blotches down her face. Her eyes are swollen shut, and her lips puffy and parted, letting out a soft breath that hitches even in her sleep.

There's a pivotal time in your life that you won't know until it happens. You won't even believe it until it happens.

It's happening...

I'm falling in love with Jules.

Or I'm already in love.

Standing here, looking down at my girl, there is no way I'm walking away from my beautiful, sweet girl. Seeing her here in my house, with Claud sleeping upstairs, makes so much fucking sense to me now that I wonder how the hell I've been such a fool to have wasted my time worrying about the what if's.

Mine.

I always knew it. It only took me a minute to wrap my head around it.

Finally, I'm listening to what Camila has been trying to tell me. I'm taking life by the fucking reins, and I'm claiming my girl.

"Harrison?" Jules's raspy voice croaks quietly as her eyes flutter up. "You're home?"

Leaning down, I put my arms around her, easily picking her up, pulling her to my chest, and then walking us toward my bedroom.

I kiss her cheeks, then forehead, letting my lips linger against her warm, smooth skin. "I'm home, baby."

In every sense of the word.

I lay her down on her side of the bed, walk back to lock the door in case Claudina wakes up early or has a nightmare, and then undress Jules. "W-what are you doing? I can't sleep in here."

"You will, and you won't fight me on it. Tonight we sleep. Tomorrow we talk."

Jules's eyes widen in surprise, though she still fights me. "I can't, Harrison. I want to, but I can't."

Her raw, shaky words have me pausing. "What do you mean by that?" I frown.

Her eyes are downcast as she plays with the hem of her shirt. "I can't do this anymore. I can't lie in this bed beside you and pretend I'm okay with it. I thought I could, but I can't do casual, Harrison. I can't do anything less than all in with you. What we had before was…"

"Was not enough." Her hopeful eyes lift to mine. "I'm not letting you go, *mon petit papillon*. This is it. This is where you belong. With me, in this bed, in my home, and in *our* life."

"Harrison. *What?*" She gasps, and the most beautiful sight of happiness crosses her face.

"Tomorrow, Jules." I kiss her red pouty lips. "Sleep now, baby," I tell her as I get in behind her and pull her close to me, never wanting to let her go.

Tomorrow, we start our life together.

Then I call my brother and tell him I'm breaking our promise because I've found my forever girl.

18

Juliette

MORNING LIGHT SHINES in my eyes, waking me from one of the most sound sleeps I've had in a while. I'm face down, snuggling into Harrison's pillow, breathing in his manly scent—my all-time favorite way to wake up.

I stretch my body, letting out a loud moan as my core begins to tingle with pleasure.

My legs part naturally, and I clench down hard, rocking onto the mattress with every swipe through my center.

"Bonjour, Juliette. T'as bien dormis?"

My head pops up, and Harrison is there, his blue eyes boring down into mine as his strong fingers linger and circle over my clit. He repeats that a few times, then drags them down, impaling me with three fingers.

Dear god, I love that move.

How long has he been doing this? I'm already about to come.

Actually, who am I kidding? He's made me come in under a minute before. His fingers are magic.

My mouth opens, but no words come out. I'm breathing hard

against the pillow, staring into his dilated eyes, not believing I'm awake right now.

"I asked how my girl slept," he growls.

"I-I slept well. Ohhh, I thought this was a dream," I cry out.

He leans over and bites my ass cheek. For some reason, it's the hottest thing ever, and it causes a gush of wetness to my sex and the throbbing between my legs to intensify.

"Oh fuck yeah. Your cunt knows exactly what I need. Give me that cream, baby."

Ahh, what's with the dirty talk first thing in the morning?

My sex tightens around his fingers.

"Not yet."

What does he mean not yet? I can't stop this. I clench again, so he slaps my ass. *Hard.*

"I said not yet," he growls, then pulls his fingers out and drags my wetness from my opening to over my behind, circling my tight hole.

Holy shit. I freeze. He's never done this before.

His other hand palms my ass cheek, spreading it open wide so he can watch his handy work. I look over my shoulder to see his mouth hanging open and his breathing erratic.

He's loving this.

We've talked about it. So. Many. Times. He has talked about it. But he's only ever teased.

His movements increase in speed, causing me to tense, but he doesn't falter; if anything, he increases the pressure, causing the tip of his finger to slip in.

"Not a dream, baby. Now be a good girl and let me in." He spits onto my behind and pushes deeper into my ass.

Oh my god. Good morning to you, too, Harrison.

Who is this naughty man?

Now I know what they mean when they say knuckles deep.

When I let out a soft, breathless moan, he picks up his pace, moving his fingers in and out, stretching my forbidden area until it burns. It doesn't hurt, it feels better than I ever expected, and quickly pleasure starts to build. I bite the pillow so I don't scream loudly, knowing it could wake the neighbors, let alone Claud.

"Fuck yes. I love it when you're like this. Submitting to me without question. Trusting me to give you what I know you'll love."

"Oh, ah. God, Harrison." This is not supposed to feel this good. Everyone I talk to says this doesn't feel good.

What the hell have they been doing this whole time?

A slow, sexy smile widens across his face. He's being all cocky, loving himself sick over this.

"It feels good." He doesn't ask.

"Yes." I breathe through my nose as he slides in another finger.

"Hips up, baby," he demands.

When I don't move fast enough, he positions himself behind me, grabbing my hip with his free hand, pulling me up so I'm doggy style, head still in the pillow.

I turn to the side, and oh *fuck me*.

Harrison's dick is sticking out of the top of his briefs, red, stiff, and swollen, leaking so much pre-come it looks like he's about to burst.

He reaches his free hands around, and just before his fingers touch my clit, he slowly pulls out of my ass, drops his face down, and licks up my behind with his thick tongue.

He swirls around, causing me to shudder and shivers to crawl up my body. Then suddenly, his fingers are on my clit, and it's too much, I explode. Without any warning, my body is shaking, my ass is pushing back into Harrison's face, and I'm screaming bloody murder into the pillow.

I lie there, my body liquefying into the mattress, trying to catch my breath while Harrison steps away to wash his face.

His strong hands wrap around me and attempt to pull me up, but I'm too exhausted, so I flop onto his chest. "Good morning, beautiful Juliette." He leans down and kisses me passionately like he's missed me for a lifetime and can't hold back.

Kissing Harrison gets better every time.

He leans back, and his eyes glow with a deep affection that wraps around my heart. I can feel by the look in his eyes that the words he spoke yesterday were true.

"Are you okay?" He smiles, proud of himself. "That wasn't supposed to happen, by the way. I woke up next to you, looking so tempting, and only wanted to make you feel good, then I got carried away."

"You definitely made me feel good," I mutter. "What was that?"

Suddenly embarrassed, I bury my head in his neck. It's as if I'm two different people with him, and the one in the bedroom is way more wild and free than I ever thought possible.

He lowers his voice. "That was me claiming you. A predatory need has taken over to have and own every inch of your body. I wasn't waiting another second, and soon." He pauses, running his hands over the globes of my ass. "I will take you here with my cock."

I swallow the lump in my throat and nod, agreeing even though his sheer size makes me nervous as hell. Having him own me and pleasing him has always been aphrodisiac to both of us.

Harrison maneuvers me, then palms his dick, squeezing hard to calm himself.

I move his hand and attempt to mimic his movements, but surprisingly, he pushes me away.

"I'm waiting for later, baby. We need to talk about us and what happened to you yesterday."

I freeze. How does he know?

Oh god, did the dance school call him? I know I was acting strange, but I never thought I made that much of a scene.

"I don't know who told you what, but I promise you, Harrison, I didn't let it affect me until after Claud went to bed. I just couldn't hold back my emotions any longer. Everything lately feels like it's coming up, boiling to the top, and I finally snapped. I'm so sorry." I cry into his chest.

He pushes me back and looks down with a furrowed brow. "What are you talking about, Jules? What happened?"

I wipe the tear that drips down my cheek. How it's even possible I have any left in my body is beyond me.

"What do *you* mean? Why did you come home early?"

He moves my hand away so he can dry my tears, then leans over to kiss me lightly. "I saw you crying in the hallway, on the security cameras."

"Security cameras? You never told me..." My eyes widen with a thought. "Who sees these videos?"

"Me? Why?"

"Well, the things you've done to me in your hallway aren't exactly something I want to share with the world."

A deep rumble vibrates through his chest. "You think I would ever chance sharing you with anyone else? Never, ever will that happen. And they were only installed the other day."

Wait. "You left your meeting because you saw me crying? That meeting was important, Harrison."

He cups my cheek and looks at me with a look that warms my insides. "Not as important as you. I told you, you're mine."

"Harrison..."

"You told me you could only do all in. I'm all in, Jules, and I will always be here for you without a second thought. I will always take care of my girls."

"Although this all sounds amazing, I'm confused," I admit.

He swings his legs off the bed and places me against the head-board. "I know my girl can't function properly without her breakfast. Stay here, and I'll grab us something, then we'll talk." He ties his robe around him, then he's out the door, and I wish he hadn't left. My imagination runs wild when he's not here, and I need the calm he brings me.

I get up and walk into the bathroom, figuring freshening up might distract me. I smile inwardly when I open the bottom cabinet, and my stuff is still there.

Even though I haven't been here in weeks, and things have been confusing between us, he kept everything of mine.

I brush my teeth, then wash my face when a memory comes barreling forward. *"This is where you belong, with me, in this bed, my home, and our life."* Harrison enters the bedroom, holding a tray of food, coffee, and green tea.

"You said you want me in your home and *our* life," I blurt out.

He sets it down, then stalks over to where I stand in the bathroom doorway, pulling me into him in an embrace.

"What do you think all in is, Jules? If we're doing this, we're doing it right. We're not half-assing it."

"But—"

"Are you having second thoughts?" He leans back to look at me.

"What? No? But…I don't know. This is all coming out of nowhere. I thought you were subtly trying to end things with me, and now you want more. So much more."

"Clearly, I have a lot to explain. Tell me one thing first, baby, are you in or are you out?"

He's asked me this once before, and just like then, there is no hesitation. "In." *So in.*

He lets out a desperate growl and aggressively takes my lips, smashing our bodies together to make us one, yet all too soon, he pulls back.

"Claud is my entire universe, and we're a package deal. You going to be okay with that?"

Is he joking with me? I cross my arms, annoyed, and walk around him. "I'm not even entertaining that question. It's almost insulting you would ask me that."

When he mutters a soft *fuck*, I realize I'm completely naked.

"Stop distracting me." He slaps my ass, chuckling as he picks me up from behind and carries me back to bed.

Before he comes to lie next to me, he passes me oatmeal, exactly how I love it, with berries on the side topped with cinnamon and maple syrup.

He takes a deep breath and leans back with his eyes closed.

I sit and watch, unsure of what he's thinking.

"We need to just get to it and stop wasting time. To do that means I need to start from the beginning and explain about Sebastian and how my life has changed over the last five years since Claud was born. But before that, know I never wanted to end things with you, Jules. You drive me fucking crazy. I've never felt this way for another woman."

"Not even Rachel?" I mumble and immediately want to kick myself for my immature insecurities.

Get your shit together, Juliette.

"Don't ask stupid fucking questions. I've told you this before. She and all the others were nothing more than an easy fuck." My stomach drops at the thought of him with other women. He squeezes my hand, sensing my hurt. "I didn't mean to say it like that. I'm sorry. Truly, she means nothing."

I nod. I hate feeling jealous, but can't stop it whenever I think of another woman in his arms.

It makes me physically ill.

"Baby, look at me." I cast my eyes up to his, full of sorrow. "It makes me crazy too. I should have realized, but I hate the idea of you comparing yourself to her or anyone else. You are on such a different level than any woman I've ever been with. No one could ever compare to you."

I nod my head in agreement, something I know I need to work on, and we have more important things to discuss.

He takes a deep breath, struggling to get the words out. "You know me and my brothers, however, you don't know we also had a sister, Camila. She died of ovarian cancer five years ago."

Instantly, tears prickle in my eyes. "I'm so sorry, Harrison."

He smiles with a hint of sadness. "She was Claudina's mother, and...I am not her biological father." My mouth opens, but no words come out. "Camila fell pregnant after a one-night stand while she was in remission. Although as protective brothers, we weren't thrilled on how it all went down, we were still ecstatic to bring a little Camila into this world. She would have four uncles who would be there to protect and love her, and she would never need a father." He takes a deep breath. "God, we were crazier than Camila. We read every book and took turns taking all the pregnancy classes. We were equally invested. Then, while pregnant with Claud, her cancer came back."

"Oh my god." A lump forms in my throat. "Treatment didn't help?"

He runs his hands over his face and clenches his jaw to hold back his emotions. "She refused treatment until her third trimester. By then, we all knew it was too late," he mutters.

I rub my chest as pain radiates through me for his whole family. "She gave up her life so her daughter could have one," I whisper, and he nods, confirming.

Silence hangs in the room before he continues.

I've always loved Claud, but now, I love her mother as well—what a selfless, amazing woman.

"She didn't want Claud to be both mother and fatherless, so she put my name on the birth certificate. She and I were best friends, and she was closest to me out of all the brothers. Since I wasn't blood-related, it made sense. Then, when the time came and shit got real, we needed a plan for Claud. I knew deep down she was always mine. It was never a question. I was even ready to fight for her. But I had to tread lightly with Sebastian since he was Camila's older biological brother."

I interlock our fingers and hold his hand for support when I see him struggling, "Keep going," I encourage.

"As Camila got worse, Seb became extremely depressed and still is, if I'm being honest. He's had a hard journey navigating his feelings, and because of that, Camila chose me as the father. Seb ultimately agreed when he realized what a bad place he was in."

"Does Claud know?"

"That I'm not her biological father? No. Definitely not. I don't even want to think of the day I need to tell her, if ever. She knows all about Camila, though. We talk about her almost every day. I never want her to forget her."

"Don't ever stop. It is exactly why I talk to my dad at night. Their memory stays alive through the people who remember them the most. And from learning how selfless Camila was, never ever let her forget."

Harrison smiles softly. "I won't."

"I never told you, but my dad also died of cancer. It happened so fast that we didn't see it coming. He was misdiagnosed, and then it was like a whirlwind of events, and he died." I sigh, all cried out at this point. "I had never felt agony like that, but I remind myself it's nowhere near the pain he was in, physically and mentally."

He rubs his fingers along the curvature of my face. "We're a sorry pair, aren't we?"

I smile sadly. Life is truly unfair. "Now it makes sense what Claud said yesterday."

"What's that?"

"That her mom would have loved to be there at ballet. She mentioned that she thought she would like me."

His eyes bulge. "She said that?"

"Mmmhmm, and when I asked where her mom was because I was freaking out since you had never told me anything, she told me she was everywhere."

He chuckles. "Rosa told Claud that Camila is her guardian angel, who is everywhere she is to protect her." He takes a sip of his coffee, then inhales a deep breath. I drink my tea, letting him take his time to get everything out. "Do you remember I told you about the ex I have a restraining order on?"

"Yes, of course."

"That happened right before Claud was born. When I signed all the legal papers to become her father officially, Seb asked me for one favor —to forgo a family of my own and make Claud my one and only person until she was older."

"What?" I whisper. "That's not fair to you."

"It didn't matter. Before he even asked, I knew I would agree to whatever it was. I knew that I had to give him anything he asked because deep down, I felt guilty for taking his niece away." His voice catches, and I know he still feels the guilt.

"Oh, Harrison." I climb into his lap and hold him tight. "You can't feel guilty. Camila asked you to do this, and it sounds as if you were the better person for the job at that time. You've given her an amazing life, and from what I've gathered, the one thing all four of you agree on is the welfare of Claudina. I think that's the takeaway from this." He nods without speaking. "How will Seb feel if you break this promise, Harrison?"

"Not good. Doesn't matter, though. I'm not living a life without you anymore. For the last few weeks, hell for the last couple of months, I knew this was so much more between us, and it's been driving me insane keeping you at arm's length. I've struggled between what I truly wanted and my promise. Then Leo gave me a significant letter that solidified it all for me."

He reaches around to his nightstand and hands me a pink letter, and before I begin reading, I already know who it's from.

I don't know how, but I do.

"Harrison," I whisper, breathing hard through my nose, tears blurring my vision trying my best not to cry as I read, and by the end, I'm sobbing hard like a baby. "She knew."

He nods. "She always did. Even about how Seb would be, she knew it all."

Her wishing she could have had longer to love Claud broke me into pieces that I'm not sure will all go back together. That line will live with me forever.

Harrison hands me a tissue. "Well, it seems like I owe Leo a thank you." I smile through my tears. "I always knew I liked him."

"Yeah, yeah. Ignore that mom stuff. I don't want that to freak you out. I only wanted to show you to better explain my struggles."

I should be freaking out. Most girls my age would be running for the hills. Not me. I feel the complete opposite, in fact.

"I'm not freaked out," I tell him truthfully.

His eyes search mine in surprise. "You should be."

I shake my head. "Harrison, you two are a duo, and I always knew you came as a package deal if we ever were going to be more. I don't know how to explain it, but I've felt a connection with Claud from before I even knew you."

"I know. I see it." He smiles softly.

"And what if Seb says no? I get heartbroken?" I lower my voice, saying the reality of it all hits hard.

"Juliette." His voice is strong and demanding, causing me to snap my head toward him. "I'm not asking Seb. I'm telling him. It's you that needs to be sure. You have to understand what I'm feeling between us if I'm willing to break this promise, don't you?"

I kiss his neck and hug him tight. "I've been sure since I looked across the room, and my heart fluttered. It's never felt so alive." I blow out a deep breath. "But Harrison, I also don't want to be the demise of your relationship with your brother when I know how close you are."

"That's not on you, baby. You wouldn't be my Jules if you didn't worry about others. You're too good for me." He cups my cheeks and presses his pouty lips hard against mine. "But I'm a selfish bastard who doesn't give a fuck, and I'm keeping you."

I chuckle, fall forward, and lean my head on his shoulder.

We're really doing this.

Ah.

"So," I mumble into his skin. "You're my boyfriend then?"

He huffs, and I know he's rolling his eyes. "Isn't there a better term for that?"

Yeah, wife, I think. *Fiancée even.*

"Nope. You're my boyfriend." I wiggle in his lap and feel him grow against my center. "I'm loving life right now, Harrison."

He stills my movements before I can grind my hips down. "Trust me, me too. However, we still need to discuss last night."

"No," I say more sternly than I mean to, but it's the last thing I want to do with the high I'm feeling right now.

"Not an option, Jules. We need to work out whatever you're going through because what I saw was a buildup of something, and it's not the first time."

I hate that he's right.

"I don't want to burst my happy bubble, H. My heart is so happy right now."

He kisses my temple, holding his lips against my skin. "Mine too, baby, but we deserve a fresh start, which means working through things together, not separately."

When I don't begin, he rubs my back encouragingly, and finally, I let it all out.

"I feel like I'm going to burst," I whisper. "Everything keeps piling up, and I don't know how to handle it. It's like suddenly I woke up, and I'm living someone else's life." Admitting it out loud is hard. "Yesterday was a rude awakening that if I put my issues in the back of my mind, for no matter how long, they don't go away. I had a break-down at the beginning of the week, too."

"What's weighing you down, baby? I hate seeing you like this."

"I've never told anyone how I feel, not even Becks," I whisper as he continuously rubs my back in support. "It started with Dad's death, and it's been a trickle of events ever since." I scrunch up my eyes in an attempt to get rid of the pain. "That night, my mom called me to come home. I told her I'd be there soon, but time got away from me. I made it only ten minutes before Dad died. I could have spent the whole night with him, but instead, I was at the studio fighting with Hunter." My stomach turns. I feel sick even thinking of this. "For months after, I was angry with Mom when I should have been consoling her. I blamed her for not trying harder to get in touch with me." I lean back to look at Harrison. "What kind of person does that? Especially when I don't blame her at all."

His sad eyes take mine. "One who is grieving, Juliette."

I shake my head, not allowing myself off the hook so easily. "No. Mom and I are a team, and I should never have acted that way. I was so angry. I put everything I had into dance, more than ever before, and for what? I ruined that, too."

He kisses my temple again. "You were hit by a taxi. That's not your fault."

"I wasn't paying attention. If I had been, maybe I could have avoided it. The night I got hit was the opening night of *The Sleeping Beauty*, a part I was so proud to have gotten, and not because I was the lead role. I grew up watching the movie with Dad, and he never complained, even if I asked to watch it repeatedly. After my perfor-mance, I stayed back before meeting my family and friends at my cele-bratory dinner. I wanted time alone to talk to him, even though my mom begged me to leave with her. I was so lost in my mind that I wasn't paying attention when I left. None of this would have happened if I had gone with Mom. I would still be dancing, pursuing my dream. Instead, I'm a baker."

Harrison pushes me back to look at my face. "You don't like being a baker?"

I shrug. "I do. Sometimes I hate it, sometimes I love it. I know I wouldn't have picked it as my career though. Recently I realized there's no going back, this is it for me, and it all hit me harder than expected."

"Going back from where? You're twenty-four, Jules. You have a whole life ahead of you. You can do whatever you want."

"Whatever I want is not an option. We don't all have the privilege of money, Harrison," I snap, taking my frustrations out on him. "Wouldn't it be nice if I could open my own dance studio, all while running the bakery with a full staff? To pay the asking rent so we don't need to move. Hell, to buy the place. Sadly, that's not a reality for most people."

He ignores my rant. "Does your mom know you're unhappy?"

"I'm not exactly unhappy. I could be doing much worse." I rub my temples. "Even if I had time to teach dance on the side, who knows if I even would. I haven't danced ballet since that night, and yesterday was a stark reminder."

"Now you have me, Juliette. Let it all go so I can shoulder some of your pain, baby."

God, I love this man. I really do.

He can be so sweet when he wants to be.

I idly rub my fingers through his hair, taking comfort in his words.

Suddenly, just from one sentence, I feel freer than ever, and yesterday doesn't seem all that important anymore. "The end-of-summer dance surprise was for the children to meet the New York City Ballet's principal dancers. Hunter and all the others were there, and I might have a bit of a panic attack."

He stills below my touch. "What happened? I'm going to fucking kill that guy."

"Calm down. Nothing bad, honestly. It was my first time seeing my replacement, Annalise, and a lot of chatter was going on. I think it was the straw that broke the camel's back, and I snapped." I think for a moment. "You know, it was my first true time dealing with my accident. Everyone walks on eggshells about it because they know how upset I get. I'm okay now, though...I can't promise it won't happen again. Today, I feel lighter after it, like I can breathe with you here by my side."

He leans forward and kisses my bare shoulder. "I want to help you through this, Jules. Whatever it takes, I'll do it."

"Thank you, Harrison. You have no idea how much those words mean to me." I run my hands through his stubble. "I think we were meant to meet and help each other."

My thought is interrupted by movement on Harrison's baby monitor, which I find adorable he still uses. He had told me once he kept it because Claudina would wake up and play independently, not wanting to disturb Harrison if he was still sleeping or working early in the morning.

Of course, Harrison doesn't want to miss any Claud time.

"You better get dressed and get out there. Something tells me she won't want to miss a second with you this morning. I'll be right behind you."

I pause in the doorway. "Harrison," I call.

He turns, and his eyes shine bright as he smiles. "Yes, baby?"

"When I was younger, my dad told me. *If he wants to...he will.* I didn't understand it at the time. You came back for me when I needed you the most. Thank you."

I place my hand on my heart to show him how much I care.

Only words could never express how much.

19

Harrison

"Noooo," Claud begs, clearly upset about the idea of Jules going home. She rarely acts like this when she doesn't get her way. I've tried my hardest with her to teach limits so she doesn't become a spoiled rich kid.

The Morales are billionaires, though they come from humble beginnings and have never let their kids forget it. Despite my parents' generational wealth, Rosa didn't treat me any differently, and I have always wanted to instill the same in Claudina.

When she doesn't stop her whining, I intervene. "That's enough, Claudina. What have I told you about that?"

She ignores me, which is a first. "Don't go home, Juliette. Please come see my mommy with us!"

I still, and the room goes silent, except for Claud's hopeful feet bouncing up and down.

Juliette glances at me and smiles softly, then crouches down so they're eye to eye. "I can't go today, sugar plum. Maybe Daddy can bring you in for a special treat later?"

"Come," I spit quickly, without thinking. Then takes Jules's arm to lift her upright, staring deep into her sultry brown eyes. "I'd like you to come with us."

"Are you sure?" she whispers. "It's okay if it's not, Harrison. This is something personal between the two of you."

"Please," I beg.

Doesn't she understand? It's not just Claud and me anymore? It's the three of us.

She hesitates. "Okay." Then she turns to Claud. "Let's go, sugar plum. I'd love to come meet your mom."

Claud skips ahead, looking back every so often, smiling so bright she may burst. I knew she adored Jules, but this is some next-level shit.

She would only hold Jules's hand when we crossed the street and changed her outfit twice so she could find the perfect skirt and white shirt, *just like Jules*.

"Daddy?" Claud calls. "Can we get lunch when we're done?"

"At a restaurant? Or a dirty water dog in the park?" I ask, my attention focused on Jules.

She blushes, casting her eyes down, hiding a smile.

"I don't want dirty dogs. Gross!" She scrunches up her nose in disgust while Jules and I laugh.

"It's what us New Yorkers call hot dogs. We get them from those stands, sugar plum." Jules points to the cart in front of us, selling hotdogs and pretzels.

Claud shakes her head like she can't believe it and runs off again.

I don't blame her. I myself only want one every ten years.

"Before you, I haven't had one since I was Claud's age. I remember my parents scoffed at the idea of eating one in the park. Rosa brought me the very next day."

"Honestly, I think my dad was in a similar situation as you. Could you imagine the Archibalds slumming it with a hot dog in the park?" She laughs sarcastically. "It's probably why he made it a tradition for us whenever we left a museum or had a weekend in the park together."

Then I remember something...

"Why do you call Claud sugar plum?" I ask curiously.

She's been calling her that since I met her.

Jules smiles broadly. "When I met her for the first time in December, she was obsessed with wearing her sugar plum outfit from her part in *The Nutcracker*. She was so cute, prancing around the bakery. I told her I was the sugar plum fairy once, and the rest is history."

I chuckle. "Oh, I remember. She begged me to sleep in it most nights, so I bought extras in case she ruined them. That happened once when she was a toddler, with her special blanket, and it was like the end of the world."

My phone dings, and it's Nate confirming they landed.

"Hey, if you're not busy the rest of the day, I was wondering if you'd do me a favor."

"Sure. I only have physical therapy planned." She smiles, linking our pinkies so Claud doesn't notice.

"Could you watch Claud again later this afternoon? She was supposed to come to the office with me, but I'm meeting Seb at my office to talk and would prefer her not to be there."

She stops walking. "Today?" Her eyes bulge.

"It can't wait another day. Claud has a big mouth, and she will tell him you babysat, and we came here all together today. He calls her almost every day when he doesn't see her."

The babysitting I could get around, but not bringing a woman to Camila's memorial stone.

"Fuck," she whispers. "I'm nervous for you, Harrison."

Me too, only I'm not going forward in life like this anymore. Seeing Claud with Jules recently and how they already have a special relationship was the push I needed. "It will be fine. We'll figure it out."

I pull out my Black Card and pass it to Jules. "Here, use this if you need anything today. In fact, keep it until I can order another one with your name on it."

She narrows her confused eyes. "Why are you giving me your credit card?"

"In case my girls need anything."

I thought it was obvious.

She passes it back to me, pushing it hard into my hand. "I may not be rich, but I can take care of myself and Claud."

Not on my watch. "I never said you couldn't, but that's not how things are going to go. I won't have you spending your money on something even as little as gum. You better get used to it."

Ignoring her grumbling, I look at my phone when Nate texts again. This time, it's a grainy picture of Leo in the club, but there is no mistake he's getting his dick sucked.

I pinch the bridge of my nose and shake my head. Those two together are bad news; they're lucky they're not all over the tabloids this morning, which would put Rosa and Javier into an early grave.

"Ah." Jules covers her eyes. "What the hell? You guys send each other stuff like that?"

"No. Only my two younger idiot brothers. They all stopped in London to look at a possible hotel site for Seb. It looks like they had some fun, too," I tell her, unable to hold back my laugh at her horrified face.

"I can't believe he's getting a blow job in the middle of a club!"

"I'm sure they had a private section." I look up to see Claud skipping too far ahead. "Claudina! That's far enough."

Jules shakes her head like she can't wrap her head around it. "Does he even know her?"

I shrug. "Who knows? Maybe, maybe not. Leo has a girl in every city. He's a bit of a modern-day Casanova. Falling in and out of love with every girl he meets."

"Please tell me you've never done that." She cringes at the thought.

"You should know I'm much more private than those two by now. The same goes for Seb. You'll never see anything about us anywhere, post-college at least."

She scrubs her face. "I wish I didn't see that. That's all I'll think of when I see him."

"Yeah. You better fucking not think of my brother getting his dick sucked." I bark.

"Well," she raises her voice and throws her hands up. You shouldn't have had it open on your phone for me to see."

"I don't care. Erase it from your memory." I warn.

My phone rings this time, and I almost ignore it but see it's Rosa calling. I tell Jules I need to take it, knowing they're in Spain and it's getting late there.

"Hi, Mom."

"You're expected at Sunday dinner the day we get home in three weeks," she quickly says.

"No hello, how are you? How's Claud?"

"I need to go, and I expect Juliette to be in attendance." She hangs up without another word.

Fuck.

I turn toward Jules, who is now hand in hand with Claud, laughing hysterically at the silly faces she's making. She turns back, with a smile on her face and laughing tears in her eyes, waving me closer to them.

I hope she's ready because she's one of us now.

There's no turning back.

"What are you two doing here?" I glance up at Nate and Leo as they walk through my office door, Skye trailing behind them. Her ears perk up when I open my desk drawer—where Claud stores extra treats and toys—quickly trotting toward me. I scratch behind her ear, causing her to melt into the floor along my feet, where I'm sure she'll lie the rest of the time she's here. "And where the hell is Lauren? I told her no one is to come back here until after I finish with Seb."

"We're here to mediate and support," Leo announces. "And you know Lauren listens to us more than you."

These two fucking idiots. "He'll lose his fucking mind if we all gang up on him. What's wrong with you two?"

Leo goes to the bar and pours four drinks. "We'll need these."

"And who the fuck told Mom about Juliette? She's demanding we come to dinner when she's home."

"Claud told her about her friend." Nate laughs with a cocky smirk. "We only confirmed she may be a little more than a friend."

Leo passes out the drinks just as Sebastian walks in. He takes the drink and looks down, confused. "Are we celebrating?"

Nate raises an eyebrow and looks between us. "Some will be, some won't be, I'm sure." He mumbles.

I lean my head back against my office chair and close my eyes, attempting to gain some patience.

"Nate and Leo are just leaving," I say as Thing One and Thing Two sit on the couch.

Leo sips his scotch. "Are we, though?" he mumbles against the glass.

Fuck's sake.

"Weren't you supposed to be away until the end of the week?" I ask Nate.

"Don't remind me." He turns toward Seb. "When did we land— five hours ago? Then I leave again in forty-eight hours."

Seb looks down at his watch. "Speaking of leaving. I need to go soon. Some fucking idiot who works the front desk at The Huxley had sex with someone from housekeeping after a happy hour a few months back. Now she's pregnant, and it's a fucking mess. So, can we get to why you called me? Is it Claudina?" he asks, then sucks back the whole glass of scotch.

Fuck. Fuck. Fuck.

Leo's eyes widen, knowing if he's drinking like that, he's stressed, and this will not go over well.

I walk around my desk and sit in one of the chairs. I know how Seb thinks. If I'm behind my desk, he'll take it as a power play, and I need an even playing field right now.

"So, I met a girl and…" I trail off, thinking of my words carefully. I'm the CEO of a trillion-dollar company, yet I can't think of a single word to say to him right now. Guessing how his face morphs into anger, he understands what I'm trying to say.

"And you what?" Seb spits in a fury.

"And…I'm in love with her, Sebastian," I tell him truthfully, saying the words out loud for the first time. Leo gives me an encouraging smile. "She loves Claud—"

He interrupts, slamming his empty glass on the table. "You fucking piece of shit. You introduced her to Claud?"

"All right, calm the hell down, and let me explain."

He grips the arms of the chair in a punishing grip and leans forward toward me. "You made a fucking promise to me that Claudina would be your one and only priority. Since when did you become so fucking untrustworthy?" He stands up and steps in front of me. "If I can't trust you with one fucking promise, how do I trust you with Claud?" he bellows, and that's when I draw the line.

I stand up to him, face to face. "You want to say that fucking bullshit. Say it to my face."

"You're a fucking liar, and I don't trust you."

"Bullshit!" Nate yells, defending me without hesitation.

Leo jumps up from his chair and pushes Seb away from me. "Shut the fuck up, Sebastian, before you say something else you'll regret. Since when have we not been in each other's corners? And since when did you become such a selfish prick? Your best friend and brother just told you he's in love with someone, and this is how you react?" He shakes his head, disappointed in his brother.

Nate stands now. "And you have some nerve questioning him as a father. That's a low fucking blow, Sebastian. Even from you."

Leo's still shaking his head. "He is the one who has always been on your side, more than anyone in this family, and this is how you repay him—by questioning his integrity. I would have knocked you the fuck out if I were him." He walks away, then turns back. "You know what. I'm ashamed we're even fucking related right now."

Sebastian's chest heaves, breathing heavily through his nose as he stands there, taking on insult after insult. Finally, he has had enough and turns toward the elevator without another word.

"I made a mistake years ago, dating the wrong woman." I raise my voice loud enough for him to hear in the hallway. "That was a long time ago, and Juliette is nothing like her. We, as brothers, take each other as we come, and now Claud and I come with Juliette. I'll give you this one pass, Sebastian, because I know I fucked up by going back on our deal and that you're still hurting. You bring up my parenting one more time, and that will be the end of everything. If you want to do the right thing, come to Sunday dinner when Mom and Dad are home and meet her before you judge her or our situation."

I walk around him and leave everyone behind when I enter my private elevator. It's time I get back to my girls.

"What's up?" I answer my phone when I see Matteo calling.

"Don't get in your car. I'm right behind you and need to talk." I turn to see Matteo running toward the curb outside our office building, with a girl trailing behind him.

Talking to him is the last fucking thing I want to do right now.

"I tried your office, but you were gone," he says, panting.

"You need to start using the gym more. You ran less than one hundred feet and look like you're about to die."

He waves me off, then playfully makes a muscle. "Gym who?"

"You're an ass."

The woman catches up to him, looking familiar, but I can't put my finger on it. She must work at Abbott, too.

"Hi, Harrison," she greets.

Wait...

I narrow my eyes. "Becks?"

"Who else would it be?" she asks, perplexed.

Which makes both of us, because why does she look so different?

"I didn't recognize you," I tell her truthfully. I'm still unable to put my finger on it.

She smirks. "Well, I guess I'm not on the clock anymore." She looks around, reaches up, unclips something, and pulls a wig off her head. "Ta da!"

Her indigo hair falls out in waves while my mouth gapes open. "Why the hell do you wear that?"

She looks between Matteo and me. "Umm…because it's the rules of the office that I do not have my hair dyed other than the normal blonde, red, or brown."

What shit is she talking about? "Since when?"

She shrugs. "You tell me, boss. You own the company."

"It must have been something my grandfather put into place. He was modern for his times, nonetheless, a formal man. I'll have Lauren, my assistant, review the employee handbook with a fine-tooth comb to see what needs to be updated. The rule stands: if you're client-facing or working on a floor with the conference rooms, you wear the wig. Day-to-day, there is no need, and that goes for any employee." I glance at Matteo. "Got it, boss?"

"Not technically her boss," he mumbles.

"Semantics. Now, my brothers are about to exit the building at any moment, and I don't want to see them. What did you need me for?"

Matteo turns and kisses Beck's forehead. "This is confidential. I'll meet you in the car." He points across the street. "My brother is idling, waiting for us there."

She thanks me for changing the archaic rules, and before walking away, she stands there, giving me the third degree with her eyes.

There is no doubt in my mind that Jules called her after I left and told her everything. Thankfully, Becks knows better than to question my intentions.

"What's going on there?" I jut my chin toward Matteo's car.

His eyes linger on Becks as she crosses the street. *I know that look.*

He takes a deep breath and lifts his shoulder. "It's complicated." After a second, he looks back and turns toward me. "I still need to dive deeper. However, I figured out who owns the shell company. The Archibald family."

"What?" I mutter in disbelief. "Are you sure?"

"Yeah, apparently oil wasn't enough for them, so they're dabbling in real estate. Greedy bastards. Does this mean anything to you?"

"It means everything. I need more information before I dig deeper. Get me the names of those running it and whatever else you can find."

My gut is telling me this is no fucking coincidence, and I need to get to the bottom of it.

"No problem." He salutes me and walks off.

"And remember, not a fucking word to anyone. Not even my brothers. I want no one sniffing around," I call after him.

I don't know what this family is playing at, but I have a terrible fucking feeling.

Juliette

My eyes flutter open, and instantly, I can tell it's not yet morning. My senses are on high alert when I don't feel Harrison wrapped around me in bed. Creeping my arm over to the other side, I feel for him—nothing —ice cold.

I stand and stretch, attempting to wake up, then wrap myself in a robe before leaving the room, not wanting any accidental naked run-ins with Claud, even if it is the middle of the night.

She doesn't know I've slept over, and I plan to leave before she wakes, so I need to be cautious as I walk through the halls.

We've decided that the three of us will slowly spend more time together so that it won't seem like such a surprise when we tell her about us. Even though I'm not sure she'll comprehend it anyway.

Peeking my head into Harrison's office, I see him sitting at his desk. His hair is mussed up from obvious distress.

"Motherfucker," he mumbles to himself and tosses his phone with gusto onto the desk.

"Hi," I whisper, not wanting to startle him. "Are you okay?" He stares with intent, not saying a word. "Harrison? What's wrong?"

He holds out his arms, so I quicken my step and settle on his lap, pulling my legs up and resting my head under his chin so he can hold me tight and use me as a stress relief.

"Talk to me. Is it because of your fight with Sebastian?" I mutter.

"There's too much going on at the moment and not enough hours in the day to deal with it all. We just lost a major international client because of my employee's lack of fucking brains." He shakes his head, frustrated. "I'll figure it out. I always do."

His computer screen is lit up with an invitation to a summer white party.

"You're going to the Hamptons next week?"

"*We're* going to the Hamptons next week," he corrects. "I hope you're ready to be introduced into the fucked-up world of the rich and famous." He laughs sardonically.

"You're not making it sound very appealing," I mumble into his chest.

"It is what it is. It's my life, and I need you by my side." He lifts my chin so I can look up into his eyes. "You ready to show the world you're mine?"

I gulp down my unease and nod. "What I'm not ready for is them digging up my past so that I have to relive it over and over."

"It's easier to stop the pictures and stories when it comes to Claud since she's a child, but I'll try my hardest to get whatever I can taken down."

"Okay. I'll ask Mom if I can get the days off." Knowing I'll kick and scream like a child until she does.

I may not be happy about the stories that will be published, but that doesn't mean I'm not giddy with joy over the fact Harrison Davenport is mine, and I want to scream it to the world.

"I'll call her if she doesn't," he says, and I laugh, thinking he is joking. "I'm being serious. There will be times I need you, Juliette. No questions asked. I will hire someone for the bakery if they need coverage. But next week, I need you there."

I reach up, cup his cheek, then playfully pucker my lips so he'll lean down, and I can reach him. "Okay, H. I'll be there." I kiss him harder, feeling the stress radiating off him.

The curtains billow from the night breeze, catching my attention, causing me to glance over his shoulder toward the open door leading to the small terrace off his office.

I climb off his lap and walk toward the door, opening it wide while holding out my hand.

"What are you doing?" he asks skeptically. "Where'd my kiss go?"

"Trust me. I'll help you forget for tonight."

"Mmm, I like the sound of that." His firm mouth lifts into a smirk before he's up, prowling toward me, a man on a mission.

I laugh out loud. "Not that you, fiend. Grab your phone." I point toward the desk, and then we walk out into the beautiful summer night, where the city is quiet and the air feels fresh.

I take his phone from his hand, unlock it—which still blows my mind that he trusts me enough with the password—and turn on Dad's and my song.

Thankfully, I don't need to worry about the volume since the neighbors and Claud's bedroom have soundproof windows.

"Dancing in the Moonlight" by King Harvest begins to play over the speakers while I take his hand in mine and press my body to my chest. Naturally, he takes the lead, and we sway to the beat of the music.

Just like I did all those late nights with my dad.

"When I was a little older than Claud, my dad would sneak me out of my room and take me to our forbidden rooftop to dance under the moonlight. It was always when I had a bad day at school or a silly fight with Becks. And when I was older, it was the nights I came home stressed about dance, boy problems, and even when I found out he was sick. He would play this song, and we would dance the night away without my mom ever knowing. It was our secret."

He leans down and kisses my forehead, then a quick peck behind my ear, on my beauty mark. "Why this song?" he murmurs.

"Dad told me that the writer Sherman Kelly wrote it while getting over a traumatic experience. He envisioned an alternate reality, the dream of a peaceful and joyful celebration of life to get him through it." I pause, giving myself a moment with the memories of my father. "He would say, *Juliette, when you dream about happiness, it will get you through anything.*"

Harrison's hand, splayed across my lower back, creeps up my body and tugs at my hair, angling my face toward his.

His lips drop, and he presses them hard against mine, holding them there until I can feel his emotions oozing out of him.

We stay like this until the song ends, held tight to one another, with our lips locked, swaying softly to a song that has significant meaning to me. Now, I get to share it with the man who now means everything to me.

"I wish I could have met your dad," he mumbles against my lips. "I love your mom. But your dad sounds exactly like the father I want to be."

"Harrison, you are already." I take a small step back to look at him in his eyes. "You're almost too good of a father. It's why you're so stressed. You don't delegate and take on too much while trying to be both parents and often even taking over Willa's role. The only thing you don't do is the housekeeper's job. You'll burn out unless you learn to let go of the reins a bit. Worry about your business succeeding and being the best CEO. You don't need to try any harder with Claud. You're already an amazing father."

His eyes glow bright in the moonlight with appreciation. "Thank you, Jules," he whispers, stepping back into my space and lightly fingering my exposed collarbone.

His broad, powerful chest rises rapidly as his fingers trace down my chest, pushing aside my robe, following a teasing pattern around the swell of my breast.

The prolonged anticipation is almost unbearable, and a visceral need to touch him comes over me. Not that it surprises me. Harrison's love language is touch, and I'm starting to think maybe mine is, too.

That or I'm just obsessed with him…both are viable answers.

I stand on my tippy-toes to swipe away the wisps of his fallen honey-blonde hair, then cup his cheek. "Take me to bed, Harrison." My lust-filled voice breathes against his lips.

He cups my behind and lifts me so we're face to face.

"How does my good girl want it?"

I glance back through the doors into his office, then turn, shooting him a flirtatious smirk, then lean in and bite his lip. "Bend me over your desk, and take your stress out on me, H."

"Fuck!" He inhales sharply and stalks inside.

I push his briefs down and rub myself on him so he can feel how ready I am.

He clenches his jaw tight, and his nostrils flare. "You better be ready…you're getting fucked hard tonight, baby," he barks and slaps my ass.

Yes…please.

20

Juliette

"You should get both," the saleswoman at La Perla says from beside me. "The coloring would complement your summer-bronzed skin perfectly."

I smile kindly. "Thank you. Unfortunately, I can only afford one. I'm going away today with my boyfriend for a couple of days, and I wanted to get something new."

"Then you must get this. It will blow his mind." She holds up a one-piece crotchless lingerie set, more risqué than anything I've ever worn.

Harrison would probably love it, except I know he loves my innocent look more than anything else.

Another sales associate walks out from the back and rushes over, interrupting us. "I'm so sorry, Ms. Caldwell. Please let me introduce myself. I'm Gloria, the store manager, and I was on my lunch break. Our new employee here hasn't yet been updated on our VIP guests."

I look between them, confused. "I'm sorry, you must be mistaken and got the wrong Ms. Caldwell. I'm in no way a VIP."

"I-I…" Gloria looks mortified. "I'm so sorry. I thought you were Juliette, that is with Mr. Harrison Davenport?"

I close my eyes for a brief moment and take a breath.

What did this man do?

"You're not wrong, Gloria. However, I don't need any special treatment."

She looks like I just dropped a bomb in the room, and I realize she most likely can't deny a Davenport request, or she would get in trouble with her boss.

"Well, I'm only going to get this today." I hold up the gorgeous navy blue and lilac lace matching set, with a demi cup bra cut so low, I know it will drive Harrison crazy. He goes wild when my areolas peek out and my hardened nipples push through the ultra-thin lace. "How about next time I ask for you directly, and you can show me what new pieces have arrived."

"That would be lovely, Juliette. Thank you." She lets out a sigh of relief, then wraps my purchase. "Here you are."

"Thank you. How much do I owe you?"

She waves me off. "Oh, don't worry about that. It goes on the house account Mr. Davenport set up for you."

"I'm going to kill that man," I grumble under my breath. "And what is the limit on this house account, may I ask?"

She looks at me, surprised.

Not as surprised as I am, Gloria.

"There is no limit, of course."

"Of course not." I smile, most likely looking half-deranged. "You know what." I turn toward the other assistant in a rage and take the crotchless piece—that I'll never wear—and then the sage green set I was looking at earlier out of her hands, possibly with too much force. For good measure, I grab another set I've been eyeing for everyday use. "These too, please."

"Oh. Yes, yes." Gloria wraps these with more enthusiasm than before.

Of course, she would. Who wouldn't, when they most definitely work off commission, and I've just spent a small fortune?

I barely say goodbye before I dial my dear old boyfriend.

"Hi, babe. I'm just finishing up here."

"I just left La Perla, Harrison…"

"Mmmm. Give me a visual. What colors did you buy?" His chair creaks, and I picture him adjusting himself.

"Who cares," I snap. "You can't spend all that money on lingerie."

"Those pieces please you just as much as me, so what's the problem? Buy the whole store for all I care."

I lower my voice when I detect hurt in his voice. "Because it's too much, Harrison." I know he means nothing by it, but having unlimited money to me is new. "I'm thankful, but it's a lot all at once. Last week a Black Card, a freaking Black Card, Harrison. Not even a platinum. Now I have carte blanche in La Perla, a store I used to save for months to buy one piece."

"I hear you, Jules, but don't read into it so much. Enjoy it. Please."

"Yeah okay…it's just…"

"What's wrong, baby?"

I step to the side so I'm out of the heavy foot traffic of Madison Avenue and lean against a brick building.

"I'm a lot younger than you, Harrison, and now you're buying me all these expensive things. You know exactly how that looks to others, and I don't ever want you to think I'm with you for your money."

"God, I wish I was there to smack that ass of yours," he grumbles. "When have I ever given a shit what others think? And I hope you don't honestly believe I'd ever think that about you, Jules. Never. Ever."

"Sorry, I don't. I think I'm nervous about the party tomorrow," I whisper.

Harrison told me the white party we are attending was a yearly event for a friend's birthday he grew up with. When I told Becks, she looked up the guest list from last year, knowing exactly who the birthday guy was. Some big-wig finance bro, as she put it.

The same as Harrison, but he works in investment banking. *Apparently, that's different.* Who the hell knew? It's all foreign to me.

We discovered this wasn't some small get-together with New

York's socialites. This party is also full of actors, musicians, and sports legends. Kygo was the freaking DJ.

"I told you already, we'll make our rounds to say hello to a few of my friends. We don't have to stay long. I promise."

I don't want to be *that* girlfriend. "We'll stay as long as you want. It's your friend's birthday."

"So does this mean I need to return the present I bought you for this weekend, orrr…"

"Harrison!"

His deep, throaty chuckle has me laughing along with him. "Are we okay? I need to get back to work before we never get to leave."

"Yes, and Harrison?"

"Yeah, baby?"

"Thank you for being so generous."

———

You've got to be kidding me right now.

I glance around and realize there is nowhere to hide, so I carefully run into the street and duck behind a random car where I can see over the trunk as I watch my Aunt Liza and cousin Amber leave the bakery.

What the hell are they doing here?

They walk toward the car, and I hold my breath, wishing on every star in the universe that they don't see me. Thankfully, the gods are on my side when they step between the cars in front of me to call for a cab.

"They've done a beautiful job with the place, don't you think?" my aunt asks.

"It's fine. Who even cares? I'm not sure why you're making such an effort when you don't even like Aunt Inès."

"Amber. That's enough." She shakes her head. "I should have made more effort when my brother was alive. He always wanted us to be close, and now that I've taken the time to get to know her after all these years, I'm regretting every second I stayed away. Inès is such a lovely woman. I never bothered to give her a chance, but better late than never."

Oh, that's sweet.

She's right. It would have made my dad so happy if they were close, and I hope he's somewhere looking down, seeing it now.

I'm glad I was wrong about my aunt. If Amber stayed away, it would be good for my mom to have close family around since she only has me.

"Can you believe she's dating him?" Amber spits with fire in her words. "Of course, she snags the billionaire."

Oh, shove it, Amber.

"Can't you be happy for your cousin? Wouldn't it be nice if you tried to be close to her, too?"

Not happening. "Not happening." We think and say at the time.

At least we can agree on that.

Thankfully, a cab comes down the street and they climb in, allowing me a reprieve from hiding so I can finally get inside and finish packing. Harrison's already on his way.

I'm flying around the apartment, shoving last-minute things into my bag as if I'm going away for three weeks. In actuality, it's three days.

Ahhh, I'm sweating bullets right now.

I spin around. "Do I look okay?" I ask Mom.

I'm wearing a stunning, white knee-length Valentino eyelet dress that is cinched at the waist, with a scooped neck and thick straps. I thrifted the dress last year with Becks and thought it would be perfect for a Hamptons birthday party until I realized it's practically an all-night rager, where people will be dressed in one-of-a-kind designer clothing.

Luckily, Becks found me a dress and is sending it with Harrison today.

I paired the one I'm wearing with a flat slingback sandal, which I'll switch to a wedge if we go out.

I'm not in the mood to hear Harrison's bitching about me in heels with my leg right now; even though I received the amazing news last week that I've finally graduated from physical therapy, he's still constantly on me about it.

I've had minimal nerve pain lately, and I'm hoping it only improves from here.

"Yes, you look perfect, my love." She smiles lovingly.

"Thank you, and here." I hand her a list of the storefronts she's going to see today. "Becks will meet you here at four, and then the two of you will meet Barbara, the realtor, at the first location. These were my favorite three I've seen so far. If you don't like any of them, we still have time to keep looking, but I want your opinion first."

Her face drops, and she nods without any words. I know this is painful for her, and if I could, I would sell my right kidney for her to keep the bakery.

The intercom buzzes, distracting us. I press the button. "I'll be right down."

"No, let me up," Harrison demands.

"I told you I'd meet you outside."

"And I told you to let me up, Juliette. I'm not having you carry down your bags," he practically growls, and Mom sniggers, reaching over me to press the button that unlocks the downstairs door.

Fuck's sake, I don't want him to come up here right now. The place is a disaster.

I open the door when I hear the elevator ping.

He walks over to Mom and kisses her hello first, then wraps his arm around my shoulders and holds his lips to my forehead. At the same time, he looks around the place.

What must he think? Our whole apartment is the size of his kitchen.

"It's homey." He smiles, and I roll my eyes.

"Oh, shut it, it's small, and you look like a freaking giant in this room."

"Hey, don't talk about my precious home like that, Juliette," Mom scolds me, and I shrink back, forgetting she was here.

"Sorry," I mumble.

Harrison picks up my bags. "As much as I would love to stay and chat, Inès, we're on a tight schedule."

"Of course, you two have fun."

Before I forget… "Mom, I meant to tell you. I overheard Aunt Liza coming out of the bakery earlier, and she was saying such lovely things about you. I'm sorry I misjudged her. You should have dinner with her one night while I'm gone."

"Oh. Okay." My mom's face lights up, but she says nothing else. She's not one to take compliments easily.

Just as we leave, she pulls Harrison back and whispers in his ear.

"What did she say?" I ask the second we're out the door.

He lifts one side of his lips. "That she's happy I finally got my act together."

"Oh god." I cover my face. "She didn't."

"Good afternoon, Juliette."

"Oh, Robert," I say, surprised. "How are you? I'm sorry, I thought Harrison was driving, so I wasn't expecting you."

"He's only driving us to the airport, not the Hamptons," Harrison answers for him.

"The airport?" I ask, puzzled. What is he talking about? "I thought we were driving straight from here."

"I don't want to waste a minute more in the city. I'm itching to get you away, so we're flying."

"What?" I squeal. "Seriously? I've never been in a helicopter."

"Well, then, I'll make sure to take you in one next time. This time, we're taking a private jet."

I stop and look him in the square in the eye to see if he's telling the truth. "Are you serious right now?"

"No. I'm lying," he says dryly.

"Harrison. Oh my god." I jump up and down like a little kid. "This is the coolest thing ever."

He rolls his eyes and hands my bags to Robert.

"What the hell is in these…dead bodies?"

I giggle and smile brightly, then dive into the back seat, excited to get this show on the road.

I have zero freaking chill right now, and I don't care in the slightest.

"Ah. I can't believe I'm going on a PJ." He looks at me deadpan. "What? Isn't that what all the cool kids call them?"

"If you mean cool as in twenty-two-year-old douchebags, then yes."

I scoot over and buckle myself in the middle, so I'm closest to him. "I'm only twenty-four, you know."

"Don't remind me," he mutters.

I bounce in my seat for the entire twenty-five minutes it takes to make it to the airstrip, ignoring Harrison's cranky demands for me to stop a million times.

Harrison gets out first, and like always, he tells Robert he's got my door. "Let's go, baby." I take his hand, and then he walks us to the stairs while Robert loads our bags.

"I'm so excited. Thank you for taking me, Harrison."

He smiles softly and lifts my hand to his lips. "*Je serais prêt à tout pour toi, mon petite papillon.*"

He would do anything for me, he tells me, in his perfect, sexy French accent, and I genuinely believe it. Harrison is a man of his word, and it makes me proud to be his.

"Davenport." God's gift to the world walks down the steps, smiling wide, popping two sexy dimples.

Holy shit, who is this man?

How is it that Harrison knows every single good-looking person in America?

Harrison drops my hand and wraps his arms around the man in a bear hug the second he gets down the steps. They stand there for, no exaggeration, at least five minutes.

Whoever this person is must be important to him.

Finally, they pull apart. Harrison shakes his head as if he can't believe his eyes, then brings the man in for another quick hug.

"I can't believe it. What are you doing here?" Harrison asks, and I think I detect slightly glassy eyes. Then he holds out his hand for me before the man can answer. "Come here, Jules."

"Yes, please introduce me to this gorgeous woman," green eyes asks, shooting me a playful smirk.

Is this guy a model? Jesus.

Harrison and all his brothers are some of the most handsome men I've ever laid eyes on, but this man is what one would call perfection.

"Don't even fucking think about it, dickhead," Harrison warns him, pulling me into his side, holding me tightly against his body. "Jules, meet one of my best friends in the world, Jackson Peters."

I hold out my hand, and Harrison's chest rumbles in warning. I elbow his side. "Stop it," I whisper loud enough for Jackson to hear, causing him to laugh and teasingly waggle his eyebrows at Harrison.

He takes my hand and quickly kisses the back of it. "Juliette Caldwell," I introduce myself. "It's lovely to meet one of Harrison's dear friends."

"The pleasure is all mine." Then he pauses. "Wait." He looks between us. "Is this the girl Leo told me about?"

There's no way I can't hold back my smile as I look up at Harrison. "Leo is seriously my favorite person."

"Good, you can have him. He's starting to piss me the fuck off."

The pilot interrupts us and tells us we need to board and buckle up before we miss our chance for takeoff.

Okay…I'm losing my mind.

A part of me wants to scream out loud that I'm currently in the most beautiful private jet. It's fully stocked with whatever you could possibly need, and the interior is elegant, with deep amber leather seats that feel like butter.

Even the flight crew is immaculate, though crazed thoughts of accidentally tripping the stewardess have crossed my mind a few times whenever she looks at Harrison.

But of course, I'm classy. I won't do that, and I need to act normal in front of Jackson, on all accounts. The other part of me is beginning to malfunction. I've stammered over my words ten times, distracted by Jackson.

Every time it happens, I wither lower in my seat from Harrison's death stares.

He knows exactly what's going on with me, and between the two of us, our jealousy is at about one hundred and psycho percent.

We're sitting at a four-top, with a table between us. I didn't even realize planes had these; I've only ever seen them on trains.

"I can't believe you're here right now. How long are you in town for?" Harrison asks Jackson.

"I came into the city yesterday for a meeting. I called Lauren to make dinner plans. I didn't want to tell you if things didn't work out. When she told me you were going to Carter's birthday party, I knew I had to surprise you, so she added me to the customs sheet for your flight. Unfortunately, I leave right after the party."

"Fuck, Mom, Dad, and the others would have loved to see you."

"I knew Mom, Dad, and Seb were out of town. But I figured Leo and Nate would also be attending the party."

"It's Nate's week with Claud. Leo and he are in the city for work, and when we leave in a few days, they will take the house over."

"How do you all know each other?" I butt in.

"Ouch." Jackson put his hand over his heart. "You've not told her about me?"

Harrison ignores him. "Jackson grew up with us, too. He's the same age as Seb and I. Though we didn't meet him until we were about nine or ten, we were instantly inseparable. When he got older, he also used the Morales household as a refuge with his sister. He has fucked-up parents too. Then he chose to go to college with Seb instead of me, so was on my shitlist for a while."

"What a fucking depressing childhood," Jackson murmurs.

Harrison shrugs. "It's the truth, and the stories that come later are not for my girl's ears." He looks down and winks at me, then turns back to Jackson.

"It's so fucking good to see you, Peters. Well, besides when you're flirting with my girl."

"God, you're just as bad as my brother-in-law. What's with the possessive shit? You really think I'd go after your girl?"

"Oh, like you didn't try to fuck all our girlfriends in high school?"

He chuckles, and there are those dimples again. "Fair. But we were sixteen. Give me a break."

I look between these two, and I can feel the closeness between them.

"Wait," Harrison suddenly says. "Brother-in-law? What the hell— we weren't invited to Sadie's wedding?"

Jackson waves him off. "They're not married yet. They've been engaged for what feels like forever."

"Promise you'll stay next time. We miss you. Mom and Dad miss you. We'll all even come to London." Harrison turns toward me. "Jackson lives there now."

I don't miss the way Jackson's face falls in sadness before he quickly masks it.

Both his phone and Harrison's phone start to blow up. "Finally, Wi-Fi. I would love to chat, but I need to work before we land. If we don't get to talk after, I'll see you both at the party," Jackson announces, then moves to another row for privacy.

"Baby, I have some work to do too. I want to get this out of the way before we get to the house."

I hold up my headphones. "Ich muss meinen Spanischunterricht nachholen." I tell him I need to catch up on my Spanish lessons in German since I have no clue how to say it in Spanish yet.

"Practice with me. I'm a much better teacher than some app."

"Not happening. You'll have no patience. I know it, and for some reason, I suck at Spanish." Then I remember I wanted to ask him something. "Can we stop at the grocery store? I know you wanted to take me out to dinner, but I would like to cook for you instead, if that's okay?"

"You don't need to do that. We have a full-time chef at the house."

"Oh. Okay," I say, disappointed.

He lifts my chin to look me straight on. "Do you want me to give him the night off?"

I nod. "Could you? It would mean a lot to me if I could cook for you."

"Of course, Jules." He leans down and kisses me when Jackson catcall whistles at us.

Harrison mutters a *fuck's sake*, and I giggle at Jackson's playfulness.

I'm glad Harrison agreed to tonight.

I know he doesn't expect anything in return for the gifts he gives me, but I'd like to thank him and show how much I care and appreciate him by doing something I love and do well.

Classical music floats through the air as I effortlessly dance around the swanky chef's kitchen. I know I had reservations about Harrison's money. However, being able to cook in this kitchen might have me changing my mind about it all.

This is some top-of-the-line shit...the best of the best, and it looks exactly how I pictured every Hamptons kitchen.

All white, bright, and gorgeous.

The fridge is organized with a color scheme system and is stocked with every high-quality ingredient you could imagine. Outside, there is an extensive herb and vegetable garden. When I saw it, my face lit up like Christmas morning, and I was off picking different herbs within seconds of seeing it.

The best part of the kitchen isn't even the kitchen itself. It's the colossal windows overlooking the property.

There's a large travertine patio, a heated saltwater pool lined with hand-painted white and baby blue tiles flown in from Spain, and sprawling perfectly mowed grass with symmetrical diagonal lines.

The whole fifteen-acre property is boxed in with high hedges, extra large hydrangeas, and every so often, patches of high grass and wild-flowers are sprinkled in, reminiscent of the English countryside.

The back doors open, so you can dine in or out with a large custom, restored teak table that would be fit for a king, where currently, my king is sitting, working, waiting for his meal.

Harrison is different here—more laid back. Something I never imagined he could be.

I've unlocked another personality and can't wait to get to know it better.

Though, now, his mood has also altered my whole menu.

I had a delicious five-star gourmet dinner planned. However, once we got here, Harrison changed into a bathing suit, a long-sleeved linen shirt, and flip-flops, and in that moment, I knew I needed to change my plan.

Instead, I decided on comfort food, making his favorites.

Herb-roasted filet mignon with a beautiful Béarnaise sauce, a melody of grilled vegetables from the garden, and roasted potatoes with an herb blend.

"What are you making now?"

"Dear God, don't scare me like that." I put my hand on my chest to allow my heartbeat to slow down.

"I called your name five times. You were daydreaming, miles away." Harrison smiles as he walks around the kitchen island and takes me in his arms.

He smells like summer—*sun-kissed and saltwater.*

I turn to face him. "A dreamy house causes lots of daydreams." I kiss his lips and try to escape when the timer goes off.

Harrison's hold on me tightens while he deepens the kiss, causing me to lose all resolve, opening up to him.

His hold is tight and possessive, but his tongue is gentle as it sweeps through my lips, and I feel it down to my toes. One hand palms my behind, pulling me into his body to feel his growing erection. The other creeps up my body, weaving through my hair to position my head in the exact way he likes it—turned to the side so he can break us apart and lick up my neck.

My knees buckle, and a soft throb begins pulsing between my legs.

"You taste fucking delicious." The deep growl of his voice vibrates against my skin, and I'm about to say fuck it to hell until my backup alarm goes off, breaking me out of my momentary stupor.

"I'm going to overcook the steak." I panic, attempting to push him away, but it's useless.

He's a brick wall of muscle. "Harrison," I whine.

Grabbing my cheeks, he suctions his pouty lips and kisses me hard one last time before a quick smack to my ass.

I take out the steak and let it rest while I plate the vegetables and potatoes.

"Take these to the table, please, and go sit. Dinner is ready."

Harrison

Fucking hell.

"Where are you going? I said dinner is ready, Harrison," Jules calls after me.

"One second, baby. I'll meet you in the dining room," I call out, needing to get to the front door before the bell rings.

I open the door in a rush and keep it ajar so our voices don't carry into the house.

"What the fuck are you doing here, and how did you get up the driveway, Rachel?" I snarl.

I'm furious right now.

How dare she show up uninvited.

She smirks flirtatiously. "Don't you remember, Harry? You gave me the code that weekend you brought me here." She reaches out to rub her fingers down my chest.

I throw her hand off me. "Do not fucking put your hands on me again. Do you understand me? And let's get one thing straight. I've never taken you here for a weekend. You were out at your house, and you came over one night. Per the NDA I made you sign, you were not to use that code again."

"Well, I heard you were in town, and I thought I'd come over and surprise you. I thought you would like some company." She pauses. "And I miss you. It's been months."

Her face falls, and for a split second, I feel her hurt. I thought she understood that what we had was completely platonic, but maybe I gave her mixed signals.

Then it dawns on me that if she knew I was here, I'm sure she knows who I'm here with.

I run my hands down my face and try to calm myself before I lose my ever-loving shit on her.

"You have some fucking balls to show up here and try to intimidate Juliette. What did you think would happen? She would run away scared because you showed up. She is ten times the woman you are, and there is nothing you could do that would push her away."

"You barely know her."

"We have been together for almost three months. Of course, I fucking know her." I bellow.

"Three months?" she shrieks.

Semantics. "Yes. So you can see for me this is serious."

My grip on the door slips when it flies open as a furious Juliette stands there glaring daggers at Rachel.

Rachels's face drops but quickly recovers, plastering on the fakest smile I've ever seen.

Juliette laces her hand through mine and places her other over my heart. "Listen to me, Rachel. We do not associate with conniving, backstabbing women like you. You are not to contact Harrison anymore. Do not call, and do not show up. Unless it pertains to his daughter and your son, you are to cut all ties. Do you understand me?"

Rachel stands there, dumbfounded.

"Do you understand?!" Juliette screams louder than I've ever heard her before.

Rachel nods, then walks away with her head hell-high. She would never show weakness to a stranger.

"Oh, and *Rach*?" Juliette says through gritted teeth.

"You step foot on this property again or so much as sneeze on the front lawn. I will personally call the police on you for trespassing. Now get back in your car, which I'm sure one of your five failed marriages paid for, and get the fuck off this property." She slams the door.

I roll my lips to hide my smirk. There she is…my sassy girl.

Juliette leans against the door and closes her eyes. I'm not stupid enough to speak to her until she is calm.

She takes a deep breath, then opens her eyes, glaring at me. *"Three months?"* She pops a brow.

I cross my arms, annoyed that's all she cares about. "Yes. I'm counting from the beginning."

"I thought you didn't remember the restaurant well. That's the beginning."

I look at her deadpan. "I never said that…I said—"

She smirks before I can finish my sentence. "I know. I'm only teasing." She takes my hand in hers. "Dinner time."

I look down at my girl in surprise. Even if it took me a while to admit it, I'm not a stranger to being jealous, and neither is Jules.

For her to be the bigger person here is…*wow.*

We just turned a huge fucking corner in our relationship.

21

Juliette

"Juliette, that was exceptional, baby. Thank you for making us dinner." Harrison wipes his mouth and tosses his linen napkin on the table.

He moves his chair back and taps his thigh.

Without a second thought, I circle the table, but before I can sit, he lifts me and positions me so I'm straddling his lap.

"Hi," I whisper.

"I'm sorry, Jules. Are you okay from before?"

I run my hands through his hair and smile tenderly. "You have no reason to be sorry, and yes, I'm okay."

"Hmm…" He lifts a brow.

I smirk. "I am, truly." He knows how jealous I can get, but I can honestly say Rachel is a manipulative piece of work. It's pathetic that she would show up here to intimidate me. I've never felt more secure in my relationship with Harrison than when he told her off.

He cups my cheek and grins. "Good." His lips drop to my breast, and he bites my nipple hard through my dress.

Ah. My sweet man has retired for the night, it seems. He reaches behind and unzips my dress, pushing away the straps so they fall, exposing my braless breasts.

Harrison hisses through his teeth, dusting the pads of his thumbs over my erect nipples, eliciting goose bumps to rise over my skin and flurries of excitement to dance in my stomach.

"Get right to it then." I sigh. God, that feels good. "We should at least clean the plates first."

He shakes his head. "Leave everything. The housekeepers will take care of them."

I don't like the idea of anyone else in the house while we're here.

"Can you give them off too? I want it just to be us two. I don't feel comfortable with them here."

"Jules, it's a big house. We need the help."

"I know." I run my fingertips along his chiseled jaw. "Please? It's only us, and we'll barely make a mess. They can come back when the others arrive."

He doesn't answer, but when he reaches around me to type a message on his phone, I know he's just made it happen.

He throws his phone down, then stands abruptly, cupping my ass, as my boobs bounce up and down in his face from his brisk walk to the other side of the table.

He lays me down on and stands there for a moment, staring down at my body. "We still have dessert, Harrison."

"First, we fuck, then I eat you, then we make love. The most perfect three-layer dessert I've ever had."

I laugh out loud. "Except I made your favorite, pavlova. Not cake."

"Fuck yes," he growls as he pushes my panties aside to swipe through my center. Completely ignoring the words coming out of my mouth.

He's in his element, and unless it's about sex, he wants to hear nothing about it.

He stands there for a moment, rubbing me back and forth, not making a move to do anything else.

"Ohhh...that feels good." My breath catches, and my hips rise as he circles my clit. "What are you doing?"

His eyes snap to mine, darkening as he tries to catch his breath. "Calming myself down." He's only like this when he wants to take me harder than he thinks I can handle.

He knows I love it, so what's the problem?

"H…please," I breathe.

He finally snaps, and in one quick movement, his bathing suit is off, and his cock shoots out, already dripping with pre-come.

God, he's enormous. No matter how many times I see it, it still wows me.

He slides his fingers through my core again, parting my swollen lips wide. "I'm obsessed with your cunt, baby. Always so pink and wet. It was made for me and only me, wasn't it?"

"Yes," I breathe. "Always. Only you."

He pushes two thick fingers inside me and begins to fuck me hard. There's no warming up…this *is* the warm-up.

Naturally, my legs open wide, and my head drops back as the feeling of euphoria takes over. In and out, he pushes his fingers inside of me, and every now and again, Harrison brushes his thumb over my clit with a steady rhythm.

The room is silent, besides our heavy breathing and the sound of my wetness sucking in his fingers with every movement he makes.

He's so fucking hot. I can't take it.

There can't possibly be a better feeling in the world than this.

He leans over and braces his left forearm on the table, dropping his head to suck my nipple. He bites down. "Ouch," I cry, and he bites harder, sending a straight shot of pleasure below. Then he quickly soothes me with slow, soothing swirls of his tongue.

Not yet…not yet, I repeat over and over again.

No…no. Please.

I reach out and take his dick, stroking it hard, matching his pace. "Oh, my fuck." He mumbles around me while he brings his knee up to the table for better leverage and begins pumping his cock into my hand.

"Shirt off!" I snap. I need to see all of him. He sits up and rips his shirt off. His head flies back, moaning loudly, as I drag my hand down to the cup and squeeze his balls.

What must we look like right now?

Half naked, laid out for the taking, that's what.

My legs are open wide and my boobs are slapping up and down as the strong muscles in his forearm strain, pumping me hard while he's also fucking my hand with his dick.

Oh lord.

The thought alone puts me over the edge. I screw up my eyes. I'm going to come so hard, I can feel it in my toes. My body begins to tingle, my back arches up, and my legs shoot out straight.

"Yes…that's it," I cry while he pushes a third finger in, and I clench around him, screaming out my release, convulsing right here on the dining room table.

His fingers pull out in a rush, and he grabs my thighs to drag me to the end of the table. Pushing my legs back, he slams into me, knocking the air right out of my lungs.

Oh…ouch.

Holding himself still, he leans over me, pushing my legs back so my knees are at my ears, and our faces are nose to nose.

He circles his hips in different directions, stretching me open. He slides out, then slowly pushes back in, repeating this a few times until I feel a rush of moisture below. "Yes, baby. There it is," he breathes against my lips, then veers back and slams into me.

"Do you know how much I adore you, Juliette?" he cries out as he hits me deep with hard, punishing thrusts. "You are everything to me."

I nod, unable to speak, my emotions completely overwhelming me.

Our eyes are locked, and even though he's fucking me hard on the dining room table, there is still a deep intimacy between us.

Without breaking eye contact, he pushes up and throws my legs over his shoulder. His hands grip my hip bones, and he holds on tight, moving me forward and back, using my body to please himself.

"Harder, H." I need more. I need everything he has. "You feel amazing."

He loses all control at my words and really lets me have it, moving at a pistol pace. His eyes scrunch up, and he turns his head to bite the side of my ankle, trying his hardest to hold back from coming.

I'm right there with you, H.

Another orgasm begins too build quickly. This one is deep down, burning through my body, ripping its way through me to escape.

"Touch yourself," he pants. "You need to come right this second."

My hand moves between my legs, I barely brush over my clit, and we orgasm in unison. Violent quivers overtake my body while his head is thrown back, groaning loudly as I spasm around him, milking every last drop.

He releases my legs and helps me sit up so we're chest to chest. I wrap my arms around him tightly and bury my head in his chest, feeling overwhelmed with emotions.

This is not a rare occurrence. I often feel like my heart could explode with pure happiness when I'm with his man.

"*Mon petit papillon.* My perfect girl, you are the light of my life," he whispers against my ear.

"It is you, Harrison, who is the perfect one." I smile softly and hold my arms out for him to pick me up.

I wrap myself around him and kiss him with all my might.

Wet lips trail my exposed back, waking me from a deep slumber. "Come on, baby, wake up."

"Mmm. What time is it?" I turn my head and see it's only five thirty in the morning. "No. Nope. Goodbye." I mumble and soon after feel myself slipping back to sleep.

"Jules, get up." Harrison kisses my heart-shaped beauty mark. "I want to take you down to the beach for sunrise."

"Oh. That's romantic." I smile into my pillow, listening to him pace around, willing myself to get out of this cloud-like bed.

He rips the blankets back, exposing the rest of my body, allowing him access to my behind. He kisses both cheeks, then trails his tongue along the crack of my behind.

Oh, jeez, he's obsessed.

He had that one moment last week, and now he can't keep his hands to himself.

He reaches down and slides his fingers through my open sex. "Oh...that feels good," I mumble, still half asleep.

All too soon, he pulls out, then swipes my moisture up and over my tight hole. I suck in a deep breath. God, I still can't believe how sensitive I am here.

He applies more pressure, and instinctually my ass pushes back, causing his finger to slip through my back opening.

"Ah." I screw up my eyes as the familiar burn electrifies my insides, one I know soon will turn to delicious pleasure. He pulls out, and I quickly turn my head. "You didn't have to stop."

"Oh. I know." He massages down my body. "But the sun doesn't wait for anyone to rise. Up you get." He slaps my ass, then jumps off the bed.

"I can't believe you, Harrison," I cry out. "You can't leave me like this." I bury my head back in the pillow and groan loudly.

"Are you coming or not?" Harrison shouts from the hallway.

His annoyed voice jolts me awake. "Sorry! I fell back to sleep. Give me a minute."

"Hurry up," he barks, then pauses in the doorway, watching me closely as I look at my naked body in the mirror. "So help me God, Juliette. If you're staring at yourself like that because you have more issues, I'm going to smack your ass for insulting my favorite everything."

"Your favorite everything?" I smirk, raising a brow.

"Yes." He crosses his arms annoyed, while his facial expression softens. He looks me up and down, slowly taking me in. "Head to toe, every inch of you is my favorite."

I bite my lip to hide my smile. I wonder if he even realizes how freaking swoony he sounds sometimes.

"Well, no, actually, I was looking at my butt." I turn around. "Like an actual butt." I widen my eyes playfully.

He chuckles. "Trust me, I know. I look every second I can."

I run my hands over my behind. "Well, I was too skinny before. I never had one. Do I look like J-Lo now?"

He bursts out laughing and grabs me around my waist, spinning me around. "Yes. Exactly like her." He bites my neck. "Now, seriously. Get dressed. We need to leave in the next five minutes to make it."

My phone vibrates, and I see my mom calling me back. "Good morning," I chirp.

"Oh, don't you sound happy. How is everything? I figured you would have slept in."

"Perfect." I smile at Harrison, and he squeezes my thigh, where his hand rests. "It is so beautiful here, and the weather couldn't be better. We're just returning from the beach, where we watched the sunrise and relaxed. Now we're going to go out for an early breakfast."

"I'm so happy for you, Juliette. But really, I want to know what the house is like."

I smile down at the phone. "House? Do you mean compound?"

"That big?" she gasps.

"You have no idea. It's huge, but it's tastefully done. You'd love it because it's not cookie-cutter. Two of his brothers are architects, so they mixed traditional with modern. I'll send a picture later."

"Tell her we'll have her out here soon. It's just as beautiful in the fall," Harrison interrupts, and I smile lovingly at him. It means so much to me that he cares about Mom.

"It's hard to hear you, my love."

"Oh yeah," I drawl. "That's because we're driving around the Hamptons in Harrison's convertible."

"Oh, you're too much." She laughs. "Jules, the morning rush is about to start. I'll talk to you later, and if not, have a fun time at the party tonight. Love you."

My stomach drops, the white party is the last thing I want to think about. "I will. Love you."

"What's wrong with your face?"

I playfully narrow my eyes. "It's my annoyed face. My mom brought up the white party, reminding me I might see Rachel again."

He rubs the inside of my thigh and pulls the car over to the side road, turning his attention fully in my direction. "Jules, baby, my goal in life is to make sure you're taken care of. If I can help it, I will never put you in a situation where I think you'd be too uncomfortable." He pushes back some of my windswept hair, smiling softly, as he pulls me in for a quick peck. "I promise we'll stay far away from her. She hates Jackson with a passion, so I'll have him stand guard. And something tells me after your Oscar-winning performance yesterday, she won't want to be anywhere near you either"

"Who could hate Jackson?"

Harrison's smile drops. "Don't."

I roll my lips. "Jealous?" I tease. "Oh, can you turn it up? This is a great song."

Harrison turns up the music, then glances at me with a twinkle in his eye and revs his engine.

"Yeah, baby. Let it rip!" I yell.

He lets out a booming, carefree laugh, and then we're off. The ocean breeze hits our faces as we speed through the empty early morning streets, listening to "Real Love Baby" by Father John Misty.d

The lyrics say, "I'm in love, I'm alive." And I feel the words wholeheartedly, deep within my bones.

My eyes close, and I throw my head back, letting my hair fly free in the wind as I sing my heart out. I reach down and squeeze Harrison's hand with meaning, and when I open my eyes and find him looking over at me, I know he feels it, too.

Harrison lets out a low, frustrated breath. "Can you stop fidgeting?"

"I'm nervous," I finally admit.

I've been trying to play it cool all day.

I walked around the property twice, sat under a tree, and started a new book. I made Harrison play backgammon six times, and then I swam laps in the pool while he worked on his tan, which then turned into some fun when he fell asleep, and I surprised him with a blow job.

But who am I kidding? It was all a distraction.

Now, we're in line to be dropped off, and undoubtedly, all eyes will be on us when we get out.

"Look at me, Jules," his deep voice commands, then he lifts my chin when I don't look him in the eyes. "You're not a stranger to the spotlight, and you know better than to let people's opinions get to you. The only ones whose matter tonight are mine and yours. We're in this together, fuck everyone else."

"You're right." I lean over and kiss him lightly. "And you're sure I look all right?" I rub my hands up and down my legs. *Shit, I'm still nervous.*

Harrison's face falls. "Do you not like your dress?"

"Like? Are you kidding me, H? I love my dress!" I look down at the new dress Harrison surprised me with.

It's a floor-length, white linen dress with spaghetti straps and a high slit up the side. He's obsessed with my legs, so that part didn't surprise me.

A peek-a-boo hole at my midriff shows a bit of my stomach, and extra fabric on the top that's tied in a large knotted bow covers my chest.

It's a one-of-a-kind dress and the one thing I'm not worried about tonight. I feel amazing in it.

"So what's the issue? You are absolutely stunning. Normally, I like your hair down, but the way you slicked it back in this wet-looking bun is fucking sexy as hell, and it accentuates your beautiful face and your freckles I love."

He takes my hand and rubs it over his crotch.

"Harrison." I snicker. "Why are you hard right now?"

"Because I can't keep my eyes off you, it's taken all my strength to keep my hands to myself. That is how unbelievably sexy you are to me."

I duck my head and feel the blush creep up my neck. "Thank you, Harrison. You always know how to make me feel good about myself. And you don't look too bad yourself." I wink playfully. Then the car comes to an abrupt stop. It's our turn to get out. "Holy crap, Harrison!" I let out a slow whistle. "What kind of freaking house is this?"

He laughs dryly. "It's a bit ostentatious."

"A bit. Dear god, it's ginormous, and not in a good way. There are ways to do luxury, but this misses the mark." It's a twenty thousand square-foot rectangle box of windows.

"I'll give you a tour, and you'll see why he did it. He has a three-hundred-and-sixty-degree view of the water with all the windows since the ocean is in the back and Mecox Bay is in the front. Though I agree, it's not for me either."

Flashes suddenly start going off. "Why are there paparazzi here? That seems very unlike the Hamptons."

"It's probable Carter called photographers, not paparazzi. Controlled chaos."

"Jeez," I mumble, more to myself.

"I'd like to open Ms. Caldwell's door," Harrison calls out to the driver. Robert had off, so he stayed in the city. "I will send a message ten minutes before we're ready to leave. We shouldn't be late."

"Yes, sir. I'll be parking in the beach lot down the road, so I'll only need a five-minute warning."

"Perfect. Thank you."

Harrison grabs my hand before he opens his door. "If you don't want to go, we'll turn around right this second. But I would be lying if I said I didn't want to show you off tonight. If we give them what they want now, they'll likely leave us alone in the city."

I nod. "You're right. Let's do it."

I take a deep breath, pull my shoulders back, and hold my head high. The spotlight here was never as intense in my former life. Nevertheless, I can do this for Harrison.

And worse comes to worse, I'll do what I always did—fake a smile until it was over.

The door opens, and when a set of dazzling blue eyes smile down at me, I immediately realize it's different now. I don't need to fake a thing, when I have Harrison by my side.

"Mr. Davenport. Over here."

"Harrison!" another person calls over all the others as we walk up to the step and repeat.

Harrison slides his arm around me and splays his hand over my hip, pulling me into his side.

We stand and smile for the cameras, and I'm surprised at how calm I am with him anchoring me.

"Harrison, this is not your first time photographed with Ms. Caldwell."

"Is there a question in that statement?" he retorts, in his Mr. CEO voice.

"Are you dating Ms. Caldwell, or will we see you with another date in a few weeks at the Rockefeller Benefit?"

Harrison's eyes sweep the room before locking with mine. His face softens, and he shoots me a devastating grin that I know they're all eating up.

The cameras begin flashing wildly when Harrison reaches up, cups my face tenderly, and brushes the apple of my cheek.

Oh my god.

My mouth curves into an unconscious smile. "What are you doing?" I whisper.

"I told you. Giving them what they want."

He turns back toward the photographers. "I can confirm that Juliette Caldwell and I are dating, and no, I will not be bringing another date to any other event in the future. From this day forward, you will only ever see Juliette on my arm. No one else...ever."

Everyone gasps, along with me.

That sounds like forever...and that sounds amazing.

This is so unlike Harrison and goes against his privacy stipulations.

He doesn't share his life with anyone, but for me, for us, and our future privacy, he's done the right thing, and I love him even more for it.

"Another champagne?" the pretty waitress asks.

"Sure. Thank you, Bianca." I hold out my glass.

I've been in awe all night that she recognized me earlier. Hollywood A-listers surround us, yet Bianca, an aspiring dancer who waitresses on the side, noticed me instantly.

So surreal.

"Not too many more. I can tell you're tipsy. I want you to remember later," Harrison purrs in my ear, biting down hard on my earlobe.

"You're tipsy, too," I protest. "I've never seen you drunk, I don't think."

"I feel more comfortable letting loose out here than in the city." He discreetly licks the side of my neck.

My knees go weak, and I can barely stand. He's been teasing me all night. "Can't it be later now? Don't you want to go home? You promised me skinny dipping." I trace my fingers along the collar of his shirt.

"Fuck. You're killing me. Soon. We're leaving soon." He pauses. "Unless you're uncomfortable and truly want to leave."

I shake my head. "I'm kidding. I've been having a great time and have met lovely people. I haven't even seen Rachel. And honestly, if I did, I wouldn't even care, screw her."

"There's my girl." He grins and then sips his negroni.

"Plus, I have an exceptional spot for people-watching. I can't move now." I nod toward the couple fighting out on the expansive lawn, and then on my other side is a guy leaning against the side of the house, making out with two women, both of whom are grinding down on each one of his thighs. "I can't believe they're doing that in public," I whisper, unable to take my eyes off them.

Harrison pinches my butt. "Stop staring."

I wrap my arms around him and hug him tightly. Kissing his chest through his shirt. "Oh my god." I push off him and do a little happy dance. "We're next."

"What are you talking about?"

"Harrison," I groan. "For the psychic. We're up next!" I point to Jolene, the psychic, who was hired for the party.

She's standing next to us, talking to Marc and Richard. They're a lovely couple I met earlier who own a famous floral company in East Hampton.

"I'm not doing it. You can. That's not my thing."

I frown. "Party pooper."

"Who's a party pooper?" Jackson grabs my drink and drains my champagne.

"Hey." I playfully punch his arm. "Harrison. He won't talk to the psychic with me."

"Oh, I'm so down," Jackson says, then grabs us two more champagnes as another waitress walks by and asks her for three tequila shots.

Harrison's going to flip out, and I'm going to throw up, probably. But it's all in good fun, and I wasn't lying before I'm having a great time.

Suddenly, a breeze from the ocean hits me. "Oh, that's nice." I open my arms out wide. "It's been so humid tonight."

"Here you are." The waitress passes out the shots to the three of us.

"Juliette," Harrison warns.

I widen my eyes and mouth *party pooper*.

Jackson dies of laughter while we cheers and shoot back the tequila.

"Hello." Jolene steps over to us.

"Are any of you interested in a reading tonight?"

"Me!" I say with a little too much enthusiasm. "And him." I point to Jackson.

"Great. Let's get started, and please keep in mind. If you've gotten a reading before, my methods may be different from others."

I smile excitedly while Harrison rolls his eyes and mumbles something under his breath.

I kick my leg out and hit his shin, shooting daggers at him. I can't wait to do this; he better not ruin it for me.

"All I need is your age and the first letter of your name."

Jackson goes first. "J, thirty-nine."

Harrison sniggers. "Old fuck."

Jackson secretly gives him the middle finger. "You're right behind me, cocksucker," he whispers.

Wait…How do I not know Harrison's birthday?

"When is your birthday?"

He rolls his lips, annoyed, and mumbles, "September twenty-first."

"What?" I shriek. "That's at the end of next month."

He shrugs while I sip my champagne nervously. I better start thinking of gifts now. This man has everything. It's going to be impossible to shop for him.

"When's your birthday?" Jackson asks.

"December eighteenth," Harrison mumbles without a thought.

"I never told you that." Then I remember he had a background check done on me. "Never mind."

"Ah, the day before Annabelle's. Sagittariuses are feisty. Be careful with that one." He tells Harrison and shoots me what I've come to learn is his signature smirk.

"Who's Annabelle?"

Jackson's face lights up, and I instantly can tell she's special to him. "One of my best friends."

"Okay, you three," Jolene interrupts and looks at me. "And your information?"

"J, twenty-four," I pause and look up to Harrison with hopeful eyes. He nods, and I chew on my right cheek and attempt to contain my smile. "And H, thirty-eight for him," I tell her.

"You're both married—"

"I'm not married," Jackson practically spits, his face goes ghost white.

Jolene doesn't say a word, but something is telling me that she and Jackson are communicating through their connected eyes.

"I see someone I know. She doesn't know what the hell she's talking about," Jackson complains, then storms away.

"What was that about?"

"No clue," Harrison answers, with a furrowed brow as he watches his friend walk away.

Jolene clears her throat to get our attention back. Thankfully, she ignores Jackson's outburst.

"We're not married either," I tell her.

She smiles warmly and takes both of our hands in hers.

Harrison is about to lose his shit, I can tell. He's only standing here to appease me but is about to hit his threshold of crazy any minute now.

"You're not married on paper. But you have the strongest bond out of anyone here at this party."

What?

"What does that mean?" I whisper.

"Your souls are married. The universe has chosen the two of you, which is more special and unique than any other marriage." I suck in a breath, and I can feel the back of my eyes tickle with tears. "You're privileged. Not everyone has a person, and those who do don't always find them. When you're born with a predetermined mate, you search, sometimes unknowingly, until you find them. Unfortunately for some, they search their whole lives and never feel complete. The two of you." She pauses. "Are complete."

She looks between us, and I can't help but glance up at Harrison, who's already staring intently at me with reverence in his eyes.

He feels this, too.

Something is happening right now.

Something extraordinary is passing through us, and if Jolene wasn't standing here right now, I know that at this moment, I would have told him I loved him, and something is telling me he would have said it back.

"That is the most beautiful thing I've ever heard," I murmur, never letting my eyes leave Harrison's.

I love this man with all my heart and feel so lucky to have found him knowing what I do.

He cups my cheek and lightly kisses my lips. "Jules," he purrs.

"You two are a lovely couple," Jolene sighs happily.

I turn my attention back to her, and I can feel the heat from my cheeks burning with embarrassment.

I completely forgot about her for a moment.

"Thank you." I take Harrison's hand and squeeze it lightly. "I feel the same way."

Without another word, she smiles again and begins to walk away, then abruptly stops and turns back. "All relationships experience bumps along the way. Hang tight. It will all work out in the end. Remember, the universe has already chosen."

We stand silently until Harrison asks if I'm ready to go home. It's rhetorical, he's pulling me out of the party before I answer.

With this new revelation, why would we ever want to stay here when we can go home to be alone together?

Ouch.

I lean over to grab my water and try to block out the morning light. My head is pounding.

"Oh baby," Harrison croons in a pained voice. "I'm sorry."

I chug my water. "What's wrong?"

He runs his fingertips down my spine. "You have cuts all over your back."

"Worth it," I mumble and snuggle closer, my back to his chest.

"It was a good night, huh?"

"The best." I yawn. "Why aren't you hung over? You went from Mr. Party Pooper to Mr. Let's Celebrate The Universe."

"I meant with a glass, not a bottle, Juliette," he accuses light-heartedly.

After we got home last night, I thought we'd be crashing through the doors, unable to contain ourselves.

Harrison had the bright idea of celebrating the universe with a drink first.

I took it a step further, jumping in the pool with the bottle. I don't know what came over me, but I wanted to live in the moment. It's not often I let loose, especially with Harrison.

Within two point two seconds, Harrison was naked, jumping in after me, and at one point, we were in the shallow end, with Harrison on his knees and my legs around his neck. That's how I got the scrapes…when he had me braced against the wall.

Harrison lifts my top leg and slowly enters me from behind.

My eyes flutter shut. "That feels amazing, H."

I don't how, but I'm always so wet for him in the morning. Maybe my body recognizes him wrapped around me in my sleep and is roaring to go the second I open my eyes.

Who knows.

He places my leg back down. "Your leg is sore?"

He can always tell. "A little," I admit.

He rubs over my hip and down the side of my thigh. "Keep it down like this. Tight together, and we'll ice it after."

I moan as he pulls out and slowly pushes back in. "Okay."

"Oh fuck. You're so tight like this."

"Don't go any faster. It feels perfect."

He squeezes his arms around my chest and buries his face in my neck. "I know, baby. So good."

Harrison's phone rings, and we ignore it. When it rings two more times, we hesitate.

It could be Claudina.

A car door slams in the near distance.

Then another one.

I look over my shoulder, and when we hear the third car door slam, Harrison pulls out as quickly and gently as possible, and we fly up, frantically trying to get dressed.

I look across the room and cover my mouth to contain my laughter. Harrison's standing there with a pained, scrunched-up face as he tries to tuck his hard dick into his shorts.

The front door slams shut, and my eyes widen. *Oh no.*

"Hello?" a man's voice calls from downstairs.

22

Juliette

"Someone is getting fucking murdered today," Harrison mutters and tosses me a dress to throw on. "Maybe stay here for two minutes, then come down so I can explain something to Claud."

"Explain what. Me?"

"Yes. She's intuitive for a five-year-old. She's going to have a lot of questions when she finds out you slept over." He walks into the bathroom, and I follow behind him.

"Well, what exactly will you say?"

"No fucking clue." He pulls himself out and starts to pee.

I throw my hands up and turn. "A little warning would have been nice."

"You're the one who followed me in here, and what's the problem? I see you use the bathroom all the time."

"That's because you have no boundaries." I huff, then walk into the closet to find another dress.

This looks like shit. It's a wrinkled mess.

Harrison washes his hands, then reminds me again to come down in two minutes.

I watch him carefully as he walks out of the room and down the hall.

I'm one lucky bitch.

He has on a pair of board shorts that ride low on his hips, and with no shirt, you get a clear view of his tanned, muscular body.

But his hair…those dark honey locks are what does it for me. It's tussled in that *I just got fucked way*, and I'd love to run my fingers through it.

He couldn't be hotter if he tried.

When he's out of view, I shake myself out of my Harrison daze and notice I have two missed messages.

The first one is from Mom.

I think this one would fit our needs the best.

Attached is a picture of one of the bakeries she visited while I was here in the Hamptons.

I click it, and my stomach knots in disappointment. Not because it's terrible but because I agree, which means this is all coming to fruition.

When I was floating in the pool yesterday, I promised myself if Mom picked a place, I would go back to the city with an open mind and think of this as a fresh start.

I only wish Le Petit Boulanger didn't hold some many memories near and dear to our hearts.

I take a deep breath and text her back.

Whatever you think is best, I know it will be great. When I'm home, we'll talk to Barbara together. xx

Before heading downstairs, I open the vague text from Becks and stare at it for a minute before replying.

> Can you come over when you're back?

> Of course, we'll be back tomorrow morning. When you're home from work, let me know, and I'll come over.

> Or can you call me later and talk?

I wish she would have given me context or would write me back. Now I'm worrying that something's wrong.

After a few minutes, she still doesn't answer, so I put my phone away and head downstairs.

"Well, do you kiss Juliette on the lips?" Claud asks Harrison with her hands on her hips.

Harrison's eyes widen in surprise. I quietly stand out of view, too curious about how he will handle this.

He's stunned, opening and shutting his mouth like a scared little guppy. Where the hell is Mr. CEO hard-ass now?

"Well?" Claud sasses.

"How do you know about kissing, little miss?" I ask and walk into the room.

"Juliette!" Claud cries.

Her dark pigtails whip wildly as she runs into my arms, climbing my body to get closer. "Claudina Davenport, did you lose your first tooth?" I ask, surprised.

How did Harrison not tell me this?

"Yes!" She smiles to show me her bottom teeth. "The tooth fairy came last night and even left fairy dust around my room!"

I glance up at Nate and Leo, who stand off to the corner. I smile, thinking of these two men walking around sprinkling glitter. "Hi, you two. What a surprise to see you…one day early."

"Surprise? More like entrapment," Harrison mumbles.

I roll my eyes. "Ever so dramatic."

"So do you?"

"Do I what, Claud?"

"Kiss my daddy?"

My lips lift in a grin at her forwardness. I love this girl.

Typically, I would follow Harrison's lead, but since he's gone mute, and I'm in their life more permanently—*hopefully*—I decide to take the reins here.

"I do kiss your dad." I raise my eyebrows. "On the lips."

"Gross!" She giggles. "Kissing your boyfriend is yuck!"

"And how do you know anything about that?" I tickle her side.

"Because Ben at school asked me to be his girlfriend, then he kissed my cheek." She shivers with disgust. "His lips were all wet."

Leo and Nate take a step forward while Harrison remains a statue.

I put my hand out to stop them. Every little girl has a boyfriend at five. They need to chill out.

"Well, if you don't like it, tell your teacher or ask him not to do it again."

She runs her fingers through my hair, playing with the ends. "I did. Now we just hold hands instead."

Okay…time to get this girl outside before her dad and uncles have a conniption.

"Hey, where's Skye?" I ask, changing the subject.

Claudina jumps out of my arms and begins to drag me outside. "She had to go potty, so she's outside. You're going to love her."

The second the back doors open, Claud runs like a wild child across the lawn to get to Skye. The beautiful shepherd perks up when she spots her and gets just as excited.

"How does she know we're dating?" I ask Harrison when he steps through the door. "I thought we were easing her into it."

He points to Leo. "This one left the gossip column open on the counter, and she saw the pictures of us from last night," he huffs, annoyed. "She's beginning to read, and it's not been easy for her, yet she knows the word girlfriend."

"Did she say anything else?" I glance at Harrison, then his brothers.

Nate walks over and kisses me hello. "No. She couldn't have been more excited. All she cared about was how beautiful you looked. Which you did."

"Smokin'," Leo adds.

"Thank you," I mutter shyly. "So I guess the cat's out of the bag for real now."

Harrison steps up behind me, drapes his arms over my shoulders, and kisses the side of my head. "It was always real, baby."

"Oh, give me a break," Nate teases.

"Not that I'm not happy to see you guys, but why are you here early?"

"They wanted to torture us after they saw the article, no doubt."

Leo shrugs. "Truth."

"Listen, Jules." Harrison ignores his brothers. "Claud's ecstatic to be here with all of us and would be devastated if we left tomorrow. Can you ask Daphne to cover you for one or two more days? I'll even give her a bonus as an incentive."

"Don't be ridiculous, you don't need to do that. It shouldn't be a problem—as you like to remind me, I'm due days off. Mom can also help. She said her hands have barely bothered her in the last few days."

"Good." He kisses me again, then looks toward the guys. "Bonfire or sunset sail tonight?"

"Boat since we have clear skies. Bonfire tomorrow, before dinner," Nate replies.

"Perfect."

Yes, perfect…everything is perfect.

Which terrifies me because nothing is ever *perfect*.

Harrison

After destroying Nate and Leo's asses in beach paddle ball, we're back at the house, lying by the pool. Tonight's our last night before we head back to the city early tomorrow.

As pissed as I was that my brothers showed up early, I have to admit, the weekend was better than I could have ever hoped for. Especially after Rachel's escapades starting our week on the wrong foot.

Juliette fits seamlessly with our group, like she was made to be a part of us. The guys love her, and I can see friendships blooming, especially with Leo.

They instantly clicked, which I should have figured would happen. Back when we first started seeing one another—the night we ran into her ex in the bar—I saw Leo take control and stand up for her when I wasn't around.

He had both of our backs.

Now, I can only hope Sebastian has the same reaction when they finally meet. How could he not? There's not one thing to dislike about my girl...she's perfect.

I'm not saying this because I'm biased. She is truly special and doesn't have a mean bone in her body. She's pure to the core.

Nate turns toward me. "Should we all go to dinner again for our last night?"

Sounds terrible. I'm relaxed in my happy place.

"No, let's do one last barbecue. There's a good chance I won't come back out for a while."

"Since you sent the staff home, I can go to the store now. I need to get up and walk around. Otherwise, I'm going to fall asleep out here. Does anyone want to come?" Leo asks.

"No," both Nate and I say in unison.

"Thanks, dicks. I'll be back."

I have no interest in moving and know Claud's in good hands with Jules; I close my eyes and attempt to take an uncharacteristic nap. It's the second one this week.

"So..." Nate says, letting his words drag.

"What is it, Nathaniel?" I ask impatiently.

He's ruining my once-in-a-lifetime relaxation time.

"Earlier, I heard you talking to Jules...you called her your little butterfly." He holds my stare. "You're in love with her? I know you said it to Seb, but truly?"

I don't hesitate. "Deeply. She's the one."

He doesn't look as shocked as I thought.

"You've told her?"

I shake my head. "No. I plan to do it sooner rather than later. She knows, though."

He narrows his eyes. "How do you know?"

There are not many people I would share my feelings with, but because Nate's already in love, he'll understand. "There is this feeling whenever our eyes lock."

"What feeling?"

"Like our souls are talking," I say and huff out a laugh. "Do you hear me right now? Who would have ever thought this is where I'd be."

"I have to admit, not me. But once I saw you two together for the first time, I knew."

Huh? "You did?"

He smirks. "Well, that's not exactly true. At first, I was blown away that you went for someone so much younger than you. Then I met her, and I got it."

"Got what?" Who cares about our fucking age.

"Jules is ordinary...and extraordinary all at the same time. If I had to pick anyone for you, she would be the one." I gulp down my emotions. I've never needed someone else's approval, but it feels nice for Nate to feel the same way. "All the other women you've been with are models, socialites...women you were expected to be with. Jules is the woman who will ground you and raise Claudina the way you want her to be raised."

"How's that?"

"She'll raise Claud in a home, not a house. She will prioritize her time and her family above all else. I already see she does, and because of that, it proves age is only a number."

He hit it spot on. "I couldn't have said it better myself. I hope Seb sees what you see."

He smiles sympathetically. "He will. Give him time."

My phone buzzes with a text from Leo.

You've got to see this.

He sends me a quick video of Claud and Jules together. I play it again, and again like I don't believe it.

Then again, while warmth runs through me.

She's dancing. And she is absolutely beautiful.

Deep down, I knew Jules had been craving this, but to finally take the step and conquer the fear of dredging up old memories...that's huge.

And after all this time, it's Claudina who gets her to face her fears.

Jules is moving around the room like an angel. You would have never known she was in an accident. Her body glides around the dance floor with an air of elegance. I wish I had seen her in her prime.

Claud is sitting in the middle of the floor, crossed-legged, just as in awe of Jules as I am.

Don't let them see you. I don't want to interrupt it.

Got it—I'm leaving now.

I think about going down there myself, but this is a moment they should have together. I don't want to ruin it.

"It's the summer. Why can't I stay up late with the grown-ups? I'm not even tired," Claud says as she yawns. She'll be out like a light in five minutes. "Where's Juliette?"

"I think she's resting before dinner."

"Oh." Her face falls. "I thought she would be here to tell me a bedtime story. I wanted to hear her special one again."

I have no clue what she's talking about. "Why don't you ask her to put you to bed? She's in my bedroom, but knock first."

"Okay!"

One minute later, she's dragging a smiling Jules behind her.

"Can you tell me your parents' fairytale story?" Claud begs Jules.

"Sure, if that's what you want, or I can read you this book." She holds up a book with a ballerina frog on the cover. "I bought this for you while shopping in Sag Harbor yesterday."

"Oh, yes! The ballerina book, please."

"What do you say, Claudina Rosa?"

She hugs Jules. "Thank you! Can Daddy read it, and you can lie down with me?" She begs with hopeful eyes.

Jules doesn't reply; she answers by climbing into Claud's bed.

Claud is half-asleep, so I skip to the end when she's not looking.

"Iris's mom tucks her in bed after a long day of dance and kisses her goodnight. I love you infinity times infinity, Iris."

"What does I love you infinity mean, Daddy?"

"Infinity means there is no end. So she loves her so much that it goes on forever and ever and ever."

"I see." She snuggles into Jules's side.

Jules's big brown eyes rise to connect with mine. She holds my attention momentarily before reaching for my hand and linking our fingers.

Her mouth opens, and she lets out a soft whisper for only me to hear. "*Infinity times infinity.*"

My breath hitches, knocking me back, completely surprised.

She loves me...

"Jules, baby." I squeeze her hand and open my mouth to tell her how much I love her, too, but Claud interrupts me.

"Well, I love you a lot of infinities, Daddy. And you too, Jules, I really love you."

I swallow the instant lump in my throat. This is it...this is my family right here in this very room. My girls. My life.

Jules smiles tenderly at me, rubbing her thumb along my skin, then leans in to kiss Claud's cheek. "I love you too, sugar plum."

"Me too, my precious angel, always and forever," I tell her, but she's already fast asleep.

Juliette

Harrison helps me out of Claud's bed, and we walk silently back to our bedroom.

The second the door closes, I look at him with uncertainty—not because I'm ashamed of confessing my love, but because I don't want him to feel pressured to reciprocate if he's not as ready to express himself as I am.

There was no plan to tell him tonight. I knew there would be a moment when I felt it in my heart to tell him, and for some reason, tonight, reading to Claud, was the time.

Everything about the moment felt right.

"You don't have to say it back. I know that you—"

"Jules, shh." He covers my mouth with his finger, then quickly replaces it with his lips. "Infinity times infinity times infinity," he mumbles against me, then steps back so our eyes lock. My heart skips a beat or two, and I'm suddenly so overwhelmed with bliss I could burst. "I love you so much, Juliette Caldwell, *mon petit papillon*. I think I have from the very beginning."

From the beginning...

I want to make a joke if he means the restaurant or masquerade party, but I'm left breathless at the thought of him loving me as I do him.

Before I know it, happy tears fill my eyes, and a smile graces my face.

He takes me in his arms, and I inhale deeply, engulfed in his masculine scent. This is one of my favorite places, safe in the arms of my love. Feeling his heartbeat against my cheek and his arms wrapped tightly around my body.

"In the last year, my life was flipped upside down, so it was par for the course when you came into my life out of nowhere." I reach up and caress his face, needing to feel him under the palm of my hand. "You were so unexpected, H, but now, I couldn't imagine my life without you. You make me feel whole again. Whenever I'm around you, I get this feeling that ignites my insides, and I suspect you're the only person who will ever make me feel like that."

"What feeling?" he murmurs.

"It's hard to explain...it's like little zaps of excitement or flutters dancing through my body."

"Like butterflies?"

I trace his tattoo over his shirt. "Exactly."

"Jules, baby." He takes a deep breath. "I've come to the conclusion that butterflies are the center of it all. You stole my breath from the moment I laid eyes on you, but when you walked in with that butterfly mask, I knew it was all over from there."

My heart hammers in my chest at his words. "I love you so much, Harrison."

He smiles softly and runs his hands through my hair. "Did I ever tell you Claudina is named after the butterfly species Claudina Agrias?"

"No. Is that why you have the tattoo?"

He nods. "It is. All the brothers got one when she was born. Then you walked into my life, *mon petit papillon*. It started to make sense… and now it's coming full circle."

"What is?" I whisper.

"If only my brothers could hear my thoughts right now." He smirks, but quickly becomes serious. "There was a missing piece to our family, and somehow, I think Camila handpicked you for us. She believed butterflies were a sign from the afterlife."

My mouth opens, but my voice catches in my throat. Goose bumps spread over my body, and an overwhelming feeling of pride fills me.

She picked me.

An urgent need to be closer to Harrison hits me out of nowhere. I put my hands up so he can pick me up, and we can be face to face.

"Kiss me," I demand.

He crushes me to his body and claims my lips with pure possessiveness. Our tongues dance together, and our bodies melt into one. *God, he is the best kisser in the world.*

They're the type you feel from your fingertips all the way to your toes.

Arousal burns inside me as our kiss deepens, and I'm desperate to feel even more of him; I rock against him, eliciting a low moan from my lips. Harrison's grip on my behind is lethal, taking control of my body, rubbing me against him in hard, deep movements.

Oh god.

Breaking out of the kiss, I lean back, panting, attempting to catch my breath. Our eyes catch and lock on each other. No words are needed. He desires me as much as do I him, and he knows exactly what we need.

Boom.

"Ah!" I jump in his arms.

A loud knock bangs on the door. "Appetizers are out. Let's go, you two. Finish whatever you're doing later," Leo calls out.

I throw my head onto Harrison's shoulder and take a breath. "Lord, that scared me half to death."

"Yeah. Fuck. I need to make love to my girl." He leans his head to the side, and kisses my beauty mark.

"We need to go down, Harrison." I sigh. Going downstairs is the last thing I want to do. "We'll feel rushed, and I want us to take our time tonight. Something tells me we'll both need some fuel for energy anyway."

"Fine," he grumbles and reluctantly puts me down on the ground.

He fixes himself and smirks.

"What?" I ask.

"I was thinking about how my body always knew you were the one."

I smile affectionately. "How?"

He thrusts his groin into me. "I barebacked you the first time."

"Oh. My. God." I slap my hands over my face. "Way to ruin the most romantic night of my life." He's ridiculous. "Let's go, you big idiot."

I can't believe he just said that.

But that's Harrison. You never know which one you'll get or what the heck will come out of his mouth next.

"You have five more minutes, Juliette, and then we're going upstairs," Harrison growls in my ear.

I'm shocked he lasted this long, so I'll take this as a win.

We're all lounging outside around the fire pit, me between Harrison's legs, while the guys relax, drinking scotch.

I couldn't even think of having another sip of alcohol after the white party. Instead, I indulged in an extra piece of the pistachio and rose tiramisu that Claud and I made earlier, deviating from the standard French pastries I'm used to.

But now, I'm in a food coma, and I could fall asleep at any moment. Though, from Harrison's tone and his hard-on pressed against me for the last hour, I know there is no way this man will let me sleep tonight.

Not that I blame him.

It's our last night before we head back to reality, and since our stay here got cut short by Nate and Leo showing up unannounced, we're in need of some alone time.

Nate and Leo's banter is hilarious and constantly entertains you, and truth be told, the last couple of days with them have been a blast.

We all went to the beach, barbequed at the house, and drove around admiring the multimillion-dollar mansions, high hedges, and perfect gardens. We even went wine tasting before Nate, who I learned has a passion for sailing, took us around Sag Harbor and Shelter Island—a small island between the North and South Forks of Long Island–for a beautiful golden sunset over the harbor.

When we arrived back in town, we ate a delicious meal at an open-aired, coastal, white-washed restaurant that had me dreaming of my next vacation.

It also confirmed my new love for Sag Harbor. The thriving, yet stuck-in-time, historic downtown is the perfect mix of the Hamptons–curated shops and top-notch restaurants, yet it keeps its old world charm, surrounded by a beautiful harbor, whaling cottages, and Greek Revival and Victorian-style homes that are protected by the historical society.

But the best part of the weekend was the quality time spent with the Davenport/Morales family, who made me feel like I was one of them. Harrison constantly reminds me that him being in a serious, committed relationship means I'm part of them now. It doesn't mean Leo and Nate have to agree, yet they've welcomed me with open arms.

Leo has even called me his little sis, and I would be lying if it didn't warm my heart.

It was only Mom, Dad, and Becks growing up, so being part of a large-knit group feels nice.

"Are you all right, baby? You're quiet," Harrison murmurs, squeezing his arms around me, keeping me warm.

"Just thinking about what a wonderful weekend I had. Thank you." I tilt my chin up, and he meets me halfway for a quick kiss.

"This is fucking weird," Leo says, and Nate nods in agreement.

"What is, I ask?"

Leo points to Harrison. "He's all touchy and kissy, it's fucking weird."

"You said that already," Harrison mutters dryly.

"Well, it is," Leo replies.

I frown. "He's not always like this? This is so normal for us."

Harrison needs his lips or hands on me at all times. I can sense he goes into withdrawal if he doesn't.

"It's been a while since I've seen him with a woman like this. If ever." Nate answers.

"Not even his crazy ex?" I lift a curious brow.

Nate laughs. "God no. She never hung out with us. I met her once, I think."

"Oh." I try to hide my smile, but I fail miserably.

Leo chuckles. "You love that, don't you."

"Yup." I wiggle on the spot. Harrison's hold on me tightens, and then he stands all in one motion with me in his arms, bridal style.

I knew that move would be his breaking point.

"We're going to bed." He looks at his brothers, but they're looking at me laughing, so I blow them a kiss good night. "We'll leave bright and early and won't see you. We already said goodbye to Claud, but keep me updated if you guys will drive or fly her back."

"Oh my god," I groan, rolling my eyes.

"What?" Harrison asks.

"*Keep me updated if you guys will drive or fly her back,*" I mock. "Most of the time, the three of you seem normal. Then you say something so ridiculous like that. Do you even know how you sound to the rest of the world?"

"Yes. Like pretentious assholes." Nate smirks. "But it's our life, and I wouldn't change it for the world. It seems like it's your world now, too."

"Nope." I point between all of them. "I'll be the one keeping you all in check."

Harrison snorts. "So we shouldn't take the private jet here next time? I believe I remember a lot of excited squeals coming from you."

My eyes narrow playfully. "Whatever, take me to bed."

Harrison

In one fell swoop, I remove Jules's lace panties, appreciating how her smooth, sun-kissed skin pebbles under my fingers as they brush down her legs. I sit back on my heels for a moment, attempting to catch my breath.

My heart is hammering against my chest in anticipation. I feel this way every time I'm with her, and if I let my emotions take over, she'll be flat on her back with her legs over my shoulders in two point two seconds. But I want to take it slow tonight, savor this moment.

She looks up at me with curious eyes.

She is so beautiful. It still blows my mind that I get to love her, care for her, and call her mine.

I'm a lucky bastard.

"Harrison," she whimpers impatiently, then peeks out her tongue and slowly traces her plump lips. Her legs drop to the side in an invitation...one I'm declining until I can get myself under control.

I'm not helping keep my self restraint as I drag my eyes away from her gorgeous face, down her body. Her breasts are perky, and her nipples are hard. I look lower and get a glimpse of her swollen sex, which is glistening with her wetness.

"Goddammit Juliette." I clench my jaw and grab my cock, slowly pumping it in my fist to ease some of my tension.

Her sex contracts and that's it. I'm only fucking human. I reach forward and swipe my fingers through her, then slowly push two fingers inside her. My girl loves when I have my hand on my cock. It turns her on like nothing else.

I pick up my pace and add another finger. "You like that, baby?"

She moans loudly in response and squeezes around my fingers. She's already close; two seconds of this, and she's ready.

I pull out, and she huffs out in annoyance. "What are you doing?" My dick jumps at the rasp of her voice, pre-come leaks down the head of my cock.

I need her now.

"You're going to come on my cock, and only my cock, tonight," I mumble as I lean down, needing a hit of my drug first. "Say you understand."

"Yes," she whimpers.

"Good girl." I kiss the scars on her hip softly, then drop my head to her sex and close my eyes, inhaling deeply. *Fuck yes...this is heaven.*

"Oh god," she cries, then subtly begins to rock her hips, searching for my mouth.

I cast my eyes up. "What do you need, baby?"

"You." Her breath shakes. "Up here."

Leaning down, I take in one more deep breath, and unable to contain myself, I pull her clit between my lips and suck hard. "The most intoxicating smell in the world is the woman you love." I lick her from bottom to top, then sit up and line myself up to her. "Did you know that?"

She covers her eyes. "You're so dirty."

I move her arm away. "Do not hide from me, ever."

She nods, shimming her body closer to me, and all I want to do is slam into her and take her hard. The urge is driving me insane.

Gentle.

Be. Fucking. Gentle.

"I need you, H," she moans.

I roll over on my back. "Change of plans. You get on top and take it slow. I want to feel every bit of my girl tonight."

Her soft, petite hand wraps around my dick, and I suck in a shaky breath as she lines me up at her center. God, her hand alone feels amazing. She shimmies side to side, opening herself. I hiss loudly as her body sucks in the head of my cock, then slowly slides down.

Her eyes catch mine, and there's a certain twinkle as she smirks. She bites her bottom lip, lifts, and slams down hard.

I throw my head back, no, no, no. "Juliette! Go easy."

She reaches down and grabs my hands, interlocking our fingers so she can use them as leverage.

She doesn't listen and repeats the movement over and over, and now I'm too far gone. I couldn't stop her even if I wanted to.

"Christ, woman. I wanted to make love," I groan through my teeth.

I'm about to blow any fucking second now. She is too tight and feels unbelievable around me. "What happened to my sweet, innocent girl I met months ago?"

I thrust my hips up, meeting her as she comes down hard. She's loving this. My girl loves it hard, just like me. This is how we do it... this is us.

"Who said this isn't making love, Harrison?" She cries. "It doesn't...oh, yes."

Her words dying on her lips as I pump into her repeatedly, taking over with a force that does not constitute making love. "It doesn't what?"

"It doesn't matter. This is how you and I make love. We feel it through our emotions. Oh god, I'm going to come. You feel so good filling me up, H."

My arm shoots out around her waist, and I flip us in one move. Her legs lock around me, pulling me in tight, as her body thrashes around, and I slam into her deep.

Her mouth parts open, and a loud guttural moan leaves her when I swipe my thumb over her clit, instantly orgasming on contact. My mouth drops to her neck, and I bite down harder than normal, not caring one fucking bit if I leave a mark. *She's mine, and I want everyone to know it.*

Fuck she can mark me, too. I'd wear it like a proud badge of honor.

One, two more hard pumps, and I'm coming deep into my girl as her orgasm grips my dick in a vise-like hold.

My eyes roll in the back of my head as I slowly move in and out, riding the aftershocks of our orgasm. Everything about her feels unreal, too good to be true. I drop my lips to hers and kiss her passionately.

"I love you, H."

I lean up to look at my beautiful girl. "I love you too." I kiss her one cheek, then the other, and drop to the side, pulling her into my arms.

. . .

My eyes shoot open from the vibration of my phone, and I quickly grab it before it wakes up Jules.

Five missed calls from Matteo.

> Where are you? I've been calling. You need to be in the office FIRST THING IN THE MORNING!

23

Harrison

"Have a good day at work, babe." I playfully slap Jules's ass to annoy her as she gets out of the car. Good luck to anyone working with her today. My girl is grouchy to the umpteenth degree.

I roll down the window. "No goodbye? Have a nice day. I love you. I'll miss you." I smirk.

She turns around, stomping back to the car, then leans in to peck my lips. "Bye. Love you," she grumbles under her breath and then turns and leaves again.

I'm tired as hell, too, but I'm used to functioning on little to no sleep. Jules, not so much.

If she has the early shift at the bakery, she's in bed by nine to get in at least seven hours of sleep. Not that I always let her; it's how I know how cranky she can be without her precious beauty sleep.

And I would be lying if I said my good mood didn't have something to do with my gorgeous brown-eyed girl—*what a weekend.*

I look up at Robert smirking in the rearview mirror. "What?"

He rolls his lips. "Nothing, sir."

"Just say it. Get it over with."

"I have nothing to say other than you look happy."

"Thanks, I feel it. And stop calling me sir. It's been ten years already." I tell him this constantly, but it will never change; he's too old school. I'm surprised he calls Jules by her first name. She must have nagged him until he caved.

"We've arrived," Robert announces, and I realize we're already parked at the curb.

My phone began dinging incessantly with notifications from the moment I dropped off Jules; it's like everyone knows I'm en route to the office.

Welcome back, Harrison.

"Thanks, Robert." I pat his shoulder. "Juliette needs to be downtown at her friend's house at six tonight. Can you drive her, then wait and drive her back uptown to the penthouse when she's done? I'll take a cab home."

"Sure, no problem. Have a good day."

I step out of the car and slowly walk up to the building, trying to catch up on any pressing emails before Lauren chews my head off for not answering her.

"Where the hell have you been, and why haven't you answered my texts." I look up to see Matteo frantically running out of the building toward me.

I hold up my phone. "I was just answering everyone from last night. Do I not get two hours a day to myself?" I look down at my watch. "And it's nine thirty in the morning. What do you mean, where have I been?"

He throws his hands up, annoyed. "For as long as I've worked here, you have been here by eight-thirty after you drop off Claud at school."

"It's August, Matteo." I sigh, already annoyed. Maybe Jules's grouchiness is rubbing off on me. "Claud is not in school, and anyway,

I'm the fucking CEO. I can get here whenever I damn well please. Now stop wasting my time and explain why you need me so urgently."

"You have a meeting right now, and they're waiting."

"Who is waiting where?"

"Lauren has them waiting in a conference room on fifteen. She wasn't sure what to do."

"Who?" I bark in frustration.

He freezes. "The Archibalds, they're demanding a meeting. One of their assistants called saying they weren't happy I've been snooping around."

"Motherfucker. You've got to be kidding me right now," I shout and can feel my blood pressure rising.

"This is why, when I text you, something is important. I mean it."

He's right. Not answering is completely unlike me, and when you're running a business, there is no time off, especially when you ask for a personal favor. "Sorry. I was a little preoccupied and lost track of time," I admit and realize I need to tell him Jules's secret. I want him in the room during the meeting. "What I'm about to tell you stays between us, not Becks, no one. I know I've said it before, but this is serious."

He nods. "I swear."

I explain Jules's family situation, how they are buying out her building, and that I'm not sure what the hell is going on now.

"Holy shit, something shady is going on for sure."

I nod, agreeing with him. "I just don't know what yet. Let's go."

"Calm down," Matteo mumbles.

"I am calm," I say through a clenched jaw while releasing my death grip on my briefcase, storming into my office, and slamming the door behind me.

Shit.

I swing the door back open, let Matteo in, and find Lauren staring at me.

"I don't have the time for anyone's shit today, Lauren. Escort the Archibalds to my office in five minutes, and do not let them out of your sight for even a second," I snap.

"Good morning to you, too."

I glare at her. "Good morning, Lauren," I mutter, then slam my door again.

Twenty minutes ago, I was as happy as could me, and now I'm about to rip off anyone's head who looks in my direction. Deep down, I know this meeting is not going to go well, and the fact that they're bombarding me first thing in the morning without a set meeting is crossing the line in my book.

"If it weren't nine thirty, I would probably suggest you have a drink. Hell, just looking at you makes me want to knock one back," Matteo mumbles as he sits in the far corner of my office.

I take a deep breath, then grab the stress ball Lauren bought me last year. I hate to admit it, but it fucking helps.

I hear voices approaching, so I cut my attention to Matteo. "Don't move from that spot. I want them cornered."

Lauren opens the door and in walk three men I've never officially met but have seen in passing, considering our families run in the same circles.

The infamous Warren Archibald, Juliette's estranged grandfather, walks in first like he owns the place, reminding me so much of my father with his entitled arrogance. If I didn't already hate him because of what he put Juliette's family through, I'd immediately hate him for that alone.

Her uncles, Conrad and Philip, follow behind like Warren's little puppets, and my first thought is to wonder if either of these two look like Jules's dad.

I walk around my desk and put my business mask on before shaking their hands hello. Matteo follows my lead and then sits back in his seat.

"Harrison Davenport," Warren says, looking around my floor-to-ceiling glass corner office. "You've done a good job with Abbott. Your grandfather would have been proud."

Of course, he's met my grandfather, but someone I don't know, especially someone I have no respect for, doesn't get to speak of him to me.

"I would ask to what do I owe the pleasure of this visit, however, I'm going to skip the pleasantries," I say while walking around my desk to sit. "Take a seat." I point to the chairs in front of me. "Please explain to me what was so dire you were inclined to barge in without a meeting first thing in the morning," I ask bluntly, scowling at all three men, waiting for one of them to speak up.

Conrad sits up straighter. "It's come to our attention that you and your people have been snooping around our business," he says, devoid of any emotion. *No shit, asshole.* When I don't answer, he continues. "As a professional courtesy, we have come here today to ask you to back off."

I lean back in my chair and cross my arms. "And why would I do that?"

The vein in Warren's old wrinkled neck pulses, clearly annoyed I'm not falling to his feet. I don't care who he is. You do not come into my building and demand anything from me. Professional courtesy, my ass.

Warren holds up his hand when Conrad attempts to speak again. "This purchase is personal, Harrison, and we'd appreciate it if you'd take a step back."

"Personal," I repeat. "I'm well aware of your personal ties to the building." I hold his eyes, telling him how much I really know.

His jaw clenches, and then he looks over at Matteo, wondering why he's here and how much *he* knows. "Matteo knows everything, so let's not hold back. Explain the importance of buying this building. I would be a fool to think you're unaware of the tenants you're kicking out."

His face changes, and the shrewd businessman with a reputation around the city emerges in a flash. "An opportunity arose to buy the building. Due to inflation, we've had to increase the rent."

"And this opportunity happens to be so soon after the death of your son?" I snarl, not holding back. I'm not here for chit-chat. "You're going to kick your granddaughter out while she still mourns her father?" I bellow, banging my fist on my desk. Philip's face drops, it's the only morsel of humanity I've seen yet. "Are you that selfish?"

"They took our son away!" he snaps, pushing his chair away to stand.

I follow his lead, standing and walking around my table to tower over him. "No, Warren, it is you who pushed your son out of your family. You are the one to blame." Conrad lets out a low rumble of rage, which I ignore. "Now, I think it's time you leave. You had some nerve coming here, asking me to back down, and now that I know the truth, you can bet your pompous ass I will do no such thing."

Warren straightens his shoulders. "Fine, if you love the girl so much. We will drop the deal with the management company if you break up with her. We've seen the pictures of you two this weekend. You care for her, and the building is important to her."

"And why would I ever break up with her? Why do you have an interest in my personal life?"

Oh....

You fucking idiot, Harrison. It all hits me at once.

Juliette was famous in the dance community but not enough to air her dirty laundry. Now that she is Juliette, ex-principal dancer, and partner to Harrison Davenport, billionaire, the vultures will dig up her past and her family, which would eventually be linked back to the Archibalds.

I smirk. This is great. "Afraid your horrid secret of disowning your child and his family will come to light? Is that it? You're afraid of a scandal."

When none of them answer, I lean back and press the buzzer, asking Lauren to escort the Archibald family out. "Let me explain something to you, gentlemen, and then I want you to get the fuck out of my office. You will never threaten me with an ultimatum again. Otherwise, you will regret ever meeting me. I assure you, I won't, and will never, break up with Juliette." I take a threatening step forward. "If you don't drop this deal, you'll be sorry, and that is *not* a threat."

Conrad opens his mouth, but I cut him off. "Get the fuck out!" I point to the door just as Lauren opens it.

I turn around and give them my back, signaling I'm done.

The second the door clicks behind them, I glance at Matteo, and his wide eyes tell me he's just as shocked as I am. "They're not going to drop it."

He nods. "I know, and holy shit, what kind of fucked-up family are they? Jules's dad was lucky to get away from them."

"I know. Dare I say they're worse than my parents?" I chuckle sarcastically. "I think we need to act fast. Go back to your office and call the management office. Do not let this sale go through, Matteo. I'm not kidding. Pay whatever you need to pay, buy the building, the whole damn block for all I care, but whatever you do, do not take no for an answer. These fuckers are not pushing Jules out of that damn building."

"On it."

"I'm going to call Jules's realtor and ask her to stall the deal."

He gives me a doubtful look. "That's not her decision."

"Money talks, Matteo. I've never been one to throw my name around, but today might be a first."

He nods. "Yeah. Good idea. I'll update you as soon as I have an answer."

"Thanks. And Matteo." He turns back. "Thank you for your discretion and keeping this from Becks. If I were put in the same situation without knowing the context, it would have been hard to keep it from Juliette."

His face falls. "Yeah...I haven't seen her much lately, so it wasn't an issue. I don't think it's going to work out between us."

"Really?" I ask, surprised. Jules never mentioned anything, and they looked like they were on the fast track to a serious relationship.

He stands in the doorway for a moment. "There is a good chance I have to work out of the London office for a while, and I don't think long-term will work."

Something in his voice is ominous concerning me. "Are you all right?"

He shrugs. "I will be…eventually."

Ten Hours Later

"Hey. What's going on?" Lauren's blonde head peeks around my doorway.

I glance at my watch. "What are you still doing here? You should have left a while ago."

"I didn't want to leave until I got a chance to talk to you. I was worried. You seem more stressed than I've ever seen before."

I run my hands down my face. "I have a lot of shit going on."

My office phone rings from Lauren's desk, so she runs back and gets it out of habit, even though she would usually be gone by now and let it go to voicemail.

"Please hold one moment," she says, then runs back to my door wide-eyed. "Philip Archibald is downstairs and would like to see you. He said to tell you he is alone, and it's important."

You've got to be kidding me.

Fuck's sake…I'm not in the mood for this right now. I'm exhausted, working on little to no sleep, and after this morning, the rest of the day went downhill.

"Earth to Harrison."

"Yeah. Let him up, and then you go home."

"Got it, boss. See you tomorrow." She salutes me and then is off to receive my guest.

I have to admit, after the shitshow this morning, I couldn't help but wonder about Philip. He didn't say one word, and his facial expressions stuck with me for some reason.

When footsteps ring out, I watch intently as he walks down the hall into my office. Earlier, I wondered if the men looked anything like Jules's dad; however, now that I have a moment to look at Philip, and who knows if he looks like her dad, but he certainly looks like *her*.

When she's with Inès, they look similar, but it's clear she's a mix of both families.

"Thanks for seeing me," he says, reaching over to shake my hand.

I wasn't planning on standing, but something about his tone had me standing to greet him.

"How can I help you?"

"Do you mind if I sit?" he asks, and I nod, pointing to the chair in front of my desk.

He leans forward and rubs his temples over his salt-and-pepper hair. This is a much different man than I saw earlier. He's distraught and similarly disheveled to how I look after the long day.

He takes a breath and glances up to look me in the eye. "I'm here to assist in any way I can. I have no interest in helping my father and brother take away Inès and Juliette's livelihood."

I suck in a breath. Neither of the men acknowledged them earlier; for some reason, hearing Philip speak their names makes it personal.

"Do you take me for a fool? Why would you help me and go against your family?" I ask skeptically.

"Because I loved my brother, Harrison. He would be devastated knowing that Inès would have to vacate the bakery she's owned for the last twenty years." When I stare at him, shocked, he smiles sadly and continues. "When my brother was disowned from our family, I was only eleven. I'm the youngest of the siblings, and we were ten years apart. Because of that, we never had the opportunity to become close, and I was influenced by my family's hatred. I didn't know any better until I was older."

"I don't understand," I tell him honestly. *What is he getting at here?*

He runs his hands through his hair. "A year before my brother died, we reconnected, and it was the best and worst day of my life. I realized that I had made a grave mistake listening to my family and that my brother was not some monster, but a kind, loving family man. Someone I wish I had gotten to know sooner, but I'm glad I had that year with him. He is someone I will always admire."

"Jules never mentioned it," I whisper.

"From what I'm aware of, she never knew. Neither did Inès. He wasn't skeptical of me, but I think he was worried about getting hurt again. Even after all these years, I can tell what my family did stuck with him. So, we took our time getting to know one another. Before he died, we had planned a whole get-together. My wife was soon to give birth, so we thought it was the perfect time to reunite and become a family. Unfortunately, he died before that could happen." He wipes a rogue tear. "My biggest regret in life will always be not reconnecting sooner."

His pain is palpable. I feel his words deep within my core.

"I'm so sorry, Philip."

"God, no. I'm sorry. I came here to tell you I'd help you, not all the rest."

"Can I ask you a personal question?" I ask.

He snorts. "Now that I've spilled my life regrets to you, it's safe to say you can ask me anything."

True. "Knowing now what you do, why are you still associated with your family?"

He leans back, crossing his legs. "Because I'm playing the long game. After meeting my family, you can imagine they're into some shady stuff. I hope to take them down one day, but trust me…I can't stand any of them."

My phone rings, and Jules's picture pops up. Philip glances down, and his face falls, so I silence the call quickly.

He audibly swallows. "I would love to meet her and have the opportunity to at least talk to her one day."

"What if that day was today?" I say without thinking. I'm already keeping a secret regarding her building. I won't keep this from her, too, and something tells me the moment she finds out, she'll want to know more.

"What?" His eyes widen. "What do you mean today?"

I walk around to the other side of my desk, suddenly realizing this seems too formal for what we're talking about. "Juliette is unaware of her building situation. I'm not mentioning anything until I'm positive I can fix this for her, so you can't ask me to keep this from her, too. And knowing my girl, she'll have a million questions. She was very close with your brother, best friends even. I think she would like to hear everything from you."

"Are you sure?"

I shrug. "There is only one way to find out." I take my phone and dial Jules's number.

"Hi, H," she answers on the first ring. I can hear the smile in her voice.

"Jules. Have you left Becks yet, or are you already home?" I ask, then hear Becks and Adriana saying goodbye in the background, which answers my question.

"I'm just leaving. I'm getting in the car with Robert now."

I blow out a breath, hoping I'm doing the right thing. "Can you have him drop you at the office? I'm still here, and I want to show you something."

She groans into the phone. "I'm so tired. Can't you meet me at the penthouse?"

"For me? Please?" I don't know what else to say without making up a huge lie.

"No one is there since it's late, right?" Her question has me lifting a rare smirk today. Ever since her out-of-character performance at the office, she refuses to come here.

"The employees went home, baby."

"Okay, fine. See you in a few minutes."

I hang up the call and see Philip eyeing the bar. "Drink to ease your nerves?"

"Please."

"She'll be here within fifteen minutes. She's not far away," I tell him.

"Can you make it a double?"

Juliette

I thank the security guard who escorts me to Harrison's floor, and then I stride down the hallway, attempting to push away all the embarrassing memories that flood my mind from my last visit.

Harrison comes into my line of vision, and I'm immediately

concerned. "Harrison." His head snaps up. "Are you okay? You don't look so great."

He stands and kisses me hello. "Thanks, baby. Are you telling me I look like shit?"

I giggle and hug him tightly around his waist. "Pretty much. Yes —" I stop mid sentence when I see a man sitting in the seat beside Harrison.

I take an unsteady step back at the familiar yet not-so-familiar face. "Jules, this is—"

"I know who this is. Why are you here?" I ask, my voice shaky, then turn toward Harrison, questioning him with a glower.

While my father was alive, I never felt the need to investigate my estranged family. Deep down, it felt like a betrayal toward my dad; however, once he was gone, my curiosity got the better of me, especially when digging into who Harrison was.

The man before me opens his mouth, but no words come out. Harrison looks between us and decides to take over, guiding me to one of the chairs and introduces me to Philip—*my uncle.*

"You look so much like him." My uncle mumbles more to himself.

"Thank you," I say for no reason other than being at a loss for any other words. I turn to Harrison. "Can you please get me some water, and can someone tell me what's going on?"

When Harrison stands, Philip catches my eyes. "You're under no obligation to stay and listen, and I completely understand if you want to leave, but I would like to tell you how I finally met my brother. Your father." Philips's pleading eyes beg me to stay. His peculiar wording piques my interest, so I nod, agreeing, too curious about what he has to say.

And I'm glad I did…for the last thirty minutes, I've sat here listening to how my uncle rekindled his relationship with my father.

He explained that because my father lived so far away for boarding school and college, my uncle was never given a chance to get to know my dad and only knew what his parents and siblings told him. He said after a year of questions and made-up information, they were all forbidden to speak my father's name.

"How did you finally speak again?" I ask.

My uncle smiles at the memory. "I was buying flowers for my wife at the florist when the door chimed, and I heard a man cursing the place down because he clumsily fell over the front mat..." He pauses. "Are you okay, Juliette?"

I wipe my tears. "Yes, sorry. I'm a crier, and I can imagine the exact scenario you're painting. Happy tears, I promise."

Harrison has been quiet, letting me take it all in at my own pace, but the small squeezes he gives my hand is a thoughtful reminder he's here.

"The second your father lifted his head, I knew he was my brother. He stood there, shocked to see me as well. I'm not sure if he had seen a picture of me or not, but I hadn't seen him since I was a child, yet we both knew."

Harrison hands me a tissue. I'm a sobbing mess now, and I can tell my uncle is trying his hardest to hold back his tears. "He bought my mom flowers every week at the same florist at the same time. He was a creature of habit."

He hangs his head, sighing heavily with anguish. "He told me. Funnily enough, I also bought my wife flowers every week...at that same florist...at the same time. My wife had an important doctor's appointment that day, so I left work early and stopped at the florist first. I only wish it happened years earlier."

Grief and despair for both my father and uncle tears at my heart. What a cruel world we live in sometimes. "I'm so sorry," I whisper. "I know you're upset that you had very little time with him, but think of it as a blessing you had, at least that. He was an amazing man, and I count anyone who crossed paths with him lucky."

Harrison scoots his chair toward mine and pulls me into him. If it weren't for my uncle, a stranger, I know he'd be placing me on his lap instead. He hates it when I'm upset.

My uncle smiles softly. "That's a beautiful way to think of it, Juliette. Thank you for passing along your positivity. I'll remind myself of it when I think about him. Which is often."

"I'm positive, but I also believe in signs, and I believe you met when you did for a reason. I'm not one hundred percent sure why, but I would like to think that you eased my dad's last year of life."

My uncle unconsciously reaches forward to take my free hand, then pulls back when he realizes what he's doing, so I reach out and take his, smiling sympathetically.

He reminds me so much of my father. I can tell he has a kind heart, and what he has said today is the truth.

He pats the top of my hand with his other, then releases me. "He brought me to one of your performances when we first reconnected. He was very proud of you, you're all he spoke about, and your mom. I could tell he loved her very much." I should be shocked, but I'm not. It's exactly something my dad would do. He loved to show me off and told me on a daily basis how proud he was. "There is no pressure, but I would love to get to know you and your mom. I know my wife feels the same, and I would like you to meet my children."

I suck in a breath. "You have children?"

He pulls out his phone to show me a picture of a pre-teen girl and a baby boy.

These people are my family…

"They're beautiful."

"Thank you." He holds my stare. "My son was born the week after your dad passed away…we named him Caldwell."

"What?" I choke out in a low, tormented voice, pressing my hand to my hurting heart.

His tears finally drop, though he smiles through them. "We call him Cal. After learning why your father left, I had never been prouder to call him my brother. I believe in true love, too, and sticking up for what you believe in. Caldwell represents your father's freedom, and I hope my son can be as courageous as Reggie one day."

"That is the most beautiful thing I've ever heard. Thank you for getting to know him. I only wish he would have told me about you. I would have liked to see you both together."

"I promise you, it was always the plan. I think we both needed time to get to know one another. Unfortunately, we didn't realize time wasn't on our side." He looks down at his watch. "Not that I want to cut this short, but I promised my daughter I would be home for bedtime tonight, and I'm already late." He passed me a card with his information on it. "I didn't know how this would go, but I'm so glad I got to meet you, Juliette. You're a lovely young woman. I can see why your father was so proud of you. I hope you call me because I meant it when I said I want to get to know you better, and I'm excited to meet the infamous Inès."

I don't know what comes over me, but I pull him into a hug. "I'm sorry." I try to pull back, but he releases a deep breath and holds me tighter for a moment longer.

"Don't be." He glances over my face one last time, smiling before shaking Harrison's hand goodbye.

We stand together, hand in hand, and watch him walk away. The second the elevator closes, my knees buckle and a sob breaks loose. Harrison catches me and lifts me in his arms, carrying us over to his chair.

I bury my head into his neck, letting go of all my emotions until, after several minutes, I am finally calm.

"Are you okay?" Harrison rubs my back.

I lean back to look at his gorgeous face. "Yes. I'm more than okay. I'm just being a drama queen." I smile, running my hands through his hair while I think. "Seriously though, I almost feel relieved that a part of my dad is back in my life. I know I've told you about my Aunt Liza, but I've never felt any emotional connection toward her. The second I met my uncle Philip, it was almost like I could feel Dad through him. I know you don't believe in all that mumbo jumbo, but I truly felt it."

"I believe whatever you tell me." He leans in and kisses me softly. "So I take it, you'll call him."

"Without a doubt." I nod. *There is no question.* "I almost can't believe it, but I look forward to hearing more about their relationship."

I put my head back onto Harrison's shoulder and yawn, the long day finally getting the better of me.

"Time to go home, baby."

"Mmm," I hum. "Let's just stay at Nate's vacant place down here so we don't have to go all the way uptown."

"Not happening. I want to go home to our bed." He stands and walks out with me in his arms, something that is becoming a regular occurrence.

Then it hits me.

Our bed.

24

Juliette

Two Months Later

A DARK SHADOW emerges in the doorway, hanging off the edge of the doorframe, gazing into the room. My pulse picks up, and excitement burns deep in my stomach from only a slight twist of Harrison's mouth.

I run my tongue along my bottom lip, boldly raking my eyes over his body, appreciating every inch of him.

Dark designer jeans, a crisp baby blue dress shirt perfectly formed to each bulging muscle in his arms, and brown suede Chelsea boots...*the man is a dream.*

The rest of August flew by, and September followed suit. Now, here I am, still in love, obsessed, and drooling over the man I'm lucky enough to call mine...every single day.

Officially, I haven't moved in, to Harrison's dismay, but *unofficially*, I've moved in.

Harrison and Sebastian are still not on speaking terms, and I know it's killing him on the inside little by little, and it's all because of our relationship. So, I can't, in good conscience, move to the next step, knowing that I'm putting a wedge between their tight-knit family.

Every morsel of compassion in my body feels for Sebastian and how he still mourns his sister five years later. How hurt he must feel being ganged up on by all the brothers, but I hope he realizes sooner rather than later that Harrison broke their promise for a good reason.

Me.

"Hi, beautiful," Harrison mutters in a deep rasp, smirking when he catches me checking him out.

"Hi, H," I whisper through a smile, holding his gaze.

"Oh god. Get a room," Becks mocks.

Harrison's eyes narrow with annoyance, which isn't new. He hasn't mentioned it *yet*, but I know Becks is beginning to grate on his last nerve. She's been at the penthouse almost twenty-four-seven since Matteo left a couple of weeks ago.

A month ago, Becks admitted she fell in love with Matteo, though she felt something was off.

Two weeks later, he moved to London, and as of this week, he stopped replying to any of her messages. I'm usually a good judge of character, and I was shocked at how quickly this escalated. Even Harrison was surprised but said he wasn't getting involved.

My bestie is a proud woman and won't admit she's hurting, so I invite her over every day after work. I'm always "cooking her favorite dinner" or needing a girl's day away from Harrison.

We both know what I'm doing, but if I know Becks like I know I do, this way makes her feel less vulnerable.

"What are you four doing in here?" he asks, glancing around the room. Myself, Adriana and Becks are lying on Claudina's bedroom floor as she puts on a show for us with her American Girl dolls.

"Oh, hi, Daddy. It's girl time. Sorry, you can't stay."

I bite my lip to hold back my laughter, even though I know Harrison will not find it funny whatsoever.

Who knew my mildly grumpy, six-foot-four man would get jealous of Claud and my relationship? I get it, though. His little girl, who he had all to himself, now four out of five times, chooses me over him.

He glares at all of us, then walks away.

"He's grumpy now." Claud giggles.

"Claudina," I lamely scold.

"She tells the truth," Becks chimes in, and I elbow her to shut up, then stand so I can get ready for the day. Today's the day I'm finally meeting Rosa and Javier at Sunday dinner.

Rosa's older sister became quite ill while they were in Spain. She was nervous this might be the last time she would see her, so they extended their trip for over a month.

"Claud, I'm going into the bedroom to get dressed for dinner. Can you please wash up and change out of your leotard and into the clothes I left you on your bed."

"Okay. Adriana, can you please do those fancy braids for me?"

"Of course, sweetheart." Then she turns to us. "Then, I'm going on a date." She hunches up her shoulders excitedly.

"No way. With who?" Becks asks, still lying on the floor with us all standing around her.

She fiddles with her phone and pulls up the Hinge dating app. "This is him."

"Oh my god. Shut. Up!" Becks cries.

Adriana's face falls. "What's wrong?"

"Don't listen to her." I kick Becks's leg in warning. "We knew him from the neighborhood growing up, is all."

"What a small world. Would he remember who you guys are? Maybe I can use you as an icebreaker."

I shake my head, giving Becks a look to zip her mouth shut. Adriana is going on a date with the nerdy guy who went to school with Becks and crushed over me all of high school.

If Adriana finds out, she'll never go on the date. She wants a boyfriend so badly but is so incredibly picky that she turns down dates left and right because they're not Mr. Right.

"It was years ago. I think you should go into your date talking about you only."

"Good idea." She takes Claud's hand and leads her into her en suite bathroom. "Tuesday night for the next dance lesson?" she asks right before she's out of sight.

"Yup, only I rented a space for the night. Harrison is having a new ballet bar installed in the home gym, so we can't use it until the end of the week."

"Have you heard anything else from her dance school?"

The simple question alone has my hackles up.

"We haven't." I blow out a breath. "Honestly, it's a good thing. I want to let it go now. Otherwise, I'm going to stress about it."

"Makes sense. I'm leaving right after I do her hair, so I'll see you then," Adriana says, and I wave her off.

A few weeks ago, Willa was sick with the flu, so naturally, I volunteered to pick Claud up from dance class. I arrived early to watch my sugar plum dance her heart out. Only once I did, all hell broke loose.

When I went to Claudina's summer dance camp a few months back, she was shy and reserved. I thought she didn't get along with the girls in class. Never in my wildest dreams would I have guessed the teacher would be picking on a five-year-old.

To say I lost my shit is an understatement, and then I left, pulling Claudina out of the class, telling her she was never going back.

Harrison should have made that call, but there was no doubt in my mind that not only Harrison, but her uncles would agree once they heard what happened.

One thing I've learned since being with Harrison is no one fucks with the Davenport/Morales family.

Harrison threatened to sue the school for negligence; of course, they assured him that the teacher would be fired and that they had no idea what was happening.

I called bullshit, so I put my foot down...Claud was never going back there again. Luckily, everyone agreed.

Now, she gets two professional ballet dancers as teachers and an aunt Becks, who she adores, as a sideline cheerleader.

"Juliette!" Harrison yells. "We leave in thirty minutes. You need to get ready."

I roll my eyes, knowing we probably leave in forty-five, but he's telling me thirty so I'm not late as usual.

"Is that my phone?" I ask Becks.

"Yeah. Mine's dead."

More like she didn't charge it to stop herself from calling Matteo.

"Barbara, the real estate lady, hasn't texted me back, has she? Or am I officially ghosted?"

"Not yet. I think it's time you start looking for a new place. You're in crunch time now."

"I know. I was hoping for a smooth transition where we could re-open right away, but I'm not sure that will happen anymore."

When I saw the place Mom and I liked best was off the market, I was concerned. When Barbara stopped answering me, I knew we were screwed over.

"Juliette!" Harrison yells again.

I roll my eyes. "Coming, dear."

I lean down and kiss Becks on the cheek. "Will I see you later? We still have five more episodes of Gilmore Girls to finish."

"No, I'm going to go see Carrie. She's working at Labo tonight. We'll catch up during the week."

"Okay, I love you, have fun, and tell Carrie I say hi. If you want to come back and sleep here later, you can. No matter how late."

"I know. Thank you, Jules…for everything."

I smile and blow her a kiss. She never has to thank me.

"Ouch!" I stand up and rub my behind where Harrison just smacked it hard. "What the hell, Harrison?"

"You need to move faster. That's the fifth outfit you took off. This is Sunday dinner at Mom and Dad's, not The Met Gala."

"Hmm…I see you're still cranky."

He walks up behind me and grabs my hip bones, pulling me into his groin. "I'm not fucking cranky. I've been watching your sexy-assin body move around naked for twenty minutes. I'm hard and need to fuck, Juliette. We haven't had sex in a week because, for some foolish reason, you won't while it's that time of the month. Which won't happen next month, I can tell you that right now. We'll go in the shower and do it there if we must, but there's no way in hell we're waiting."

"Sex maniac," I tease and roll my hips back into him, and he's right. He's rock solid.

He leans over my back, licks up the side of my neck, and bites my ear. "We need to leave now, baby. Otherwise, I'm bending you over in this closet, and you'll be walking into Mom's with come dripping down your legs." He rolls his hips with meaning, then reaches around and rubs his fingers over my panties.

Oh god, my mouth hangs open. I can barely breathe, just from one small touch. "You better stop Harrison," I warn, with little bite behind it.

"Ah, fuck. I can't, baby." He continues to roll his hips into my behind, picking up speed every second that passes. He's going to come in his pants if he doesn't stop.

From the friction of my lace panties and his fingers, it's already becoming too much for me. "I'm going to come soooo soon," I cry out.

"Hold on to the shelf," he growls and undoes his zipper.

I don't even attempt to take off my thong. I force it to the side for easy access so he can push right in. "What a good girl, so smart, baby." He lines himself up and slams in.

Ah. I screw up my eyes. Jesus, that never gets easier.

"You okay?" He slides out, then back in, slowly, hissing with each stroke.

I can tell he's already on the edge.

I push back in a silent invitation. It only burns the first few seconds, and then I warm up to him quickly. He widens his stance, bends his legs slightly, and begins hitting me with deeper, meaningful pumps, really letting me have it.

"Fuck. How close are you?" he pants, rubbing my clit with more pressure.

"Don't stop. I'm there…I'm there," I cry out, my body quivers, and my legs shake while I hold on desperately to the shelf so I don't fall as my orgasm rips through me.

"Daddy? Juliette?" The closet door handle jingles, and I freeze, thinking I might be having a stroke on the spot.

I try to pull back, but Harrison doesn't let up his pace. He presses his lips to my ear. "Stay quiet, Jules."

Then he pumps me once more, hard and fast, hitting the back of me so hard it takes everything in me not to scream the house down. "Fucckkk," he whispers, and I feel the telling jerk as he comes deep inside me.

"Hello?"

"One minute, angel. I'm helping Juliette with something," he calls out.

"Yeah. You're helping me get a one-way ticket to the insane asylum." I turn around and punch his arm, and he chuckles. "We need rules. No more sex during the day."

"I'm not being one of those parents." He rearranges himself and then zips up his pants before leaning down, using a dirty white T-shirt to wipe up his come dripping down my legs.

"It's not *those parents*. It's every parent, Harrison." My eyes widen. "Oh dear god, she probably heard me orgasm. I was screaming so loud."

"Mmm. Probably won't be the last time."

"What did you say?" I squeal.

"Hello. I'm still out here, you know," Claud calls out.

"Wear the black skirt and purple sweater. It's Rosa's favorite color." He points to one of the many outfits I threw on the closet floor.

I throw my hands up in frustration. "You could have told me that twenty minutes ago."

He winks and then opens the door and slips out before Claud can see me naked.

"I wish Mom could have come," I mumble, annoyed, as we walk down the tree-lined street to the Morales residence.

"Jules," Harrison chastises. *I know I'm being selfish.* "Did you want your mom to cancel on your uncle? She's been looking forward to spending more time with Philip."

"Ugh. I know you're right. What if Rosa and Javier don't like me?"

"I like you. Claud likes you. That's all that matters."

"No, we don't," she interrupts us. "We love her."

This girl is too cute. I bend down and pick her up, twirling her around the city street. "I love you too."

"Let me down, let me down. We're here." Claud jumps out of my arms, and we follow her as she runs up the steps to a beautiful brownstone.

"Ich bin nervös." I whisper in German that I'm nervous.

"Ne t'en fais pas." He answers in French that I shouldn't worry.

Of course, he would say that. This is much more formal than how he met my mom. We weren't even officially dating yet when he did.

"What did you say?" Claud asks.

"You need to learn German to understand." I smile down at her.

"Oh." Her face falls. "I want to learn German like you and Daddy."

Harrison rolls his eyes outwardly, annoyed.

"Don't be jealous," I tease him.

I remember he once told me he's tried to teach Claud German and French, but she only takes an interest in Spanish since Rosa and Javier speak it.

Suddenly, the door swings open, and the most beautiful, distinguished woman with silver hair and dark eyes stands there staring at me.

"Grammy, Grammy." Claud jumps up and down, overly excited.

Rosa bends down and quickly kisses and hugs Claud, her eyes never leaving mine. Then she stands up and walks in my direction; I have no idea what to do, so I stand like a statue.

She lifts her hands and surprises me by cupping my cheeks in a loving, tender way. "It is so nice to meet you, Juliette." Her smile is kind, and it eases most of my nerves.

"Thank you for having me. It's a pleasure to meet you, Mrs. Morales."

"You are stunning." She turns toward Harrison. "Just absolutely gorgeous."

"I know, Mom. Trust me." He smiles and mouths, *I love you.*

Rosa drops her hands and then engulfs me with a hug. "Thank you so much. They needed you," she whispers in my ear.

That's it. My last nerves drift away. It's exactly what I needed to hear from her...I needed to know she accepted us. That she knew I wasn't here to replace her daughter.

"Come on, Mom. Let's take this inside."

"Yes. Let's go. Everyone is inside already." Rosa takes my hand and leads me into the house, then looks back at me again with warmth in her eyes. "I'm so happy you're here."

"Can I help you clean up, Rosa?" I ask as I walk into the kitchen behind her.

"Absolutely not." She points to the chair at the kitchen table. "However, you can sit and keep me company."

"I can definitely do that." I pour myself a glass of water and then take a seat. "Thank you for dinner. Everything was delicious, and you and Javier are hilarious together. You remind me a lot of Leo, and Javier's humor is so dry. You're the perfect combo."

She chuckles, and her eyes crinkle with her wide smile. "We are the perfect combo, aren't we?"

She puts on some rubber gloves and begins washing the dishes. I've learned very quickly tonight that it doesn't matter that Rosa and Javier are abundantly wealthy. Rosa likes to take care of everything herself and only hires part-time help.

Their brownstone, which probably cost twenty-plus-million dollars, has been decorated with top-of-the-line furniture but still has a homey feel in every room. Javier uses his favorite chair in the living room, which is thirty years old, and no one is fazed that it's ripping at the seams and the fabric is completely worn out. Each room is designed with rich color and character, showcasing a plethora of family pictures that line the walls and tables.

You can tell people are very much loved in this house.

"Rosa?" I call to grab her attention.

"Yes, sweetheart?"

"Thank you." She turns her head to look at me over her shoulder. "Thank you for welcoming me into your home and your life. I'm so very grateful." I won't elaborate more. She knows exactly what I mean.

If you're *in* with this family, you're in...but if you're not, you're screwed, and I know if the matriarch of this family didn't approve, it would be much worse than Sebastian and Harrison not talking. The thought of it alone makes me sick to my stomach.

A life without Harrison and Claud would feel like Hell on Earth, and I never want to experience it.

Rosa removes her gloves and walks over to me, taking my hands in hers. "Juliette, I've dreamed of this day for a long time, and you're even more wonderful than I could have ever imagined. My son and granddaughter deserve to have a complete family. It's what my daughter would have wanted. She was selfless and only wanted the best for everyone. So, I'm the one who is grateful they met a woman with confidence who is beautiful inside and out. I can tell you love them very much and that you will be a role model my granddaughter can look up to. That's all I can ask for." Without another word, she squeezes my hands and walks back to resume her cleaning.

Claudina walks into the kitchen, quietly saunters to me, and climbs onto my lap. "You tired, sugar plum?"

She nods and snuggles closer.

Leo is behind Claud with Skye, who pushes her way under my legs and flops down, making herself comfortable. Leo grabs one of the chairs from around the kitchen table, pulls it up close to mine, and drapes his arm around me, pulling me into a side hug.

I lean my head on his shoulder, just as tired as Claud, and ask him how his date went yesterday.

"It was fine. She wasn't the right one."

"Oh please." I laugh. "You don't care about the right one. You only care about the right now."

He shrugs under my head. "I don't know, you guys look happy. Maybe it's time I settle down."

"I'll believe it when I see it, playboy."

"What's a playboy?" Claud asks over her yawn.

"Nice one." Leo chuckles.

"Umm…"

"Hey." Nate walks into the kitchen, luckily distracting Claud, then takes a seat in front of me. He lifts my legs and puts them on his lap so Claudina has more room to sprawl on top of me.

"Is Skye friendly with other dogs?"

"Yeah, why?" Nate answers.

"No reason."

No reason except trying to convince Harrison that Skye needs a sibling who lives at the penthouse. My dad was severely allergic, so we never had a dog, and now, after hanging out with Skye for the last few months, adopting a dog is all I can think of.

Leo squeezes his arm that's wrapped around me. "He'll never go for it."

"We'll see…"

"We'll see what?" Harrison asks as he walks into the kitchen, then stops dead in his tracks, glaring at Leo and Nate.

"Can you two get your dirty paws off my girl?"

No one listens to him, and Rosa is staring at all of us, smiling happily.

"He said paws. That must be a sign," I whisper to Leo.

Harrison whistles the way he does when he wants Skye to come to him, but instead, she looks up and then decides to stay near me.

I smirk at his apparent agitation. "I'm the favorite now, Davenport. You better get used to it."

He shakes his head, then kisses Rosa goodbye. "Let's go. You two look like you're about to pass out any second now."

Harrison

My phone rings, and I look down to see Seb calling, and I freeze, letting the call drop off. Then it rings again.

"Can you answer that, please?" Jules grumbles next to me.

"Sorry, baby. Go back to sleep." I kiss her forehead, then stand up and put my laptop away. It's late anyway, and I shouldn't be working anymore.

"Hello?" I answer and walk out of the bedroom into my office.

"Hey." Silence hangs in the air, and I wait, letting him take the lead. "I'm sorry I didn't come today…I was going to."

"Why didn't you then?"

He blows out an audible breath. "Because I'm a fucked-up person. I'm so fucked up in the head, Harrison, it's not even funny."

"Don't say that," I snap.

"It's the goddamn truth, and we all know it. My sister died five years ago. I need to get my damn act together. The second I got home from your office that day, I threw up because I was so sick with disgust at myself after what I said to you, and still, for some reason, I couldn't fucking apologize right away. You're a great father, the best, and I wouldn't want Claudina in anyone's hands but yours."

"I never thought you meant it, Seb."

"That's beside the point. The words should have never come out of my mouth."

"You're right, but I love you and told you I'm giving you this one pass."

"I'm still fucking pissed you bombarded me in your office. It's not even about the promise. Well, that's a lie—it is, we shook on it, and you damn well know that it was never about me. It was always about Claudina's protection. After your stalker ex went crazy, and you had to get a restraining order, I worried for all of us. We're all targets, and that's why you agreed, and then one day, I'm attacked by all my brothers, and suddenly I'm the piece of shit for getting mad. You should have come to me one-on-one before you started a whole fucking life with her. Claudina won't shut up about Juliette. I know everything that goes on. You're starting a family, and you told me last because you knew you were in the wrong."

I lean back in my office chair and take in his words. Everything he's saying is right, not one wrong word or thought.

"Before I get into it, I need you to know I never wanted to bombard you. Nate and Leo showed up on their own, and I asked them to leave several times." I twirl my pen around anxiously, thinking of a way to convince him about Juliette, but I come up short, so I tell it to him straight. "In the five, almost six, years Claudina has been alive, I have never let anyone but family or close friends enter my home. Not one stranger, woman, or delivery person. The maintenance workers were even background-checked. I had Nate and Leo draw in a separate elevator in the blueprints for my office, so she has private access so she wouldn't cross paths with most of my employees. Besides dropping her off from school, I normally don't even pick her up or drop her off at activities to keep the little anonymity she has. I have always protected her from our life. You know all of this already, so you have to understand that when I met Juliette, my life flipped upside down because, all of a sudden, I wanted to let her in. I wanted to share my life with her... but I couldn't." I pick up a glass of water from about five days ago and chug it. "I pushed her away, Seb. This wasn't a rash decision. I met her back in May, it's now October, and I'd be lying if I didn't want her from that very first day I saw her, but because I knew I couldn't, I never got her number. I never called. I didn't even know her full name. It was killing me. Without sounding like a complete fucking loser, the truth is my heart ached for her. Then another month went by, and there she was again. I knew I couldn't walk away again...I was falling for her hard, and I had to figure out how to make this work. I couldn't then, and can't now, ever live without her. She's going to be my wife, and I want your approval. I don't need it...but I want it."

"Harrison," Seb drawls.

"I know it's a lot to take in, and honestly, I never expected you to jump for joy. I only want you to give her a chance. No one says you need to be best friends, but do you know who she is best friends with?

Claudina. They are inseparable, and Juliette loves our girl whole-heartedly."

"I get it...I'm happy for you..."

"But?" There's a long pause. I can practically hear him thinking. "Sebastian?"

He lowers his voice. "I'm afraid Camila will be forgotten...that she will be replaced."

My head drops. Hearing the pain in his voice physically hurts me. How could he ever think that?

"Seb, I promise you that is not even a possibility. Camila is a huge part of our home life. I talk about her constantly. So does Mom, and I'm sure you do too. It will never happen." I hate that he lives with these thoughts on his shoulders every day. I wish I could take some of the burden from him. I hope he's still seeing a therapist; otherwise, I'm not sure how he lives day to day. "Listen, we're going to take Claudina to the playground tomorrow after school. Jules has off on Mondays, and Claud has a half day. Come and meet her there. It's informal, and you can leave whenever you want. You don't even need to talk to her. Come and hang out with me. If you hate her or feel uncomfortable with the situation, you leave. I've known you since you were three. You process things differently than I do, so I'm not expecting you two to be best friends, but I'd like you to at least meet her, and then we can go from there."

After what feels like five minutes, he says, "Yeah. Okay...I'll be there. I can't promise you anything. I still don't feel good about this. But I'll come for you and for Claud."

"That means a lot to me, Seb. I'll talk to you tomorrow. It's late. Love you, brother."

"Love you too."

I walk back into the room and find Juliette wide awake, sitting up in the dark against the headboard. She must have heard our conversation.

"I'm meeting Seb tomorrow?"

The sound of tiny feet trotting down the hallway has us pausing our conversation. Claud stands at the doorway, with one pigtail still intact, the other a wild mess, tightly holding her favorite blanket to her chest.

No words are exchanged. Juliette opens her arms up. Claud walks over, gets in the bed, and snuggles up to Jules.

"Did you have a bad dream again?" Jules whispers softly against Claud's temple, where her lips are pressed.

"Mmmhmm," Claud mumbles.

"Okay, you're safe here. Go back to sleep, sugar plum."

We silently wait for her to fall back to sleep, and I'm left standing here thinking of any possible reason in the world Sebastian could not love this woman.

"Tomorrow?"

"Yeah, baby...tomorrow." I climb into bed with my girls and lay on my side to watch them both.

"So, wife. Huh?" she teases, biting her bottom lip.

I reach my arm over Claud and run my thumb along Jules's face. "You are everything good in this world, and I'm never letting you go, beautiful Juliette."

25

Harrison

I ROLL over to pull my girl into my arms when I see Claudina lying in Juliette's arms, wide-eyed and ready for her day. I put my finger to my lips so she doesn't wake Juliette, then take a breather to calm my body before getting out of bed. I forgot Claud came in here last night and was two seconds away from taking off my briefs.

Fuck, that would have been bad.

Slowly, I get out of bed and put on my workout clothes, then quietly lift Claudina out of bed.

"Shh," I whisper, then walk us out of the bedroom and into the kitchen, sitting her down on the kitchen island.

"Good morning, my precious angel." I kiss her on her forehead, then her right cheek, and left. "How did you sleep?"

"Good." She smiles, kicking her legs back and forth. "I wish I could sleep with you guys every night."

Sounds fucking terrible.

Mornings are my favorite time of the day with Jules. When we wake up, we are too tired to talk, so instead we make sweet love, half asleep and cuddly while I take her from behind in my arms.

"You're a big girl, Claud. You need to sleep in your own bed."

"I know." She pouts.

I'm relieved when I open the fridge, and it's stocked with what I need. "Do you want to make Juliette breakfast, and we can all have breakfast in bed before school?"

"Yes, yes, yes," she chants. "Does she like pancakes?"

"Of course, who doesn't? Can you cut the fruit, please?" I hand her a bowl with her child safe knife and begin preparing the batter. "Don't forget that Jules will pick you up from school today, not Willa."

"Oh yeah. How come?"

"School is only half the day today, so Jules will pick you up and bring you to the park. Then me and Uncle Sebby will meet you there."

"Uncle Sebby?" she squeals, and I have to shush her again. "Oops. Sorry, Daddy. This is going to be the best day ever. When we get home, can I paint your nails? Look…" She picks up her hands. "Juliette painted ours yesterday. They're glitter."

"I have a meeting tomorrow, so you can't paint my nails, but you can paint my toes."

She giggles. "Okay."

I put the batter on the griddle, turn the kettle on for Jules, and then make myself an espresso. "Do you want orange juice?" I ask Claud.

"Mmmhmm."

After flipping the pancakes, I arrange the breakfast trays and ask Claud to pick flowers from the bouquet the housekeeper put in the entryway on Friday. "If you can't reach, I'll help."

She brings two peonies. "This is Juliette's favorite, and mine now too."

I smile at the memory of our Fourth of July date when the rooftop was filled with them. It seems like yesterday, but at the same time, so long ago.

"Do you want yogurt too?" I hold up her favorite strawberry kiwi yogurt.

"No, thanks."

"Angel, your birthday is next month. What do you want to do for your party?"

"You said when I turn six, I can have an ice skating birthday party with hot chocolate."

How the hell does she remember that? The last thing I want to do is watch a group of kids almost break their necks.

"You don't want to do a dance party? You can bring Juliette and show off a real ballerina to all your friends," I suggest, feeling not one bit bad using Jules as bait.

"Nope. I really want to go ice skating at the big one," she pleads.

"The one in Central Park?"

She nods enthusiastically, "Yup. That one and Juliette promised to bake me a cake."

Well, at least that's a plus. Wollman Rink is large and not as touristy. There was no way in hell I would bring her to Bryant Park or any of the others.

"Okay, Claud let's go. Can you open the door for me, and I'll hold the trays?"

She stops in front of her room. "One sec, I want to put on my slippers."

It feels like she's taking three hours. "Claudina, let's go. My arms are going to fall off."

She skips out of her room, wearing slippers that look like pointe shoes. "That's silly. Your arms can't fall off."

"It's an expression because the trays are so heavy. Let's go."

Claud pushes open the door and screams good morning, then runs and jumps in the bed to wake up Jules.

"Good morning, sugar plum," Juliette rasps, and I have to think of anything but the sound of her voice with my daughter in sight.

My dick is like one of Pavlov's dogs when it hears the deep rasp of her voice in the morning.

"We made you breakfast in bed." Claud bounces up and down.

"You did." Juliette tickles her side. "Thank you. What time is it? Don't you have school?"

I walk around the bed and lean down to kiss my girl good morning. "Claud and I woke up extra early today. We have plenty of time," I tell her when her phone buzzes, and I see red.

Who the fuck is Isaac?

Hey baby girl, see you today at Ten! Xo

"Who the fuck is Isaac?"

"Bad word!" Claud shouts.

"Sorry," I say through my teeth. "Answer the question, Juliette."

She's blinking at me like I have ten heads, but then she shakes herself out of it and sits up straight, glaring daggers at me.

"I thought we were both getting over this jealousy crap."

I lift a brow. "Says the woman who almost plowed down the lady at the grocery store."

She waves me off. "That's different, and Isaac is my hairdresser, Harrison. So you can calm down." When I don't retreat, she sighs, clearly exasperated. "My very gay hairdresser. Now shut up so I can enjoy my breakfast."

"Fine." I crawl in next to Claud and grab one of the strawberries off her plate.

"Just to confirm, pick-up is at eleven forty-five today?" Jules asks through a mouth full of pancakes.

"Yeah. Call me when you're heading to the park, and I'll meet you there. Seb is coming at one, so Claud has time to change after school if she wants."

She stares at my leg, shaking with nerves. "Why don't you go to the gym and calm down? A run will do you some good. I'll get Claud ready for school and drop her off today, too. Mom has a doctor's appointment at eight-thirty a few blocks away."

"Are you sure?" I ask, already out of bed. I'm so amped up for today's meet and greet that I need to expel some energy.

"Yes. Before you go, can you grab me a painkiller?"

I hand her the bottle and some water. "What's wrong with your leg? You haven't had pain in weeks."

"I was in such a deep sleep last night, I don't think I moved once and put too much pressure on it."

"Do the heat therapy, then the stretches before you leave, and what's wrong with your mom?"

"We're a sorry pair, her and I. She's had a few bad flare-ups over the last couple of weeks, so the doctor is going to give her a Corticosteroid injection. She's gotten them before."

"With the new doctor? I don't want you to go back to the old one. She didn't know what the hell she was talking about."

"Yes, you control freak, we're going to the doctor you picked. Now go work out. Goodbye." She smiles and swats me away.

Please...I'm not a control freak because I want to care for all my girls, which now includes her mother too.

I kiss her and smile down at her. "You're beautiful, did you know that?"

"Uh-huh." She laughs and wiggles her brows playfully. "You're not too bad yourself."

I look up to see Claud smiling at our interaction. She loves affection. I lean over and kiss her next.

"Come say goodbye before you leave."

Juliette

"Your name, again?" the nasty school attendant asks when I tell her I'm picking up Claudina.

"Juliette Caldwell," I tell her for the second time. My last name starts with a C. It's at the beginning of the list, for god's sake.

I can't take it anymore. I point to where I'm listed.

"I see it," she snaps.

Sure you did, old lady.

"Juliette!" I look up to see my sugar plum racing out the door. "I love your hair. Can I cut mine shorter?"

Over my dead body. *Literally.* Harrison would kill me if I cut off her long, thick hair.

"I'm going to grow it again after this, so you need to keep it long so my hair can match yours. Plus, if you cut it now, we won't be able to do all the fun braids we've been testing out."

She runs her hair along her fishtail braids. "Yeah, you're right. These are so cool."

"They are. Do you want to change before the park?" I ask.

She puts her hand in mine and swings it back and forth with a sparkle in her eye. "How about we go to The Little Baker instead and get a treat before the park."

"Only if you say it the proper way. Le Petit Boulanger," I say in French. "Repeat it slowly—Le."

Her face drops. "Fine. Le."

"Petit."

"Petit." She says perfectly, even with a slight French accent.

"Bou-lan-ger."

"I can't say that word." She stomps her foot.

My sweet girl takes after her father when it comes to perfection. "Try it once, please, and go slow."

She does it. It's not perfect, but for someone just learning, it's great.

"Good job, you're a natural, Claud." I put my hand up to high-five her, but she pouts and keeps walking.

"I didn't say it like you. It was bad."

"No, it wasn't, I promise. It takes time to speak it the way Daddy and I do. Do you know who else speaks French?"

"Who?"

"Inès, and you can practice with her anytime you want. She's the one who taught me."

"Oh. Okay." She smiles. She loves my mom, and I think it would be better if she taught her how to speak French and German rather than Harrison or me. She needs a neutral setting where she doesn't feel pressured. "Is your leg okay?" She looks at me, her expression quickly changing to concern.

"It's okay, Claud. Some days are worse than others."

"Okay." She looks down again. "We can walk another day."

I squeeze her little hand. She's like a mini-Harrison. "Walking and stretching sometimes helps, and it's not a far walk."

"Okay, but first chocolate cupcakes!"

———

"Stay where I can see you, and if you need help on the monkey bars again, come and ask me so you don't fall and hurt yourself." I point to the bench. "This is the bench I'll be sitting on."

"Okay." Claud gives me a thumbs-up and runs toward a little girl she often plays with at the playground.

"Hey," I answer my phone, "Are you almost here?"

"Your incompetence will not be tolerated in my company," Harrison's CEO voice booms over the phone. "We're at risk of losing the account because the portfolios you manage haven't been performing. You better figure out a way to adjust the strategy to fix this. Otherwise, it's your ass on the line, not mine." Then I hear a phone slam down.

"Um, hello?"

"Shit, sorry, baby. I thought the call was over when I dialed your number."

"What the heck was that?"

He takes a deep breath. "It was nothing. I don't want to talk about work. I'm only leaving now, so I'll be late but still be there before Seb."

"Okay, no problem. I know you only like riding with Robert, but take the subway at this time of the day. You'll get here in half the time."

"Yeah, not happening. I'll see you soon. Love you."

"Okay, love you too."

Claud comes running over to me after twenty minutes of playing. "Do we have any chalk? Some of the kids are drawing over there." She points behind the swings.

"I'm sorry, Claud, we don't. We can bring some next time, or maybe one of the kids can share with you."

"Hi. Sorry to eavesdrop," the woman next to me interrupts and points over to the kids. "My daughter is in the pink sweater, and she has extra. She'd be happy to share with you."

"Okay, thank you!" Claud calls and runs over so fast I'm worried she will trip and fall.

I'm watching her closely when something at the corner of the playground catches my eye.

Turning my head, it looks like…no, it can't be…

What the hell?

"Amber?" I call after my cousin, completely confused, but she doesn't react. Her eyes are laser-focused on the children drawing with chalk. Fear knots my stomach when I see her take a step forward, swiveling around until her gaze locks on Claud.

"Amber!" I scream as I jump up and rush toward them.

She raises her head, and a slow, malicious smirk lifts at the corners of her mouth just as she takes another step closer to Claudina. *Don't you dare.*

"Claudina," I scream, running as fast as I can. *Why isn't she listening?*

Amber's mouth moves, and Claud nods.

My heart is beating out of my skin, and I can feel bile rising in my throat. *Just a few more steps…*then, right before my eyes, Amber bends down, grabs Claudina, and brings her tight to her chest. Claud cries for help just as I burst through the swings and leap, lunging forward to stop them.

My foot hits the pavement, and a searing pain shoots up my leg, debilitating my movement, crippling me to the ground. Everything happens so fast. My knee smacks the concrete, and unable to put my hands out, my head slams down hard into the ground.

Dots blur my vision as I watch a man come out of nowhere, grab Claudina out of Amber's arms, and knock her to the floor.

"Claudina!" I attempt to call out again, but my voice gets lost in my throat, as blackness starts to take over. *Nooo…*

No. No. No.

Claudina screams my name, but I can't move. I'm helpless. And then, there's nothing.

Light flashes in front of me, causing my eyes to flutter open. I hear someone beside me take a gasp of relief while a strange woman shines a flashlight back and forth over my eyes. "Welcome back. I'm June, a paramedic." She smiles. "Can you tell me your name, please?"

"Juliette," I murmur.

"Can you follow the light with your eyes, Juliette?" she asks, and I do…or at least I think I do.

"You're doing, perfect Juliette."

"Juliette!" I hear Claud cry from a distance. I attempt to sit up, and June pushes me back down.

"Please stay down until I work you over."

"Where is she? Is she okay?"

"She's okay." Harrison's voice croaks next to me. "Are you okay?"

"H? Where are you? I can't see you."

He walks around, and his horrified face stares down at me, and I burst into tears. "Is Claudina okay?" I sob, tears blinding my eyes. "I'm sorry. I'm so, so sorry."

"Sir, I've asked you multiple times now to take a step back. I'm almost done here." June says as she waves someone over, then turns toward me. "Juliette, do you remember what happened here today?"

"Yes. Amber tried to take Claud from the playground," I utter, the vision fresh in my mind.

"Okay, that's great. Now, I need you to please lay still while we get you to the hospital."

"What? Why?"

"You've taken a hard hit to your head, and you have an open wound that needs to be cleaned out. It will also need to be stitched. They will probably want to do a CT scan while you're there to be safe."

"I'm not in pain, though," I tell her.

"That's because of the adrenaline. Give it some time," she says and then begins to push the stretcher that I'm lying on over to the ambulance, Harrison following along.

Before they put me in, Claud comes into view. She is crying hysterically, trying with all her might to remove herself from Sebastian's arms.

I recognize him now from the pictures—he's the one who saved her from Amber.

"Seb, give me her so she can see Juliette. Otherwise, she's going to freak out more." Harrison puts his arms out, and Sebastian takes a step back.

"Absolutely-fucking-not. Over my dead body, is she going near that woman."

My heart drops at his words.

He blames me…and he has a right to. *This is all because of me.*

My cousin, my fucked-up leg…none of this would have happened otherwise.

My head is secure, so I can't turn, but I move my eyes toward June and ask her to please put me in the ambulance. I need to get out of here.

Harrison is screaming at Sebastian, Claud is crying, and I feel like my life is falling apart right in front of my eyes.

Claudina could have been kidnapped today because of me…

"So, what you're telling me is that she has a disabled leg, and you left Claudina in her care? You jeopardized Claudina's life because of a fucking woman?" Sebastian shouts. "She could have been kidnapped!"

"Stop it!" Claud cries.

"Come here, sweetheart." Leo's voice suddenly appears, and I hear Claud's cries move further and further away.

"It is my fault, not Juliette's," Harrison bellows. "It's not because of her fucking leg. How close-minded can you be? How are you not seeing the bigger picture here."

I screw up my eyes and weep. I don't want to hear anymore. "Get me out of here, please."

A hand rubs my foot, and my eyes fly open to see Rosa's sad face staring back at me. She looks at June and asks if she can ride with me. "No, Rosa. Be with your family."

"Sweetheart, you are my family now. Let me come."

I have no fight left in me. "Can you call my mom, please?" I cry and wish away the tears.

"I did. She was downtown near Battery Park, so it will take some time for her to get up here. She's going to meet us at the hospital." Just as June closes the doors, Harrison screams to wait, but luckily, June does not listen. *I can't face him right now.*

We arrived at the hospital in less than ten minutes, and I couldn't say a word to Rosa the whole ride. She just held my hand silently and let me be.

I want to say something, but sorry doesn't seem anywhere close to good enough.

They rolled me straight to a room, and now I'm laying here, my head and neck braced, while Rosa fills out all the paperwork for me before they take me back for a scan.

I'm pretty positive I heard her threaten staff with words and names like Davenport and donation when we arrived, and then suddenly, I was being rushed around and promised the best doctors.

There's a knock on the door. I can't turn to see who it is with my head stabilized, but I'm praying it's my mom. Rosa gets up and comes to my side. "How can we help you, Detectives?"

"Detectives?" My voice is hoarse.

"We're here to get a statement from Ms. Caldwell on today's attempted kidnapping."

"You will need to come back at a later time. She is about to go for a scan." Rosa points behind her to the hospital orderly.

The detectives move to the side when I get pushed out. Rosa follows beside us, reassuring me she's not leaving my side.

When we pass, the detectives stare down at me, and the taller one glares at me with a look of suspicion, causing the hairs on the back of my neck to stand up. What the hell was that about?

"Rosa, I appreciate you being here with me, but maybe while I'm in the scan, you can go back to the room and wait for my mom? She's going to be frantic, so I don't want you to miss her. She'll be the one screaming the house down in a French accent."

"Of course, sweetheart. Anything you want." She leans down, kisses my forehead, and then returns to the room.

Miraculously, I'm taken right in for the scan, and it's done seamlessly. I'm not a stranger to hospital stays. Nothing goes smoothly, especially in a big city hospital, so it only confirms what I thought Rosa said earlier.

While I'm alone, waiting for the orderly to push me back, my mind starts racing, and I now wish Rosa had stayed with me to distract my frantic thoughts.

How is my sugar plum?

What could I have done differently?

Where is Amber? Did she get arrested? Was she on drugs? Did she forget to take her medication? Why did she do this to me? How did she know who Claud was?

But most importantly…how will we ever move past this?

"*You jeopardized Claudina's life because of a fucking woman.*" Sebastian's words play repeatedly in my head, and suddenly, this is all starting to feel like the beginning of the end. There is no way to fix this. Sebastian's right…Claudina's life was in my hands, and I failed her.

"Are you ready, miss?"

"Yes. Thanks," I mumble.

While I'm rolled back into the room, my mind doesn't stop, and I'm becoming more anxious by the second. Harrison will never trust me again. *How could he?*

What would have happened if Sebastian didn't intervene?

"What's wrong? Are you okay?" Harrison's worried voice startles me as I'm wheeled into the room. They took off the stabilizer, and although stiff and sore, it feels good to move my head.

I glance over him, and it's the first time I'm getting a good look at him. He looks so unlike my usual put-together man; his vibrant blue eyes are dull and sad. His hair is disheveled, and his clothes are askew, covered with blood and muck.

"What are you doing here? Why aren't you with Claudina?"

He furrows his brows. "What do you mean, what am I doing here?

Did you expect me not to be by your side after I watched you unconscious on the ground with blood dripping out of your head?" he says, hurt laced through his words.

"Yes. Claud is more important than me. You should be with her." I reply with no emotion, turning my head away from him. The second I see the disappointment of what I've done, it will break me in half.

"Claud is fine. She has no idea what happened today and thought the commotion was because you were hurt. That's the only thing worrying her right now." When I don't answer, he takes my hand in his, and I attempt to pull it away, but he won't let me. "Look at me, Jules. What's going on?"

Two women with white coats, who I presume are doctors, walk in the room. "Hello, Ms. Juliette Caldwell?"

"Yes. That's me."

"I'm Dr. Valentine, and this is Dr. Lead, the hospital's head plastic surgeon. I've looked over your scans, and luckily, there was no internal bleeding, and you only have a concussion. I will have a nurse come in shortly to clean your head wound and knee, and then Dr. Lead will be back to stitch up your wound."

"Juliette!" My mother comes barreling into the room and stops short when she sees the doctors. "Oh, pardon me. I'm Juliette's mother."

Dr. Valentine smiles in her direction. "I was just finishing telling your daughter. She has a mild concussion, and we will discharge her after stitching her up as long as she has someone to keep an eye on her overnight."

"Dieu merci," she cries, realizing quickly she spoke French, which makes me hyper-aware of how worried she was. "Sorry, thank goodness. I was so worried."

"Two detectives are waiting for a statement. Should I send them in now?"

"No," Harrison answers quickly.

I sigh, not wanting to do this at all. "It's fine, we should get it over with."

The detectives ask my mom and Rosa to leave, and neither is happy about it by the grumbles I hear as they walk out.

"Can you tell us everything that happened today from the second you arrived at the park?"

I went over every detail I could remember, from when Claud tied her shoe to the smirk on Amber's face. They write it all down, and I think that would be the end, but the detective that gave me bad vibes from before takes a seat and turns his chair toward me.

"I have a few more questions."

"About what?" Harrison snaps. "She gave her statement. She needs rest."

He ignores him and continues. "Is it correct that Amber Allen is your first cousin?"

"Yes."

"What?" Harrison's voice raises. "Who is Amber? I thought it was Ashley who attempted this."

"Who is Ashley?" I ask.

We're looking at one another, confused, and then glance back at the detectives for clarification.

"Harrison, is it correct to say you dated Ashley Allen and then had a restraining order placed on her six years ago?"

"Correct."

The detective writes some things down and then looks back at me. "Ms. Caldwell, did you conspire with your cousin to aid the attempted kidnapping of Claudina Davenport?"

"What?" I shout and instantly regret it when the pain radiates through my head. "What the hell are you talking about?"

"This is absolutely preposterous. What kind of question is that?" Harrison barks. I can see the anger steaming out of him.

The other detective shakes his head to signal that's enough.

"Harrison, were you aware that Ashley's birth name is Amber Allen, Ms. Caldwell's cousin."

We look at each other again with confusion.

Harrison sits there in shock, processing everything. This all makes sense now. Harrison mentioned his ex began acting strange, like a different person, even erratic at times.

That describes Amber to a tee.

And what the hell is this crap about her changing her name to Ashley.

"I have a question," I say.

"Sure."

"How did Harrison file a restraining order against Ashley? Wouldn't her legal name come up in court?"

"She legally changed her name seven years ago."

What? This is all too much for me right now. "Do you have any other questions? My head is hurting, and I think I've had enough. I can't take anymore."

The detectives look at each other and then back to us. "No. We'll be in touch if we need anything else."

"Wait," I call out. "What happens to Amber?"

"She'll be transferred to Bellevue Psychiatric Hospital, where she will be under watch."

I nod, anticipating that response. While I'm infuriated by her actions today, I also recognize that when she's off her medication, her cognitive abilities are compromised.

When the detectives leave, my eyes stay locked on the door. "So your *crazy* ex-girlfriend is my mentally unstable cousin?" I whisper.

There is no going back, I think, the second the words are out of my mouth. I will never be able to face his family after this. All I've brought into this family is hurt and pain. Most importantly, Sebastian, his brother and best friend, will never get over this. I heard it in his voice, this was my last chance with him.

I've said it once, and I will say it again. I will not come between them.

"Why won't you look at me, Juliette? You're scaring me."

I scrunch up my face and let a few tears that have been pooling in my eyes escape.

"I'm so, so sorry, Harrison."

"Baby," he croons, carefully touching my face. "This has nothing to do with you. She broke her restraining order and came after Claud because of me."

"Not because of you," I snap. "Because she was jealous of you and me together. I remember hearing her talk to my aunt, and she was bitter I was dating you. She's been like this my whole life."

"She would have been bitter if I got serious with anyone, Jules. Don't you see that?"

"Okay, and would that other person have a fucked-up leg and fall to the ground when they try to get to Claud?" I don't let him answer. "I think not. How will you ever trust me with Claud again? How?" I howl.

"You were trying to save her. You falling was an accident. It was not your fault." Tears fall from his eyes because his words are a lie.

He knows I'm right.

How will I ever feel confident to take care of Claud again?

She'll never be safe with me.

Emptiness spreads through my body as the thought of them not in my life takes over my mind. Harrison's standing within reach, yet I still feel like I'm miles away from reality. Somewhere locked between a nightmare and hell.

"When I get discharged, I'm going to go home to Mom's," I state, void of feelings. If I show one ounce of any emotion, he'll pounce on it and won't let me go.

This is what is best. Time away from me...time for him to repair his bond between his brothers.

26

Juliette

PUTTING a smile on your face and pretending you're okay can only last so long. Eventually, the numbness wears off, and your world begins to crumble.

It's been two weeks since the hospital, two weeks since I last saw my love, and one week since I started therapy.

Something had to change. The uncontrollable sobs and sleepless nights were getting to be too much.

The emotional damage finally took its toll on me, and I needed help.

It's not been easy staying true to my decision when my eyes close at night, snuggled in bed, wrapped in my dad's sweatshirt, missing Harrison's arms around me.

All I see is the image of his haunted expression.

The tears in his eyes.

The disappointment.

All puncturing my heart deeper and deeper as the days went by.

He'd never cried before, even when he spoke about Camila, yet I hurt him so badly, he couldn't hold back.

"Don't leave me...don't leave us," he cried, his devastated eyes begging me to stay.

Should I have let it play out and hoped Seb came around? Did I make a mistake giving them space?

There's no way I could live with myself if he didn't.

I would constantly worry that Harrison resented me for the fallout of his brotherhood, and worst of all, I'd be concerned that the distance between them would hurt the rest of the family, mostly Claudina.

Those thoughts, on top of the constant blame I put on myself, weren't healthy, and I see that now with the support of my therapist.

I've seen her four times in only one week, and it's helped tremendously.

She went back to the beginning, when Dad suddenly got sick, and reminded me that from then on, a series of tragedies unfolded, each weaving its own web into one significant heartache. Those tragedies transpired in such a short amount of time making it natural for my mind to struggle when bombarded with these challenges.

She assured me it was perfectly normal and that I was not alone, constantly validating my feelings. Since then, we've been working on restructuring my outlook, specifically surrounding the attempted kidnapping. The events that happened don't define me; they aren't my fault, and healing is a gradual process.

Something she mentioned that has stuck with me most is that if I don't have self-compassion, I'll never move on from my past. Apparently, I easily understand others and give grace when needed, but not with myself.

Maybe that's true...I don't know.

All I know is even with all this new self-discovery, I'm miserable without Harrison.

I want to call Seb myself and tell him to get his head out of his ass and realize I'm a good person and that he's putting a strain on both Harrison and Claudina.

I've spoken to her every night, and she's devastated I'm not there. She doesn't understand what's going on; she thinks I'm at my mom's to let my injury heal.

It's true in a way, but I can hear how much she misses me in her voice.

Mom, unsurprisingly, has been by my side every step of the way. I'm not sure she understood why I walked away from Harrison, especially since I told her my future was with him, but she still supported me full-heartedly.

When I explained that sometimes you need to heal yourself before you give yourself to another, I think she finally got it.

Believe it or not, my other biggest supporter has been my uncle Philip. He visits every morning before work and walks with me in the park, even on the days I don't want to get up. He forces me to get out of bed and distracts me with stories of him and Dad, his kids, and life in general.

When he saw the incident on the news, he was at the apartment within the hour of my hospital release. Every local news outlet and newspaper had it running—billionaire baby nearly kidnapped.

No one could miss it.

Well...besides Becks.

The night before the accident, while we were at the Sunday dinner with Rosa and Javier, she got a call to be ready first thing in the morning. She was taking the place of a sick employee on a three-week work trip to Hong Kong.

Un-freaking-lucky for me.

"Juliette, my love." My mom knocks on the door, thankfully interrupting my thoughts, holding my phone in her hand. "It's been going off nonstop."

I nod, acknowledging her. Why does she think I left it in the kitchen?

No part of me wants to talk to anyone.

"It's Leo."

She hands me my phone, and *it is* him.

Huh.

"Hello?"

"Get your cute butt downstairs. We have things to do, places to be," he chirps. Then I hear the familiar sweet giggle of my favorite girl, and I'm out of bed without thinking.

I need to see her.

Quickly, I wash my face, careful not to wet my stitches, and then throw on a warm sweater and jeans before telling Mom I'm leaving. If my leg weren't still sore, I'd be running down the steps, busting through the front doors, but it takes me a little longer than usual.

"What are you doing here?" I ask Leo, then turn around to find Claud, but I don't see her.

Leo brings me in for a tight hug that almost has my resolve breaking on contact. "I figured you'd be wallowing around like your other half."

I don't have a second to ask him how Harrison is because Claud comes running out of the bakery with a macaron sticking out of her mouth. I should have known that's where she would be.

Leo has to warn her to slow down so she doesn't hurt my leg, but to have her in my arms right now would be worth the pain and cheaper than going to my therapist.

She hugs me tightly, chewing loudly in my ear, putting a smile on my face. "Hi," she mumbles through a full mouth. "I miss you. When are you coming home?"

My eyes glance at Leo, and he frowns, as if he's wondering the same thing.

Claud's smart, so I need to be honest. "I'm not sure, sugar plum. Hopefully soon." She doesn't answer. Instead, she tightens the hold around my neck when she's done eating. If I know anything about Claud, it's that she wants me to hold her and carry her to wherever we're going. Claudina is ultra-affectionate, and being held tightly by someone she feels comfortable with is her safety blanket.

As much as I want to keep her in my arms all day, I won't be able to. Soon, my knee and leg will start throbbing. Leo must think the same thing, so he takes her out of my arms.

"Do you want to come see the stars with us?" she asks, and I look at Leo for help. I have no idea what she's talking about.

"Claud wants to go to the planetarium at the Museum of Natural History. She likes to lie back and look at the stars."

"Sure, I'd love to, sugar plum." At this age, the show at the planetarium would be hard for her to grasp, but when I was younger, I thought it was the coolest thing just to sit back and watch.

"Should we take a taxi?" Leo asks, glancing down at my leg.

"Let's walk. I won't be able to spend time roaming the museum after the show, though, and I'll take a taxi back."

This is what I needed today.

To spend time with my sugar plum, hearing her giggles and holding her in my lap while we watched the stars.

There came a point where I needed to rest but didn't want to go home, so I read in the park while they explored more of the museum, and then all three of us had an early dinner.

Now we're waiting for our car, and I can see Leo's itching to talk to me; he's been a jittery bundle of nerves all day, trying his best to hold back, but I can't stand it anymore.

"Just spit it out already," I say.

"Claud, sweetheart, can you go play on the grass? I need to talk to Jules for a moment."

Claud skips off without questioning him, bouncy pigtails and all. As she gets further from us, my heart rate skyrockets and my body goes into panic mode.

"No, Claud!" I scream and freeze, realizing what I've done. It's as if all of Manhattan has just gone silent. People are staring at me, and Claud is stuck in her spot, wide-eyed.

Leo puts his arms around my trembling body. "Breathe, Jules, it's okay. She's okay." He rubs my arm to soothe me. "She's right in front of us. Nothing's going to happen."

"I know," I whisper. "I'm working on it. I promise."

"Go ahead, Claudina, it's okay," Leo says, then points around the park. "There are bodyguards here. She is safe."

I nod, acknowledging I know he's right. Wait, did he say… "Bodyguards?"

"Come on," he says, walking us to some chairs near where Claud is doing cartwheels in the park.

"You haven't noticed them? You have one, too."

I frown, confused. "What? Since when? Why?"

He smiles at Claud when she waves to us. "They started the morning after the incident. They're temporary, hopefully. With the heightened attention around us, we all felt more at ease having some protection."

He's right. It does make me feel a lot better. Even though Amber will be in a psychiatric facility for a while, it doesn't mean there aren't other threats out there.

"Of course, one of you snaps your fingers, and poof, bodyguards appear within hours," I tease.

He chuckles because he knows I'm right. "It's a good thing to have connections. This time, though, it was Jackson who helped. He works closely with a security company in London. They work worldwide, so a team was sent out that night."

However they got them, I'm grateful. It gives me peace of mind they're here.

"Where is the car? I feel like it's taking forever," I ask.

Leo grabs my hand, pulling my attention from Claud to him. "Don't worry about the car. First, you'll tell me why you're doing this, silly girl. You and Harrison need each other. You need to go back to him."

I drop my head and take a deep breath. "I can't be the one who comes between a family as close as yours, Leo. Your whole relationship is based on the bond you all have, and I can't be the driving factor behind a family divide. I wouldn't think twice if Claudina weren't in the picture, but they need to be good for her sake." I lean back and think about Harrison. "Has Seb been giving Harrison a hard time?"

"They're not talking much to be honest." He sighs. "It's a delicate situation. The world views Sebastian as this strong cutthroat hotel mogul, which he is. But I see the hurt he lives with every day and how hard it is for him to live without Camila. For all the shit he's been putting Harrison through, it's only because family comes first, and his knee-jerk reaction was to protect Claudina."

I hesitate before asking my next question. "Can I ask you something without sounding insensitive?"

"Of course."

"Why has Camila's death affected him more than the rest of you? Even Rosa and Javier have moved on and live a full life celebrating her."

He drums his fingers on this thigh. "I'm not sure there's a real formula to understand an individual's grief. He was close to Camila but no more than Harrison. Who's to say Harrison wouldn't have been the same if he had not had Claud to care for." He pauses to think, then continues. "I often wonder if Sebastian is his own worst enemy. When Camila passed, he was in such a bad place that it soon became a vicious circle. He was depressed and mad at himself for it, and now it's like he can't break the cycle."

"Then I came along and interfered," I murmur. "And Harrison broke the promise."

"Oh please, that promise was fucking dumb."

"Leo." I laugh.

"It's true. Protecting Claudina from our depraved world is all of our number one priority. Harrison didn't need to shake on it to ensure that."

This is true, each of them, including myself, would do whatever it takes to protect her from anything.

"After Harrison speaks to Seb, what happens if he never comes around to the idea of the two of you?" Leo asks.

"If Seb doesn't want to make an effort, that's a different story. Harrison and I are forever, so it's not a question of *if* I'm going back. It's when. I know that deep in my heart, and truthfully, it's not only about Seb. The incident brought up a lot of issues for me, too. Working to be the best version of myself is important for my relationship with Harrison and Claud." I shrug. "I was spiraling in the hospital, and maybe I made a knee-jerk decision, but at the end of the day, it was the right choice."

He stares at me for a moment. I can see the wheels turning in his head, thinking about what I said, and I know he understands when he gives a slight nod.

He stands, helps me up, and wraps his arms around me. "You're a good person, Juliette Caldwell."

My love, if your leg isn't hurting, can you go downstairs and check on the stoop for a bag of groceries? I think the delivery boy left them outside instead of buzzing up.

I'll check now, Mom. Hopefully, you ordered ice cream. LOTS of ice cream.

Of course, my love.

I take the elevator down and open the door to our building. I don't see any groceries, but what I do see is Harrison sitting on the bench across the street.

I hesitate, and as if he can sense me, he looks up, and we lock eyes. Like a magnet, I'm pulled to him, and my heart responds instantly, thumping steadily against my chest.

"What are you doing here?" I whisper.

"I'm sorry, baby. I thought you'd be inside for the night." He shrugs. "I-I was missing you and sitting here makes me feel closer."

My heart stops. "You've been here before?"

He hangs his head. "Almost every night."

My strong man looks so alone and dejected, breaking my heart all over again. I need his touch, his closeness, so I walk closer and sit next to him, interlocking our fingers.

"I miss you too," I murmur, placing my head on his shoulders. "We're going to work it all out soon. I promise."

We sit like this for what feels like hours, silently soaking in each other's company, until his phone buzzes, and he sighs, unimpressed. "I need to get back. Leo is dropping Claud off at the house now."

We sit for another minute until I turn and lightly kiss his lips.

"Infinity times infinity," I whisper.

His breath hitches, and I don't try to dry my tears. Both of our emotions are fragile at the moment. He understands my tears.

"I love you too, *mon petit papillon*." He brushes away a slight wisp of hair and kisses me again. "Come back to me soon, Juliette. I'm waiting for you."

The days are long, but the nights are longer when you're all alone in your head.

It's been another two weeks since I've seen Harrison, and my insecurities are at an all-time high. He has Claudina call me every night, and I can sometimes hear him in the background, but he never asks to talk to me, and my stubborn ass doesn't either.

If I hadn't known he'd been calling Mom to check in on me, I would have wondered if what we had was even real.

But I'm ready to go *home* now…I'm mentally more vital than ever before, and my therapist thinks I've given Sebastian enough time to come to terms with his feelings. Now it's on him to make an effort.

She's helped me with personal priorities, and we're working on putting myself first, which includes taking steps to get back into the dance community.

Teaching Claud a few days a week apparently doesn't count. It was some of my favorite times of the week, and now that my injuries have healed, I can't wait to get back to that special time with her.

But besides all that, I've been more stressed over a different issue. *Our lease.*

It's coming to an end sooner rather than later, and we still don't have a new location secured.

After Barbara ghosted me, Leo set me up with a realtor he knew, and he's shown us some great places. Only Mom hates most of them, or when we make an offer on one we do like, someone outbids us.

I'm tempted to take my Black Card that's burning a hole in my pocket, buy us something expensive, and call it a day.

I would never. Even if Harrison would prefer it.

Either way, I'm not letting it upset me anymore. I'm moving on, and Mom and I are going to start a new chapter in our book.

And hopefully, by this weekend, Harrison and Claud will be a part of it.

I'm ready, Harrison.

Harrison

"You look like fucking dog shit." Nate hands me a beer and sits between me and Leo on the couch. "I don't understand what you're doing and why you haven't gone and dragged her home yet."

I frown. "I only got half of that. What did you say?"

"For fuck's sake," Leo sighs deeply and rolls his eyes. "You're a miserable bastard to be around, and you need to get your girl back. Who cares about that fucking idiot." He nods over his shoulder toward the bathroom where Seb is.

I sip my beer and glare at him. "I'm miserable? Have you taken a look in the mirror?"

Nate smiles around his drink, unable to hold back his laughter. "Ask Leo why he looks like shit."

I turn my attention back to Leo. "What is he talking about?"

"Nothing," Leo snaps.

I smirk, looking at Nate to answer. "He had a repeater last night. She looked at him and said… *Oh, I thought it was bigger last time we were together.*"

For the first time in a while, I let out a real laugh, imagining how it went down. Leave it to my brothers to finally get a smile out of me.

Leo scoffs. "Please. I met her years ago at a club. She's a party girl. The only thing she remembers is how to snort coke." He crosses his arms, annoyed. "And we're talking about this idiot. Not me."

"You say it like you don't know exactly what I'm doing and what my plan is," I say.

"Well you're taking fucking forever."

"Forever for what?" Seb asks as he walks back into the room.

"Nothing," I mutter, and the conversation goes dead.

"Oh fuck. Look at his arm." Leo points to Mason, our quarterback friend. "He's killing it this season."

"Leo, can you come here for a second?" Nate calls from behind me.

When the hell did he get off the couch?

Leo leaves, and suddenly you can cut the tension with a knife. Things are...complicated with Seb.

"I'm seeing my therapist regularly," he says, breaking the silence, still focused on the football game.

"Why is there a point if you won't listen to them?" I'm happy he's still going, but it seems useless if he isn't going in with an open mind.

He takes a long sip of his beer and blows out a breath. "Why? Because I realized I was hurting my niece by being a selfish bastard."

"Seb."

"Don't. I know I am, and I admit I might have overreacted over the Juliette situation. I'm not happy about it, but I'm trying to figure my shit out."

Juliette sacrificed her own happiness for mine. For that alone, I love her more than humanly possible. Her decision wasn't what I wanted, but she didn't give me a choice. She would rather burn us to the ground so my bond stays tight with my family...but she's our family now, and I'm not losing her.

I nod. "I'm glad you're coming around, but I need you to know that no matter what you said, I was getting her back. It's Jules who was giving you time, not me. I appreciate you putting in the effort now, but Juliette is my family just as much as you are, and she deserves to be back with me and Claud."

With Seb starting to wrap his head around the idea, I'm putting this in motion. *Now.*

"Nathaniel, Leo? It's happening...tomorrow," I stand and call out. "So you better have the plans all drawn up."

Leo points to his drafting table. "All set. You might want to add a puppy to the grand plan."

I stop dead in my tracks. "What are you talking about?"

"She wants one, even made sure Skye was dog friendly. I think she was waiting until she officially moved in to ask."

I think this over and realize it's already late, and I'm not sure I have time to contact a rescue. "Send me the information on the dog rescue you got Skye from."

Then I walk to my office and call Inès, telling her I need her help tomorrow.

But first, tonight, I need access to their rooftop.

"Jules's baby." I softly trace her freckles, rousing her from her deep sleep.

"Harrison?" she rasps, and I smile, happy to hear that voice again. "What are you doing here?"

"Come with me, baby." I put my arms around her, lifting her out of bed.

She rubs her eyes and snuggles into my chest. "I can walk," she murmurs.

"And I can carry you." Which I do, all the way to the rooftop.

"Oh my god," she gasps.

"Dancing in the Moonlight" by King Harvest is playing over the speakers of her rooftop.

The blankets in the corner I put up here earlier catch her eye, so I place her on the ground and wrap her up to keep her warm on this cold autumn night. Then I hold out my hand. "Dance with me?"

She smiles softly and takes my hand so I can twirl her around into my chest. Her in my arms is the best feeling in the world.

"What is this?" I rub off some hardened pink stuff she has smeared on her face.

She looks down at my hand and chuckles. "I fell asleep before washing my face. It's frosting from the cakes I was taste testing for Claud's birthday this weekend."

I pull her closer, burying my face in her hair. "Even with everything going on, you were still going to make Claud a cake?" I mumble.

"Are you kidding me? Of course I am. What we're trying to work out has nothing to do with my sugar plum. She deserves the best."

She's right, she does. They both do.

We stay like this, silently swaying to the music until the song ends. Juliette once told me her favorite part of the day was lying in bed with me late at night, talking about nothing. *Just talking.*

My favorite is this, the silence. It reminds me that I found someone I'm so comfortable with that no words need to be exchanged. I'm happy to just be in her presence.

"You told me that your dad said *when you dream about happiness, it will get you through anything.*" I kiss her forehead. "He was right. I dream about you every night, which has gotten me through the past few weeks. You're my happiness, and now I'm ready to make my dream a reality. You're coming home, Juliette. It's time." I kiss her again, then carry her downstairs and put her back to bed.

"You're not staying?" Her voice catches.

I shake my head. "I'll see you tomorrow, beautiful Juliette. Sleep sweet."

"Everything's going to be okay," she whispers before I leave.

"Yeah, baby. It is."

27

Juliette

THE ÉCLAIRS ARE BURNED. *Shit.*

Mom's going to kill me. It's the third thing this morning I've screwed up, too dazed and confused about my life.

Ever since last night, I've been completely out of it, wondering if I'm losing my mind. Was I dreaming, or did Harrison actually come to visit?

He said he'd see me tomorrow…which is today.

When, today? Is he coming here to the bakery? Or…

"Juliette!" I jump out of my skin at my mom's tone. "You're lucky you're my daughter, or you would be fired. A customer is asking for you. Get up there, and I'll fix these."

"Are you sure?"

"Juliette. I love you. Now get out of my kitchen." She playfully whips me in the butt with her towel.

I quickly wash my hands, remove my apron, and hang it up before heading to the front. I'm more suited for the front of the shop today, with my dazed mind—as long as Mom is feeling up to baking, I'll be more useful up here.

"Hi, baby."

I spin around at the familiar deep voice. "Harrison," I gasp, placing my hand over my heart. "You're here."

He steps around the counter and cups my cheeks. "I told you I'd come." He leans down, and I lift my chin, aching for him to kiss my lips. I've been dreaming about how they make me feel when they are pressed against mine.

Instead, he tilts his head and kisses *his favorite*, my beauty mark.

I throw myself into him and tightly wrap my arms around him, clinging to him for dear life.

"I missed you so much." I squeeze tighter, not wanting to let him go.

I feel his body relax under my hold as if he's relieved, then he pulls back, looking down at me. The depths of his blue eyes catch mine, holding me captive. "I can't tell you how happy I am to hear that." He bows his head and finally kisses me, allowing his plump lips to take mine with full suction before leaning back and raising a questioning brow. "This shit's over, baby. You're coming home, and you'll never leave us again. Right?"

"I didn't—"

"I know why you did it, Jules, but never again. Never. Ever. I can't fucking stand being without you." He pulls my head into his chest and holds it against his wildly beating heart. "You're *our* family now. If anyone has an issue, it's them breaking our bond, no one else." I suck in a breath at his declaration.

My love for this man is boundless, with a passion that words can hardly capture.

Being encased in his arms floods my mind with memories, while his touch reminds me that no memory or image could ever replace being consoled by his actual touch.

"Come outside with me for a moment," he mumbles, grabbing my jacket from the closet and helping me put it on.

"Let me tell Mom where I'm going."

He zips up my coat. "She knows. Don't worry," he replies. Then he leads me the opposite way through the back door into the courtyard area, which is alive with colorful mums and cabbage that Mom and I planted for the fall season.

With his hand pressed against my lower back, he walks me to the corner, where a large wooden table stands with papers stacked on top.

What the heck is that?

He takes a deep breath, and it's the first time I've gotten a good look at him in the light.

"Are you all right?" I frown.

He maneuvers me in front of the wooden table. "I need to talk to you about something important, and I've been dreading it."

My heart drops. "What is it?"

For a split second, an alarming feeling of anxiety plummets to the pit of my stomach, thinking maybe he saw Rachel again.

Only Harrison would never do that to me, so I have to believe it's something else.

He rubs his temples. Whatever it is has him stressed.

"A while back, when you told me about being pushed out of the bakery, something didn't sit right with me. My staff and I did some investigating and found something unsavory to say the least."

He digs out his phone and places it on the table in front of me, with a movie queued up to play. "What is that?"

"Your estranged asshole of a grandfather was still so bitter he decided to hurt your mother after his son died by taking away her favorite thing. It was your grandfather who was buying the building and pushing you both out of here."

My eyes widen at his words. "What? Are you sure?"

Who in their right mind would ever do that?

The thought of it validates every feeling and reason why my father disassociated from his family. It's mind-boggling that he was ever even related to such hatred. My father was the kindest man. He didn't have a mean or vindictive bone in his body.

"Not only that, but he thought he could outsmart me. He came to my office and gave me an ultimatum: Break up with you, or he'd kick you out of the bakery."

"What the actual fuck," I shout, annoyed. Can this get any worse?

"I don't even know the man, and I already hate him. Why would he go to you? What do you have to do with this?"

"He was scared that now that you're with me, people will dig around and figure out you're an Archibald."

"I am not an Archibald," I say with meaning.

He smirks. "I know, baby, I mean by blood only. Anyway, watch this." He presses play on his phone, and I stand in shock, watching the security footage from Harrison's office.

I gasp in horror about fifteen times.

Who could be this cruel?

When I'm done, I stare at the black screen momentarily. "Wait… what was Uncle Philip doing there?"

Harrison waves me off. "He came back alone and has been helping me ever since. As you know now, he hates your family. He's putting on a show to collect enough information to expose them and hopefully take over one day."

My nerves settle slightly. I would have been so disappointed if my uncle had been involved. In the couple of months I've known him, he's already become incredibly important to me.

To have a part of my dad with me again is a blessing and has helped my healing process tremendously.

"So what now? I hate the idea of them taking this away from us. They'll knock it down to spite us."

That has a smile stretching the width of his face. "Now they can go fuck themselves because you and I own the building."

"What?" I shriek, and he hands me over the deed to the building. "Harrison Davenport. What did you do?" I cry.

"Now the building stays in the family, and the treasured spot that is so important to you and your mom will always be yours."

My hand flies to my mouth to hold in my sob. "I can't let you do this. It's too much."

A whole freaking building?

"Juliette, it was nothing. Pocket change." He winks.

"But—"

"No," he firmly cuts me off. "You're not fighting me on this. It's a done deal. Get used to this, Juliette. It's your life now."

There's my man.

Demanding as hell, and I wouldn't take him any other way.

I interlock our fingers and bring the back of his hand up, pressing my lips against his skin. "Thank you, H." I can't react properly because I'm still stunned. I shake my head in disbelief, then continue. "I'm thankful not only for the building but also for you having my back and sticking up for me to my estranged family. It means the world to me."

"You're welcome, baby. I've told you before I would do anything for you."

"So we can stay? Mom can keep her bakery?"

He pulls over a stool that comes out of nowhere and sits me in front of the table, rolling out blueprints that look an awfully lot like this building.

I scan over everything before he explains, and my eyes snag at the words on top.

"Harrison?" I ask cautiously.

"I said we're keeping the building. Not the bakery."

I whip around on my seat to face him. "What are you talking about? Why would you do that and take it away from us?"

"I'm not taking it away from you, baby. I'm passing it on to you so you can start your future. Your mom and I spoke in-depth over the last few weeks, and we've decided that it's time for her to take a step back so you can start your legacy right here in the same space your mom did. Take back hold of your future, and do what you love, not what you think people want you to do." He smiles softly and runs his thumbs along the apples of my cheeks. "In the new year, your mom is retiring, not only herself, but the bakery. It's time."

Oh, Mom...

I glance back to the blueprints and reread the heading.

Petit Papillons School of Dance.

Little butterflies.

He points to the all-glass storefront. "We're going to build a dance studio for you to teach and finally do something for yourself. You can hire Adriana and whoever else you want."

"I—I…" I'm at a loss for words as I stare at this beautiful man, completely in awe. "At the masquerade gala, you asked me if I thought you were beautiful, and I said I didn't know you well enough to say."

"I remember." He grins. "I was highly insulted."

I playfully smack his chest, then leave my hand pressed against him, rubbing circles over his heart. "I said beauty is not about looks but the whole package, and you, Harrison Davenport, are the most beautiful man I have ever met. Thank you for being you," I say, then hesitate.

"What is it?"

I watch my fingers tracing over his sweater, unable to look him in the eyes. "I'm worried I won't be able to do it…"

"You're ready, Jules." He lifts my chin and cups my cheek. "I never told you that I saw you dancing in the Hamptons. You were like an angel floating around the room, and I couldn't take my eyes off you. It would be an absolute shame to hide the beauty of your talent, and you're a phenomenal teacher. But it's your choice. We can keep it a bakery and hire more staff. Whatever you decide, it's yours."

I shake my head. No, I want to do this…I want to teach Claud in my studio and immerse myself back in the dance world, like my therapist said.

I'm ready to feel alive again.

"Wait…what about all the places we looked at to rent?"

"The ones the realtor said were exclusive, they were fake listings. The ones your mom didn't like were real. I was worried you'd look them up in detail online." He winks. "A perk of knowing people in high places."

God, did he think of everything?

"I can't believe the bakery will be gone, but you're right. I think it's time."

He points to a small part of the blueprint. "Here we can build out a kitchen, so when you're not teaching dance, you can still teach your baking class."

"You're amazing." I smile, grateful for this man. "I don't want to give that up. I love teaching that class. Thank you, Harrison, for thinking of everything and giving me everything I could ever desire."

I hold out my arms for him to pick me up. "I need to be close to you and kiss you properly."

"There's one more thing." He picks me up but swiftly puts me on the ground before I can wrap my body around him.

"There is nothing else I need, Harrison. You've given me too much already."

"Not even this?" He drops to one knee and opens a velvet box, revealing an enormous, pear-shaped diamond ring. "Juliette Caldwell, will you marry me?"

"What?" I whisper.

My mouth hangs open in shock as the world around me suddenly stands still.

His blue eyes hold mine, shimmering with hope and happiness. "You opened up my eyes to a life that I never imagined. You broke down my walls and crawled straight into my heart and my daughter's heart."

"Harrison." I croak and drop my forehead to his.

"Marry me, Jules." He takes the ring out and holds it up to my trembling finger. "Make me the happiest man on earth."

"And me!" I turn to see a wide-eyed Claud standing in the door-way, with Nate's hand now securely over her mouth.

"Sorry," he cringes.

With tears streaming down my cheeks and a smile on my face, I turn back toward Harrison and nod. "Yes. Yes, I'll marry you."

He slips on the ring, then stands, pulling me into his arms, and kisses me in a way he's never kissed me before.

I faintly hear people clapping and cheering in the background, but I'm too lost in my own happiness to see anyone but Harrison until I'm almost plowed over by a little body crashing into my legs.

Harrison picks up Claud and pulls us all into an embrace. "My girls. My family. My loves." He kisses Claud and then me.

My heart.

"Hi, sugar plum." I lean in and kiss her, too.

"Show her, Daddy, show her!" She bounces in Harrison's arms. "Please."

He smirks at her enthusiasm, and places her back down on the ground. He takes off his suit jacket, and hands it to Claud, then unties my favorite pinkish tie. Whenever I see him wear it, it brings me back to the first time I slept at the penthouse, and the beautiful memories to follow. He begins unbuttoning his shirt…now I'm confused.

"What are you doing?"

He ignores me, then pushes open his shirt, exposing his toned chest, and a dusting of chest hair…and then I see it. "Oh my god." I reach out and trace over his tattoo *and* his new one. "H," I breathe.

Now, a second larger butterfly is intertwined with the smaller one meant for Claudina.

"Do you like it?" he whispers, sounding unsure.

"I love it. So much."

There's no way to truly measure someone's love for another. Still, Harrison permanently tattooing a butterfly, something so meaningful to him, tells me everything I need to know about our love.

What's even more remarkable is how he wove it with Claudina's butterfly—his precious daughter, who is untouchable to the rest of the world.

I hold my hand out in front of my face to admire my ring, and I can't help my goofy smile. "This is freaking huge." I laugh, not that I expected anything less from Harrison. "But so stunning."

"I'm glad you like it. Claudina picked it out with me, and I've never bribed her so many times in my life not to tell you. We all know she has a big mouth."

Claud giggles and smiles up at me. "You did a good job, sugar plum. It's beautiful."

She nods. "So pretty." Then runs back into the bakery.

Then it hits me…

"Holy crap. You're my fiancé." I widen my eyes to get my point across. "I can't believe this is real life." I laugh and look down at my ring again, wiggling my fingers.

He chuckles at my excitement. "Don't get used to it."

"What are you talking about?" I frown.

"You won't be my fiancée for long. I'm not waiting to marry you, Juliette. I want to start the new year with you as my wife."

"Are you crazy? It's already November."

He shrugs. "So that means you have six weeks to plan it."

I stand there shocked, but an exhilarating feeling runs through me —next month, this man will be my husband. Oh. My. God. I want to jump around and scream it to the world.

With how often I say he's my end game, I wonder if I manifested this because his proposal never once crossed my mind. Which I'm glad for.

One of Becks's coworkers recently got engaged, and she knew it the whole time, or at least suspected it. In preparation, she got her hair and nails done.

To me, being surprised had so much more meaning behind it.

"I'm kicking myself in the ass now that I invited everyone here to celebrate." He leans in closer as the doors bust open. "We need to have engagement sex. A fucking lot of it."

Oh god, I need that too.

"I'm surprised they waited this long."

"All right, you two love birds. You had your moment," Leo calls out with a big smile on his face.

There are few people here, but it's hard to make out the faces in the small courtyard, with Harrison towering over me.

Where's Mom?

I turn around in circles until I spot her, and I immediately get choked up when I see her face.

Without a word, she takes me in her arms and holds me tightly. We stand in an embrace until I break the silence. "I can't believe you knew."

She leans back and wipes a rare tear that's slipped down her cheek while neither of us attempts to stop my waterworks. We both know there's no use. "There was nothing that could get me to spoil this for you. I'm so happy for you, my love, for both of you." She takes my hands in hers. "Bonne chance et bonheur. Que votre amour dure éternellement."

Good luck and happiness. May your love last forever.

"Hey, let me in." Becks wraps her arms around both Mom and me, pulling us into a huddle. "Look at you snagging the elusive billionaire."

"Rebecca," I sigh.

"I'm kidding." She kisses my cheek. "In all seriousness, Juliette. I'm so happy for you, and for the first time in my life, I can admit I was wrong."

"About?"

"You haven't romanticized your life because you are truly living your fairytale, and if anyone deserves this happily ever after, it's you." She pulls her arm away from Mom and throws it around me, squeezing me tight. "I love you so much. Congratulations."

"I love you, too," I mumble against her shoulder. "Don't ever leave me for three weeks again. I missed you terribly."

Every part of me wants to ask if she's all right, but I know this is not the time or place to bring it up.

She came home from Hong Kong the other night and had been thrown right back into work. Today is the first day I've seen her in person, and her blue hair is gone, and in its place is her natural color. I haven't seen Becks with a full head of black hair since I was twelve years old. Which only means my best friend is hurting more than she's let on about Matteo.

"Stop hogging my little sis." I don't even have to look up to know it's Leo.

"Does no one care about me?" Harrison grumbles.

"Not particularly," Nate chimes in, and then they both take me in their arms.

"There is no lack of hugs today," I joke.

There is so much love around us that I could burst with happiness.

After the rest of our guests—Rosa, Javier, and my uncle Philip—have congratulated us, we're ready to say our goodbyes before

Harrison drags me out of here in front of everyone when suddenly the back door opens, and a familiar face walks through.

Rosa gasps beside me, clearly as shocked as I am that her other son showed up.

Harrison walks over to me and wraps a protective arm around my shoulder.

Today has been a whirlwind, so we've been unable to talk about what's happened over the last month we've been apart. Nevertheless, if he came here to start a future with me, he and Sebastian had to have at least talked.

How well that conversation went is still up in the air.

Seb puts his hand out to shake Harrison's, and then Harrison pulls him into an embrace while we all stand quietly and watch the emotions radiating off these two.

Seb pulls back first, rolling his shoulders, then turning his attention to me. "Congratulations, Juliette."

"Thank you," I whisper.

He bows his head once, then turns and begins to walk out. To someone on the outside, they might view Seb as rude.

To us, this was monumental.

"You're leaving already, Uncle Sebby?" Claud runs over to him, pulling at his hand.

From the corner of my eye, I see Harrison mouth something to Nate.

"Why don't you take her with you?" Harrison calls out. "She was going home with Nate, but you should take her. You only have to stop at Mom's for her bag."

"Are you sure?" Seb asks Nate, who nods. "Yeah, okay." He leans down and picks up Claud, who smothers her uncle's face with kisses.

I see Sebastian's change in an instant; that effect Claudina has on all of us works like an immediate stress reliever for him, too.

Claud jumps out of his arms and runs to us. "Bye. I love you," she says, hugging both our legs quickly and then running back into Seb's arms.

"Are you ready, fiancée?"

"Yes. Take me *home*, H."

———

"Hi, Robert," I call out happily when he opens the car door for me.

He gives me a warm look, glancing down at my ring. "It's good to see you, Juliette. I hear congratulations are in order?"

"They are, can you believe it?" I grin ear to ear.

He looks at Harrison, then me. "I wouldn't have believed it if it were anyone but you."

"I love that answer." I wiggle on the spot, I'm so freaking excited I can't even stand still.

"Let's go." Harrison pats my behind, then gets in behind me, leans over, and buckles me. I don't even attempt to swat him away, too lost in my happiness bubble.

I hold out my hand, staring at my ring again.

I hope I'm not about to wake up from a dream because it sure does feel like one.

"How many times are you going to stare at it? It's the same ring it was three minutes ago."

"You're not allowed to be grumpy today," I chastise, handing him my phone. "Now, take a picture of me so I never forget this moment."

He takes the photo and stares at it briefly, smiling to himself.

"You're stunning, Jules."

"Words can't describe how happy I am, Harrison." I hold up my camera. "Let's take a picture together."

"I'll take it for you two," Robert offers, reaching in the back seat for my phone. "Say cheese."

I hold up my ring and look at Harrison. At that exact moment, he glances down at me, and Robert snaps the picture.

Without even looking at it, I already know it will be my favorite of all time.

"Robert, can you pull over on Fifth Avenue, anywhere along the park," Harrison requests.

"What are we doing now? I thought we were going home."

He reaches over and interlocks our fingers. "We are soon."

Robert pulls over, and we quickly get out, trying not to hold up any traffic. Harrison leads me over to one of the benches that line the front of the park.

"When we go home, I want to walk into our apartment with nothing in our way. A fresh start to our new life." He lifts my hand and kisses it lightly, holding my eyes. "How are you, Jules? Truly."

"Better than when I saw you last, I can tell you that. I won't lie and say everything is great. I still have flashbacks to the day at the park, but I'm working on it, I promise. I started seeing a therapist. She's amazing, and I wish I had started when my dad died. Life is starting to make sense again, and she's helped me navigate my feelings over everything that's happened to me over the last year or so." When he doesn't respond, I ask him something that's been on my mind. "Are you mad at me?"

He takes a few deep breaths as if contemplating his answer. "About what?"

I shrug. "I can make a list, but off the top of my head, for not saving Claudina before Seb or for walking away from us."

"Juliette, not even for one second did I blame you for the park incident. It was an accident, end of story. So no, I'm not mad about Claudina. You love her and have always had her best interest at heart."

"But...?"

"I understand, in a way, why you handled things the way you did. However, I would be lying if I said I wasn't mad after you left the hospital...or maybe hurt is a better way to describe my feelings. You left me. You didn't let me care for you or to help you navigate this time with you. We were supposed to be a team, and I didn't like feeling helpless."

"We *are* a team," I croak.

"You had physical injuries that needed tending to. It should have been me helping you, not your mom. I love Inès, but that's my job now."

"I know." I drop my head. "I'm sorry."

"Baby." He cups my cheek, lifting my head. "I'm not mad

anymore, I promise you. But you asked, so I wanted to be honest about my feelings. Emotions were high for everyone involved after the park incident."

I nod. "I know."

He leans in and kisses my lips gently. "God, I missed you so fucking much. You have no idea."

"Trust me, I felt like I was missing a limb, but I'm a better version of myself now."

He scoffs. "You are perfect, then and now."

"*Then*, had you shown me the blueprints, I would have freaked out and never even considered teaching."

He's silent because he knows it's true. I might have taught Claud with Adriana, but I would have never considered teaching others.

"And Seb?" I ask tentatively. "I can't believe he came today."

"I didn't know how much I wanted him there until he showed up." He squeezes my hand lightly, and I can feel the weight of his shoulders fade. "That was his olive branch, his blessing in a way, and I'm grateful. He's struggling with a lot of the same issues as you from the day at the park. I know you're not *healed* from your memories or even your injuries. But for Seb, it's just adding to a huge pile he's still trying to overcome."

It's not lost on me that we haven't said the word *kidnap*, and keep referring to it as the park incident.

Knowing Claudina has no idea what almost transpired and that Amber is getting the treatment she so desperately needs is helping with all our healing processes.

"So we're all good?"

"Better than good, Jules. You're going to be my wife. I'm the luckiest man in the world. No matter what's been happening, I couldn't fathom having you come home without a ring on your finger."

My heart swells in my chest. I love this man so much.

Harrison walks me backward toward the bed with his lips locked on mine and his hands full of my behind. The second we entered the penthouse, our clothes were ripped off in a frenzy as we attempted to navigate toward the bedroom.

Now, I can feel him trying to slow things down as he picks me up and lays me on the bed. He's standing at the end, breathing heavily, staring at me like he can't believe I'm actually here.

"How did I ever live a life without you?" Harrison whispers, and I roll my lips to hold back my tears.

I need to get myself sorted.

I can't continue crying all night...only being here again with the love of my life has me feeling completely overwhelmed.

Harrison walks to his side of the bed, and I track his every move and muscle that flexes, staring at his new tattoo. It's absolutely beautiful...it's my new favorite thing about him.

He shuts off the lights and gets in bed. I turn on my side, mimicking him, and he pulls me tight to his chest. The familiar feeling of us skin to skin warms my soul, and I can feel the power of our love when he presses his lips against mine.

"We'll go to your mom's tomorrow and bring the rest of your stuff back. Besides the few pieces Claud stole, most of it is untouched in the closet." He smiles against my lips. "I found her playing Barbies in her room, wearing one of your dresses."

"You should have taken a picture. I hate that I missed it." That's a core memory we should have experienced together.

"You'll have the rest of your life to make memories with her, baby. Don't worry."

Harrison pulls back and sweeps the hair off my forehead, studying my face. Our eyes are locked while my hands roam over his skin, tracing his broad chest and chiseled stomach, then up through the light dusting of chest hair. "I missed you so much," I mutter.

He palms my nape, running circles with his thumb over my beauty mark, then leans in and rests his forehead against mine. "I never want to feel broken again. You're my other half. I can't live without you, Juliette. Tu me complètes." *You complete me.*

He kisses me, and it turns desperate quickly. His groin tilts up, and I feel his erection against me, leaving a trail of pre-come as we begin to rock into each other.

"Harrison," I moan.

He picks up my leg and throws it over his hip, opening me up wide, then swipes his fingers through my core and slides two fingers deep inside of me.

"Ah." I wince.

He brushes a few kisses across my face as he picks up speed. "Relax. I need to warm you up, baby. You're too tight."

He slides his thick fingers out, and we both watch with open mouths when he easily glides through my rush of wetness.

"Fuck yeah, baby," he whispers.

"Harrison. Now," I whimper. There's just something about him turned on and staring at my sex that has me feeling desperate.

Slowly, he pulls his fingers out and puts them to my lips. "Suck."

I smirk, then wrap my mouth around his fingers, deep-throating them in one pass, twirling my tongue on the way up. "You like that, H?" I purr when he moans loudly.

"Such a good girl, Jules. Taste yourself, and suck those fingers dry," he demands, then lifts my legs and positions himself at my entrance.

He pauses. "My leg feels fine, Harrison. I promise." I lean in and peck his lips, and that's all he needs to hear.

He surges forward, impaling me in one swift movement. I screw up my face and throw my head forward, resting it on his shoulder. Shit, that burns.

"I'm sorry. I'm sorry." He stills, rubbing my back.

"Couldn't you have had a normal-sized dick, or I'd even be good with a medium size," I mumble into his skin.

He chuckles deeply. "Thank fuck, I don't."

He slides out slowly, then pushes back in a few times until he senses I'm open and relaxed for him. "Put your foot up on my thigh," he murmurs but decides quickly I'm not spread open enough. He runs his hand up the side of my thigh and grips the back of my knee, pushing my leg up and apart, testing all my dancer flexibility.

He slams into me deep, holding still, and rotates his hips so his groin rubs against my clit. *Ah.* Sparks of pleasure ignite through my whole body, and I know I won't last long.

It's too good.

It always is.

I rock against him, searching for more, and he clenches his jaw as he watches me pleasure myself against him. "Fuck yeah, baby." He pulls out slowly so that I can feel every inch of him sliding through me with measurement movements, then slams back in, over and over. He's controlled, but I can sense he will lose it at any moment.

We were apart too long not to be affected by this feeling and the connection we have for one another.

My eyes close, and I throw my head back. "So good," I whimper. This man is a freaking sex god. No matter which position or speed. He's perfect.

"Fuck, you feel amazing. Jules," he growls, tightening his grip on my leg.

My eyes roll back in my head. I can't hold it.

"I'm going to come," I stammer. "Yessss." This is too good of a feeling to stop it. I glance down, watching as his dick disappears inside me, and it puts me over the edge.

I clench hard around his length, crying out with our eyes locked and my body convulsing violently. His eyes darken like the deep depths of the sea while he pulls back and slams into me hard. I feel the telling jerk when he comes inside me, moaning loudly, crying out my name in bliss.

He lets go of my legs and pulls me into a tight embrace. We pant, trying to catch our breath as I cling to him.

"I love you, Jules," he whispers and kisses me in a sweet and tender way. *Pure perfection.*

I rub his tattoo, feeling his heart match mine, as they beat in sync for one another.

28

Harrison

Five Weeks Later

I STRETCH over to Jules's side of the bed, then curse under my breath when I remember she slept at her mom's last night with Becks and Claud. It gives me anxiety not having her in our bed after the month of being separated from one another.

Today is our wedding day, and she insisted on the archaic tradition of sleeping apart from your soon-to-be husband the night before.

My phone rings, and I grab it quickly, but it's not my girl.

Nate.

"What do you want, fucker? It's six in the morning."

"I knew you'd be up. I wanted to see if you wanted to run in the park."

I narrow my eyes. "Why? You've never asked me that before, and you also live all the way downtown."

"Well, I figured Sebastian would be lacking in his best man skills, and I'd need to pick up the slack of taking care of you today."

"Oh, for fuck's sake, what are you, a child? You said you were fine with this, and you and Leo will be each other's best man."

He scoffs. "Whatever. I still would have been the better choice. A run, yes or no."

I'm not particularly keen on it when I can work out in the warmth of my own home, but…by the time he gets uptown and we head out, that's about the time Jules likes to take her morning walk.

"Yeah, fine. Let me know when you're close."

"I need to tell you something, in case it comes up later," I announce over Nate's loud panting. "And why the hell are you so out of breath?"

"It's the cold air, it hurts my lungs."

I roll my eyes at his dramatics, and just to be a dick, I pick up my pace, knowing his competitiveness won't let him lag.

"Mason called the other day and asked if he could bring Maddie Grace as his date."

Nate stops dead in his tracks. "What did you say?" he spits.

"I said I didn't think bringing his sister was a good idea. That I didn't want any drama between you and her." When he clenches his jaw and looks like he's about to burst, I hold up my hand to stop him. "This is not about you, Nate. I know you're dying to see Madeline. But today needs to be drama-free. I can't have anything go wrong. Jules deserves the perfect day."

He blows out a breath. "Yeah. Fine. Why the fuck did you even tell me?"

"Because if Mason mentioned it, I didn't want you to blow up at him after a few drinks."

"I want to throw up." He points to the exit. "I'm leaving."

"You know I'm right," I call out when he runs in the opposite direction of me.

I'm about to head home myself. We have a long day ahead of us, but instead, I make a quick detour, running around the reservoir, up and over the bridge, into Gilder Run Path, where Camila's memorial stone lies, and then freeze.

Slowly backing up.

Jules is here, sitting on the bench by herself. I can't hear her, but I can tell she's talking to Camila. Her smile is broad, but she wipes her eyes a few times. I have no doubt she's crying. My girl is sensitive and isn't afraid to show her emotions.

When a man in all black circles the corner and sits next to her, my legs move without thought to reach her. But when her face lights up, and she throws her arms around him, I stop, confused, while anger burns deep in the pit of my stomach.

What. The. Fuck.

I'm about to lose my shit when he pulls off his hood, and a very familiar face appears.

Leo.

He says something that makes Jules's face drop, and when he reaches into his pocket and pulls out a pink envelope for her, I know why.

The overwhelming feeling grips my heart like a vise. I drop my chin to my chest and breathe in through my nose, then turn back and go home. Every inch of me wants to demand that she show me the letter, but even I know that's wrong, and for once, I need to use restraint when it comes to her.

This is a private moment between her and Camila.

Juliette

"Leo." I throw my arms around him. "How did you know I was here?"

He motions his head to the left, and I frown until I realize he means my bodyguard. "He must be good at his job because I almost always forget he's here."

"He better," Leo mumbles. "Harrison is paying them enough."

He removes his hood and blows air into his hands to warm up, even though it's pretty mild for a December day. We've been so lucky with the weather so far.

"This morning, I was planning on coming to your mom's, but when I heard you were here, I knew I had to give you this now. There is no better place to read it than here."

He unzips the pocket in his jacket, and I suck in a deep breath and lean away when I see the pink sticking out.

"Leo," I whisper.

He handed me the pink envelope addressed to soon-to-be *Mrs. Davenport*. "I was under strict instructions to give this to you on the morning of your wedding day and no later. She didn't want to be the cause of tears that ruined your makeup."

I'm speechless.

Leo kisses my forehead. "See you later, *bride*." He winks and leaves me to read it by myself.

There's no hesitation; I rip it open to find beautiful cursive and read it immediately.

To The Woman Who Captured Harrison's Heart,
(I'm sorry for not addressing you properly. You know…
I'm dead, so I have no clue what your name is.)

Oh. My. God. I chuckle.

Just from that one sentence, she reminds me so much of Leo.

Sorry, that may have been too morbid.
On a serious note…
Congratulations. You're marrying my overbearing brother,
and I say that in the best way possible. If you're

438

special enough to gain Harrison's attention, he will protect, cherish, and love you with all he has for the rest of his life.

I hope you don't find this letter bizarre. Something in my heart told me I had to write to you.

Believe it or not, this is the second letter I've written to anyone.

First Harrison, and now you.

In Harrison's letter, I told him I trusted his judgment and hoped he'd picked a woman who could be the best role model for my little girl. Who would love her wholeheartedly, like she was their own.

But honestly, as I write this letter, something inside me tells me you've already been chosen.

Harrison won't pick you...the universe has already done so.

Claudina deserves to have a mother figure in her life, and I can't thank you enough for being there for her when this cruel world will eventually rip me away from her far too soon.

But I'm lucky enough to be left with the gut feeling that you will be all she ever needs. It's a selfless act to be the mom to someone else's child. But it was natural for you, wasn't it?

Since I've been sick, I've been getting these crazy feelings of insight. Right now, my body is lighting up with warmth, knowing you're an angel on earth with my baby. Somehow, I feel connected to you, and I have no idea why.

. . .

I pick up my head and stare at her memorial through my heavy stream of tears.

I'm right here, Camila…I can feel you, too.

Maybe the connection is through Claudina… If my intuition is correct, by allowing myself to release my role as Claudina's mom, you have already taken it over.

I will always be her mother but thank you for being her mom. I hope that even when I pass, I will feel this connection with you, and maybe you'll feel it with me.

So to my new sister…I love you.

Thank you again for loving Harrison, Claudina, and my brothers. You're part of the best family in the world now.

Enjoy today, and forget about the minor nuisances. Be in the moment because you never know when it will be taken away from you.

Know that you carry the legacy of love and resilience. In every shared laugh, exchanged vow, and dance tonight, may you feel my presence, a silent witness to the beauty of your union.

All my love,
Camila

With my eyes locked on her memorial, I sit in awe of this beautiful soul. And before I leave, I thank Camila for granting me the greatest gift of all.

Acceptance.

"I'm nervous," I whisper to Mom, who links her arm with mine.

We're waiting for the cue for Mom to walk me down the aisle so I can finally marry the man of my dreams.

"Don't be, my love. Everything will fade away once you walk down that aisle except you and Harrison." She kisses my cheek. "I'm so proud of the woman you've become. Every day, I'm reminded of how honored I am to be your mom."

"Mom," I whisper-whine. "I told you no emotional talk yet; I can't cry."

She smiles, then points to Becks, who has just made it to the altar.

I'm next.

We're getting married at a small Gothic-style church in our neighborhood filled with stained glass and maroon velvet cushions on the pews.

It's so beautiful even John F. Kennedy and Jacqueline Kennedy Onassis were parishioners here.

I glance around the curtain and see Claud and Becks standing to the left and my handsome man to the right.

Of course, his tuxedo was custom and fits his body like a glove. To his side are Sebastian, Nate, Leo, and Jackson.

The music starts, and I suck in a breath. Here we go...

And just like Mom said, the second I step out from the curtain, everything around me fades away, and I zero in on my man, who is standing at the altar with tears in his eyes and a face full of admiration.

"Hi, H..." I whisper.

"Beautiful, Juliette. You look...like a dream." He shakes his head like he can't believe his eyes. He takes my hand and puts it to his mouth. "Are you ready to be my wife?"

"More than you can ever imagine." I smile.

"I, Juliette Caldwell, take you, Harrison Davenport, for my lawful husband, to have and to hold from this day forward, for better, for worse, for richer, for poorer, in sickness and health, until death do us part."

I say my vows proudly while Harrison can't stand still. Anticipation runs through him. I've never seen him so excited that it has me giggling out loud after my vows.

I cover my mouth, embarrassed. "Oh god." My eyes widen. "Not God." I cover my face.

"Sorry," I mumble.

What the hell is wrong with me?

Everyone laughs, including the priest. Harrison's over-the-top smile as he takes my hands in his calms me.

He repeats his vows, and then the priest says the best part.

"I now pronounce you husband and wife. You may kiss the bride."

Harrison steps forward and cups my cheeks. "I love you," he whispers for only me to hear, then kisses me with such tenderness that I feel it all the way to my toes.

It's the most perfect wedding kiss of all time.

He pulls back and smiles softly while everyone in the church cheers loudly.

"Now we celebrate."

"You have to go over and officially meet Lauren. Otherwise, she'll bombard you when you least expect it." Harrison hands me a glass of champagne.

I cringe. "I'm still embarrassed."

"Too bad I'm not having my wife hide away from the business I own, and soon I want to fuck you over my desk."

My eyes widen, and I look around to ensure no one heard him. I almost die of embarrassment when I realize my uncle is talking to Becks behind us.

"If Uncle Philip heard, you're dead meat," I warn, and he chuckles.

"It was nice of you to ask him to do an uncle-niece dance."

I look back at my uncle, then back to Harrison. "In a way, it's to honor my dad. I'm so lucky to have met my uncle. I feel like Dad's here with us through him." I pause, wondering if I should bring this up again. "And you're sure it won't cause problems that your parents aren't here?"

"My parents are right there." He points to Rosa and Javier. "The other two are inconsequential."

I nod and sip my drink. He's right.

"So, what's the plan for this place? You haven't done anything to it," I ask.

We both look around the usually unfinished space, which is, for today, beautifully decorated for our reception. It is filled with candelabras and all-white peonies.

It's where we spent a beautiful evening getting to know one another at the masquerade gala. When Harrison suggested we use it for the wedding, I immediately said yes due to the place's deep meaning.

"Do you want to live here?" He looks at me over his negroni as he takes a sip.

"Do you?"

"When our family grows, yes," he says.

I bite my lip but can't hold back my smile as I nod. *Family.*

Speaking of family.

I notice Sebastian standing in the door leading to the terrace, looking lost in his thoughts.

I know this is my chance.

I go up on my tippy-toes and kiss Harrison. "Can you wait here? I'll only be a moment."

I walk out onto the terrace and close the door behind me. "Do you mind if we talk?"

Seb nods, then turns back to look over Central Park.

I take a breath to steady my nerves.

"I know that we had a rocky start, to put it lightly. But I wanted to tell you that I love Harrison and Claudina very much and will always treat Claudina like my own. However, I will never forget the woman who brought her into this world. We will always celebrate Camila's life in our home. We will speak of her daily, and Claudina will always know how much her mother loves her."

He nods and, with a clenched jaw, answers, "Thank you."

I pause, wondering if I should say the next part. I think he'd appreciate it.

"I visit her...alone." He looks down, and I know I have his attention now. "Harrison and Claud don't know, but I do often. I wanted to feel closer to Camila. I go there, and I talk. I tell her about Claud and myself, too, so she'll get to know and trust me, too."

I think I shocked him.

"Juliette...it's not you, it's me."

I smirk. "Did you just give me the break-up line?"

He laughs, and it's beautiful. I'm already seeing a different side of him. "I realized it the second they were out of my mouth. But—"

"You don't have to say anything now, Sebastian. I only wanted to tell you so I can join this family with you, knowing I have the best intentions." I turn and walk out, but I stop when I hear my name being called.

"My sister would have loved you."

I scrunch my eyes and continue walking, not wanting to make a big deal of his words.

Because they are huge...monumental even, and I know it's mine and Seb's turning point.

"Everything all right, baby?" Harrison pulls me into his side.

I nod. "Everything is perfect."

The band slows down, and there is an announcement that cocktail hour is now over, and we should take our seats, along with removing our masks if we choose.

I glance at Harrison in his *Phantom of the Opera* mask while he traces my butterfly one. "Let's keep them on for a little while longer." He moves in and whispers against my mouth. "These masks remind me that if you take chances in life, you may encounter something incredible, and tonight, they will bring me lifelong memories."

I smile against his lips. I love this man.

For so long, after my accident, I was worried I would struggle to find my purpose again. I went along with life, not truly living. Only I had to wait a little longer to find out that two people, a gorgeous older man, and the most precious little girl, would flip my world around and give me life again.

EPILOGUE

Juliette

One Week Later

WITH A HOT CHOCOLATE in my hand and a sleeping Claud in my lap, I rock back and forth in my chair, watching the snow fall over Aspen Mountain. It's serene and calming, and I can see why Harrison and his brothers love to spend the holiday season here.

It's Christmas Eve, and Harrison and I arrived in Aspen, Colorado, earlier today to meet the whole family—Claudina, Nate, Leo, Seb, Rosa, Javier, Mom, and, of course, Becks.

We'd been on our honeymoon in Napa Valley for the last five days and stayed in a small, quaint town called St. Helena.

We left soon after the wedding, which happened to be my twenty-fifth birthday, and had the trip of a lifetime.

Harrison knew the owners of a few vineyards, so it was a special treat to get private tours from them. We also explored new-to-us wines around the Napa region, relaxed at the spa, and even did a sunrise hot-air balloon ride.

And of course, the only thing Harrison cared about was the sex… *lots of sex.*

The hotel cottages were perched high up on a hillside, and ours looked into the most beautiful valley, with lush vegetation and vines growing along the slopes.

It was lavish, and the resort décor was exotic…five-star all the way. Not that Harrison knows how to do anything less.

He originally wanted to go somewhere secluded, with beaches, but I wanted to do something unique we wouldn't normally do with Claud. So we compromised and did Napa in the winter, and we've booked a family trip to the South of France this summer, where Harrison has us staying on a mega yacht.

A yacht…a freaking yacht!

We're going to hold a small party while we're there to celebrate our nuptials with my French family. With such short notice, only my aunt, Mom's sister, and two cousins could make it.

"Hey, baby," Harrison calls out.

"Shhh. She's sleeping."

He kisses the top of my head and takes a sleeping Claud from my arms. "I'm going to put her to bed. Meet me in the living room. My brothers and I want to give you your Christmas gift tonight."

"Gift as in singular?" I widen my eyes, excited. It must be good if they are all chipping in together. "Is it a puppy?" I ask excitedly.

He shakes his head, ignoring me, and walks upstairs toward Claudina's room. He can't say no to me for long. We're going to get a puppy. I know it.

"Oh, good," I say to Nate as he lights the fire in the fireplace. "I'm frozen from sitting by those windows."

"Here." Leo hands me his blanket, then gets himself another.

"Thanks." I sit on the floor with my back against the couch and call Skye over to lie with me. Harrison walks into the room, scoots me forward, and sits behind me, pulling me back into his chest.

It's just the guys and me. I'm not sure where everyone else is, but when Nate's done and sits in the chair across from me, I can feel the air change.

Leo walks over and hands me a thin box tied with a bow. "Merry Christmas, Juliette."

I hold the box in my hands, staring at it like it will bite me.

I don't know why I'm nervous to open this.

Slowly, I untie the bow, open the box, and push away the folded tissue paper when my heart stops, and my hand flies to my mouth in shock.

"W-Wh…" I mumble, unable to speak through the lump in my throat.

I take the papers out of the box and hold them in my shaky hands, scanning the words repeatedly.

The State of New York.
Petition for Adoption of Minor
Claudina Rosa Morales Davenport… Juliette Brigitte Caldwell

"Oh my god, is this…" I cry. "You want me to adopt Claudina?" I turn to look at Harrison through my tears.

He nods, blinking back tears himself. "We all do." He points to some of the paperwork. "All you need to do is sign, and our lawyer will file for us. It will be a process, but it's what we all want."

I glance around, and there is not a dry eye in the room. When my eyes connect with Seb, I linger there, silently asking if he's okay with this.

He nods, and I don't miss his lips turning up in a slight grin. This breaks my resolve, and I sob into my hands and throw myself into Harrison's body.

I've never felt like I do now. This is true happiness.

I wipe my tears on Harrison's shirt, then stand up and hug Nate, Leo, and Seb, lingering with my arms around him a second more than the others.

We haven't spoken since the wedding, but his agreement on this means everything. "Thank you," I whisper, and he squeezes me lightly in response.

I take a deep breath and look around the room, and I notice the rest of the crew in the doorway, all crying and smiling.

Interlocking my fingers with Harrison's, using him as my strength to calm my emotions before I address our family.

"I am so touched by the trust you have extended by asking me to adopt our precious Claudina, my sugar plum. It means the world to me that you have the confidence in me as a parent." I pause and take a breath. "I have always loved Claud as my own, and I will continue to love and care for her for the rest of my life. Not a day will go by where I won't include Camila in our life. That's my promise to you. By adopting Claudina, she will now always have two moms who have and will always put her first."

Things felt like they couldn't get any better…until now.

Twelve Years Later

"What's that noise?" Colette asks Harry.

"Mom's crying."

Colette's hand reaches up to touch my arm. "Are you okay, Mommy?"

Harrison's worried eyes turn to mine while I can hear the panic in Colette's voice.

I reach back and take my sensitive girl's hand, giving her a reassuring squeeze. "I'm okay, sweetie. Today is an emotional day."

"What is it?" Harrison whispers.

I hesitate to tell him. He thinks it's strange that I do this. "I was thinking of Claud, and then I was talking to Camila."

He holds my eyes, and for the first time, I think he wants to know what about.

"I was telling her she'd be so proud of our girl. That Claud's living her dream and never gave up hope. That she's grown into a beautiful woman that I'm so incredibly proud of, and now she's in Paris performing for the world to see."

He smiles sadly. "She knows," he whispers, then places his hand over his butterfly tattoos. "I've never felt this. It's like my heart hurts but in the best way possible."

"He's probably having a heart attack," Harry mutters to Collette, ruining the moment.

"What?" Collette shrieks and starts to cry.

"Harry," Harrison snaps. "Shut your mouth. Jesus, I'm not having a fucking heart attack."

"Bad word," Collette mumbles.

Harrison turns toward the back row to take Collette's hand from me. "I'm sorry, sweetheart," he croons while his eyes shoot daggers at Harrison Jr.

Harry is eleven going on twenty-one, and he's trying our patience every step of the way. Harrison and he butt heads over everything.

Harry might look like me, but he and his dad are the same person. Meanwhile, Collette, our seven-year-old, and youngest Vivienne, who is four and not here today, are me to a tee.

"Okay, both of you, stop. Today is about Claudina, and when you're older, Harry, you'll understand what a big deal this is," I say and start crying again.

I'm so emotional today.

It could also be because I'm seven months pregnant with our second boy or because my sugar plum made it big time, and I couldn't be prouder of her if I tried.

Today is Claudina's eighteenth birthday, which, in itself, has me losing it…how is she eighteen? But most importantly, today is her debut performance with The Paris Opera Ballet.

I can't even freaking believe it.

It's the most challenging ballet to get accepted into, so we all had doubts.

Not that she didn't deserve it. Claudina is better than I ever was.

However, she was up against the best in the world, and they were only accepting one male and two female ballet dancers this year.

When she was younger, we rented a summer house here in France so she could attend the kid's summer program. After that, she was accepted to audition for the school program, so naturally, she begged us to send her to the dance school in Paris during her high school years.

Harrison, Seb, Leo, and Nate flipped out and said no without consulting me. But now, they have me to answer to, and although I knew I would miss her terribly, I also understood that this was her chance to make it for herself.

And no serious dancer turns down Paris. They just don't.

Luckily, my cousins all live in Paris now and hosted Claud during her stay, which eased the guys' anxiety since she was staying with family.

"We're here, *mon petit papillon*." Harrison grabs my attention.

I look out the window, and I can't believe it.

I turn back to the third row and look at Colette and Harry, dressed in their little tuxedo and gown. "Are you two ready to watch your big sister shine brighter than all the stars in the sky?"

They both nod excitedly—*even Harry*.

Harrison helps me out of the car, straightens his velvet bow tie, then fixes my stunning custom gown while I stare up at The Palais Garnier.

I reach aimlessly for Harrison's hand, and we stand there, taking in the magnitude of it all.

It doesn't matter that I lived this life years before. It still has that overwhelming effect, and this...this is Paris.

"I love you, Harrison." I look over at my gorgeous husband, who hasn't aged a day besides his graying hair.

Harrison Davenport is still pure perfection.

His eyes hold mine, and if he said no words, that would be okay; I can see all the love in the world through them.

They've always spoken to me.

"Tu es l'amour de ma vie, Juliette."

You are the love of my life.

We're escorted to our seats front and center. The uncles and their significant others, along with Mom, Becks, Rosa, and Javier, are already here.

Leo chuckles when he sees my tear-streaked face. "Cut it out. All your pictures are going to be terrible."

I elbow him as I sit. "Shut up."

"Can I sit with Uncle Sebby?" Colette whispers in my ear.

I look down the row at Seb and point to Colette. He nods, and I tell her it's okay.

"I have butterflies in my stomach," I whisper to Leo.

He sucks in a deep breath and takes my hand in his, squeezing it lightly. "Me too," he mutters, and then I turn toward Harrison.

He must have heard me by the way he's staring at me. "They haven't stopped fluttering since we got in the car."

My other hand takes his and I close my eyes and take a deep breath.

Camila's here to watch her baby.

When I feel like I might lose it again, I lean over Harrison to talk to Harry and distract myself. "Did you know the first-ever performance occurred here in 1875? Pretty cool, huh?"

"So, Dad's age?" he deadpans.

God, he's so naughty, though that was a good one.

"Harry, you're lucky we're in public. Otherwise, I most likely would strangle you," Harrison mutters dryly through his clenched jaw while Leo tries his hardest not to laugh out loud.

The curtains begin to open.

This is it.

Merde, sugar plum, I wish her luck. *You got this*, I think, sending her good vibes.

Harrison

She did it.

My precious angel is a professional ballerina, just as she swore she would be when she was a little girl.

Claudina is flawless up there.

Over the years, Jules has taught me so much that I know Claud is perfecting every move effortlessly.

Even Harry is sitting here in awe of his sister. He can't take his eyes off the stage.

He's my son. I love him with all of my being, but he's a tough one, constantly grinding my gears, and I'm trying to be better with him.

I don't want him to hate me when he grows up. I want a relationship with him like I have with Rosa and Javier, but I don't know how to get through to him.

I rest my forearm on the armrest between us and place my palm facing up. I don't look at him, but I can feel him contemplating.

Come on, Harry.

He puts his hand in mine, and quickly, I close mine before he changes his mind.

We sit there hand in hand, the whole performance, without him even trying to escape my hold.

Maybe it's because we're in the dark, and no one can see.

Either way, I'll take anything he gives.

Baby steps.

We're waiting backstage for my angel, and I spot her before anyone else.

She's gorgeous—the spitting image of Camila, with the delicate air of Juliette.

With her head held high, she looks around until she sees our large group. Her smile stretches over her face, and she waves excitedly.

Every bone in my body wants to open my arms for her, but I have finally given up the idea that she wants to see me first. That stopped thirteen years ago, now there is one person more important than me.

"Mom," Claud cries and flings herself into Jules's arms.

"Congratulations, sugar plum. I love you." Juliette barely gets out through the tears.

I place my hand on Jules's back so my pregnant wife doesn't topple over. "Careful."

Jules is sobbing now, and there is no way she can control it. I can tell she's squeezing Claud within an inch of life. "Jules, baby. Let Claud breathe," I tell her softly.

Claud shakes her head. "Don't," she mumbles into Jules's neck, and they stay there having their moment while the rest of us stand and watch.

These two have built an incredible bond, and every time I see them together, it confirms that Camila handpicked Juliette.

Besides loving Claudina unconditionally and Claudina being utterly obsessed with my beautiful wife, Juliette didn't come into this relationship only for me.

She undoubtedly was made to be Claud's other mom.

Glancing over our family, a sense of pride washes over me.

We're all here as a unit.

Everyone is happy, loved, and thankful. It took a while after Camila died, but we've all learned never to take life for granted.

And what a life it is…I wouldn't trade it for the world.

The End.

ALSO BY J R GALE

The Taylored Men Series

London Lovers (Wills and Sadie)

Destined Lovers (Declan and Nora)

Lilacs and Lovers (Lola and Matthew- Novella)

Secret Lovers (Jackson and Annabelle)

The Bonded Brother Series

Mr. Unexpected (Harrison and Juliette)

Mr. Persistent (Pre-order Nate's story)

The Jetset Twins

Her Rival (Pre-order Olivia's story)

AFTERWORD

Thank you so much for reading. It means the world to me to have your support.
If you enjoyed reading Mr. Unexpected, please consider leaving a review!

Don't forget to check online for other releases and my website for my newsletter and updates.

Read on for an excerpt from London Lovers

ACKNOWLEDGMENTS

I will always start by expressing my gratitude toward the incredible and selfless T L Swan. You're an inspiration, and I wouldn't have written these words without your guidance.

Sara, the best PA, and friend. Your support from day one has been invaluable. I appreciate it and you beyond words! xx

My betas, Kathryn, Sara, Jaclyn, Lizzy, Danielle, and Andi—Thank you! Your words and support over the last few months made this book what it is today.

Michael, family, and friends thank you for putting up with my workaholic ways and inflexible calendar!

Last but not least, to you, the best readers around.

Thanks for being the biggest part of everything I'm doing and for choosing to read Mr. Unexpected. This is not possible without you.

J R Gale xx

ABOUT THE AUTHOR

J R Gale is a contemporary romance author obsessed with the happily ever after.

She is a native New Yorker, residing in New York City with her husband and rescue pup, Cali.

When she's not thinking of your next alpha book boyfriend, you can find her traveling the world—romance book in hand.

LONDON LOVERS EXCERPT

Chapter One

Sadie

Finally! The wheels hit the ground, and I'm instantly bouncing in my seat. Anticipation runs through me, excited for what's to come. But it's taking freaking forever to get off this plane.

It's been eight hours since I've left Manhattan and eight hours since I left my old self behind.

Now, I'm excited to get the hell away from New York and to start my annual girls' trip.

But I'm especially excited to see my best friend, Annabelle—it's been almost one year since I've seen her last, the longest stretch since we have been kids.

Finally, the seat belt light switches off, and all the passengers jump up to grab their carry-on bags. Lining up, eager to head off the plane.

"Bienvenu en France," the stewardess kindly welcomes me as we disembark the plane, and I thank her.

"Merci beaucoup," in what I can only hope sounded French.

I walk out onto the tarmac, waiting for the shuttle to bring us to our terminal, and that's when I'm hit with that familiar feeling I always get when I arrive at my final destination.

It's that buzzing energy and eagerness you feel from other travelers excited to start an adventure.

I take a minute to check out my new surroundings, and almost everyone looks the same. Eyes wide, backs tall, heads high, smiles wide. No matter where you land in the world, everyone does it. It's the magic of traveling.

For some, it's the excitement of starting something new, maybe a honeymoon or a well-deserved holiday they've saved for. But, for others, it's a feeling they've escaped whatever it is they are leaving behind. And, unfortunately for me, it's the latter—the cheater ex-boyfriend and parents who aren't worthy of holding the title.

An hour later, I finally exit the customs area after getting stuck behind the loudest New Yorkers known to man. Not exactly the way I envisioned this starting. But I'm off to retrieve my baggage, where Belle should be waiting for me.

"Sadie, darling, I'm over here!" she screams across the baggage claim, waving her hands like a crazed woman.

She isn't hard to miss. I spotted her instantly, along with half of the airport.

I'll never know if people are staring because she's screaming or because of Belle's looks. She must have been a model in her former life; Tall, blonde, and perfect—inside and out.

Growing up, we spent every summer together, and all the boys fawned over her, giving her the unfortunate nickname of "BB" or "Double *B*" for Bombshell Belle. Luckily the only time she ever hears that now is if my brother is trying to piss her off.

I walk over to where Belle is still waving her arms. I love this girl with all of my heart, but I can already see her enthusiasm is at level one hundred. And, after my long overnight flight, I'm not exactly ready for it.

The saying "opposites attract" is not just about romantic couples. It applies to best friends too.

Annabelle has that larger-than-life attitude. She's a busy bee, Miss Popular, career-driven, and all around good person with a strong backbone. On the other hand, I tend to be more reserved and shy. I probably could use a little of Belle's charisma in some instances.

That's what this trip is all about, breaking all my bad habits of letting everyone walk all over me and finally doing what's best for me. Although I don't love being the center of attention, I am still a strong, independent person. I just lost my way a little, and I am finally set to be back on track with my life.

And, with Belle by my side, I know it will happen. She is the only person in the world I want to be right now, my bestie and sister soul mate. The best support person you'll ever need in your life.

"I've missed you so much," I mumble into her hair.

"Oh, Sadie. I've also missed you so much. I can't believe it's been so long."

"Please, Annabelle, don't start. If you cry, I cry."

I need to go into this trip with good happy vibes.

I've felt terrible that I canceled going to London to see Belle and my brother for Christmas. Instead, I was suckered into staying for my mother's charity luncheon, her charity banquet, her charity cocktail party, and who knows what other event she made me attend for appearances. *But no more.*

"Right, right, well, let's get your bags and make our way to the hotel. Our driver is waiting right out front."

We drive a short distance to our hotel located on the Cote d'Azur in a small town called Antibes, located somewhere between Nice and Saint-Tropez.

Initially, I rented a country home right outside Avignon, where I could reset, think things through, and try to understand how I let myself get steamrolled by my family and Colton, my ex, time and time again.

But unlucky, for me, lucky for Belle, the house caught fire a few months ago, and Annabelle insisted on staying here. Which now isn't looking so bad, after all.

We enter the property down a long, tree-lined driveway, barely making out the hotel in the distance. This place is top notch, I can already tell. But then again, I did not expect anything less from Annabelle.

We might have grown up "upper class," but I try to live a more reserved lifestyle. Belle, on the other hand—not so much.

The bellhops walk out to meet our car while the hotel staff waits with champagne and warm towels.

"Welcome, you must be Ms. Hughes," the one attendant says to Annabelle.

"Yes, and this is my friend, Sadie Peters."

"Welcome, please let us take your luggage while my colleague Jacques escorts you to reception to check in."

I pinch Annabelle's side and raise my eyebrows.

Jacques is gorgeous, and if I know Annabelle, she will jump right on that.

"Jacques," she purrs. "What a beautiful French name. Where are you from?"

Paris pronounced Pa-ree in his beautiful French accent

I walk away to explore the hotel before catching Annabelle go into full flirt mode.

And, wow, I am lost for words. This hotel is beyond gorgeous.

After you pass through the two massive front doors, the reception area is entirely open, greeting you with the most spectacular view of the Mediterranean Sea.

The lobby is done mainly in sleek white marble and glass walls, adorned with huge flower arrangements of orchids, white roses, and I definitely smell jasmine somewhere. White-and-beige linen curtains blow from the sea breeze, giving it a relaxing but romantic feel. This place is perfect.

I make my way over to the beautiful lady waiting for us to check in. *Geez, do they only employ good-looking people here?*

I look down at my overnight flight outfit, realizing I probably should have freshened up and changed at the airport before arriving at the hotel.

After giving our information to the front desk attendant, Annabelle wanders back over.

"Holy shit, Sadie!" she whisper-screams.

"What? What's the matter?"

"Did you see who's here?"

"Who?" I ask, turning my head, looking to see someone familiar.

"Well, knowing you, you probably were more worried about the decor and floral arrangements than paying attention to anyone else."

I roll my eyes. "Oh, shut it, Miss I Need To Flirt With Every Man I See."

"Well, don't look now. But Wills Taylor and three other extremely good-looking, probably also rugby players, are standing over to our right, about to check in."

"I have no idea who Wills Taylor is, Belle," I say in a huff.

She knows everyone and their mother. Why would I expect anything different now that we are in the South of France?

I slowly move my head to check out this Wills Taylor she is talking about, and holy hell, she wasn't lying.

There are four massively huge, very attractive men over on the other side of the hotel check-in area. Usually, the big muscle type is not my cup of tea, but no one can deny how good-looking these men are. They are all dressed perfectly in crisp summer suits and loafers, but one of them is just that much more handsome than the others. He looks like he should be in an old Hollywood movie, the James Dean of our time, but with a very muscular, athletic body. It's hard to move my eyes away. It's like I'm glued to him. But just when I go to turn back to Annabelle, he slowly turns to me, and his eyes catch mine.

Oh god, this is like a bad car crash, where I can't look away. He slowly lifts one side of his mouth with a too-sexy smirk, and I can feel the heat of embarrassment spread through my body.

"What the hell?" Belle snaps me out of my gaze. It's also when I realized I've been holding my breath.

"What's the matter?" I widen my eyes and act surprised.

"I just told you not to look, and you were staring right at Wills. Now he is staring right over at us. Actually…"

"Actually, what?" I snap a little too fast.

She raises her eyebrows slightly and says, "He's staring at you, and he just tapped one of his mates. They are both looking at you right now."

"You need to get your eyes checked, Belle. I'm standing next to you, and I'm in yoga pants and a T-shirt. Let's go. Our room is ready."

I start to head toward the elevator, not waiting for her. I need a shower and a glass of wine to relax in our suite. I can't be thinking of any guys.

"What does that mean? You're standing next to me?" she huffs once she catches up.

I roll my eyes at her. "It meant nothing, just that you're standing here dressed like we're about to go out to a garden party, all perfect and beautiful, and I look like I just did an hour of hot yoga."

I press the elevator for one of the top floors where all the suites are located; we are sharing a two-bedroom suite that Belle says is "to die for."

As the doors are closing, I catch another glimpse of this Wills she keeps going on about, and my stomach drops. He really is strikingly handsome, all serious and mysterious looking. But fortunately, the doors shut before I could think any more about him. I am here to turn over a new leaf, not troll for men.

"Sadie, are you even listening?"

"Huh? No, I zoned out for a minute, sorry. What were you saying?"

"That you need to stop being so hard on yourself—you are your own worst critic. You're beautiful even with yoga pants on. Plus, I would die for your bum." Belle laughs and pinches my behind.

"Okay, okay, enough about me. Our room is here, number 1414."

We walk inside, and again the beauty of this place has me lost for words.

Our bags are already up here, and the porters must have opened all the windows so we could smell the fresh sea breeze. We walk through the white-and-gray marble foyer that leads to the balcony.

Holy crap, this is bigger than some New York apartments. We have a small dipping pool overlooking the sea, a dining room table, lounge chairs, and a small bar area. We could probably stay here the whole vacation and never leave.

"Wow, Belle, you did good. This place is amazing. This is the exact place I need to be right now."

She settles up next to me, leaning over to give me a side hug. "I'm glad you're happy. You deserve this trip more than anyone. But I know you're exhausted, so go jump in the shower, take a power nap, and get ready so we can relax, catch up, have some drinks before dinner. Woo!"

"Take it down fifty notches until I get that nap, crazy!" I laugh as I head toward the shower.

"Love you, too!" she yells.

I find my room, and holy crap, it's filled with multiple bouquets of flowers. Well, there goes the no-crying rule because the tears are already streaming down my face. I know this is Annabelle's doing. I walk over to the small arrangement next to my bed with fresh lavender and read the attached small card.

My darling Sadie,

I think each of our paths is already set for us when we are born. We may not understand the whys and reasoning behind our journeys yet, but we will all go through things in life that set us up for what is meant to be. You have already overcome some obstacles that have only made you stronger. So, please don't let anyone erase your spirit and sparkle that makes you, you.

You are the most selfless, kindhearted person I have ever had the pleasure of knowing in my life. What comes next for you on this life journey will only bring you happiness and love. I know it. So please embrace whatever comes your way next. I am so proud of you. You deserve it all.

I love you.

Your sister soul mate,
Annabelle

Now sobbing, I take the note and store it in my bag to avoid losing it.

Between Belle and I, we have more emotions than a romance novel. But I don't know what I would do without her, always knowing exactly what I need to hear. People could only wish to have an Annabelle in their lives.

After I shower and nap, I stroll out to the balcony where Belle is relaxing, sipping some champagne. I walk over to her and hug her tightly. She kisses my cheek, and I whisper, "I love you."

"I love you, too, Sadie."

We sit there hugging for a minute until Belle decides it's time for more champagne.

"A toast is in order!" she shouts. "Cheers to the almost birthday girl. Let's make this trip the best one yet. Sleep all morning, beach all day, drink, dance, and have sex all night!" She clinks my glass.

I hit my hand to my forehead and laugh. "I am not having sex all night, or sex at all. You're lucky that I'm agreeing to party, *sometimes*."

"Sadie, you need to let loose on this trip. Why can't sex be in order? The way Wills was staring at you made it very clear he would be interested. It just so happens, I think I know one of his friends. I'm going to invite them out tomorrow night if I have the chance."

I ignore her and continue to drink my champagne. I feel a blush creeping up and butterflies in my stomach. The feeling I got when Wills just glanced over was something I am certainly not used to.

But he looked like he would be all too consuming and a little intense for my liking. I practically roll my eyes at myself.

Yeah, right, Sadie, you liked exactly how he was looking at you.

I ignore those thoughts and stare out over the balcony. I take in the view before me, thinking about what this trip means to me. Belle and I take a few weeks' vacation every year, but tomorrow, I turn thirty and I promised myself I would start doing what was best for *me* now.

I am finally going to open my own floral design shop, it's something I've dreamed about my whole life. I want to volunteer more and travel even more.

Belle has been trying to get me to move to London for some time now, and honestly, it isn't the worst idea. A place to start fresh. Plus, my brother, Jackson, lives there, and I miss him a ridiculous amount. So I know it's the right move, I just need to woman up and take the plunge.

Besides being close to Annabelle and Jackson, the other major perk of moving would be to distance myself from my parents and our toxic relationship.

The other reason would be I wouldn't have to see Colton anymore. Since I caught him cheating, he has tried to get back together numerous times, claiming it was only that once.

But little does he know—I know the truth. It's been going on for more than six months, and honestly, I'm not sure I even care. Which tells you… I'm done.

I clearly didn't love him anymore, and it took an unfortunate circumstance to show me that. At the end of the day, I was more embarrassed than heartbroken with what he did.

He was what my parents always wanted, a rich boy from a high society family with strong political ties. We met when we were twenty-four and were good friends first. Both of us were so carefree and enjoyed many of the same interests. I did love him. But he grew to be everything I hate about the social circles our families run in. Caring more about status and appearances than me.

Annabelle tops off my champagne, not saying anything. She knows when I just need to process things by myself.

Maybe it wouldn't hurt if I let loose this trip and lived untroubled like Belle? I know how to go out and have a good time. It's just not my priority like her. Plus, I don't have many friends in Manhattan that I enjoy letting loose with like I do with her. Since she lives over three thousand miles away, it's easier to have quiet weekends with a good book and wine. On occasion, a nice dinner, or if I'm forced, my family drags me to events to be "seen."

So, to let loose and have "Annabelle type of fun" is just not second nature to me.

But maybe it's time to set out and try.

"Let's go shopping tomorrow, Belle. I think I need something sexier and more birthday appropriate if we aim to go out dancing tomorrow night."

She couldn't whip her head faster toward me, clapping her hands like a little kid.

"YES, YES, YES, let's do it! When we head down to dinner, I'll ask the concierge where the best shopping is. And on that note, let's go inside so you can get ready for dinner," she says as she tops us off with even more champagne.

I'm jet-lagged and now tipsy. We better leave soon. Otherwise, I'll be passing out again.

I'm finishing up my makeup when Belle comes into my room looking freaking gorgeous.

"Belle," I moan. She always does this. "You said we were getting drinks and dinner at the bar downstairs—nothing fancy tonight."

She looks down at herself and smirks. "You know me, fancy is my middle name."

"I'm almost done, and to be clear, when we get downstairs, I want no more talk about me. I only want to hear about you—you can catch me up on this new guy you're dating."

"Dating is too serious of a word. I'm not tying myself to anyone right now."

Of course, she's not.

"Done! Let's go."

My stomach rumbles loudly as we leave. It's only now I realize I haven't eaten since the plane ride.

We make our way to the hostess stand to get seated for dinner. I'm still in awe of the decor in this hotel. The beach theme continues throughout but adds different elements as you explore.

The restaurant reminds me of beach meets Paris, all-white flowing linens, but high ceilings and beautiful moldings. The bar is a white marble with brass hardware fitted with mauve-colored velvet chairs. I think I need to recreate this at home somehow. It's classy, simple, yet super sexy all at the same time.

The hostess is an attractive young girl—*shocker*—and not the friendliest. Nevertheless, she's giving Belle the once-over, and I can already tell this will be an issue.

"I am sorry, but we are very backed up tonight. So, you will need to sit at the bar and wait," the hostess says in a short, clipped voice.

"Well, that's not good enough. How long will it be? We traveled all day and have a reservation for right now," Belle explains.

"Madam, I do not know. You need to move to the bar now. I have other customers to help."

"Annabelle, let's just get a drink first, then eat." I hate confrontation.

"Fine." She glares at the hostess. "One drink, then our table better be ready."

We walk off to the lounge area near the bar. "Don't get all worked up," I warn.

"She just hit a nerve. She kept looking me up and down. It was as if she just decided right there and then that they were busy and we couldn't sit."

We switch from champagne to some slightly dirty martinis. I can already predict most of our drink orders—champagne, wine, martinis, and lots of spicy margaritas.

"So… spill the tea, Belle. Starting with this new man of yours."

We may talk every day and get caught up with each other. But it's just not the same as an in-person gossip sesh.

"Ugh. He is not my man. I am still a single woman. But I think there is potential there. I met him through a coworker of mine. His name is Trey."

"Trey?!" I spit my drink out, laughing. God, why am I laughing? That's so mean. But I can't help it, I can't stop. "Trey has to be listed as one of the top ten douchiest names, right?"

I cannot see Miss High Society Annabelle with a "Trey."

She starts laughing now too. "I know it's terrible, isn't it? But he is rather handsome, so it makes up for his name."

I take a deep breath. "Okay, okay. Sorry. Tell me more. Give me the rundown."

"He is older by a few years and very close to his family. Which, by the way—they have a house in the Alps, so now we have a ski house if this works out. He is an only child, lives in Mayfair, has many good-looking friends for you, and he's a barrister." She takes a deep breath. "He's just over six feet, so tall enough for me, which is crucial."

Belle, being probably around five feet ten, needs someone tall, no question about it.

"He has more of a runner's body, but still muscular, dark hair, light eyes, light skin. Proclaimed foodie. No faults so far, except he works a lot. And he lives a lifestyle a little closer to yours." She winks. "Probably better off since I am always out and about at events and openings all around London for work and fun. If we both lived a similar lifestyle, it wouldn't work."

Belle is in public relations, which suits her perfectly.

"Well, even though I will probably never be able to say his name without laughing, I am glad you're happy and giving this guy a try." I smile at her softly.

"You've been killing it at your job, and now you have someone that seems just as successful. Who, hopefully, won't feel threatened like other men in your past."

"Boys, Sadie, not men. Too emasculating to date a woman that's more successful than them."

She chuckles and adds, "Plus, they all had small dicks. I can't work with that."

She is too much. I'm laughing hard again—god, I've missed this girl. At least my abs are getting a workout tonight.

We finish our martinis when I feel someone's eyes on me. I turn to the bar and spot Wills's friends all standing ordering drinks, but I don't see him.

But for some reason, I just know he's here somewhere. I'm getting the same feeling I had when we were in the lobby. So I take another look around when a deep voice whispers in my ear, sending a shiver through my body.

"Looking for me?"

I slowly raise my eyes. Jesus, he is freaking hot. His gorgeous gray eyes bore into mine, and he raises an eyebrow in question.

"Huh?" I hear him chuckle a little. Jesus, I can't even put together a sentence.

"I asked if you were looking for me? I saw you looking over at my friends. Then it seemed like you didn't find what you were looking for."

So smug.

"I, um, no. I was looking for the waiter to order another drink," I say.

Belle's eyes are as wide as saucers right now, and I am trying to telepathically tell her to jump in here and say something.

"Wills Taylor." He reaches his hand out for mine.

I extend my hand to him, and he kisses the back, leaving his lips there a little longer than expected.

"And you are?" he says in his posh British accent.

"Sadie. And this is my friend Annabelle."

He doesn't even glance over at her. This is very intense. *He is very intense.*

"Can I buy you ladies another round?"

"No," "Yes," Belle and I say in unison.

"Yes, please." Belle beats me to it.

"Okay." He chuckles. "I'll be right back." He drops my hand. I hadn't even realized he was still holding it. But the second he lets go, I feel an instant loss.

What the hell is that all about?

"Holy shit, Sadie! That was freaking hot. I told you he wanted to devour you."

What do I even say to her? She's right. He looked like he wanted to eat me alive, right there and then.

I glance back to the bar and catch a glimpse of Wills talking with his friends. He's in the perfect position for me to see him full on now.

He's wearing a different suit than earlier and has undone a few top buttons for a more relaxed feel. His chest is broad, where you can see the outline of his muscles and a dusting of very light-brown hair. But his legs, holy hell! The way they fill out his suit is just, wow.

I think Belle mentioned he played rugby, and I can see it now.

I realize I'm staring, so I slowly turn my eyes back to a very smiley Belle. "Don't start. That was too intense. I could barely form a freaking sentence," I mutter.

"That's because you're turned on. Look at you—you're beet red."

"I am not," I deny. But I know I am. I can feel the heat radiating off me. And I can't help but reach up and touch my face to confirm. "I was just taken by surprise, that's all."

"Well, I don't believe that one bit. Anyway, Wills is coming back over now, with his three friends."

I jolt up and fix my dress and hair quickly.

I think I hear Belle murmur, "That's what I thought." But I ignore her. I can't have her in my head right now.

All four guys make it to our table with our drinks. Wills hands me mine.

"Thank you, Wills," I whisper and look down at my drink. His stare is too intense for me.

"Annabelle Hughes, it's lovely to see you. How are your brothers?" I hear one of Wills's friends ask Annabelle.

Now, I remember she mentioned she may have known one of his friends.

"They are trouble, as usual." She laughs.

"George, this is my best friend, Sadie Peters. We are here on holiday for the next few weeks."

George walks over and kisses both my cheeks.

"It's a pleasure," he says.

Behind him, Wills is staring daggers into the back of his head. What the hell is that about?

"Seems like you met Wills. These are our friends Leo and Declan. Lucky for you girls, we are also here on holiday for a few weeks." He winks, and I shake the other two's hands, introducing myself.

Leo and George seem like fun boys. Declan seems just as intense as Wills but with a gentler side. I'm getting this feeling that there is more to him than meets the eye.

"Anna, it's been so long since I've seen you. I'm surprised I recognized you," George states.

"Ah! Anna, I haven't heard someone call you that in a long time." I laugh, and she glares at me. She would rather be called Double *B* than Anna. Not sure what her hang-up is, but she's hated it for as long as I can remember.

"You've known each other a long time?" George asks.

"Yes." Belle smiles over at me. "We have been best friends for twenty-five years."

Wills still hasn't said a word since walking back here, but I can feel his eyes on me. I don't chance a look because I'm afraid I'll start drooling or do something equally as stupid.

"Why don't you ladies join us for dinner?" Leo chimes in.

"No can do, boys. The first night is always just Sadie and me. No matter where we travel, it's our rule. Just her and I." She grabs my hand and squeezes lightly.

We made that rule when we were teenagers, as our life got too busy. Whenever we saw each other, throughout the years, the first night was always to catch up and just spend time together.

"But I have an even better invitation," she adds. "Tomorrow, it's Sadie's thirtieth birthday, and we are going dancing. Meet us at the club after dinner? I can send you the details, George."

They all nod.

"See you boys tomorrow, then!" Belle giggles and blows kisses to the guys as they walk off like she's known them for years.

Wills is still beside me, so I finally look up as he leans down toward me. "Good night, Sadie, until tomorrow, beautiful," he whispers, then kisses my cheek with a slightly open mouth, lingering there for a second.

I'm speechless. Again.

What the hell was that? *And why did I want to turn my head so my lips could feel his open mouth?*

Printed in Great Britain
by Amazon